WHISPERS, WHISKERS, & WINE

WHISPERS, WHISKERS, & WINE

Imogen Knowed

Cover by Sariel Castaño Díaz

ISBN: 979-8-9874825-1-3

Dedication

To all the women in tech who know that the cartoony villains in this book are, unfortunately, realistic.

And, to my muse, Megan Thee Stallion. Her music pulled me out of a dark place, and I hope the universe brings her eternal happiness.

Content Warnings

This book has explicit descriptions of sexual acts.

While all sex is consensual, some acts may be considered dubious or coerced.

There is mention of sexual assault and childhood assault; however, it is not described in detail.

Events in this book center around various mental health crises and coming to terms with sexuality.

Body shaming and some ableist language are also present.

If you have any questions or comments about these content warnings, feel free to contact me. You can find me at:

https://www.instagram.com/imogenknowed/

1

ADLEY

Snow falls outside the window to my desk's left—a thick white curtain swirling into view. I blink back tears as I attempt to focus on the snow and appreciate its beauty. *Breathe. Just breathe.* I pace my breath and try to bring down my heart rate. The only thing that matters is the rhythm of my breath. It'll be okay.

The voice of my boss, Daniel, barks from within my headphones. "Adley! Are you listening?" I snap my attention back to my laptop monitor.

"Yes, I am," I say with the plastered-on smile of a complacent worker drone.

"Then explain why the hell the game is fucking broken! We have a demo this afternoon, and we don't have a working build!" he yells furiously.

I grit my teeth and reply, "It seems someone committed code late last night, causing the build to fail." Even though no one on the team was supposed to commit any code changes after lunch yesterday—to ensure this exact thing didn't happen. We have these processes in place for a fucking reason. I internally sigh but externally smile. "No worries, I'm on it. I think I know what the issue is. I'll fix it."

"Why haven't you fixed it yet?!" he yells. "This is your job, Adley." My heart thumps harder. I can feel it in my ears. My watch vibrates on my wrist. I don't even have to look at it to know why it's alerting me—my heart rate is up. Way up.

Because I was a-fucking-sleep, you fucking prick. Why are you even awake right now? Keep the smile on your face and lift your tone. You got this. Breath. "I will jump on it as soon as we get off this call. I'll just undo the change, and everything should be fine."

"It better be!" he says.

I want to say his boyfriend is the one who broke protocol and committed code after we ensured everything was stable and ready to go. I want to say that his boyfriend is a fucking moron. I want to say that I'm just one developer on a team of many, and this is actually NOT my fucking job. But I say, "No worries, I've got it," and jam my thumb hard on the edge of my desk—soothed ever so slightly by the pain.

He huffs, obviously wanting to keep deriding me, but my response has quelled him a bit—less wind in his pissed-off sail. But he's still mad. He's likely madder that I didn't give him what he wanted: tears. But I'll smile for the camera and cry when it's off.

"Alright," he says with slightly less aggression, "I'll see you this afternoon for the demo."

"Bye!" I say with all the saccharine charm I can muster.

He doesn't even respond; he simply disconnects from the call. I log off as well and close out Zoom. I flip the cover on my camera and stare at my pink mechanical keyboard. The rainbow lights dancing behind the keys feel like they're mocking me—flaming the rage and panic bubbling within me. I want to scream. I want to cry. But first, I'll fix this fucking code.

Dream job? Ha. Video games are supposed to be fun. This isn't fucking fun.

=^..^= ♥ =^..^=

Fixing the code calms me slightly, but not significantly. James made the same kind of mistake he makes every-fucking-time. I've mentored him about this on countless occasions, but he still half-asses everything. I'm starting to think it truly is weaponized incompetence.

It took me longer to fix than I hoped. The plan was to just undo the change. However, upon further inspection, I realized it was a pervasive problem woven into multiple systems. Undoing his work from last night would have made a successful build, but once someone played the game for more than ten minutes, it would have crashed.

There was no quick way to remove the tumor that was James' shitty code without going through the code base and adjusting everything it touched. I could have rolled back his change and just pretended I didn't see the enormous red flag, but as the team's honorary scapegoat, I'd be blamed for it somehow. So I fixed it. Because of their insistence that everything is somehow my fault, my responsibility, I am angry at myself for not catching this problem earlier. I try to forgive myself with a reminder that I can't personally review every line of code that guy commits. *It's really not my fucking job.* Oh well, at least it's fixed, and the new build is in progress.

I check my clock and then my calendar. It's 8:15 a.m. and the fix I've committed should prepare the game for the demo this afternoon. I thought working for a company two time zones behind me would mean I got to wake up a bit later, and getting emergency calls at 6:30 a.m. wouldn't be a thing. But instead, I still somehow manage to get reamed out before I've had my morning coffee. Why was he even up at 4:30 a.m. checking on the build? I don't even officially start my day until 9 a.m.—I should take a long lunch or leave early today because fuck this job.

But before all of that. Coffee. I need some coffee.

I start the K-cup and contemplate my carbon footprint while browsing my phone. I usually try not to check social media until after lunch, but Daniel has my morning all out of whack, and fuck it, I need the dopamine hit right now. I scroll through Instagram, double-tapping every cute cat video that graces my feed.

The sound of roiling water fills the air as the machine churns. In a moment of weakness, I switch to my alternate account before the machine even has time to spurt out its dark liquid. *Downward spiral, here I come!* I know this is a bad idea, but I do it anyway, convinced this time will somehow be worth it.

I scroll through image after image, and while my feed contains the occasional celebrity, most of the feed features my exes and other people I want to stalk "anonymously" on the internet. If anyone ever took the time to review the follower list of this account, they'd know it was me instantly. All you have to do is compare it to my list of my past lovers and enemies (same thing, really), and it's one-to-one. The few celebrities I sprinkled in there to throw people "off my scent" aren't fooling anyone.

All my exes have, for one reason or another, accepted my friend request—either not noticing the glaring signal it is me or being so self-involved that they want me to see their posts. Wanting to rub their success in my face. Given my history with lovers, both are equally likely. I tend to gravitate to two types. Type 1: sweet and dumb. These are the folks who definitely wouldn't notice the pattern. Type 2: cruel narcissists. These are the ones who would post things knowing full well I am creeping and will post things with the explicit intent to hurt me.

Or is this train of thought all indicative that I'm the narcissist—assuming I'm the main character in everyone's life, and all their actions revolve around me? *Hmm.*

My fingers swipe upward, scrolling through pictures of people way happier than me. I stop on an image of a woman, cropped to show only her extremely pregnant belly and her hand resting atop it—wearing a huge fucking engagement ring. My heart sinks before I even look at the poster's name. I already know it's Veronica. My heart pounds in my ears as I read the accompanying text, "38 weeks! I can see the finish line!" followed by a ton of emojis and hashtags like "#blessed, #manifesting #hotmama." 38 weeks? I do the mental math. She got pregnant way before July.

My heart sinks at the memory of Bryce lying next to me in bed. He stroked my belly and told me he'd never want children. His hair fell across his face in a way that made this ex-emo swoon. I'd never been with anyone so classically handsome. I was willing to do whatever he wanted because I knew I didn't deserve him.

He joked it was good we wouldn't have children because I would probably have difficulty losing weight after. He said the last thing I needed was more belly fat. Before I could reply, he sunk his fingers inside me and said, "Plus, you can't loosen this up anymore." Yeah, I know he sounds like a cartoon villain, but this dude actually said this shit to me. I really tried to believe him when he said, "I'm just joking. Would I be fucking you if I didn't think you were at least a little attractive?" with emphasis on "little."

Bryce constantly compared me to my best friend, Veronica. How much thinner she was. How much longer her hair was. Then, when she cut her hair, how she better pulled off short hair because her jaw was more defined. "Snatched," to quote him. He claimed he said these things to motivate me to better myself, but now I realize he just wanted me to be her.

Well, good for fucking them. I hope they're fucking happy together. No, I don't. I hope they fall off a fucking cliff. Well, after the baby is born. The baby doesn't deserve death by cliff—despite being a genetic blend of two awful people.

I click on her profile picture to see her other posts.

Pinned is a picture of Bryce kneeling in front of her, kissing her pregnant belly. Further down are pictures of them together, in my home. There's a picture of the two of them sitting at my table on the Fourth of July. I'm cropped out, but my arm is still in the frame. Fucking assholes. *I know you know how to use Photoshop, Bryce.*

A selfie of Veronica topless in bikini bottoms, her bare chest pressed against his, appears on the screen. The angle is high enough that I can see his hands on her ass. He is kissing her neck on the side opposite the camera, obscuring his face, but it's obviously him. I know instantly where and when this picture was taken. The ground beneath her matches the bathroom tile from our hotel room during last winter's trip to Thailand. *On my birthday? What cruelty.* They planned the whole trip for me as a surprise—even though I hate surprises. But was it just a trip for them to hook up?

They told me that this Fourth of July was the first time they slept together. A neighbor who illegally shoots off a barrage of fireworks every year had just started doing so. All our friends—all Bryce's friends—were in the backyard eating hot dogs, waving sparklers, and sinking deep into drunkenness. But they were nowhere to be found. When I went looking for them, I found Bryce sunk deep into Veronica, bending her over on my bed.

Because I'm a glutton for punishment, I click on Bryce's tag in the photo. His first post is a picture of our cat, Mittens, in a box, looking cozy in front of a fire. Well, his cat now. When he ran out on me, he also ran out with my cat.

I'd like to say I was the one who kicked him out. That fucking my best friend in my home was the last straw and the moment I toughened up and stood up for myself. I'd like to say it. But I can't. Instead, I was a blubbering mess. And when I was at my absolute lowest, he took the cat, claiming he was afraid I'd hurt her to spite him—which is ridiculous. I needed her. I still do. *Fucking prick.*

In the days following, I was in a flurry of desperate, self-loathing, calling Bryce non-stop, begging him to come home. When he refused, I found solace by burning my bedspread in my backyard and tossing all the leftover sparklers on the heap. I received a stern talking-to from a hot firefighter. A few days later, Ethan (a.k.a. "hot firefighter") showed up at my house with a fire extinguisher and a face made for riding.

In an attempt to run from my feelings, I switch back to my main account. Only to find a picture of HotEthanHatesFires at a party with a beautiful blonde draped around his neck, kissing him hard on the cheek. *What the fuck, Instagram? Do you hate me?* I still held out a small hope that Ethan and I could have a real relationship. Or at least return to the booty-calling and reviewing fire safety we had throughout most of the Fall. *He is a nice guy. Why can't I lock a nice guy down?*

I close Instagram, trying to block out the awful feeling building in the pit of my stomach and sending waves of despair throughout my body. I consider putting my phone away entirely, but the anxiety of sitting here with my feelings is too intense. Posts of friends announcing their indie game releases and award nominations instantly turn this dopamine chase into a full-on crash. I try to be a mature, good friend. To stamp down the bubbling, festering jealousy. I want them all to succeed. And I know life isn't a competition, but fuck if I'm not failing.

Leslie, an old college acquaintance, announcing her game's release cuts particularly deep. She began development on it after I started working on my game, *Harem Hex Healer*. I was on track to finish it over two years ago. But then, Veronica and I got the brilliant idea to move across the country to start fresh. I had just started working remotely for my current job, and we took that as a sign that we should go live wherever we wanted. So we traded palmetto trees for 10,000 lakes. It all seemed so perfect: a bigger paycheck, nicer city, best friend. And then I met this "amazing guy, Bryce."

Unfortunately, the job ended up being a toxic waste dump of bro culture despite the interviewers promising me diversity and mental health were important to them. I now never have enough energy to even think about working on my own game after hours. And the mortgage company and student loan lenders don't care if you go from a two-earner household to one, so quitting the shitshow isn't an option right now. I couldn't even afford to hire an artist to make the rest of the art for my game if I wanted to.

And that explains the slow descent that led to my downfall. Friendless. Boyfriendless. Catless. Completely alone. Working a job I hate so fucking much just because it pays well. Well, well-ish, anyway. Not well enough to sustain my dreams.

Ok, Adley. Get your shit together. I blink back tears yet again as I start to spiral—reminiscing about how I had it all, had my shit together, was going somewhere, and it all fell to shit.

I'll never be good enough for anyone. I don't work on my passion project. I don't do anything but work, sleep, and drink. So what even is the fucking point of waking up every day?

I gaze out the sliding glass door by my kitchen table and attempt to recenter myself. I whisper, "Get it together, Adley." Holding my coffee in both hands, I move the cup to my chest to absorb the heat. It comforts me slightly. I close my eyes firmly and take deep breaths, focusing on the sensation. In through my nose. Out through my mouth, making a little 'o' with my lips. I try to focus on the coffee's smell and the cup's warmth against my hands and chest.

Veronica taught me this. Well, tried to teach me. I've always sucked at this whole mindfulness thing. I can't ever focus on the here and now. My past haunts me, and my future taunts me—my mind flitters between regret for the past and anxiety for the future.

I've got to stop moping. I start work in half an hour, and my job sucks enough without adding my being a weepy mess to the mix. The dude-bros on my team would never let me live it down if I started crying during stand-up. They finally stopped calling me "Sadley" after I cried last time. I swear they compete over who can be the most cruel and misogynistic without getting reported to HR.

Maybe I should take the day off. Use a PTO day. Do I want to use one now, or should I try to save it for one of the inevitable and numerous days that I will feel so much worse? I could lay around, drink too much wine, and paint my nails. Maybe I could light a fire, really live it up. Or I could pretend to be a fully functional and stable human and clean my house.

"Come on, Adley. You don't have time for this," I say, slapping my cheeks, trying to snap myself out of it. I need to make some breakfast, brush my teeth, and do my morning skincare routine before work starts. I can make some quick scrambled eggs and scarf them down while standing over the stove. If I do that, I'll have time for grooming. If I don't do my morning routine, my whole day will be thrown into disarray. *It already is, though.*

I shuffle to the window, still gripping my coffee to my chest as a tear rolls off my chin into it. The snow is coming down hard. Maybe I need to stare out the window, watch the snow, and let myself have a good five-minute cry. I could go one day without brushing my teeth or applying the whole cabinet's worth of serums and lotions that I've somehow convinced myself my aging skin needs.

I try my damnedest to silence my mind. Stop the racing thoughts and checklists. Stop the flashing images of Bryce calming me when I would get worked up. Or Mittens sitting with me at my desk while my coworkers made fun of me. Or Veronica lecturing me about how I need to manifest my ideal self.

Veronica would tell me constantly that my negative thoughts would be my downfall. "Not to victim blame or anything, girl, just you're doing, like, the opposite of manifesting. You become a self-fulfilling prophecy with all this negative self-talk. You gotta put the energy you want out there." Bryce said pretty much the same thing, just not as nicely when I walked in on him balls deep in Veronica.

Veronica looked back at me with a massive smile as Bryce pulled his dick out of her. She seemed so… pleased with herself. His dick was still hard and glistening as he told me that it was my fault he was fucking her. That my self-esteem issues made him less attracted to me each day, "Add that to the fact you let yourself go, and how could I not fuck her?" When I tried to explain his saying stuff like that to me was part of why my self-esteem was so fucked he asserted it was actually my communication issues that were the problem. "It's because you're autistic and just don't get the nuance of communication, Adley," he said with an eye roll. Then he grabbed his keys because he "had to get away" from me and my "negative fucking vibe!"

Alright. Fine. I'll ask the universe for what I want. I close my eyes and say with as much confidence as I can muster, "Okay, Universe. First, could you make Veronica realize she's a fucking cunt? Then, could you send me someone to love? A cat? A man? A woman? I'm not picky. Maybe Ethan? I'd even take Bryce back at this point. But, preferably not Bryce…" I lower my tone to a whisper, hopeful the Universe can't hear this part, "Well, maybe Bryce."

The snow's density increases suddenly. There must be a whole extra foot of snow than there was when I started staring out this window. That can't be true. I haven't been standing here that long. I check my phone for the weather forecast. "Winter storm warning. Travel is not advised." Well, it's a good thing I don't have to go anywhere. Not that I could because Bryce also took my truck. *He took everything from me.* It was the only vehicle I had that could drive in this shit—electric cars are great for the environment but nearly useless six months out of the year in this winter wonderland.

Something in the distance grabs my attention. I can make out a golden shape on top of my fence, but it's nearly impossible to see due to the snow. *Is that a cat?* The window is fogging slightly, and I wipe it away to get a better look. As with everything I do, my efforts are in vain. I still can't get a good look at this theoretical cat.

It must be a neighbor's cat. But why would they let it out in this storm? It stops moving and falls. It doesn't leap. It falls. It falls over on its side, instantly buried in fresh snow.

What the fuck? Is it okay?

I flick my wrist up nervously to check my watch. My first meeting of the day starts in fifteen minutes. *Fuck.*

What should I do? It might be hurt.

In a moment of uncharacteristic decisiveness, I open Slack and send a quick message on my team's group channel: "Will be late to meeting. Must save a cat."

2

ADLEY

With a burst of determined energy, I fling the door open and launch into the snow. As I trudge forward, the winter gear I hastily threw on provides little protection against the biting cold. I struggle against the waist-deep snow, creating a trench in my wake.

I try to zip my coat, but my gloved fingers fumble against the zipper. I'm uncoordinated and trip as I lift my legs, pushing against the weight of the snow. Fuck it's cold. I stop moving forward to focus on closing my coat, trying not to fall.

I nervously stare at the cat and try to send it good vibes. *Don't worry, I'm coming.* Frustration builds, and I fling off my gloves, watching them disappear into the snow. Well, add that to my list of regrets. I finally manage to seal my coat, but the cold is already gnawing at my exposed hands.

Retrieving the gloves is pointless; I don't want to waste time digging for them. I pause and look back to my house, contemplating whether getting another pair of gloves is the wiser move.

But with panic rising inside me, I face the cold. *This is stupid.* Panic clouds my thoughts while the snow seems to fall faster and harder. I attempt to shield my frozen fingers by pulling them into my jacket sleeves, but it's not particularly effective.

I push toward the cat. My face stings from the frigid air, and my eyelashes are freezing together. Doubts creep in—was it really a cat that fell? Or did I just hurl myself out here for absolutely no reason?

I finally reach the edge of my yard, approximately where the cat fell. With a sense of relief and urgency, I spot a divot in the snow that hopefully indicates where it landed.

Please don't be dead.

EZRA

The world's sounds have returned, but my vision remains lost. The whooshing, plaguing my brain since I fell from my balcony, now more closely resembles a gusting wind. It grows louder and more forceful as my consciousness returns to me. *How could Sarah have pushed me?* Yeah, I was being kind of a dick, but pushing me off a balcony was extreme, even for her.

I try to move, but my limbs are frozen—not just in place, but literally frozen. A cold has seeped so deep into my bones that I worry all warmth has left the world. It takes me a moment to realize my vision is returning when all black is replaced by all white.

Snow? Where am I? What is going on? The last thing I remember was the ocean's waves fast approaching and bracing myself for the impact that never came. How did I end up in the snow?

A loud crunching noise interrupts the dull roar of the blizzard. With great effort, I manage to turn my head towards the source. With blurry eyes, I see a dark silhouette slowly making its way towards me. Exhaustion overtakes my body, and I resign myself to whatever fate awaits.

As the figure draws closer, their form becomes clearer through the curtain of snow. They're bundled up in thick winter clothing, movements awkward and strained as they trudge through the deep snow. Each step seems to require significant effort. Clouds of condensation escape from their mouth with every labored breath.

Am I dead? Is that an angel coming to collect my soul?

A melodic feminine voice carries over the wind, "Oh, kitty. Please don't be dead." The figure approaching me must be a woman. She's almost within reach, as her strides seem more purposeful, more hurried, and less graceful—not that they were graceful before.

Why would she use such an endearing term to describe me, though? Kitty? "I'm coming, kitty. Just hold on," she says through labored breaths. Her voice is comforting. Beautiful.

Either she's an angel, or she has me confused with someone else. I am not her kitty. But I welcome her approaching presence. She's obviously trying to help me. I don't understand why I can't move. But I'm definitely going to freeze if she doesn't help me.

Suddenly, she stumbles in the deep snow and falls toward me, her face planting into the soft white powder. If I weren't so exhausted, I might chuckle. She awkwardly pushes herself up, struggling to regain control of her body. A stream of expletives spews from her mouth. *Maybe not an angel.* When her face lifts to gaze at me, our eyes meet.

The most beautiful grey-blue eyes I've ever seen, sparkling like diamonds against the crisp winter landscape, pierce through me, causing my heart, already slowed from the cold, to fully stop. Her activating gaze spreads warmth through my entire body, arousing parts of myself that, if she were an angel, I'd most assuredly go to hell for. All thoughts of cold and danger disappear. My mind and body are consumed by those grey eyes.

"Motherfucker!" She breaks my trance with another stream of obscenities that oddly make me find her even more endearing. She pushes herself awkwardly upward, hitting the snow angrily on her way up. She chides herself, "Get it together, Adley!" How is this so fucking adorable?

The shape of her body is more apparent now, despite being bundled in heavy winter garb that removes most of her shape. She's voluptuous. So voluptuous. I'm about to freeze to death, but my blood is boiling with lust. I find myself wondering what her breasts look like, what the shape of her hips is like.

She struggles toward me, desperate to reach me. *That's it. Come to me, baby.*

I picture ripping her fluffy coat off and entering her with my full length as she screams, "Motherfucker!" in ecstasy. What is wrong with me? How can I be thinking of that when I'm about to die?

She hovers over me. I am unable to break my gaze from her. I can see the full details of her face now. Pink with cold. The most adorable nose sits in the middle of rosy, youthful cheeks. Her lips are full and chapped. I want to kiss them to warm them. Even chapped, they're beautiful and perfect. I picture them wrapping around my dick when I'm at my full anthro height, towering over her.

My breath, previously slowed from certain death, morphs into a pant. I pant for her. My hurried breath begins to condense, too. "Oh, thank God! You're alive," she says as she reaches toward me.

She gently touches me and then pulls back, unsure what to do. She unzips her coat, revealing a tight, low-cut t-shirt stretched by large breasts. What is she doing? Exposing herself to me? She picks me up with the most delicate, gentle hands.

No one has ever carried me in my ailo form before. I instinctively want to thrash about. The lack of control I have over my body while she holds me makes me panic. She brings my limp body to her breasts and nuzzles me between them, then zips her coat around me.

She smells like nothing I've ever smelled before. It reminds me slightly of roses. And catnip, which, despite my only having the opportunity to partake in once, has burned into my sense memory. The scent is intoxicating and arousing. I rest between her breasts, delirious as the warmth of her body and the warmth of lust overtake me. I want to transform right now and bury myself in her warm cunt. But I'm still too weak.

She treads in the snow again, in the direction from whence she came. I'm not sure where she is taking me. I can barely think straight. My mind is racing with thoughts of sex. My senses are overloading with the feeling of her breasts through her shirt against my sides. As her arms swing, they press harder into me, threatening to suffocate me. I could die happy here between these breasts. I wish I could be against her bare skin. The warmth and smell of her engulf me. I close my eyes, and a deep purr vibrates from within me.

She places her arm on my back over her coat and says, "Don't worry, kitty. I'm bringing you home."

I've heard men talk about when they first purred for their fated mate, but nothing can describe this feeling. I was starting to think I'd never find one. Believe me, I've tried with enough women. To find one at a time like this is not ideal, but I won't complain. She is taking me to her home and no doubt she and I will spend the next few days fucking until we have fully explored each other's bodies with our tongues. I don't hear her purring, though. *That's weird.*

She should be purring, too. She hasn't even mentioned my purr. You'd think she'd be overjoyed that I have purred for her. Does she not find me attractive? That can't be. Maybe she is too concerned with saving my life at the moment. *What a sweet woman.* She's able to set aside her lust for me to save my life. From the stories I've heard of the purr, most would not have the self-control to do anything other than drop everything and fully succumb to ravishing each other.

I hear the faint muffled sound of a sliding glass door opening, and the air around me instantly warms—we must be inside. She quickly unzips and places me atop her discarded coat. It's soft and smells of her. What a gentle woman taking such good care of me.

She removes her boots and throws them aside with a loud, wet splat.

"Okay, kitty, let me get you a towel. I'll be right back," she says. It's evident to me by now that she's talking to me. I'm "kitty." She must have purred for me already. That's why she's calling me kitty and not purring right now. I can't wait until I am warm enough to transform so we can consummate our fate while she calls me "kitty." I hope she's an ear-puller.

She turns her back to me and walks toward a hallway, pulling her puffy pants off while she walks. I am excited to see the curvature of her voluptuous body without the coat and pants. It is the most enticing, gorgeous body I've ever seen.

The pants hit the floor, and the curve of her ass is revealed to me. But wait. No tail? What? She throws off her hat. No ears? She has no ears atop her head! She stands on her tiptoes, looking in her hall closet for something. She pulls her hair back and tucks it behind her vestigial ears.

Is she actually an angel? Did I actually die? Did Sarah actually fucking kill me? Is my fated mate an angel? That's kinda cool. But also, that would mean I am dead, which is decidedly not cool.

"My shirt is soaked," she says at the wet spot pooling around her breasts where she stored me. Her nipples peer through her shirt, and I let out a moan of pleasure, unable to quench the lust stirring my loins.

"Oh, poor kitty, don't worry. I'll be there in a second." She makes a harrumph sound and removes her shirt. Her tits bounce as the fabric releases them for me to see. Her nipples are large and pink, almost the color of her cheeks rosy from the cold. I make a pathetic, needy, wailing noise as my brain short circuits at the sight.

She looks at me with deep concern, "I know you're scared. Don't worry, I won't hurt you," she says.

"Babe, I am not scared. I don't mind a little pain. My safe word is marbles," I tell her, but she doesn't respond.

I push inside myself to trigger my anthro transformation so that I can grab her in my arms and lick those beautiful large nipples. But for some reason, I cannot transform. Am I too weak from the cold? My body aches. Oh, how I wish I could ravage her. I would give anything to be able to do so at this exact moment.

She runs toward me and slides on her knees until she kneels before me. Her tits hang in my face, and I almost explode from the sheer beauty.

"What a good boy, don't worry. I'll take good care of you," she coos. *That's it. I'm dead. I've gone to heaven.*

ADLEY

Despite being a popsicle, he is a gorgeous cat. I'm pretty sure it's a "he" since he's orange and orange cats tend to be boys. His hair is long, and the icicles that had accumulated around him are melting, matting his hair around him.

I search my phone for the vet's number. I realize I'm standing shirtless in front of my window, and as I scroll for the number, I return to my bedroom to put on a shirt.

The vet's number is still in my phone from when I had a cat. I note the time: 9:15 a.m. I'm super late for my meeting. I open Slack on my phone and send a message that I won't be making the meeting at all. I'll probably just take the whole day off. I was looking for an excuse to bail on this day, and a popsicle cat I need to take to the vet is as good as any.

I close the app, not waiting for a reply. Faint pings from the laptop in the other room furiously sound, indicating someone obviously had something to say about my missing the meeting.

I wait for the vet's phone to ring for a long time until I get a voicemail saying they don't open until 9:30. "Hi, this is Adley Blaze, Mittens Blaze's mom. Owner. Well, Mittens's ex-owner, I guess. Anyway, I found a cat frozen in the snow and need to bring him in. I also need some advice on what to do. Please call back."

Have the roads been plowed yet? I check the window at the front of my house. *No, they have not been plowed. Well, fuck.*

I really don't know what else to do at this point. I return to the cat, and I gently pet him with the towel. "I'm so sorry, sweetheart. I'm sorry you landed in the yard of a useless, panicked loser who can't even figure out what to do." An overwhelming sense of grief and self-hatred floods over me, as I begin to wail.

My eyes are closed, and I am lost in my pit of despair, which, let's face it, is my default state lately. Something touches my leg. I open my eyes, and the cat has reached his paw out to my knee. He looks at me with the brightest blue eyes I've ever seen on a cat. They almost sparkle. "Your eyes are so beautiful."

He meows, breaking me from my self-pitying pit. I go to the basement and find some of Mittens' old stuff: a litter box, litter, food bowls, a bed, and so on. I set it all up in my upstairs bathroom. Then, get a heating pad and place it on the cat bed.

I return to the cat in the kitchen, and he does not break his eyes from me. He must be terrified. And he hasn't moved, so I'm worried his back is broken or something.

"Okay, sweetheart. I'm just going to pick you up and put you in the bathroom until I hear from the vet."

When I lift him, he does not fight me—further cementing my fear that his back is broken. But he does stiffen once I bring him to my chest. "Don't worry, I won't hurt you. I'm trying to help you." Almost as if he understands me, he pushes his face into my breasts and nuzzles, purring. "Aww, aren't you sweet," I say.

He howls when I place him on the heating pad atop the cat bed. "Omg, did I hurt you?! Is it too hot?" I put my hand between him and the pad to test the temperature. He nuzzles into my hand and purrs even louder.

"Wow, you have the loudest purr I've ever heard," I say with a laugh. "I guess you're just lonely. Don't worry, I won't leave you."

I pet his face in gentle strokes, and he nuzzles against my hand aggressively, his body still limp. "Can you move?" I ask.

He looks at me as if to say, "Talk to me all you want; I can't understand." He howls when I remove my hand, so I place my bare foot beside him. "How's this as a replacement?" He seems appeased and gently presses against my foot.

"Would you like a treat?" I reach into the box of stuff I brought upstairs and pull out some Churu.

Moments after I open it, his head lifts for the first time. His eyes laser focus on the tube in my hand.

"Oh, I guess you do want a treat," I laugh while backing toward the door to try and put some space between us while taking a cross-legged seat on the floor. "Well, come and get it, pretty boy."

He raises himself effortlessly as if he was never hurt to begin with. "Were you faking it?" I ask.

He pauses and shakes his head. What? "Wait. Did you just shake your head? Can you understand me?"

He freezes and stares at me as if trying to decide whether or not to answer me. Then his eyes return to the treat. "Of course you didn't. It's okay; you can have some. Come here, good boy." I say in a cooing voice.

His demeanor instantly changes to that of a confident cat. And he slowly slinks toward me, appearing to strut and show off. He stalks toward me, maintaining eye contact, and I feel as if he might eat me, not the treat.

He places his paw on my leg and moves as if he is going to climb up my chest, ignoring the treat. I put the treat in front of his face, stopping him in his tracks. He sniffs it, then grabs the whole tube, backflipping to the ground with it. He flops on the floor with the tube, pushing the pâté out with his paws and licking it furiously.

"I guess you were super hungry," I say. He nuzzles the tube as if he's never tasted anything as delicious in his whole life.

3

EZRA

"Please don't piss all over my house and make me regret not locking you in the bathroom," she says while walking to a room with two computers in it. Interesting. Does she live with someone? I will kill them. *Jeeze, Ezra. Tone it down. She's your fated mate, but you don't have to resort to murder… yet.*

"Babe, why would I piss all over your house? As you can see, I have full control of my body now. I'm all good," I tell her, twirling around, but she does not respond. Instead, she sits at one of the computers and types something.

"Whatcha doing, babe? Telling all your friends that you have finally found your fated mate and he's the hottest guy in the world?" I ask, leaping onto her lap to view the screen. I know it's uncouth to sit in a woman's lap while in my ailo form, but she's my fated mate, so I doubt she'll mind. We're going to be doing significantly kinkier stuff in due time.

She opens a messaging app I've never seen before and types, "Found cat almost dead in the snow in my backyard. Taking a personal day."

"Cat? Babe? I'm not the smartest guy in the world, but calling me a cat is a bit harsh, don't you think?" I say to her. A stream of messages pings away in response to hers. They all appear to be from men. I leap to the keys to tell all of these fuckers they have missed out, she's mine now, and they need to leave her alone.

She giggles at me. "Hey, don't walk on my keyboard," she says, placing me on the ground and shutting the laptop. The sensation of her holding me sends a tingle through my whole body.

"How are you doing, kitty?" she coos at me. Her calling me kitty is hot as fuck. Who am I kidding? Everything this woman does is hot as fuck.

"I'm just waiting for the vet to call me back," she says. I rub myself against her leg, unable to stop myself. "What a sweet boy you are." When she leans down to pet me, the hair on my back vibrates at her touch.

I can see up her shorts and look toward the soft mound being held from view by tight panties. I want to transform, throw her down, and rip them off her with my teeth.

"You're obviously someone's pet. You're so clean and sweet. I definitely need to take you to the vet so they can see if you have a microchip. Maybe I should post on the local Facebook page asking if anyone has a lost cat."

"Babe, why do you keep calling me a pet and talking about taking me to the vet? I'm all for roleplaying, but you really should let me in on the scenario. We should talk about consent and boundaries if this is going to work out."

She points her phone at me, and I pose to show her my good side because a man must always look his best for photos.

"Damn, you are so photogenic. You're like a cat model."

"Not like a model, babe, I am a model," I coo at her and rub my scent on her legs some more. I can barely contain myself; my purr is so loud that I'm surprised it's not rattling the windows.

"Oh, the vet should be open by now. Should I wait for them to call me back?"

"Babe, stop worrying about that vet and just sit down so I can nuzzle into your lap. I want to bury my face in that sweet cunt," I say up to her.

"Gosh, you're talkative," she giggles. Well, that seals it. She definitely can't understand me. You can't talk about burying your face in a woman's sweet cunt without getting a slap or at least a nervous giggle. What is going on? She obviously speaks English, so I'm confused why she can't understand me.

She nervously hits some buttons on her phone and holds it to her vestigial ear—well, for her, I guess it's her only ear. She impatiently taps her fingers on her leg in a very specific pattern while also tapping her foot.

She waits quietly, her face contorting. "Oh," she says dejectedly, "Oh, um, I'm so sorry. I called and left a message already, but this is Adley Blaze. I found a cat in the snow. I don't know if he's injured, but he might be. I'm not really sure what to do." Pause. "Yes, yes, I'll do that. Thank you for your help."

She visibly deflates as she removes the phone from her ear. "She seemed annoyed. I should have waited for them to call me back. Stupid, Adley," she says to herself.

She turns to me, and her voice changes to one less harsh than the one she used to herself. "They're open and suggested I bring you in to get you scanned for a microchip. Maybe if they scan your microchip and find your owner, the owner can pick up the bill. Is that shitty of me? To take you to the vet and then foist the bill on them?"

Why does she think I'm a pet? "Babe, I'm so confused about what's happening right now," I say.

She looks at me for a long while. I turn, letting her get a good look at me. I strut with my tail held high and puffed out. *Yes, I know, I'm handsome. Take it all in, babe.* She quirks a half smile, then walks to the window, flinging the light-blocking curtains open. The sun casts a warmth on her face that makes my heart melt.

She stomps her foot in an absolutely adorable way. If I were a better man, I'd not notice how it made her tits and ass jiggle, but it appears finding my fated mate has removed all hopes of me ever being a better man. "Fuck, the roads still aren't plowed," she says while she hits herself on the leg. "What am I going to do? The roads aren't plowed. I can't leave."

Tears stream down her face, and I really don't know what to do about it. Is she crying because she wants to help me and can't understand me? I walk toward her, trying to show her how well I feel. "Look at me. No injuries. No worries, babe. Please stop crying," I say, knowing she can't understand me but hoping she gets my intent.

She calms and says, "Maybe I can call Bryce and see if he can take us to the vet. He likes cats. God, he's going to lecture me about how useless I am and is probably gonna want some payment for helping. Knowing him, he will say he'll only do it if I blow him."

"Blow him?!" I wail in frustration. She is mine. My mate. She will not be blowing anyone but me.

"Oh my God, are you okay?! You are hurt! I knew it! Let me call Bryce and have him take us to the vet." She's spiraling again and now flipping through her phone.

"No!" I howl loudly. I jump onto the counter next to her and knock the phone out of her hand.

She looks at me in wild bewilderment. That was a bit forward of me. She probably thought I was trying to hit her. If she could fucking understand me, I'd explain I would never hurt her. But since I can't explain shit, we just stare at each other for what seems like an eternity. I must convince this woman that I am not just some pet and not injured.

Her smell is intoxicating. She looks so cute with that dumbfounded look on her face. Well, someone has to say something. "Meow!" I say and prance around with my tail held high. I give a great view of my ass and then look behind myself. "Meow," I say again. This is so embarrassing, but I know this is irresistible to the ladies. Why they like this baby talk, I will never understand. But, hey, we all have our kinks.

She reaches out and places her hand in front of my face with her fingers curled under. I purr and rub my face against her hand, unable to stop myself. "Are you feeling okay? Are you just scared?" she asks.

I need to convince her I do not need medical attention. I cannot let her call this man Bryce and defile herself for my sake. If he steps foot in this home and demands oral sex from my mate, I will murder him. I need to convince her I am alright. I need to buy enough time to figure out how to communicate with her. I also have to figure out why I can't enter my anthro form because the next dick that enters her will be mine.

"Would you like some food? What about a litter box?" *What the fuck is a litter box?*

She runs her hand down my back, and the sensation of her rubbing my body is almost enough to send me over the edge. I must get it together. I freeze and tense my body, willing myself to transform. I must have her. But alas, I still cannot. *Damn it.*

"What a good boy," she says. *Good boy?! What are you doing to me, woman?* I leap down and run to hide under the couch. I have to get away from her. I can't embarrass myself and pop a boner as an ailo. Once I can go anthro, I'll show her all there is to me. But I really don't want my mate to see my dick for the first time… like this. That would be mortifying. That's really more of a second or third-year after-mate bonding kind of thing. Like after you start leaving the bathroom door open kind of thing.

She tiptoes after me and leans down on her hands and knees to peer under the couch at me. I can see her tits through the top opening of her shirt. She's not wearing a bra. I moan loudly in absolute pain at the beauty.

She looks at me concerned and lowers her voice to something soothing, "Sorry, kitty. I didn't mean to scare you. I'm sorry you're hurting. Don't worry. I'll get you to the vet soon." Fuck, she keeps thinking my wails of lust are wails of pain. I need to figure something out fast. I need to figure out why I can't transform. Then I will sink my dick so far up her that it will do all the talking necessary between us.

=^..^= ♥ =^..^=

It's dawning on me that I've died and entered some kind of other place. I'm not sure if this is heaven or if I'm in an alternate dimension. But the way her ass curves just right where her tail should be leads me to believe this is heaven. However, I don't know why heaven would force me to remain in this form while my fated mate bounces around in those shorts in front of me. Or why heaven would make it so I can't talk to her.

She leaves me in my spot underneath the couch. I hear rustling out of sight before she returns and places a box in the corner of the room. She says, "Here's your litter box, kitty. You can go to the bathroom here." *What? Go to the bathroom there?* She's got to be kidding. Is this some sick joke?

Did I die and get reincarnated into a world where men are viewed as pets, women can't understand them, and people shit in dirt boxes? That's weird.

"I suppose I can't keep calling you kitty. What should I call you?" She taps her finger to her lip and scrunches her face in thought.

"Ezra, you should call me Ezra," I say, but I know by now that she doesn't understand me.

"How about Cheddar since you're yellow?" she says. *Are you fucking kidding me? Cheddar? I liked "kitty" better. And I'm not "yellow." I'm cream.* I start to make a gagging face, but I'm afraid she'll freak out thinking I'm dying again, so I stop.

"My name is Adley. You could call me that if you could talk," she says, giggling.

"Adley. What a beautiful name," I say—to myself, obviously.

"Let me get you some food." Okay. This is my chance. If I eat, she'll assume I am well enough not to be seen by a doctor and won't call that pervert who demands blowjobs for rides.

She exits my sight and presumably goes to the kitchen. A can opens, and she makes a clicking noise with her mouth. "Cheddar. Here, kitty-kitty. Come get some food." *Now's my chance.* I can show her I am well. Not that I could resist her calling me kitty-kitty.

A delicious aroma hits my nose, unlike anything I've ever smelled, and I am further enticed out of my hiding place. It smells even better than that ecstasy in a tube she gave me earlier. This must be heaven because this place is filled with non-stop pleasure. Well, except for the torture of not being able to fuck my mate.

She leans down and places a dish on the ground with what looks like a pâté. The food on the dish looks unappetizing, but the smell is out of this world. I look at it with apprehension, unsure what to do. She backs away slowly. "It's okay; it's food. You can eat it. I won't hurt you."

I lower my head to the bowl and sniff at it. It looks like it should smell like shit, but it's the exact opposite of putrid. I'm a personal chef, five-star meal kind of guy, and this looks super gross. I look at her out of the side of my eyes, and the smile on her face is so exhilarating that I feel an intense desire to please her. I open my mouth slightly and stick my tongue out just enough to touch the food with the tip of my tongue. The texture isn't terrible.

She squeals in delight and stops when I pull back and look at her. She does not want to scare me. She must think I am the biggest—for lack of a better term—scaredy cat that has ever existed. I lower my head again, careful not to remove my eyes from her. I'm hopeful to see her tits bounce again as she squeals in pleasure.

I open my mouth and decide just to dive in. I grab a huge bite, and an explosion of flavors fills my mouth. How could this slop taste so good? This is somehow scientifically engineered to be the most delicious fucking thing on the planet. How have I never tasted this before?

I take another bite, and she does a cute little celebratory dance. How is this woman so adorable? I purr with lust and pleasure. *Stop. Stop, Ezra.*

"Can I look at you? I just want to make sure you don't have any injuries. If you seem okay, I'll feel better about waiting until the roads are plowed to take you to the vet." I nod my head in acceptance.

"Ha, you keep nodding and shaking your head at me. It's so cute."

I lower my head back down to the food and enjoy my meal. When I'm done, I'll think of a way to convince her I'm not a pet.

Nodding seems to be making some headway… no pun intended. She approaches me cautiously and looks around my body. "You are such a handsome kitty," she says, and my heart completely melts into a delicious lustful purr. I've never felt such joy from a compliment in my life. And I fucking live off of compliments.

"You look okay. Maybe we can wait until tomorrow to take you to the vet." *Yes! Let's do that!*

"Do you prefer ear rubs or back strokes?" she asks. *Babe, you can rub and stroke literally any part of me.* I cannot stop myself from arching my back to meet her hand when she reaches out to me. The sensation of her touch reverberates throughout my entire body.

"Good kitty. Such a handsome boy," she coos. I love this woman. I love her. I have never felt such contentment in my life.

4

EZRA

Adley leaves the room and returns with a laptop—different from the one she messaged on earlier. She sits at the table and flings it open, glancing at me as she pulls open the computer. How many computers does she have?

I want to see what she's up to. Hopefully not messaging the blowjob demanding douche. I sigh a sad goodbye to my meal. As much as I want to finish this, I must ensure she is not messaging that guy. I rub my scent on her feet and look at her inquisitively. I make a questioning mew hoping she'll tell me what she's doing.

"Well, if I'm not working today, maybe I can do some work on my game," she tells me. Her game? What's she talking about?

I leap atop the table and position myself in front of the computer screen so I can see what she's looking at. "Hey, I can't see," she says, gently nudging me to the side.

I sit next to the laptop and am pleased to see no messages from men. I rub against her hand, marking it as mine. Is she a programmer? A black screen with what looks like code stares back at her. She switches windows, and crudely drawn characters are placed throughout the screen. Is this a video game? *Awesome.* Does she make video games? *That's so cool.* I paw at the screen, hoping I can get her to talk about it.

"Cheddar, stop. You'll scratch the screen," she says.

"Babe, my claws are retracted. Don't worry about it," I say to her and knock her chin with my forehead.

"Cheddar, I can't see," she laughs at me.

"Come on, babe, I wanna know what this is." Maybe I can walk on the keyboard and type, "Not a cat, hot fucking dude," or something equally insane.

I place my paw on the 'N' key but am immediately lifted and placed beside the laptop. I harumph at her. "Wow, such a mad boy," she giggles.

"You can sit with me if you want," she says, patting her lap. *Score.* I slink down, careful not to hurt her, enjoying the softness of her flesh under my paws. I curl up in her lap. The feel of the crevice between her thighs against my side makes my body melt into her.

She shifts windows with a sigh, gazing absently at the code. When her phone vibrates, she checks the screen, grimacing before placing it face down. Pushing her laptop aside, she rests her arms on the table and lays her head down, peeking at me through her arms. With her eyes shut, she appears on the verge of tears. Her hair falls around her face like curtains. *She's so beautiful.* I stand in her lap, rubbing my face against hers. "What's wrong, babe?"

She sits upward and brings her legs into a crossed position on the chair, wrapping her legs fully around me. She stares blankly at the wall while stroking me. I'm obviously enjoying this; in fact, this may be the best thing that's ever happened to me. But she's unhappy, and I cannot enjoy being nestled against my mate's pussy and wrapped in the embrace of her legs if she is unhappy. "It's okay. Whatever has bothered you, I will fix it," I say, knowing she can't understand me, but I don't care. Commence *Operation Destroy Whatever Has Made My Mate Unhappy.*

It was the phone or the laptop that upset her. *Let's start with the laptop.* I stroll behind it, pressing my back against it until it shuts. She chuckles. "Yeah, I wasn't getting work done anyway. Thanks, Cheddar."

"No prob, babe."

Now for the phone. It's face down, so I gently push it off the table, hoping it will land face up, allowing me to see the message. *Score!* It falls face up. "Cheddar!" she scolds me.

"No, it's okay, babe. I got this," I say and leap down to the phone, unlocking it with a swipe.

A message from someone named "Bryce" is front and center. *Is that a dick pic?!* My blood boils, and every strand of hair on my body stands on end. With a low violent growl, I attack the phone. How dare this motherfucker send my woman a dick pic! Adley reprimands me once more, "No, Cheddar! Bad boy!" I recoil, not in fear of her, nor truly hurt by her words, but… I admit, they do sting. I don't want her to see me as a bad boy. I want to be her good boy.

"Aww, baby. I'm sorry, did I scare you?" she asks.

She lifts me to her chest and holds me like a baby, my belly raised. At first, I am quite uncomfortable having my belly exposed like this, but her reassuring gaze makes me feel so at ease. I smush my face under her tits, further reducing my uneasiness.

She strokes my belly, and the need to sink into her is so overwhelming. I need to transform immediately. I cannot take one more minute not inside of her. Why can't I fucking transform?

She carries me to the living room and sits still, cradling me against her breasts. I'm tempted to take a nibble of the underside, but I really shouldn't bite her until I learn how to ask her if that's okay.

"Wanna watch TV?" she asks me.

"Sure, babe, whatever you want, as long as your tits stay on my face, I'm a happy man," I respond.

"I'll take that as a yes," she says, which is good because it was. Maybe she's starting to understand me.

The TV illuminates the darkened room, and she opens an app I've never seen before. She scrolls through the options, and I stand in her lap, my attention now on the TV. "Oh, you like TV?"

"No, I just… I've never seen any of these shows before," I say. "Fuck, I really am in another world, aren't I?"

"I'll take that as a yes, too," she says. She's wrong in her translation this time, but one for two isn't bad.

I leap from her lap and approach the TV. As much as my body misses the warmth of her thighs and tits, I want to get a good look at these shows. Something seems off. I'm not sure what it is. As I get closer, I realize what it is. Absolutely none of the people in the small previews have ears or tails. What the actual fuck?

"Babe, am I dead? Are you an angel?" I ask her.

"Oh, you don't want to watch any of this?" she asks.

"No, that's not what I said!" I return my gaze to the TV as she switches to another app. The new app contains only animated shows. She clicks through a few different things, and my attention is drawn to a panel of a show called *Fruits Basket.* It shows a young girl with two boys standing behind her, one with orange hair and another with black. She's also holding an orange ailo. The description says something about a family that can transform.

Wait a minute! I paw at the *Fruits Basket* panel before she can navigate away from this screen. "Hey, I wanna see this one, babe! Let me see this one!" I scream.

"Woah, Cheddar. Calm down. Do you want to watch *Fruits Basket*? Okay, that works for me." She presses select, and we watch the show together.

At one point, she laughs and says, "Oh, dang, I should have named you Kyo," referencing the male lead with orange hair. A sinking feeling in the pit of my stomach builds as I watch the show.

I stay transfixed next to the TV, waiting for it to explain what's going on with me. I watch until almost the end of the episode before I finally see what I've been waiting for: the boy with orange hair, Kyo, transforms into an orange ailo. Well, not an ailo—a cat. When the young girl, Tohru, touches him, he transforms into a cat. She freaks out and picks him up, saying he needs to go to the doctor.

Is this what has happened to me? Do the women transform their men into cats and then take them to the vet? No, that can't be it. Tohru was really surprised when Kyo transformed. Does Adley think I'm a fucking cat? When she called me a cat earlier, I thought she was being cheeky, but now… can she not transform into an ailo form? Is that why she can't understand me? Is that why she doesn't have a tail?

Fuck. Am I stuck in this world as a goddamn cat?

Adley sighs and leaves the living room. I want to keep watching this show because, despite the existential crisis it is forming within me, I'm enjoying it. I follow her back into the kitchen area—reluctant to let her leave my sight and also kind of hopeful she'll give me some more of that food. Instead of getting me food, she sits back at the laptop at the table.

I leap into her lap. Something on this laptop is stressing her out, and I want to comfort her as best I can.

Curled up on my mate's lap, I begin to doze off in contentment with the beat of her heart soothing me. My eyes drift closed as I watch the snow fall out the glass door, contemplating my fate. I'm worried maybe I'm stuck like this forever. And if that's my fate, I suppose it isn't so bad. The snow is beautiful. So is my mate. The food is great. I guess if I have to be stuck like this, it's nice that I'm stuck here. *Just me and my mate. Forever.*

A movement flashes by in the backyard, snapping my heavy lids open. *What the fuck was that?*

I leap from her arms onto the table, hopeful to get a better look. The snow is dying down, but it still obstructs my vision. I slink down, ears back, squinting into the snow. *Pounce mode activated.*

A black figure makes its way slowly through the trench in the snow Adley's path made during my rescue.

I crouch down, hoping to conceal myself. It's another Ailura! A male. His powerful form slinks forward with grace. *Who is that? How did he get here? Is he here for my mate? She is mine.* I cannot protect her from the men in her computer, but I can protect her from whoever the fuck this guy is.

A low howl seeps from my chest as he approaches. He does not see me yet and continues to walk toward the house. Adley moves beside me. "What's up, Cheddar? Do you see something?" she says and leans forward, peering through the window.

The Ailura sees her, and his tail and ears shoot straight up. Without a moment's hesitation, he launches himself forward, galloping down the path. His four paws move so fast I wouldn't know they hit the ground if it weren't for the trail of footprints left behind him.

I jump off the table and stand at the base of the window. I steel myself for the approach. What will he do? Will he transform and open the door? Should I transform and open the door to cut him off? *I can't fucking transform. This is such bullshit.*

There is no sense in trying to remain quiet now. I scream at the top of my lungs, "Stay back! Don't you dare come into this house!"

Adley coos at me in that soothing voice she uses when trying to calm me, "Aww, Cheddar baby, it's okay."

"No, Adley, please stay back; it's not safe!" I shout at her.

"Are you scared, Cheddar? What's going on? Why are you crying?" She asks as she kneels to get closer to my level. A loud thump slaps against the glass door as the other ailo's body slams against it. He is at the door and staring at Adley with such intensity he doesn't even see me.

His demeanor instantly changes, as a shiver runs down his spine. His ears tilt forward, and his eyes widen. His pupils dilate, fully engulfing his irises. *I know that look.* That is the look of a man purring for his fated mate for the first time. His hair lowers, and so does his body. He rolls to his back showing her his belly. His purr is loud and low—lower pitch than mine.

"Oh. Wow. The cat distribution system is working overtime today," Adley giggles.

This fucking guy. How dare he show his belly to my mate!

I leap in front of Adley and throw myself at the glass door so hard it shakes. "Cheddar, calm down!" She says with a tone of anger. Why is she mad at me? I am protecting her. Has this fucking rake won her over?

Slamming my body onto the glass causes him to finally notice me. He slowly stands to a less languid pose. Then, his ears and tail shoot straight up as they did when he spotted Adley. He freezes in place, staring at me. His disposition changes after a moment, and now he looks like he wants to kill me. His ears are laid flat on his head, his fur is raised, and he yells to me, "How are you alive?!" *What?*

Adley pushes me aside and squats in front of the glass door. "It's okay, Cheddar. He won't hurt you. He's outside. There's glass here." He freezes when she moves in front of him. His eyes lock on her crotch. Damn, those fucking sexy shorts—giving him an eyeful.

He stands and rubs his body against the door, marking his territory. How fucking dare he. I leap at him again, yelling, "No! This is my mate!" The glass shakes with a loud thud.

His tone completely changes, and a smoothness that emanates intense lust rolls out of him, "You are incorrect. That is my mate. I have purred for her." He continues to rub against the glass and now looks at Adley. "Hello, my name is Marshall. What is your name?"

"Aww, he's so cute. Cheddar, can I let him in?"

"No!" I plead with her. I turn back to the douche behind the glass. "She's my mate. I purred for her first. I have already claimed her," I yell back and smack at the door.

The sugar in his voice subsides only slightly, "Then why does her hand bear no mate-mark?"

Why? Because for some fucking reason, I can't transform. But I can't tell him that. If he knows I can't transform, he'll take advantage of the situation and probably kill me. *Why did the most fucking astute motherfucker in whatever universe this is have to show up on my mate's door?*

"It seems you haven't fully claimed her, or she's not really your fated mate."

"She is my fated mate! I will kill you," I hiss.

"I don't think you will. If you were going to, you would have come out here and done so already," he says in a flat tone.

I have no response for that. I cannot admit I can't transform.

"Are you too weak to transform? Oh, well, I guess that means I can claim her first," he says cooly. He pauses and tenses as if he is about to hack up a furball.

"What is happening? Why can't I transform?" he shrieks.

"Ha!" I laugh back. "Fuck you!" I howl.

"Cheddar, baby, you need to calm down. Be a good boy," Adley utters.

She cracks the door ever so slightly, and I leap on the chance to throw my claws at this ugly motherfucker's face. Unfortunately, he has the same idea: our claws scratch at each other painfully.

"Please let me in. I can be your good boy," he says as he flops on his back again.

"Aww," Adley coos. "Okay, sweetheart, don't worry. I'll let you in. First, I need to do something about the man of the house." She reaches down and picks me up. My muscles instantly relax as I melt into her soft flesh. She holds me against the swell of her breast, and all rational thought leaves my head. Lust overpowers me, and I forget about that other guy. As I forget about everything, I purr, nuzzling my face into her breast.

"Wow, what's gotten into you? Are you trying to butter me up so I won't let him in?" she asks.

She's walking me toward her bedroom. When we get in there, I will reveal my anthro form to her. I will use every ounce of my strength to transform. Once she sees me, there's no way she'll choose him over me. I will claim her, and we will live happily ever after.

She strokes my head and coos at me, "It's okay, my good boy. He won't hurt you."

We are in her room, and I am ready to try transforming again, but I have to wait for her to put me down so I don't hurt her. She gently lays me on the bed. Does she know what I'm thinking? Does she want to make love to me, too? I straighten my body, preparing for the transformation. And nothing fucking happens. *Fuck*!

She backs away from me toward the door. "Don't worry, Cheddar. I'm just going to let him in to make sure he's okay. I'll lock him in the bathroom for now." *Wait, what? She's going to let him in?*

She quickly jumps backward through the door, pulling it shut. *What the fuck?! Did she just lock me in here?*

I leap from the bed and try to peer under the door.

"Adley, no! You can't let him in! You are mine!" I howl.

She ducks close to the opening under the door. "Be a good boy, Cheddar. I know you're jealous and think this is your territory, but I need to check on him." *Think it's my territory? What does that mean? This IS my territory.*

I'm sure you will be the best of friends," she says.

"No, the fuck we won't!" I howl back.

I watch her feet disappear down the hallway and toward the back door. Deep sinking helplessness overwhelms me as I howl for her to return to me. "Please, Adley! Please! Don't choose him over me! I'm sorry I knocked your phone off the table!"

Is there something in this world blocking my transformation? Am I doomed to be stuck in this form for the rest of my life, unable to consummate my love with my fated mate? Am I truly in hell?

5

MARSHALL

She left with Ezra. Of course, she'd choose Ezra over me. He's perfect. He's everything I'm not. Even my fated mate won't choose me! I stand at the glass door, and wail as the sorrow overwhelms me, "Please choose me! I promise to be the best mate! I will do anything you need! I will cook! I will clean! I will even do your taxes! I will be a good lover!"

I have never felt such despair. I finally found my fated mate, finally found a woman whom I am instantly attracted to, and she is off being fucked by Ezra. I will never be able to compare to him. I thought he was dead. Is this where he has been for the last ten years? If so, why hasn't he mate-marked her yet?

The smell of his lust has me in a state of arousal that I am struggling to recover from. Flashes of them mating and me within the mix quickly flicker through my head. I try to repress the thoughts. I try to focus on what I can do to get her to come back. I picture her beautiful smile looking up at me, ready to take my cock in her mouth, while his smile beams brightly next to it.

A purr rips through my body, a distinctly different feeling than the anguish in my head. I thought I was over Ezra. I thought getting a fated mate would pull this obsession with him out of my head. *Why do I feel even more attracted to him than ever?*

Just as I think the pain of loss will become unbearable, she is once again in view. Ezra is nowhere to be seen. *Where is he?* She smiles at me, and my sorrow melts. I feel a warmth the likes of which I have never felt. Did she choose me?

She slowly approaches the door, and I sit patiently—afraid moving will startle her. "I'm going to open the door. Will you be a good boy for me?" she asks.

"Yes. I will be very good. You can let me in," I respond.

She giggles, "I'll take that as a yes."

"Please take me," I say as I envision entering her. My ears fall, and the purr rumbling through my body relaxes all my muscles and threatens to stiffen my cock. I've heard purring for your fated mate for the first time can whip you into a sexual frenzy, but I always thought everyone was exaggerating. This is maddening. All I can think about is sinking my dick into her and putting my mate mark on her. Hopefully, she'll let me. And hopefully, she will let me soon.

In my research of the portals, I found mention of women with beauty unmatched by any of our world. I assumed they were fanciful legends. Masturbatory fantasies conjured by men with too much time on their hands and not enough interaction with women. There was never any proof of the portals, let alone the women on the other side, but now I see both the portals and women were based in truth. She resembles the paintings of angels in chapels. I wonder if those who claim to have seen angels also saw through the portals.

The blood rushes to my cock at the thought that I've been fated with a literal manifestation of a goddess, an angel, a being with beauty so unparalleled that she has been written as a legend.

It would be my luck that Ezra has also bonded with her. I have to get rid of him. I can't share her with him. I have no idea how I'll do it, but I must. The thought of the three of us embraced in a pile of lust sounds appealing, but it's not what I want for myself.

I have never seen a woman like this. I sound so cliché, but I've never been instantly attracted to a woman. To anyone. She has a sparkle in her eyes absent in my world's women. I think, perhaps, it is related to her irises. I could spend my whole day staring at her eyes—staring at the swell of her breasts. She has a hold on me. I must study her face and determine precisely what it is that is so beautiful about her.

She squats in front of me, and the opening of her shorts hangs at an angle such that I can see the slight curve of her ass cheek. She shifts slightly, spreading her legs, and I focus on the soft skin on her inner thigh. I melt toward the ground and show her my belly. *Oh, please, please open the door.*

"Aww, you're so sweet. Okay, I'll open the door. Please don't scratch me."

"If anyone ever thinks of scratching you, I will destroy them," I say softly. I must control my tone. Women like it when you speak softly.

The door slides open, and the smell of pure bliss wafts toward me. Her smell is like nothing I've ever experienced. It takes every ounce of my willpower not to launch myself so that my face is buried deep between her legs. I try to transform to take her properly, but I cannot.

This is… unfortunate.

I am broken from my lustful stupor by Ezra loudly yelling, "I swear to God if you hurt her, I will kill you and your whole family!"

I stiffen at the sound. He dares to threaten me? I have no family, so that doesn't bother me. But hurt her? That would never happen.

She notices my reaction and says, "Don't worry, he's locked in my bedroom." He's in her bedroom? I want to be in her bedroom.

"Can I pick you up?" she asks as she tentatively approaches me, hands outstretched.

"Yes, you may," I say while I stand on my hind legs and stretch myself toward her. It's taboo to be held in this form, but I give all of zero fucks right now. This is actually quite nice—to be so deliriously in love.

"Omg, you're just like my Mittens!" She says and reaches down toward me. *Mittens? Who is that? An ex-lover?* Jealousy ripples through me. She pulls me close to her chest. I feel a comfort and pleasure I did not think was possible. My purr grows louder as I nuzzle myself into her neck.

"Oh, you sweet boy." A small tear begins to escape the corner of her eye. I study her face, trying to determine what she's thinking. She seems happy, yet sad. I'm not sure what's going on. It's an emotion I don't know the name of. Maybe she lost someone recently, and I am bringing her relief? I need to set aside my lust for a moment and show her some empathy.

I headbutt her, wiping the tears with my face and lick her nose gently. "I'm sorry you are hurting, angel. I will do everything I can to ensure you never hurt again."

"Alright, Romeo," she giggles. I don't know what that means, but it seems like a good thing.

She carries me into her home, and I don't pay much attention to my surroundings, but when she stops, I realize we are in a bathroom. She puts me down on the counter.

"I'll be right back. Please wait here." She snaps a picture of me with her phone.

She shuts the door gently behind her, and I am alone. *Why did she lock me in here?* I guess I'm stuck in here until she lets me out, or I can transform and let myself out. Ezra has finally stopped yelling. *At least there's that.* I'll explore for a bit while I wait.

Her hairbrush is on the counter. I approach it and feel guilty about what I'm about to do, but her smell on it is so intoxicating I cannot help myself.

I'm sure she won't mind. If she does, I will wash it for her. *That would be upsetting.* I rub my face against it, finding pleasure in the sensation and mixing my scent with it. *You will be mine, sweet angel. What is her name?* I suppose I should find out.

I'm lost in the sensations of the brush when she returns. She has a box of dirt, some bowls, and a can. *What's this?* I stop brushing myself to get a better look at what she's up to. She doesn't immediately scold me for scenting her brush, so she must like me.

"I'm sorry I didn't request your name earlier. As you know, the purring causes males to be… well, a bit stupid. But I am a scholar, and I can control myself. I'm sure Ezra has charmed you with his looks, but I can be a much better mate. I promise. Oh, um, my name is Marshall," I ramble at her, not as clear-headed as I want her to believe, while she begins arranging the things.

She places the box on the floor and then fills one of the bowls with water. *Oh, is that for me? Does she think I'm thirsty?* This woman is so sweet. She's helping me remain comfortable while I am stuck as an ailo. I've never hated this form more. God. I'm so fucking useless right now. But that's okay. We are mates now. We will work together to help each other.

"Thank you, sweet angel. I actually am quite uncomfortable as an ailo and prefer not to take this form. So, it means a lot to me that you are trying to improve my comfort," I continue to ramble at her. She simply smiles at me and proceeds with her tasks.

She opens a can with a clack, and a smell almost as intoxicating as hers hits me. *Is that food? Oh, wow. This place must be heaven.*

She empties its contents into the other bowl on the ground. I cannot help myself—I instantly jump to the bowl. I take a deep whiff before sinking my teeth in.

"Well, you must have been hungry," she laughs. "Okay, well, I'm going to leave you in here for a bit," she says, running her hand down my back. If I died right now, I would die happy. I am in pure ecstasy. *Is this what every moment with her will be like?* Every moment spent getting my PhD and researching the portals to this dimension has been worth it.

"Okay, I've got to go check on Cheddar. Once y'all seem to get along, I'll let you out. You're so sweet. I wish I could keep the two of you, but you're obviously both someone's pets."

Keep us? What does she mean? I stop eating and look at her. She's already halfway out the door. *Wait. She's leaving me in here? She's going to make me leave?* She gently shuts the door, and I remain here dumbfounded.

I run toward the door and push my paw under it. "Angel, please don't lock me in here. I promise I will be a good mate," I plead. Stretching my arms as far as I can under the door.

Not far from where I am, she says, "Okay, Cheddar, he's in the bathroom. You can come out now."

Who's Cheddar? A door opens, and the thunder of running paws approaches me. Instantly, claws sink into my outstretched arms. I wail out in pain and bring my hand in.

"Stay the fuck away from Adley!" Ezra yells.

Oh, Cheddar must be what she calls Ezra. *That's weird.*

"Oh. Her name is Adley. Adley is a good name for a mate," I say.

"No!" he screams and swats at me under the door. "She is my mate!"

"Well, unfortunately for you, she is my mate, too," I say, trying to sound intimidating, but knowing I'm failing.

"I'll just let you boys get to know each other. I'd appreciate it if you kept it down, though," Adley says. The sound of her soft footsteps wander away from the door.

I beg her, "Adley, please don't leave me in here. I'm sorry I rambled and talked about myself. I was nervous. You're so beautiful! It frazzles my brain thinking of us mating." And at that, my brain frazzles thinking of our body parts intertwined.

Ezra hisses. "She can't understand you, you fucking idiot," he says, pressing his nose under the door. I could pop his cute little nose, but I don't want to scar his face. And I'm too sad to deal with him right now. I sink to the ground and wail in desperation. He doesn't seem to be a threat to Adley and can't seem to transform, so I don't have to worry about him claiming her, at least.

"You will not touch her!" he says.

"I'm going to touch her… a lot," I say back as cooly as I can. I try to conjure up visions of bullies that get laid a lot and emulate them, "You'll be sitting on the sidelines crying, stroking your cock, and I'll be filling her up with so much of my seed we'll start a whole colony of hybrids. I wonder if they'll have my ears or hers," I chuckle. *Damn, that was good. Nice work, Marshall. Very intimidating and confident.*

"You are not good enough for her!" Ezra hisses.

"Nor are you! All you do is fuck women and leave them, Ezra! I know you. Your reputation precedes you."

He doesn't say anything. He just stands there with his nose under the door, huffing. Still angry. I hate that I think his nose is cute, but I'm happy I've upset him this way—and on purpose. Usually, I upset people without meaning to.

"Boys, I know you're both big, strong men who need to show each other who's boss, but would you mind keeping it down?" Adley yells from another part of the house.

"As soon as I can transform, I am going to get out of this room, and I am going to make love to her until she forgets you ever existed," I say to Ezra with a growl. *Ha! If only my speech teacher could hear me now. She wouldn't be proud, but probably impressed.*

He hisses and claws at me, but he can't reach me. He screams, "Wrong! I have never met a woman that I couldn't make love me. I will make her love me, and then I'm dragging your ass back home so I can be with her without you bothering us."

"Back home? Didn't you notice your portal closing?"

"Portal? Gone?"

"Yeah, your portal is closed. It's gone. We're stuck here. Permanently. There's no getting rid of me," I say.

As I say this, I realize there are quite a few other ways he could get rid of me. None of which would be too extreme for a man protecting his fated mate from someone trying to take her from him. He could kill me. He could kill Adley. I know he won't do that. A man would never kill his mate, no matter how deranged he is. But me? He could definitely kill me. Well, he could try, anyway. I won't go down so easily. This resolve is unlike any I've ever experienced.

"We'll see about that," he says and slinks off toward the direction of Adley's voice. "Have fun shitting in your gross sandbox." *What? Why would I shit in the box?*

6

ADLEY

Fuck, I really don't want to call Bryce. But now that there are two cats here, I feel like I should take them to the vet and find their homes. Waiting much longer would only be cruel to them and their owners. I've been doing my best not to text him—not cave to the booty calls. But now that Ethan doesn't come over anymore, I don't have anything left to distract me from my toxic draw to Bryce.

I call him, but am immediately sent to voicemail. He's hung up on me. I don't know why I called, he won't answer. I'll text him. A message on my phone pops up before I even get a chance. "I'm at work. What do you want, Adley?" the message says.

"Two cats showed up in my backyard. I need to get them to the vet but the roads still aren't plowed. I was hoping you could maybe take me in the truck," I text back.

"I guess I could come over in a bit," he responds, following up with a winky face. What's with the winky face? Shit. I forgot about the dick pic he sent me earlier. Cheddar somehow accidentally deleted it. I didn't even realize cat paws could trigger capacitive touch.

"Thanks so much!" I text back then put my phone away. I sit on the couch and pull out a book to read while I wait. Cheddar sits next to me, glued to my side. "You're so sweet. I bet you're lonely, huh? Don't worry; I'll find your owners soon enough," I say and stroke his back. He nuzzles against me, flopping around as I pet his body. I pull a blanket over my body, chilled by the weather and my minimal clothing. He makes biscuits on the blanket against my leg and eventually falls into a contented trance at my side.

We sit like this for a while and it makes me wish I could keep him. Long moments pass, and I'm really getting into the steamy scene of my book. I reach under the blanket and gently press at my clit to suppress the arousal. I'm not sure what's going on, but I've been so extremely aroused all day. I'm not ovulating, but my hormones are running rampant.

I moan, and Cheddar wakes, standing right at attention. I laugh, "Sorry to wake you."

My phone vibrates in my pocket. A new message from Bryce: "Wut you up 2?" *Has he been thinking of me?* He sends me dick pics often. His response can go one of two ways: he can find a way to make me feel bad for wanting him or find a way to make me feel bad for NOT wanting him. And unfortunately for me, I almost always want him. I miss him. I've lost count of how many times I've let him come over, remind me that he broke up with me for a reason, and then have what he calls "pity sex" with me. God, I'm so fucking pathetic. I know I'm worth more than this. I don't know why I am stuck on him.

I sigh. Am I desperate enough to flirt back? He'll be here soon. I need a ride to the vet, and I think maybe I also need to get laid. I could pretend I didn't see this message. Feign ignorance when he arrives and insist we leave for the vet immediately. Or…

"What do you think, Cheddar? Should I message him back?" He doesn't respond—obviously. I chew the inside of my cheek and think about the last time I hooked up with Bryce.

He has always been an excellent lay, even if he is a total douchebag. Also, I get a sick sense of satisfaction sleeping with him while he's with Veronica, given the history of her stealing him from me. The guilt over her being pregnant while I sleep with her fiancé does keep me up at night, though, and every single time I vow will be the last. But, discovering today that the baby was conceived while he and I were still together, makes me feel quite a bit less guilty. So, maybe I shouldn't feel bad about fucking her man—she fucked mine, after all.

I miss her too, if I am being honest, but her betrayal seems less forgivable somehow. Not that I forgive Bryce. I just want to fuck him. That's not forgiveness. That's just getting a basic need met. It's medical.

My pussy still aches from the arousal my book has stirred. I wiggle slightly on the couch, arousing myself with memories of Bryce. I stand, trying to remove any pressure from my pelvis. I slip my hand into my panties and press hard against my clit. *Fuck. Yeah, I am desperate enough.*

"I guess I am," I say to Cheddar.

"Touching myself thinking of you," I text back with the hand not in my pants.

"Ooo rly? Can I get a pic of your wet pussy?" He responds.

"I can do you one better," I respond. I send the pictures that I took of Cheddar and Romeo. "Two pussies for the price of one. They're dry, though, sorry."

"Funny," he responds with a smirking emoji. "But really, I wanna see your tight wet pussy. Send a pic." Damn, he must be desperate to call it tight. Typically, he finds a way to insult me. Calling me loose is his go-to insult—right after fat.

"How about you see it irl?" I respond.

He messages me with an eggplant emoji and the letters "omw." I place my phone on the coffee table, and Cheddar jumps up to look at the phone.

"Looking at your picture?" I laugh. "You're cute, huh? Bryce is coming over. We'll take you to the vet and hopefully find out who owns you." He begins pawing at the phone, the messages scrolling quickly.

"Stop that, silly. You'll accidentally text him. You already deleted one of the pictures he sent," I say, turning off the screen. I flip it upside down just to be safe. Cheddar looks like I stole his favorite toy and wails at me. "You sure are emotive," I laugh.

I catch my reflection in a nearby mirror. *Fuck, I look like shit.* I run to my bathroom, and Romeo sits on the sink counter waiting for me.

"Good news, Romeo, I'm taking you and Cheddar to the vet. They'll scan you for microchips and hopefully figure out who your families are."

Cheddar appears at the door and howls, inciting a growl from Romeo in response. "Fuck," I say and close the door. Romeo jumps down and continues to howl at Cheddar from under the door.

I swipe a brush through my hair and brush my teeth. Suddenly, the howling stops and Romeo is by my feet, rubbing against my leg while I slap on some lotion and a little mascara.

I open the door cautiously, trying to stop the impending firestorm of fur and claws, but Cheddar blocks my path, rubbing against my legs.

They look at each other and continue to rub against me. "What, y'all are friends all of a sudden? Worked it out under the door?"

Cheddar looks at me and nods. "That nodding is so creepy, Cheddar. Fuck, he'll be here soon. I've got to change." They rush in front of me and stop, rubbing against my legs and mewing. It's almost like they're trying to stop me from leaving the room.

"You're going to trip me. What has gotten into you, two? Bryce is coming over. Yeah, he's a pretentious douche, but he can't talk if I'm sitting on his face." They continue to howl and whine.

I rip my shirt and shorts off and throw them in the basket. While I stand at my underwear drawer, I notice the howling has stopped. The two are on my bed, side by side, staring transfixed at me. "You two are so weird." It's almost like they're ogling me. *That is deranged, Adley. Don't be so desperate for sexual attention that you think your cats find you hot.*

I pull up a pair of sexy undies and hold it up for them. "How are these?" I say, holding the panties against me. They blink slowly at me, unmoving. "I'll take that as a yes, I guess."

I remove my current undies. "Fuck, they're soaked," I say. Two howls and purrs come from the bed. They show me their bellies. "You're both so cute," I say, stroking them. "But I can't just sit here and pet you. I have to get ready."

The cats watch me with the intensity of a burning sun as I frantically change my clothes. I slip on a quick sundress because this should be easy to get fucked in. I'll have to change into something else when we go to the vet—it's like negative ten degrees outside.

I look into the mirror and check myself out. "What do y'all think? Do you think Bryce will like it?" They both stand, their hair rising. "What's gotten into y'all?" I exclaim as they start zooming all over the house. "Can y'all please get your zoomies out before Bryce gets here?"

MARSHALL

Ezra says, "She can't do that. She can't invite a man over here!"

"She can do whatever she wants. And it seems she already invited him," I say.

Ezra yells at me, "Why are you being so cavalier about this? We have to stop her. We can't sit here while she…" he gulps, "sits on some other dude's face!"

"Shut up for a minute. I'm thinking." My brain reels, considering ways to get around this.

"Thinking about what?!"

"I'm trying to figure out how to stop this, you moron."

"Maybe I can pretend to be hurt or sick. When she found me, she took off work to care for me."

"Shut up," I snap. Actually, that's not a terrible idea. It's better than the idea I have, which is nothing.

"Fuck you. I'm going to vomit in front of the door." Ezra runs towards the door and heaves. His back arches and his eyes bulge. Is he able to make himself throw up? Wasn't he part of an anti-bulimia campaign?

I run toward him, unsure what to do.

"Cheddar! No, not now," Adley says, exacerbated.

She stands above us. Ezra looks up at her and freezes mid-gag. *Why did he stop?* I look up and am greeted with see-through underwear, slightly moist and glistening. I too am frozen in lust.

The doorbell rings, breaking us out of our stupor. We slam our bodies against the door, trying to block Adley from it.

Ezra howls, "No, Adley. Please. I love you. You are ours. Don't let another man touch you." He said "ours," not "mine". *Interesting.*

"Okay, sillies. I need to open the door now," she says, gently pushing us to the side with her foot so she can reach for the door. She swings it open, forcing us between the door and the wall. I'm stuck in the corner and cannot see anything except the fluff of Ezra's tail. Ezra is squished against me, howling. The feeling of his body against mine like this makes me gasp.

"Ah, you wore that dress I like," the faceless man says. I hear a noise that sounds way too much like a slap on the ass for my comfort. "But, you've put on some weight. Might need to retire it," he continues.

I leap over Ezra to get a look at this man. I am stunned by his size. He's the opposite of Ezra and me. We're lean, but he's all hulking muscle. What the fuck is this guy? A bodybuilder? His hand is up her skirt, with a whole fistful of her ass squeezed between his fingers.

I puff myself up as big as possible, turning my body to the side. *Be big, Marshall.* I hiss. Ezra follows suit.

"These the cats you need me to drop off at the pound for you?" the hulk says.

"What? No. I need you to take us to the vet," Adley responds, confused.

"Oh, I didn't realize I was signing up for all that," he says.

"I swear that's what I texted you," Adley says, walking toward her phone on the nearby coffee table. He grabs her arm, stopping her.

I howl, "Don't grab her like that!"

He says, "It's alright. I'll take you. But first, I have some major blue balls from those sexy texts you were sending me. I know you're desperate now that I'm gone, but I was at work."

She cuts him off, "You sent me a dick pic."

"Well, you started texting me about that wet pussy of yours. I'm just a man, Adley. I can't ignore a message from a desperate slut," he says.

I howl and hiss at him. I want to claw him up, but Adley is in the way, and I can't safely get to him without hurting her.

"Fuck you, bro! You texted her a pic of your dick, and she sent you pictures of us!" Ezra growls up to him. "Who the fuck does this guy think he is? The king of gaslighting?" Ezra asks me.

"We must kill him," I howl, entirely on the same page with Ezra, ready to join forces to take this colossal motherfucker down. How we will do that in our tiny ailo forms when I doubt we could even do it in our anthro forms is beyond me, but I am willing to try for my Adley. Honestly, this guy is such a cock I would probably do it for anyone.

"As soon as Adley is safely away from him, *Operation Take Down the Big Guy* is a go!" Ezra howls.

"Right!" I respond.

"I'm not going to argue with you about the chain of events, Bryce," Adley says. *Why not? And why are you letting him talk to you like that?* She turns to us and says, "Gentleman, can you please calm down? Do I have to lock you in the bathroom?" She reaches towards us, and we each relax, not wanting to hurt her, but scurry away to avoid being caught. I hide under the couch, and Ezra jumps on a lower shelf of a bookshelf. We glare and growl at the man.

"Well, as much as I love an audience, I don't know if I can get it up with all this racket. Let's go to your room," he says.

"Yes, let's," Adley says. She grabs his hand and leads him towards her room. Ezra tries to scratch him as he walks by, but his outstretched paw is easily avoided. I rush to the bedroom door, blocking their path with as much of my body as possible.

Adley laughs and says, "It's almost like he understood you." *Why are you doing this, Adley? He's such a jerk!* I must stop this.

He slinks toward her, cornering her against the wall. He snakes his hand between her legs and traces the edge of her lace panties, eliciting a moan from Adley that makes my hair stand on edge.

"I have to admit, sometimes I missed this sopping wet cunt," he says into her neck.

I have a perfect view of everything his hand is doing to her. He uses his middle finger to push her panties aside and plunges into her with his other fingers. The sight feels like a stab through my heart as Adley arches forward, pressing her body against his.

She bites her lip and says, "We can fuck, but then we need to go to the vet, okay?"

"Alright. I'll fuck that fat ass right here," he says and grabs her aggressively, turning her away from him. He slaps her ass hard. "I love watching it shake. Bend over for me."

She obliges.

"Touch your toes. Or are you even capable?" he laughs.

"Come on, Bryce. I've told you I don't like when you talk to me like that," she says and bends forward.

"But you still do it. Because you're a needy slut who wants my big dick. Aren't you?" She doesn't respond. "Aren't you?!" he says louder and slaps her ass even harder this time. She lets out a whimper.

My heart breaks when she responds, "Yes. I'm a needy slut who needs your big cock. But, please, not so hard. We've gone over this."

"You think that's hard? Just wait, slut. I have something hard for you," he says while pulling out and stroking his, honestly, not very impressive, dick. My heart stops. I don't know what to do. Ezra stares down and appears to be in shock, unsure of what to do either.

"I'm going to bury my fat dick so deep inside you, your insides are gonna' get rearranged. I know how you like it. You like it rough, don't you, you dirty fucking slut?"

Why is she letting him talk to her like this? Does she like this? She rises slightly and says, "Bryce, I don't need this shit."

"You do need this. You need it so bad. That's why you stalk me on that alternate, huh? You think I didn't know? Come on, Adley, I know you. I've pounded that pussy more than anyone. Now take this dick." He grabs his dick and moves toward her.

Without thinking, I lunge toward him, ready to scratch his eyes out, my muscles ripple and my fur recedes, as my body stretches to my anthro form midair.

I scream, "Don't you fucking dare," as I collide with him, my naked body hurls against him.

In that same instant, Ezra jumps from the bookshelf and is full anthro before he even hits the ground. "I'll fucking kill you," Ezra screams. We throw ourselves onto this guy who's twice our size, probably put together, and push him away from Adley. She turns, facing us, eyes wide. We both grab ahold of him, naked flesh slapping together.

Bryce seems horrified. "Eww, gross. What the actual fuck?! Where did these guys come from? I'm not into gang bangs, Adley. Learn to respect some boundaries, you fucking bitch."

Okay, so he was horrified that two naked men were on top of him.

He pushes us away from himself, causing Ezra to fall to the ground. I am able to maintain my balance.

He scrambles to his feet and pulls up his pants. "Don't fucking text me again, you freak," he shouts and runs out the door. "Your pussy is too loose anyway, and you need to lose weight," he screams from the front porch, having left the door open.

I run toward the door. "It's scientifically impossible for a vagina to be loose. It stretches to accommodate what is placed inside it," I yell back. And, in an attempt to be more insulting and less pedantic, I add, "There is such a thing as a small dick, though!"

Ezra yells, "Yeah! And your sexting game is weak, bro!"

I help Ezra from the ground, asking, "You okay?"

"Yeah. Did he really think we were trying to fuck him? Shit, that's embarrassing. Are we really so unintimidating?"

I look Ezra up and down, trying not to focus on his nudity. *Is he intimidating? Yes.* But not because he looks like he can hurt someone. He's intimidating because when you look at him, you feel like you're standing in the presence of perfection. I open my mouth to say something, but only an "uhh" emerges. *Nice work, Marshall. Very articulate.*

"Never mind. I don't want to know," Ezra says, waving me off.

A weak whimper sounds to my left, and Adley stares at us wide-eyed, pressing her body as close to the wall as possible.

Ezra smiles at Adley and outstretches his arms. "Okay, so… let me explain."

7

ADLEY

"Don't come any closer," I squeak at the two incredibly hot and incredibly naked men standing in my hallway.

"Babe, it's me. Cheddar. Well, Ezra," the tall blond one says, placing his hand on his chest. He walks toward me and grins so wide that I can almost see all his teeth. Dazzling. His arms are outstretched as if he plans to embrace me. He also has a massive erection—an impressive erection. Despite his face looking friendly and his body being appealing as fuck, he's still a fucking man—therefore, he cannot be trusted.

The even taller brunet one says, "I think you're scaring her." My bedroom is just a few feet away. I need to get behind that door.

Undeterred, the one who claims to be Cheddar says, walking toward me, "Adley, seriously, it's me, Cheddar. I've been trying to talk to you all day." He reaches toward me.

"Don't touch me!" I yell out.

"Okay, okay, I'm backing off," the one who claims to be Cheddar says.

He backs far enough away that he could no longer reach out to me, so I leap through my bedroom door and slam it behind me, locking it quickly.

"I'm going to call the cops! Get the fuck out of my house," I scream.

"Babe, we're not going to hurt you," the one who claims to be Cheddar says.

"You shouldn't have approached her," the other one says.

"Dude, it's real easy to criticize when you aren't fucking offering any other suggestions. All you did was stand there."

"I was trying not to scare her. Two naked men materializing would be scary to any woman."

"But… she's my fated mate. I need her to talk to me," the blond one whines.

"You will not be mating with me, you fucking assholes! Get out of my house!" I scream, even though sex with them would likely be magical, and I wish my door was glass so I could look at them a little longer.

"You're not doing a very good job talking to her," says the dark-haired one.

"Fuck you, dude! Do better then!"

"I'm calling the cops!" *Fuck.* My phone is in the living room.

"No, you're not," the dark-haired one says.

"That sounds so ominous and rapey, dude!" says Blondy. "What he meant to say was, 'You left your phone in the living room.' Remember, you flipped it upside down on the coffee table? When I tried to text that asshole and tell him not to come and mess with you."

Wait, what? "How do you know that?" I ask.

"Because it's me, Cheddar," he pleads.

"I swear, if you hurt that cat, I will kill you," I say.

"Aww, babe, you'd kill for me?"

"You can't just keep telling her you are Cheddar. She does not believe you. She will not suddenly start believing you," chimes in the brunet.

"Dude, offer solutions or shut the fuck up," the blond one says.

"So, what is your plan? We just stand here and wait for her to come out?" the other says.

Suddenly, I recall the bat under my bed. I slide over to the side of my bed and pull it out, gripping it tight. I want to remove the dust bunnies that static-cling to the knee-high Sailor Moon sock slipped over it, but there's a time and a place for that kind of anal retentive behavior. This being neither.

"I talk to her. She'll come out once I fully explain that she's my fated mate and all that entails," the blond one says.

"I don't know if you can charm your way out of this one," the other says.

"Well, she'll have to come out eventually. There's no other exit," the blond one says.

"There's the window," the dark-haired one says.

The window! I run to the window, bat in hand, and open the curtains.

I have no idea how to open this fucking window. Since I have lived here, it has never been ajar. The bat is under my armpit while I frantically fumble at the latch, trying to figure out how it works. I think I finally have it when the incredibly hot blond one runs up to the window, naked, clearly freezing in the snow, waving his hands frantically. *So fucking handsome.*

"Seriously, I won't hurt you. Please just talk to me! I am your fated mate!" he says. I wonder how many of my neighbors are getting a show right now.

I refuse to be the woman who is killed in her home because she didn't appropriately suspect the insanely hot naked guys who broke in and attacked her ex-boyfriend. I scramble back from the window, falling on my ass and gripping my bat even harder.

If he's outside, that means only the other one is at my bedroom door right now. I'm going to have to fight him off. Maybe I can get my phone.

I resolve myself and stand—my socked feet slipping on the hardwood until I get my balance.

I hesitate a moment before willing myself to open the door. I swing it open and grip my bat, ready to hit some fucking balls.

"Oh, she's left-handed," the tall, raven-haired one says as I kick the door open.

"Dude, how is that relevant right now?" the blond one says, rushing back from the outside. He must have seen me go to the door through the window.

"Just an observation," the brunet shrugs.

"Babe, seriously, we're not going to hurt you," says the blond. The noiret one backs away, but the blond one stands his ground. He must not think I will hit him. *I will smash that pretty, smug, fucking face in.*

I swing my bat, ready to knock his fucking head off, but Blondy grabs it. He looks at me stunned, dumbfounded. "Ow, babe, come on," he pleads.

Too bad for him—I read that one article explaining why I should put a sock on my bat. I pull back the bat, causing his grip to get lost under the sock.

"Shit," he says as realization dawns on him.

I swing again, this time even harder. And he flinches downward, covering his head, until suddenly he is no longer there. *What the fuck? Where did he go?*

I look around, confused. I approach the brunet, ready to cave his head in, but he points downward. And there's Cheddar. He meows at me.

"Cheddar, are you okay?" I ask. *Oh, thank God.* I was worried these weirdos hurt him.

Cheddar then turns into the hot blond, nervously laughing, "Babe, you almost got me."

"What the fuck?!" I shout, startled, stumbling backward and almost falling.

"Whew, I was worried I couldn't transform," he says, shaking his limbs. Then, to the other man, he says with a little bounce, "Bro, looks like I can do it again!"

"Wha…" I gape.

"I told you, I'm Cheddar," he says, but I swing again. He transforms into Cheddar again, narrowly dodging my swing, and runs off, jumping onto my couch.

I rush toward the dark-haired one, swinging. But before I can hit him, he turns into Romeo and jumps onto the bookshelf.

Cheddar turns into the man again and says, "Listen, I know this is really weird and scary." I swing, he transforms, and he jumps to the other couch as a cat. My bat crashes down on a vase.

He becomes a man again and says, "I gathered from that show we watched earlier, *Fruits Basket*, that this is not something people in your world can normally do." I swing again, and he transforms again.

Romeo howls. The blond one yells to him, "Dude, I don't know! I'm trying here. Maybe you could fucking help." Swing, transform, leap, transform.

"But, I promise, we will not hurt you," Cheddar says.

I am exhausted. I don't know how much more I can keep swinging at this guy full force.

"Babe, you're going to hurt yourself. Please just put the bat down and talk to us," he pleads. I swing again, only for him to transform and leap out of the way again.

"No, I'm going to hurt you," I say, pulling the bat high above my head. Something grips the bat, stopping it from moving. I turn to see the brunet holding my bat with one hand. I pull with all my might, but he's overpowering me—with just one hand. I'm fucked.

"Please sit down and let us talk to you," he says, staring down at me. I fall back and sit on the couch.

"Happy?" he says to the other. "I helped."

"Thanks, bro," the blond one says with an annoyed sigh.

I fall onto the couch, panting, my heart racing, worn out from trying to kill them with a bat. They stand over me, dicks fully in my face. My fear must be apparent, because they both back away from me, giving me a bit of space. The dark-haired one stands at the entrance to the living room, blocking my exit. But the blond one sits on the opposite couch, leaning back, cocky as fuck.

"Oh, geeze, Ads, that was a workout," he looks around. "You broke your cute little vase," he says, pointing at the pile of ceramics on the ground. *It was a cute vase. Dang it.* Not the worst of my problems right now.

"I think maybe you should shut up and give her some time to process this," the brunet says beside me.

"Oh, okay. That makes sense," he says. "I'm sorry, babe, take all the time you need." He leans back as if he's presenting his body to me.

I catch my breath and get a good look at the two of them. They do look like those cats—like men-versions of Cheddar and Romeo. In all the excitement of trying to murder them with my bat, I didn't really register the ears atop their heads and the tails. I was distracted by the attempted murdering—and the dicks.

"Are you really Cheddar?" I finally ask.

"Sure am, babe," he says, transforms into Cheddar, and then prances around in a circle on the couch. He meows, and the other grunts in response—I'm guessing they can talk to each other.

He transforms and says, "But my name is actually Ezra."

"And you're Romeo?" I ask the tall, dark-haired one.

"Marshall," he says directly. He doesn't transform to prove the point. He doesn't need to. He just stands there covering his dick.

These really are the cats that showed up in my backyard.

"How? Why? How?!" I ask.

"We're from another dimension. We came through portals in your backyard," Marshall says, looking down, not making eye contact. *Is he shy?* He's covering his junk with both hands. Hmmm, a home-invading rapist wouldn't cover his junk.

"There are portals to another dimension in my backyard?" I ask excitedly.

Marshall responds, "Were. There were portals to another dimension—our home—in your backyard. They closed. I believe they were one way."

"Why would you go through a one-way portal?" I ask.

"Well, I didn't know it was one way. I went through because I was curious," Marshall says abashedly.

"Well, you know what they say about curiosity and the cat…" I say, trailing off.

"No, I do not. What do they say? And we are not cats," Marshall says.

"That it killed it. That curiosity killed the cat," I respond.

"Interesting. How would the construct of curiosity kill a cat?" he says looking to the side, obviously contemplating the saying.

"Um… it's an idiom. I recommend not thinking too hard about it," I retort.

"Okay. But please do not call us cats. It is rude," Marshall says.

"Dude, chill. They like cats here," the blond one, Ezra, says.

"Perhaps you do not mind being called unintelligent, as you so obviously are, but I take offense to it," Marshall says.

"Okay, I apologize. I will not call you cats," I say.

"Thank you," Marshall responds.

I look to Ezra, "And you? Why did you go through a one-way portal?"

He shrugs and says, "I didn't choose to go through any portal. I didn't even realize I had gone through one until this guy showed up and started yelling about portals. I just kind of ended up here." He looks at his nails, avoiding me as if he has more to say on the matter but has chosen not to.

The difference between the two is shockingly apparent. One stands, shy, a man of few words. The other lounges like he's lived here his whole life.

"Okay, so you're not cats, and you're not humans. What are you? What is your species called?" I ask.

Marshall responds, "Ailura is the name of our species."

"Okay…" I say, trailing off and trying to absorb this whole thing.

I look between the two of them. Their naked bodies are on full display. They both have similar builds: tall, lean, and muscular. From this angle, I can see the way Marshall's ass curves from his leg, and holy fuck that's a tight ass. I can feel the redness of a blush enter my cheeks, and I turn to Ezra. He's even harder to look at, leaned back on my couch, ankle crossed over his knee, arms splayed out, and dick fully erect.

"Um…could you, like, put a pillow over that or something?" I ask, kind of not wanting him to.

"You sure you want that, babe?" he says with a Cheshire grin.

I want to ask if they can read minds, but if he can't, that would definitely admit what I was just thinking. I avert my eyes. "Yes, please."

He shrugs, evaluates the pillows on the couch, and chooses the frilliest one to cover himself.

"Can you hand me that one?" Marshall asks, pointing at one of the other pillows.

Ezra throws it at him. He catches it, realizes he is uncovered, and covers himself quickly.

"You're welcome, bro," Ezra says.

"Thank you," Marshall responds.

Now that their dicks are covered, I can get a better look at them without distraction. Perched atop their heads are furry ears that twitch and turn as they talk and blend seamlessly into their hair. Their tails are covered with the same hair as their ears and seem to have minds of their own. Marshall's black, sleek, powerful tail flicks anxiously behind him. In contrast, Ezra's tail sways casually at his side—so fluffy.

They are absolutely gorgeous. Flawless skin. Sinewy muscles. Toned. *So toned.* Images of the two of them ravishing me run so quickly through my head that I think the neurons in my brain short-circuit. I squeeze my legs together hard, relieving at least a little of the lady boner I am getting.

I bite my lip, trying to think of how to ask what I want to ask without sounding like a horny, needy slut, all of which I kind of am right now.

"You got something you wanna ask us, babe?" Ezra says, leaning forward, elbows on the pillow. Marshall also appears to lean closer. Moisture pools under me as my pussy does everything it can to tell me, "Hey, brain, let these two dudes fuck you. You'll like it."

"Um, earlier, you kept saying something about fated mates," I ask meekly, squeezing my legs together again and trying to tell my pussy to shut the fuck up.

He leans forward, mouth cocked into a half grin, and purrs out, "I did say something about that, yes." His personality seems to have changed since earlier—when he was trying to talk to me through the door. Earlier, he was excited—childlike. Now he seems cocky—suave.

"So, umm… that's not a thing here. But, I watch a lot of anime and read a lot of smut, so I think I get the general idea of a fated mate, but, umm… how do you know I am your fated mate?" I ask.

"You like to read smut? Is that what you were reading earlier when you started touching yourself," Ezra says with a half-smile, trying to derail the conversation.

I blush, embarrassed, unsure how to respond.

"We purred for you," Marshall says, and Ezra cuts him an annoyed glance for putting the conversation back on the original rail.

"Don't cats purr all the time?" I ask.

Marshall says curtly, "We are not cats."

"Oh, um. I'm sorry. Do Ailura not purr all the time?" I ask again.

"We only purr for our fated mate. I've never purred before," Marshall says.

"Have you?" I ask, looking at Ezra.

"Not until I saw you," Ezra responds, licking his lips. "Fated mates are kind of a one-time thing," he adds.

"Well, actually, in rare cases, very powerful female Ailura have been able to collect multiple fated mates," Marshall says, correcting Ezra. Ezra shoots him a "shut the fuck up" look.

"Okay, so I'm your fated mate. Are y'all also fated mates of each other?"

"NO!" They say in unison, glaring at each other. If this were an anime, lightning would be shooting between their eyes.

They return their attention to me, but Marshall glances back at Ezra, his expression saying something I can't quite distinguish. However, Ezra does not see this look as he stares intently at me.

"Technically, we could be fated by the transitive property of our relationship, but we'll never be able to mate-mark each other. Males can only have one first-degree fated mate," Marshall explains further.

"Transitive property?" Ezra asks at the same time that I ask, "Mate-mark?"

Ignoring Ezra, Marshall responds to me, "After we claim you, we will place a mate-mark on you."

Before considering what he's just said, I answer Ezra's question, "The transitive property is an algebraic property that states, 'if a and b are related, and b and c are related, then a and c are also related.' So, to put it simply, if you are my fated mate, and I am his fated mate, then you and he are also fated mates."

"Oh, thanks, babe! See, it's not so hard to answer a question, bro," Ezra says, smirking at Marshall.

Marshall looks at me in admiration, then turns to Ezra, "Well, I did not think you would understand it," he barks at Ezra.

"Then why'd you say it?" Ezra asks with a hiss.

In all the smut I read, whenever a woman has a fated mate, he is very possessive. These two obviously don't like each other. Will they be bickering and fighting each other until I choose one of them?

"Does this mean that you are going to fight over me until one of you can 'claim' me and 'mark' me?" I ask, punctuating "claim" and "mark" with air quotes.

"Um...," Marshall says and looks at Ezra, unsure what to say. Ezra looks back at him. His wheels are turning. Marshall may call him dumb, but I see a calculating man before me. I also see Marshall relying on him to lead the conversation. Ezra's face contorts momentarily, revealing he has determined the best path forward. "Here's the thing, babe. Like he said, we only get one shot at this. You're going to consume our thoughts until the end of time. We will always be drawn to you. So, yes, we will fight for you. The fated mate bond is the ultimate form of love and pleasure. We need you. We crave you. No other person will ever be able to satisfy us. In fact, we'll be in sort of a lust frenzy over you until we can claim you. Some men have been driven mad by an unclaimed mate bonding. Fighting over you? Well, that's up to you."

"Frenzy?" I ask.

"We'll be driven mad with arousal until we can... satiate the desire," Marshall says averting his eyes.

Hmm, interesting. I guess that explains all the blushing and boners. "And what do you mean it's up to me?" I ask Ezra.

He sighs. "Well, it is your choice. You could choose not to let us claim you—it can only be consensual, you understand. In which case, we'd probably fight to win your affections until you died. Or, you could choose one of us, in which case we'd fight each other—until one of us died. And, then, there's the last choice. I can't believe I am about to say this. You could let us both claim you, and we'd just have to learn to get over it." He shrugs and leans back, seeming to concede.

Okay, I can have neither of them, one of them, or both of them. I don't know anything about them. I definitely want to fuck both of them. But, "mate bond" with them? I don't want some magical ball and chain attached to me just so I can get laid—even if it is with the most ungodly attractive men I've ever seen. Men that cause my whole body to tingle with lust just looking at them.

I need to get to know them. I don't have to know them to fuck them, though, do I? I suppose I should learn about this. They look at me expectantly, like they want me to say something. "That's a big decision," I say, biting my lip.

"Do you not want to be with us?" Ezra asks.

"I didn't say that," I respond and look at them in a way that I am sure they perceive as eye fucking because Marshall fully blushes and pushes his pillow tighter to his crotch while Ezra licks his lips.

"So, are you saying you do want to be with us?"

"I also didn't say that." But yeah, I am kind of saying that because every molecule in my body begs these men to enter me.

Ezra leans forward and places his hand on my knee, his posture one of casual seduction. The feeling sends shockwaves through my entire body, and it takes every last bit of my willpower not to moan. He asks, "What can we do to help you decide?" *Lick my pussy and make me scream!*

"We'll see," I say, not ready yet to say yes. Definitely not ready yet to say no. "For now, let's get you two some clothes." Dear God, please don't let this be the stupidest fucking thing I've ever done. Dead in a ditch, murdered by models.

They look at each other disappointed, then to me. Marshall nods, and Ezra stands, saying, "Sure, babe, we'll put on some clothes, but I doubt we'll be wearing them for long."

"I think I have some clothes that might fit you two," I say, looking at their naked bodies, embarrassed to let my eyes linger for much longer. I lead them to my bedroom, still a bit weary of them, but honestly, it's hard not to believe dudes who can magically transform into cats. Also, if they were going to hurt me, they definitely would have by now.

Ezra invades my space like he did as a cat and croons at me, "Do you really want me to get dressed?" He tilts my face toward his with gentle fingers on my chin. I avert my eyes because eyes are even more challenging to look at than dicks.

"For now," I say with a nervous giggle. Pulling away from his touch, which, surprisingly, isn't particularly bothersome—I usually cringe at the touch of people I don't know.

I turn away from him and bend down to look through the drawer where I keep my pajama bottoms. "I have some men's shorts that might fit you," I say.

I pull out two pairs of men's basketball-style shorts. When I face them again, they both look pained and are covering their dicks. "What's wrong?" I ask.

"That ass," Ezra says.

Embarrassed, "What's wrong with my ass?!" I ask, reaching behind myself.

"Absolutely nothing," Marshall says with tears in his eyes and a voice dripping with lust.

Ezra moves closer and says, "Babe, that is the most perfect fucking peach of an ass I've ever seen. It's taking every ounce of my self-control not to bite into it."

I blush, unsure if I believe all this, and laugh nervously. These men are hot. Unbelievably hot. Like "Am I dreaming?" hot. To hear them say such a thing to me is a bit outlandish. But I suppose two cats I found in my backyard turning into hot dudes is just as outlandish as hot dudes being into me. I'm still a bit incredulous and squint at them as if they're full of shit.

"Here you go," I say, giving the shorts to Ezra. The enthusiasm on his face upon noticing me watch his dick as he releases it is adorable. It is challenging not to ogle him. I toss the other shorts to Marshall, who stands rigidly upon noticing me look at him. It's as if he wants me to look at him but doesn't know what to do with his body. Now, side by side, they wait, dicks at attention, not putting their new shorts on. They're probably expecting I'll change my mind and say, "Actually, boys, don't put on the shorts, fuck me instead."

I raise my eyebrows at them as if to say, "Go on then." Their faces cloud with disappointment. Maybe I should have complimented them and said something like, "Yes, boys, you have imposing members." Ezra almost leaps into his shorts with the exuberance of someone with infinite energy. But, Marshall puts his on in a more reserved, controlled way. The shorts are too small on both of them.

Their members are outlined perfectly. So, I still get to see what they're packing and honestly, I'm not mad at it. I'm kind of wishing I had given them some smaller shorts.

I give them shirts that might fit them. Ezra slips a pink *Fruits Basket* shirt over his head and points at his chest, "Hey! I know this!" and laughs. Marshall puts a black tee that says "C#" on with such controlled, deliberate movements that it's as if he's in a slowed-down commercial, trying to sell me that shirt. *Sell it to me, baby.*

The shirts do not reach their shorts' edge, exposing their midriffs in such a small, slight way; the eroticism of it makes me reconsider my stance on school dress codes. Teen boys and their inability to concentrate in the face of midriffs suddenly makes sense to me. *I get it, teen boys; I get it. It is distracting as fuck. But, still, stop objectifying girls.*

I can probably see the heads of their dicks pop out if they shifted just right since they seem to have tucked their erections into the waistline of the shorts to keep them from standing straight out. A twinge of great arousal rushes through me. Somehow, the idea of their dicks sneakily poking out their shorts is more arousing than their dicks out in full force and in my face.

Ezra gazes at himself in my full-length mirror. He asks, "Is this how men dress here?" turning to check out his ass. He looks incredulously at Marshall, recognizing that they do both look a bit ridiculous.

Without waiting for an answer, probably knowing from the smirk on my face what the answer is, he asks, "Where should I put my tail?" The shorts are pulled down below the base of his tail, exposing the tops of his ass cheeks.

He stuffs his tail down one of the short legs and pulls the shorts up to the appropriate place on his waist. The shorts now being correctly positioned, further accentuate his dick, but the fluffy blond tail wiggling out the bottom looks so ridiculous I can't help but laugh.

He spins around, poking his butt out at me. "What, this look isn't doing it for you, babe?" he laughs.

"Actually, it kind of is," I say and laugh. "Hold on just a sec." I find the sewing kit in my office closet and return to him, pulling the scissors out. He looks concerned momentarily when I say, "Turn around," but returns to his flirtatious demeanor pretty quickly as the realization of what I am aiming to do crosses his mind.

"Yes, ma'am," he says, grinning at me and pointing his ass at me. I pull out the waistband, squatting down to eyeball the location of his tail at the base, and cut a vertical hole approximately three inches long along the seam. I grab his fluffy tail through the hole, noting my fingers as they graze his ass, and thread it through.

He shivers, doubling over and bracing himself against the bed with one hand and clutching at his dick with the other.

He pants, "You gotta warn a guy before you do that, babe." He composes himself quickly and pulls me close, jamming his cock into my side and stroking my cheek. I swoon when he says, "Don't make me blow my load before I have a proper chance to make you come first."

Deflecting, I say, "Oh, well, don't come in the shorts. I don't think I have any others that will fit y'all." Ezra is disheartened, but not deterred by this rebuff to his advances and continues to smirk at me, gripping me tightly and pressing into me.

I pull away and say, "Marshall, should I cut a hole for your tail, too?" I hold the scissors up as if I'm about to challenge him to a fencing duel. Ezra's smile falls when my attention is turned to Marshall.

Marshall clears his throat and nods. He croaks out, "Yes, please," but does not look up from the ground.

"Don't be shy, bro," Ezra grins. "She'll be gentle with that tiny tail of yours," He snickers then scowls, obviously not wanting me to help Marshall.

Marshall turns his back to me, but not before cutting Ezra a glance that could melt ice. I cut the hole for him, then lean forward and unable to stop myself from teasing him, I whisper seductively, "I'm going to pull it through now." And to further tease him, I say with a gasp, "Are you ready for it?"

He clutches at the edge of the dresser, bracing himself, his body rigid and the muscles in his neck tensing in a way that makes me want to lick him. With a nod, he whimpers, "Yes, I am ready."

I drum my fingers into a firm grip around the base of his tail. It's thinner than Ezra's bushy one, making it much easier to feel the powerful muscles undulate under the fur. As I thread it through the hole, a gasp releases from Marshall, making me wonder if he actually came. Maybe I should have given him something to bite down on. The reaction is so deliciously arousing.

He wipes the sweat that has beaded across his forehead, and says, "Thank you," in a way that oozes with so much gratitude I can't wait to hear him thank me for fucking him. I stand close to him as he turns to me. I am taken by the height difference between us. His towering form makes me want to drop to my knees so that he can tower even higher as I suck his dick. As I consider him, he averts his eyes. It seems I'm not the only one who struggles with eye contact.

I desperately want to sprawl on my bed and say, "I was just kidding, guys. Please pound into me so hard my brain rattles in my skull." But I really need to continue our previous conversation and learn more about these guys before I fully slut it up with them.

Perhaps some social lubricant (aka wine) will help me get over whatever is still holding me back from believing what's happening. "Let's go in the living room and chat. Would y'all like some wine?"

8

EZRA

I think that's the first time in my life a woman has ever talked me into my clothes. I would be discouraged, but I see the way she looks at me. She wants it. Unfortunately, she also looks at the guy on the opposite couch the same way.

The two couches in the living room sit perpendicular to each other, adjoined by an end table. Additional tables sit on their opposite sides, and another coffee table sits in the middle. Marshall and I choose opposite couches and sit on opposite sides—an attempt to put as much space between us as possible. We have formed an unspoken truce of sorts, but an air of animosity still lingers between us. I'm definitely ready to throw down if necessary.

I realize that by sitting on opposite couches, Adley will have to choose which of us to sit with when she enters the room. My heart races in anticipation of her return, confident she'll pick me to sit with. Well, mostly confident.

Adley scurries between the living room and the kitchen. The spaces are joined by a small partition separating them, but they're mostly visible to each other. She returns with three wine glasses intertwined between her fingers and an ice bucket holding a bottle of wine. She lays the glasses on the coffee table, a neutral zone that doesn't yet signal where she plans to sit, before returning to the kitchen momentarily.

This time, she returns with a tray, bending in front of me to place it on the coffee table. I want to rise and sink my dick so deep into her that she screams in Marshall's face, but I'm a gentleman. Mostly…

The tray has what appears to be snacks—a charcuterie board. It is adorned with varied fruits, cheeses, and crackers, most of which are recognizable to me. She's placed them on the tray in an aesthetically appealing way, and I can't help but wonder if she's trying to impress us with her domestic skills. I am impressed, but I'm much more impressed by the ass that is once again in my face as she plucks a purplish bulbous fruit from a bushel. I'm not quite sure what it is. A faint memory of recognition flits at the back of my mind, but I cannot place it. It looks kind of tasty. I mean to ask her what it is, but before I get a chance, Marshall rises from his seat and forcefully grabs her hand, shouting, "Adley, no!" effectively scolding her like a child. This action causes the fruit en route to her mouth to fall to the floor.

As it rolls lazily toward my feet, I recognize it for what it is. *A grape!* I stand, alert, and kick at it, sending it under the coffee table and not wanting it near me or my woman.

"Hey!" she says, offended at his intrusion and jerking her hand from his grasp. "What the fuck, Marshall?"

Marshall looks thoroughly chastised, and I am happy he's the one she yelled at, not me. I got yelled at enough with my attempts to thwart cell phone pervs earlier today. She rubs at the spot where he grabbed her and backs away from him, moving closer to my space. *I shall protect you from the big mean man, babe!* I consider using this moment to my advantage, shielding her with my body, pressing against her lustfully, of course, and saying, "Yeah, Marshall, what the fuck?!" Fully feigning ignorance so that she'll choose me, and we'll go back to her room and live happily ever after—at least two times.

Marshall does not meet her eyes and stares at his toes, looking like a little kid being yelled at by his mommy. I'm annoyed at how cute it kind of is. Adley looks like she's ready to tear him to pieces if he doesn't provide a valid explanation for his actions immediately, and I appreciate that his inadvertent cuteness does not squelch her rage.

"It's poisonous, Adley," he states meekly.

"What are you talking about? Grapes aren't poisonous," she says, annoyed, still rubbing her wrist. A look of understanding crosses her face when she says, "Oooh, grapes are poisonous to cats," while snapping her fingers and looking to the side.

Marshall opens his mouth at the word "cat," but before he can protest, she says, "I'm sorry, I'm not calling you a cat. I know you're not cats. But they are my only reference. It's hard not to draw parallels." After a moment's pause, she continues, "In my world, cats are our pets. We love them. I love them."

"It's cool, babe, comparing us to cats is fine. As long as you don't call us cats, it's not that insulting," I say. Marshall looks like he may protest, but doesn't.

"Oh, like the difference between calling someone a bitch and saying they're acting like a bitch... but, I always found both to be equally insulting." Before I can tell her that comparing us to dogs and bitches is actually way worse than cats she changes the subject.

"I suppose y'all evolved from them or something?" she asks.

Marshall shakes his head, "No. Cats exist in our world but are extremely rare and a scientific anomaly. They are from a completely different branch of the evolutionary tree than Ailura. In fact, cats are so distinct genetically from all life that they appear to have evolved on their own singular evolutionary tree. Our ailo forms share many traits with them, but we don't share any known common ancestors. Our genetic blueprints are so different we might as well share no traits at all."

I chime in with a shudder, "They have these dead eyes. They're super creepy."

"Well, they're prolific here," she says. I hope I can avoid ever seeing one in person. They are terrifying.

She says, "But, back on topic. Grapes aren't poisonous to me. I love grapes. I promise I'll be okay. Do I need to remove them from the room? Will it hurt you if I keep eating them?"

I'm incredulous, but I will try to trust her because why would she have them if they would kill her?

"Oh, no, as long as we don't eat them, we should be okay," Marshall says. He gently brushes his fingers at the reddening ring around her wrist. She does not pull away but lets her hand hang at her side, allowing him to touch her. A low growl resonates within me at the audacity of him to touch her, and at the pain she is inevitably feeling due to his actions.

"I'm sorry if I hurt you," he says, tears welling in his eyes.

"It's okay. Just a little misunderstanding. It probably won't be the last we have." She laughs at this, unconcerned while pouring a glass of wine. "Oh, I suppose that means you can't have wine. It's made of grapes."

"You make wine with grapes?!" I ask, taken aback, sticking my tongue out in disgust.

"Yeah. It can be made with other fruits, but I've only had wine made from grapes. We make spirits from other foods, like wheat, barley, rice…," she trails off. "What is your wine made of?"

"Mostly apples," Marshall says. "It's interesting how similar our worlds are." He looks around in fascination, taking the whole room in with his eyes. "We have the same fruits, and even our furniture and technology are extremely similar. Everything is just… slightly different," he says as he sits back in his spot. Distracted, he leans over and inspects the table's wood to his side. "What kind of wood is this?"

"Absolutely no idea," she says, not taking her eye off the glass she is filling to the brim. Her glass is nearly overflowing now, and she sits on the couch Marshall is on, balancing her wine so it does not spill.

My heart sinks at her choice of seating. I sit back in my spot, and she says, "I'm sorry, I don't have any wine for you. But can you eat the cheese and crackers? Oh, are you hungry? I should have asked. I can get you something more substantial."

"No, the food you gave me earlier was delicious!" I say.

"Yes, the food from earlier was more than sufficient," Marshall says.

Adley giggles, but I'm not sure why. Is there something funny about us eating that canned delicacy?

She places her glass on a coaster atop the table to her left. I realize the coaster is an island in a sea of random stuff—a tablet device, glasses, headphones, vitamins, hand lotion, books, hair ties—all things that indicate to me that the spot Adley sits in now must be where she generally sits. No other table has personal items on it—just vases and coasters. Awesome. She sat there just because she always does, not because she wanted to be near Marshall.

I shift down to the opposite end of my couch so I can be closer to her and lean as far over the armrest as possible, spilling onto the table that's holding her wine and other possessions.

She sips her wine. The movement of her throat as the liquid glides down the inside of her delicately curved neck, attached to her soft shoulders, is so lurid. Well, actually, it's the vision of my semen shooting down the back of her throat that this swallow conjures that is lurid, not the swallowing itself. I appreciate that she is being modest in her willingness to just give herself to me, but this has honestly been the hardest I've ever had to work for a lay. And for her to be so incredibly intoxicating while also withholding her sweet cunt from me is torture—really, it's damaging my pride a little. But, I recall the saying that goes something like, "Nothing worth having is easy," and I know that in Adley's case, the saying is true. She'll make me work for it, and it will be even sweeter for it. Not that I would judge her for just giving it to me, mind you.

Turning my focus from her throat to her breasts, I am incredibly grateful she put this dress on—even if it was for that colossal asshole. It is silky and hangs on her tits in a way that makes me think even the fabric itself wishes it could break so that it could reveal those beautiful tits to the world. My eyes are locked on the point where the small, thin strap holds the fabric stretched over her breasts. If only it would snap. *Where are those scissors?*

Marshall, no longer enthralled by the curiosities that are "types of wood," notices me leaning closer, my breath bouncing off Adley's breasts. He scootches closer to her and smirks at me, indicating that he is as aware as I am that, for him, there is no table between them.

She looks between us and giggles, "This is so weird. Y'all are looking at me like I'm some kind of goddess or something."

"You are," we say in unison.

"Sure," she laughs into her glass and then drinks.

Before we can protest her dismissal of our compliments, she says, "Okay, I think y'all need to explain to me how you came here. You mentioned one-way portals." She pulls her legs up to sit cross-legged and fluffs the dress to form a small tent over her knees. *Would it be inappropriate for me to transform and hide in there? Yes, the answer is yes, right?* She then grabs the pillow behind her and places it in her lap. Oh, how I wish I were that pillow.

Marshall positions himself as if he is about to begin what will obviously be a dorky, arrogant speech, so I chime in before he can, "Oh, well, I don't know too much about how I got here. I was having a party at my house, and the next thing I knew, I was here in the snow." Marshall eyes me with a dubious expression. *What, bitch? Got something to say?*

"That was ten years ago. Where have you been since then?" Marshall asks. *This fucking guy.* I guess he did have something to say.

"What!? It was this morning. I have only been here a few hours. However, it was nighttime during the party," I respond, thinking about what the change in time, not just weather, could mean.

"Ten years ago, Sarah Chance was charged with your murder. The investigation was prolonged due to them never finding your body. I guess this is where your body has been this whole time," he says.

"Really? Was she found guilty?" I ask. The memory of her shoving me flashes before my eyes.

"Yes. There were enough eyewitness accounts to determine her guilt. She was sentenced to life in prison," Marshall responds.

"Oh, I feel kind of bad about that... but she did push me off a balcony over a cliff. I guess I fell through a portal, and it saved my life," I say, trailing off and imagining that princess of a woman in jail, and a twinge of sadness flits through me.

"So, I guess time works differently here," Marshall trails off, and now we both seem lost in thought.

"Why did she push you?" Adley asks. *Damn, this woman really cuts to the chase, doesn't she?* I like that. I can't tell her I was super fucking drunk, prancing around on the edge of the railing when my girlfriend pushed me off the balcony in a fit of jealous rage. Well, ex-girlfriend, I guess. We were literally in the process of breaking up.

Instead, I say flippantly, "You know how women can be," with a shrug. Apparently, that was not the right thing to say because Adley looks offended. I am striking out. I need to take control of this conversation.

"Witnesses claimed they were fighting about his infidelity. He broke up with her, saying he was going to go fuck other women at the party. So, she pushed him," Marshall states. *Damn, dude, give a guy a break.* Adley looks at me, repulsed. *Well, fuck.*

"I did not cheat on her! I have never cheated on anybody. She was super insecure about it, though, and constantly accused me. I was trying to break up with her, yes, but not to fuck other women. I was fed up with the accusations," I say. Fucking Marshall. It's hard to pass myself off in a good light with this story in the open.

"How do you know all this, Marshall? Do you know each other?" Adley asks.

Not letting him answer because the dude is really fucking this conversation up for me, I respond, "Nah, babe, I don't know him. But it's understandable he knows me. I'm kind of a big deal," I grin.

"Really?" she asks.

"Yeah, babe, I've been voted hottest man alive. Twice. Once for my anthro form and once for my ailo form," I say and lean back, grinning, giving her a good look at my bod—that even in this ridiculous outfit is pretty great.

"Anthro form? Ailo form?" Adley asks, luckily more interested in learning about my species than my past.

"Oh, yeah, this is my ailo form," I say, transforming quickly. I wiggle out of the pile of clothes left in my wake and sit atop them. I put my paws up on the table and coo at her. "I'm super handsome, aren't I? My long hair is rare and coveted."

"She can't understand you, moron," Marshall says. He follows the insult with a gentle bite of the cheese she laid out. Testing it for poison, I suspect.

I tilt my head at him, "Oh, I forgot".

Adley giggles and says, "Yeah, all I hear is 'meow.'" She looks positively smitten with me. I walk on her lap and rub against her chin to really seal the deal before popping back into my anthro form.

Now butt naked and sitting on my pile of clothes, I am excited to have a dick out that I could plunge into Adley properly again. I put my elbows on the table and say, "You seemed to kind of know what I was saying earlier today."

"I can just read cats really well. Sometimes, I think I understand them better than people. Oh, sorry. I have to stop comparing y'all to cats," she says, gently slamming her fist into her leg while sipping more wine. I'm cataloging her defense mechanisms and mannerisms. This knowledge will be vital if she lets me mate-mark her and chooses to let me be with her for the rest of our lives. I reach toward her hand, wanting to ensure she doesn't hit herself again, but she casually pulls it from my reach. Hmm, she must be a bit reticent now that she knows my last girlfriend tried to kill me.

"And this is your anthro form, I take it?" she asks, pointing at me. Oh, she wasn't pulling away from me. She was just using it to gesture at me.

"Yeah, which do you prefer, babe? I'm guessing this one due to the whole...," I trail off and gesture to my body like I'm presenting a gift to her in the form of a large, erect dick.

She giggles, "Yeah, could you, umm, put the clothes back on?" she says with a blush and averts her eyes. Damn it. I shouldn't have been so cocky—pun, fully intended.

"Sure, babe." I stand and I take my sweet time, hoping she'll get an eyeful and eye fuck me the way I've seen her do numerous times already. She looks towards Marshall. I turn, pointing my ass toward her face, and make sure my tail swipes her nose. I need to seduce her, and I need to seduce her now. My dick gets even harder, and I hope she'll take this bait. I slowly bend to pick up my clothes. Maybe she's an ass chick?

"Alright, that's enough of that. Stop posturing and put your fucking clothes on," Marshall snaps, but he seems to be blushing and wants to look, too.

"You sure that's what *you* want, bro?" I say as I stick my ass higher in the air and twitch my tail at him.

He swallows and replies curtly, "Yes."

I shrug and jump into my shorts, trying to do so in an athletic, graceful way. I probably look like a dork, though. Let's see how long before she asks me to put my shirt back on. I just can't draw attention to it.

"So, you didn't see the portal?" Marshall asks. Oh, we're back on portals? Cool, that should help this shirt stay off.

"Portal? Nope," I say and lean back into the couch. I tense my muscles slightly, trying to accentuate my features.

"But you were in your ailo form when you fell, right?" Marshall asks.

"Yeah, I was," I say, grabbing a piece of cheese.

"But you saw a portal?" Adley asks Marshall.

Marshall sits taller, pride exuding from him. Now it's time for him to posture, I suppose. He starts, "Well, yes. Let me backtrack and explain that I am a scientist. My life's work has revolved around the study of alternate dimensions." His chest seems to inflate at how proud he must be of himself. He's still got his shirt on, though, so I've got a leg up. But Adley looks at him transfixed.

I lean back. I know the type. He's going to info-dump on her. Luckily for me, women hate all this mansplaining bullshit. So, I sit back and just wait for her to start looking bored with him, a small smile on my face. Once her eyes glaze over, I'll redirect her attention to me and then fuck her. *Flawless plan.*

Adley turns to him and actually seems quite interested. "Oh, wow! That's so cool. You must be really smart, huh?" I deflate a little. I'm not liking how interested she seems in him.

"I am," he says with dorking arrogance, "I have a PhD in theoretical physics." If he had glasses, this is where he'd push them up his nose. *Nerd.*

"Oh, awesome! I have a Ph.D. in computer science," she says proudly. *Well, fuck.* Of course, my fated mate would be brainy and into this stuff. That's going to make this a bit harder of a competition.

"The portals, bro. Get back to explaining that," I say, annoyed and gesturing at him to hurry up because I am interested, too. Adley nods vigorously, excited to learn more.

"There are numerous accounts of old coots claiming they saw great beauties through shimmering windows in the world only visible when they were in their ailo form. In many of the stories, these men lament a great loss. The windows closed quickly, but not before revealing their fated mate in the form of what some called 'an angel.' The window closed, and their fated mates were never seen again. They spent the rest of their lives, sad shells of men, never finding another beauty that could compare and never being able to get over the loss of their fated mate."

"That's so sad," Adley says.

He continues, "And there are stories describing men purring then disappearing into thin air—"

I cut him off, "So, what's that got to do with your fancy degree, bro?" I ask. Damn, this fucker is succinct most of the time, but when you actually want to get some information out of him, he won't get to the fucking point.

"Oh, well, yes, I wrote my dissertation on quantum superposition. I postulated that a random subatomic—"

"Bro, explain in a way normal people can understand!" I snap.

"Um, I was studying parallel universes."

"See, was that so hard?" I hiss.

"When I was collecting resources for my literature review, a book from a discredited physicist accidentally made its way into the bunch. He postulated that the various anecdotes of men seeing their fated mates through shimmering windows were actually men seeing rifts in our dimension, essentially, portals to a parallel universe."

"His name wasn't Schrödinger by chance?" Adley asks, laughing.

"No. Why?" He asks.

"Never mind. Just a joke," she says, sipping her wine, looking a little embarrassed.

"He spent the rest of his life trying to prove the theory, trying to find his fated mate in another universe, but he died a disgrace," Marshall continues.

"That's so sad!" Adley whines.

"At first, I brushed the stories off as hoaxes and his research as junk science, a fantastical concoction of a horny, lonely man. But I just couldn't shake the idea that maybe there was some truth to some of it. Initially, it was just a casual curiosity. But it evolved into a secret obsession. I read any account or report about these occurrences I could. A few months ago, I was reading a news article about a man who had seen a portal. The article noted the location. And that's when it clicked for me. There was a pattern." I yawn, wishing he would wrap this shit up.

"Anyway, long story short—" he says.

I scoff, "Already a long story, bro."

He continues as if I had not interrupted him, "I calculated where I suspected the next portal would be and as you can likely infer, my calculations were correct. I was weirdly drawn to it. It was like the universe said, 'Go through the portal. You will find happiness.'"

He laughs and looks away as if he's considering something.

"So, you had to turn into an ailo to see it?" Adley asks.

"Yeah, they are this precise mix of colors. We can't see them when our eyes are this shape," he says, pointing at his eyes.

"So that's why you were in your ailo form when you came?" She asks.

"Yes," he says and continues. "In my haste to jump through the portal and see what was on the other side, I had forgotten something vital: the stories all state that they close quickly. The moment my feet touched the ground, it snapped shut behind me," he says with frustration. "It was stupid. I should have planned better. I let my enthusiasm, curiosity, and arrogance get the better of me. But then again, I would not have met you had I been more careful," he says, smiling at Adley.

"So you're stuck here?" she asks.

"It would appear that way," he says.

"But you can find another one, bro. Just reuse that fancy math to find out when it will open again. Then jump through it and go home," I say, hoping he will do just that.

"Actually, I can't. The portals appear in a very specific pattern, but I have no data about where they have appeared here. I can't project their future path without past data points to calculate the projection. And, since you and I are the only ones who can theoretically see them, I doubt I'll find any records of others seeing them. I'm almost certain we are stuck here."

"What do you mean only you and I can see them?" I ask.

"Well, it would stand to reason we are the only Ailura in this world; therefore, we are the only beings that can transform into ailo forms—the only beings that can see the portals. Adley has given us every indication to believe that changing into ailo form is not something her species can do. Perhaps, these...," he cringes, "cats can see them, but based on how Adley describes them, I doubt they can tell us."

"Oh!! I wonder if the cats in your world are actually from mine! Like they jumped through the portals and got stuck there," Adley says excitedly.

Marshall thinks momentarily, "That could explain why they are scattered worldwide and don't share much genetic sequencing with us." He stares off into the corner of the room, obviously lost in thought.

I don't know shit about genetics, but if their genes are so different because they're from a different world, does that mean Adley would be too genetically different to conceive children with us? Is that what Marshall is so lost in thought about? I think I want kids. Can I definitely not have them now? I look at Adley and consider bringing it up. Seemingly invigorated by the concept of portals, however, and not wanting to stop the chat, she interrupts our pondering by asking Marshall, "Why didn't you change to this form, your anthro form, sooner?" she asks.

"I couldn't. It's like going through the portal stunted my ability. Maybe it took a lot of energy, I don't know. It also seemed to take all my belongings, so... yeah, that part I haven't figured out yet," Marshall says.

"Like it sapped your magic? And that stopped you from being able to transform?" she asks.

"Magic?" he chuckles arrogantly. "It's not magic. It's science. Do you call rain magic?" And there it is, the pretentious fumble I was waiting for. Adley deflates slightly and sips her wine, not as interested in continuing the conversation now.

Marshall doesn't seem to notice the slight change in her composure. Or if he does, he doesn't know what to do about it because he just sits there looking at her with a dumb expression on his face.

I change my posture and lean toward her, ready to throw down my moves. "So, now that we know all about the portals. Would you like me to teach you about fated mates?" I say with all the charisma I can muster, and if experience has taught me anything, it's a lot. I pull her into a standing position, hugging her body close to mine.

I bring my mouth close to her neck and breathe in her scent, the frenzy taking hold of me as my purr vibrates through me. "Rather than explain, let me demonstrate," I say huskily into her neck.

9

ADLEY

I literally swoon. His voice carries a shock wave from my neck straight to my pussy, and a moan of pleasure escapes my lips. The wine has made me more comfortable and less nervous; it's dulled my senses that usually make the world a little too much—a little too loud, a little too bright, but it hasn't turned down the electric sensation I feel at his touch.

"You feel that, don't you?" he says in that same husky voice, which is different from his normal voice. My hands are pressed against his chest, which I realize is still bare. The smooth skin is so soft with stiff pectoral muscles behind it.

Marshall sits bolt upright and growls.

Ezra puts his hand in front of Marshall's face, "Shh, you had your turn to talk. Now it's mine." The same hand gracefully glides to my chin and tilts my head to his face.

He looks into my eyes, and for once, I don't balk at the eye contact. I watch his eyes as they dilate and sparkle. His other hand reaches down toward my ass, and with a handful, he pulls me closer to his middle. His hard dick jams into my stomach, and God, I wish I were taller so that it would line up with my pussy.

Ezra's demeanor has changed entirely. Up to this point, he has been jovial, a little silly, but now he has the aura of James Bond, and something about the jarring switch in character is highly erotic.

He moves to my ear and whispers, "You feel that, Adley? Do you feel that pull toward me? How your pussy wants to wrap itself so hard around my dick that it would take all your strength to let go?"

"Uh, huh," I say, biting my lip.

"That is the draw of a fated mate."

"Oooh," I say, unable to say much more.

"And when I kiss you, it doesn't matter where I kiss you; your whole body will feel it. May I show you?"

"Yes," I sigh out, hypnotized by his seduction.

He gently kisses the area under my ear, and a wave of pleasure pulses through my body, instantly soaking my panties.

He slinks his face back to my mouth and whispers, "You're getting wet for me, aren't you?" His mouth is so close to mine I could lick it.

"Yes," I swoon.

My face is still tilted upward, frozen in place, despite his no longer holding it. I cannot move. The sexiness has entirely stunned me. I am prey, paralyzed by his words, paralyzed by his beauty, waiting to be eaten. He grins at me. I cannot see his mouth, but I see the crinkle in the corner of his eyes, and the fact that he is smiling at me makes my heart and breath, the last parts of my body still working, stop. *Death by sexiness.*

"I'm going to claim you now, Adley," he says, pulling my hand to his mouth and kissing my fingers.

"Okay," I say, literally unable to say anything else.

"Stop!" Marshall roars, standing.

Ezra hisses at him, and his voice changes, "Bro, you had your fucking turn to seduce her. You talked *at* her. It didn't work. She doesn't want you."

He's ripped from me, and I fall backward onto the couch, apparently unable to stand without him holding me up. Damn, did he really paralyze me?

"Wow," I say. "Y'all sure you don't have magic?"

"It's not magic; it's pheromones and sound. It's a form of conversational hypnosis," Marshall barks at me, and I flinch at his raised voice, retreating slightly into the couch. He doesn't yell exactly, but the aggression in his voice is apparent and scary. I am instantly sober from my lust despite the wine still clouding my senses.

"Don't yell at her, dude! It's not her fault you're so lame you couldn't get a pussy wet with a bucket of water," Ezra laughs and falls back into his chair. "Calm the fuck down. Can't you see you're scaring her," he says with less joviality.

Marshall looks at me and deflates. "Oh, Adley, I am sorry. Sometimes, I don't recognize the tone of my voice," he says, sitting down in a slow, controlled way further down the couch than he had previously.

"Remember, from her perspective, we're two large dudes who 'magically,'" he says magically with air quotes, and Marshall tries to protest, but Ezra cuts him off with a hand wave and continues, "appeared in her house and told her we're going to fuck her silly. Can you imagine how potentially scary that could be for a woman? She's being incredibly cool and chill and understanding with us, but do not fucking push it, bro."

Ezra turns to me and gently says, "I'm sorry, Adley, I got a little carried away. I should have known he'd react that way."

"It's okay," I say, shifting in my seat, trying to relax.

The vibe fully killed, Ezra attempts to lighten the mood and regain control of the situation. "Being fated but not bonded makes males a bit crazy." He says with a dismissive laugh, rolling his fingers around next to his head. "Once we claim you, we'll chill out a bit, I promise, babe," he says.

"So, what exactly does claiming entail?" I ask hesitantly.

"Well," he smirks, "there's two parts to it." He holds up a finger, "First, we have to give you a mind-rocking orgasm."

I shift, my arousal making me uncomfortable, "And the second part?"

He points up his second finger, "We have to mark you," he says matter-of-factly.

"You have to expand," I respond.

"It's a bite. Once we leave our mate marks on you, you are officially ours. This will cause us to feel more secure in our relationship with you and remove some of the anxiety causing all this… tension," he says, giving Marshall a side-eye.

"Bite me?! Why? I'm sorry, I know you said it wasn't magic, but it all sounds… like magic the way you describe it. Why can't you purr for anyone else? Why are you in a frenzy until you 'claim' me? Why can't you just mate-mark someone else? Like, why does a fated mate have to be the one you bite? Can you please explain the science?" Marshall looks like he wants to answer, but is still too ashamed to speak.

Ezra responds, "It's something about compatibility of chemicals and bodily fluids, bro, you explain it."

Marshall states, "Your pheromones stimulate our larynx, which give us the ability to purr. Each Ailura has a unique chemical composition that can trigger this in them—but not all find a mate who's pheromones can cause it."

I ask, "So, you can mate with someone who is not your fated mate?"

Ezra chimes in, "Yeah, we can have sex with whomever we want. But, once we find a fated mate and purr for them, sex with anyone else would be… unpleasant."

"What do you mean?" I ask.

Ezra responds, "Once an Ailura unlocks the ability to purr, to orgasm without purring is… bland. So, sex with anyone you cannot purr for is possible, but not preferred. Our bodies will crave that ultimate pleasure."

I ask, "And why will sleeping with me reduce the frenzy?"

Marshall responds, "Mixing our bodily fluids with yours will reduce the frenzy, because it will change your chemistry just enough to stop us from being in a constant state of arousal."

I ask, "And why can't you mate-mark someone who is not your fated mate?"

Marshall responds, "You can only cause a mate-mark if you are purring. Purring is required to mix the mate-marking chemicals in our saliva. Otherwise, the scar will just be a scar."

I ask, "Why do you need to do the mate-mark? Where does the mate-mark go?"

"Mate-marking is kind of… psychological. It's like a pledge," Ezra states. "We could technically bite you anywhere; it's up to us—up to you. It's ritualistic and depends on culture, but most Auilra do it around a finger. So," he grabs my hand. "I'd take your finger in my mouth, usually this one," he says, stroking my ring finger on my left hand, "confess my love to you, pledge an oath to protect you, purr, then bite down, leaving my mark. This will signal to all others that we are bonded not only by lust, but also by love."

"Oh, so, like a wedding ring?" I ask.

"Sorry, I don't know what a wedding is," he says.

"Oh… um, here, whenever a couple wants to pledge their love to each other and tie themselves to each other 'until death do they part,' they get married. They have a big party called a wedding in which they invite all their friends and family and vow to be together forever. They wear a ring around this finger to indicate to the world that they are married."

"Oh, yeah, it is like that!" Ezra says excitedly. "Except, for us, the bonding is done in private. It's frowned upon in our culture to fuck in public. But I have to admit, the idea of fucking in front of a bunch of people is interesting." He strokes his chin, "I don't know if I'd want to do it in front of my family, though," he says with a disgusted face.

I laugh, "Oh, no, we don't fuck during weddings. We fuck after, in private. It's called 'consummating the marriage.' Actually, now that I think about it, I do think it used to be done in front of people—a long time ago. And maybe only with rich people."

"Why did they have to be rich to fuck in front of people?" Ezra asks. "Did people charge to watch? That's weird; you'd think it would be the other way around. Like people would pay to watch." Marshall leans forward, interested in hearing my answer.

"Well, it was a way to ensure that the consummation actually occurred. I don't know much about it, but I think marriage has only recently become something people do for love. Usually, it was for economic or political reasons, such as to tie two families together. It also helped with making sure property was passed down to heirs."

"So, wait, people would just be married, and they weren't in love?" Ezra asks in confusion. "They'd be stuck together forever, and they might not even like each other."

"Yeah, love is not required for marriage. It's mostly a legal thing—even now. Now, at least you can get divorced if you are unhappy."

"What is divorce?" he asks.

"They break up."

"What?! And then they are doomed to be alone forever?" he jumps to the couch I am sitting on, putting himself between me and Marshall. He turns his back entirely to Marshall. Marshall slaps his tail away as it settles near his face.

"Um, well, no, you can get married again."

"This is confusing...," Ezra says. "So, they don't have to love each other, but they still experience the sexual pull, right?"

"Eh, no…sexual attraction is also not required," I say, feeling like I'm doing a shitty job explaining this.

"That sounds miserable!"

"I suppose for some people, it is," I say, sadly.

MARSHALL

I've fucked this whole thing up. I want to impress Adley. I want her to choose me. But I'm nervous and intimidated by Ezra. I keep trying to interject myself into the conversation, to ingratiate myself to Adley, but it's even harder now that Ezra is between us on the couch. His back to me, not turning to even acknowledge me. I'm fully iced out. It's been like this for the last half hour: me sitting here quietly, him chatting with her, making her feel special.

His warmth permeates the area around him; he still doesn't have his shirt on, and I have a full view of his back. There was a time when I would have given anything to be this close to him. His tail smacks against me when he excitedly jumps to talk to Adley. It is so soft; I want to grab it and rub it against my face with purpose, not in this teasing, unintentional way it's happening now.

Adley has drunk an entire bottle of wine now, and she has gotten very animated. She is much louder and quite funny, giving Ezra a run for his money in the charm department. I believe the wine has helped her become more comfortable. Now I understand what she meant when she jokingly called it "liquid courage" and "social lubricant." If it weren't made of grapes, I could probably use some, too.

"I'll be right back, boys," she says. We must look heartbroken because she says, "I'll be back! Just going to the bathroom. Don't kill each other while I'm gone."

"We'll try," Ezra laughs.

The moment she is out of sight, Ezra hops into her seat, putting more space between us. He turns to me, arms splayed out in that arrogant way, and takes up as much space as possible. He leans back, crosses one leg over the other, and splays his arms across the back of the couch. His posture is open, intimidating, and fucking sexy as hell. I can't help but notice the way, despite sitting, his abs are still perfectly outlined. His chest heaves slightly, ready to fight me.

Any power I may have had in this situation is gone. I've lost. I've lost wholly, and I might as well just give up. The corner of his mouth cocks upward at me in a smirk that oozes confidence. He's dazzling. I try to hide the fact that I am downright ogling him.

"Like what you see, do you?" He says with a level of arrogance that raises my hackles. Embarrassed and unable to think of a good comeback, instead of addressing his comment, I choose to change the subject. "I get it, Ezra, you've won. No need to be a dick and rub it in."

Only momentarily, his posture deflates slightly as if what I said has affected him. Is he just putting on a show? Is this bravado faked? Is he trying to intimidate me? Well, now that I've seen the crack in his facade, I am not quite as intimidated. I can put up a facade, too.

"Yeah, I have won. So, maybe you should go so I can; what was the word she used? Consummate this thing," he says.

"I'm not going anywhere," I say.

So, what's your plan, Marshall? Just hang around here, pumping your dick in the corner of the room, watching while I fuck Adley?"

"No," I say, unsure what my plan is. But the scenario he described doesn't sound terrible.

"Instead of embarrassing yourself, why don't you just leave?" he says.

"I told you, the portal closed," I say.

"You can go somewhere else. You don't have to stay here," he says.

I don't want to leave. I want to be with Adley. "She is my mate, too!" I yell.

"Then why are you acting like such a fucking asshole to her?"

"I'm the asshole? You've iced me out of the conversation! You've put me down every chance you got."

He thinks for a moment, and then his face changes in realization, almost as if he's determined a new direction to take this conversation. I've seen him do this a few times during our conversation. He shifts his personality and approach to meet the needs of the conversation. "I know you want to fuck me, too," he says with a smirk and a brief chuckle. He jerks his head to the side to flip his hair out of his eyes and stares into my eyes.

His beauty is on full display—so close I could touch him. I could jump across this couch and throw my whole body atop him. I've wanted this for so long: to be with Ezra—not that I'll ever tell him that. And now, as he confronts me about it, that he has figured me out despite my attempt to hide it, I am blinded by rage.

"That's not true...," I say, my voice quivering with fury.

"You can deny it all you want, but your dick doesn't lie," he says, eyes fixing on my junk. These shorts hide nothing. And they certainly aren't hiding my body's response to his half-nakedness.

The sound of a door opening pierces the silence, followed by Adley belting in a sing-song voice, "I'm going to get more wine," from the hallway out of sight.

We sit in cold silence and await her return. Ezra stares me down with a look of confidence and smugness. I want to punch him in his fucking beautiful face. I will not let him win. I will bond with Adley.

She enters the room, and Ezra's demeanor changes entirely. This guy is a social chameleon morphing and changing at a whim to fit the situation. Two can play at this game. Before Ezra can return to his spot, she plops between us. Splitting us up.

"So, Adley, what do you do for fun?" I ask, emulating Ezra. I get it now.

I realize that trying to impress Adley by talking all about myself isn't the best move. I'll approach this as he does. He focuses the conversation more on her, interjecting with his own takes and questions. She responds much more favorably to that. I will try to only go into my spiels when she asks me to elaborate.

10

ADLEY

Here's the thing about me: Bryce wasn't wrong—I am kind of a needy slut. I like romantic attention. I like to be doted on. I like having sex—a lot. I need a boyfriend. And I don't mean I need a boyfriend right now; I mean I need a boyfriend *always*. I have never been single this long, and it's killing me. The loneliness is unbearable.

I jump into relationships with my whole heart quickly. Bryce was just the last in a long… and I do mean long… list of people I've hitched my sexual wagon to and just went along for the ride with. I want more. I want something good. I want something that's not just me falling in love the moment a person says something nice to me and then bending my whole world to make sure they stay happy and never leave. Chasing the compliments and the orgasms that ultimately dry up and leave me feeling worthless. I want someone who won't leave—someone who won't find someone better because they'll think I am the best.

This fated mate thing is kind of perfect for me. Two guys who are going to like me no matter how crazy they ultimately find out I am. Knowing they'll never want to leave—that's freeing in a way. I don't have to hide myself. I can show them my whole self, and they'll stay. Because they'll find me so fucking irresistible they'll ignore the rest of it. They'll be so unquestionably devoted to me—in the same way I am. And that is so fucking hot.

We've been chatting for hours. The tension that was initially in the conversation has vanished. Granted, I'm a little drunk, so I might just not be noticing.

We've spent most of the conversation chatting about the differences between our two worlds. Still, I've learned a little about their general personalities and interests from how they directed the conversations or the topics they wanted to focus on the most. It seems Marshall likes science and technology (no surprise based on his explanations of portals), but he is also fascinated with the differences in our history and art. Interestingly, our two worlds have developed in remarkably similar ways. Ezra, on the other hand, is more focused on the present. He wants to know about pop culture, fashion, and media. I'm unable to fill in all the gaps for them, only really being interested in technology, science, pop culture, and media. We all seem to enjoy video games, though. I was particularly interested in learning how theirs had developed in a very similar, yet slightly different way than the ones I'm familiar with. I'll definitely be asking them more about them in the future.

Is there a future? What happens tomorrow? Do I let them stay here? They can't go to their dimension, but does that mean they live here—in my house? *You can't go home, but do you have to stay here?* I feel weirdly responsible for them. They showed up in my yard. They fated mated (is that a verb?—I'm still trying to learn the lingo) with me?

They told me I had four choices: neither of them, just Marshall, just Ezra, or both. And as I sit here looking at them, I reflect on their differences. I don't know which I prefer. I don't think I prefer either. I like them both. I want them both. I don't want to choose between them. I want to see how this all pans out. I'm getting a bit ahead of myself. I'm already thinking about the whole marriage, white picket fence, 2.5 kids, and a dog thing—with both. Well, I guess in this case, it would be a mate-mark, white picket fence, not sure if kids are even possible, and they probably wouldn't want a dog.

I want to feel them both inside me. I want to have four hands grasping me, pleasuring me, loving me.

I've wanted to fuck both of them since I first laid eyes on them—even when I was scared of them and trying to bash their brains in. But I try not to be a desperate, impulsive, needy slut. But now I don't know if I care anymore. Will waiting make me less desperate? Probably not. Less impulsive? Yes. Less of a needy slut? Definitely not. And do I really care?

I'm feeling so much more comfortable with them. So why not? Why not just fuck them and see what happens? I really, really want to fuck them. The sexual tension has been building, and I just don't think I can take it anymore. *Time to make a move, Adley. You can do this. They've made it extremely clear that they want to fuck you, so fuck them.*

First, I need to freshen up. "Sorry, boys, I'll be right back," I say and excuse myself to the bathroom. I check myself in the mirror and use some wet wipes on all possibly questionable regions of my body to ensure ultimate freshness. I try not to linger on my reflection because doing so would likely cause me to evaluate myself in ways I don't have time for right now. *No, talking yourself out of this, convincing yourself you're too ugly, not worthy, Adley. You got this.* I spritz a little perfume because why not?

When I return to the living room, Marshall and Ezra are standing facing each other down and appear to be on the verge of fucking or killing each other. "What's going on?" I ask them. Maybe this is a bad idea. They obviously hate each other and have just been playing nice for my sake.

"We were having a discussion," Marshall says.

"About what?" I ask.

"You," Ezra says.

"Oh," I say, unsure how to respond. I think they've argued almost every time I've left the room. I would like for them to stop fighting. I want to find a way to rush past this awful tense part and get right to our happily ever after—the three of us.

We all stand frozen in place. Each waiting on one of the others to do or say something. All night, Ezra has taken the lead and moved things along. But he seems to be holding back from overtly trying to have sex with me now. I think he's waiting for me to do something. And also trying not to provoke Marshall too much.

I want to move this forward but don't know how to flirt. I don't know how to be coy. I am direct and always have been. Fuck it, maybe I just tell them what I want.

"So, I think I am ready for the two of you to claim me," I say quickly. Tugging at my dress and balling the fabric in my hands. Using the sensation against my fingers to soothe my nerves. "But, just the sex part. We need to hold off on the whole biting thing for a while." Even though, honestly, I'd probably be down for that, too.

They look at each other for a long moment, a silent argument storming between them, and I think they're going to turn me down. They said they'd be okay with me being with both of them, but they obviously didn't mean that.

"I'm sorry. Was that too forward of me? Never mind. We don't have to...," I say and start to sit back down.

Ezra's expression changes suddenly, and he glides toward me, dick slowly rising with each step—easily visible in those tiny shorts. "No, no, babe! I want to. I want it so bad. I just want to be sure I understand. Do you want us both to fuck you, Adley?"

"Yes, please," I say enthusiastically. Ezra's face twitches; I can't tell if he's disappointed. "I want you both inside me." At these words, a loud purr emanates from both of them, vibrating through my body. *Oh, this feels nice.*

It's like they're able to make the atmosphere a sex toy.

Ezra raises an eyebrow at me, intrigued, and Marshall's eyes widen in surprise. Neither says anything for a long moment as they contemplate their next move.

"Would being with both of us make you happy?" Ezra asks.

"Um… I think so. I want to feel beautiful. I want to feel like you truly mean all those nice things you've been saying. Could you, um, both, maybe make me feel like you do really think I'm some otherworldly goddess?" *God, I am so lame.*

Ezra hesitates no longer and lunges at me. He embraces me, burying his head in my neck and inhaling my scent. He moans and presses himself hard into me. He hugs me as if he's reuniting with a long-lost lover. The desire in his embrace is palpable.

Marshall stands, staring wide-eyed and lustful. He almost looks sad with a longing in his eyes. He definitely wants to come over here, but something is holding him back. I can see the confusion on his face as he seems to be trying to decide what exactly he should do.

"Do you want to join us?" I ask him. He nods his head. I reach my hand to him, and he tentatively moves toward me. He seems terrified.

"Marshall, are you okay? We do not have to do this." At those words, Ezra pulls away from me and looks to Marshall. Waiting to hear his response.

"I want to." Marshall stammers, "I just…I haven't…I mean. I don't know what to do. I'm sorry. I'm nervous."

Ezra's scowls at him, "You can just watch if you want." I knew this was a bad idea. They're just going to fight, and I really don't think I can get off if there's a catfight happening right on top of me. Ezra looks at me, and his face softens. I should just call this off.

I leave Ezra's side and hold Marshall's hands. "Marshall, I'm serious. We don't have to do this. We can spend the rest of the evening talking."

"No!" he says in almost a shout. "I really, really, really want to."

The fear on his face makes me feel terrible. Are we pressuring him? Is the whole fated mate thing too much for him? Then, realization dawns on me. "Marshall, have you never had sex before?"

He shakes his head in what seems like shame. "Oh, Marshall. It's okay. Is this too much for you? Let's just sit down and talk. We can take it slower. Maybe try some other time, okay?" I say as I sit on the couch, trying to pull him beside me.

Marshall stays standing, resisting my pull to the couch, and looks at Ezra for assistance, a desperation in his face. This is not how he wants it to be, but I don't know what to do.

Ezra sighs loudly. "It's okay, bro. I'll help you. Just follow my lead, okay?" Marshall's face lights up.

"Does that work for you, Marshall?" I ask, still seated, still holding Marshall's hands.

"Yes!" he says, nodding his head.

"Okay, then—" I say. At that, Ezra pulls me from the couch back into the passionate embrace he had held me previously, picking up where he left off. Marshall still stands frozen—separate from us. And I'm not sure if he really is ready. I look at him, having a hard time focusing on Ezra, as I am still worried about Marshall.

Ezra pulls back and looks at me. "We will worship you like the goddess you are," Ezra tells me gently. Then, without breaking eye contact with me, he says in a less loving tone to Marshall, "Come." He points behind my back, indicating what he wants Marshall to do.

Marshall doesn't hesitate. The electricity of his arousal and anticipation is palpable. He slides up behind me and gingerly places his hands on my shoulders. "Kiss her. Compliment her," Ezra says.

Marshall gently kisses my neck and exhales loudly like he has been waiting his whole life to do so. "You are the most beautiful creature I have ever seen. Thank you for letting me touch you. I will do my best to prove I deserve this honor," he says. It seems Marshall, normally curt, can be a bit poetic in the heat of the moment. That's cute. He continues to massage my back and plant tiny kisses on me as he goes.

"Take off her dress," Ezra says. Marshall grabs the straps of my dress and pulls them to the side, making it drop to the ground effortlessly.

Ezra holds my face in his hands and looks at me with the intensity of a man who has never seen such beauty. A girl could get used to this level of adoration. "So, fucking beautiful. We are so lucky." He closes his eyes and kisses my mouth, our tongues dancing together in lust. My body writhes, wanting to push him down and jump on his dick, but I wait. I am going to let Ezra take charge here—he seems to have a plan.

Ezra breaks our deep kiss so that he can gently kiss my cheek. He moves slowly around my face, moving around my jaw while stroking the other side. His other hand is gripped firmly on my hip, insisting that my body remains against his at all times.

Marshall is still gently massaging my back and kissing my neck—less assured than Ezra in his kisses but no less grateful. He hovers over my ear; his breath twinged with excitement and nervousness, "An angel. Perfect." I can feel a slight tremble in his grasp, and it is so fucking hot. He kisses my ear gently, then lets his kisses softly explore my body.

Marshall hasn't pulled me close like Ezra has. I'm reminded of middle school dances—when I first realized that boys were interested in me sexually. There were two types of boys: the ones who followed the rules, keeping their distance, and the ones who didn't, jamming their pelvises against you in a sly self-confident way that defied the rules and said, "fuck you!" to the chaperones. Marshall is the first type. Ezra is the second.

Ezra places a gentle kiss at the center of my throat, causing me to moan and arch forward, trying to bring my body even closer to his.

Ezra backs away, dropping his shorts to the ground and kicking them to the side. He nods at Marshall, wordlessly indicating that he should disrobe, too. I can't see, but I sense Marshall does just that.

I reach for Ezra's dick, but he pulls away and says, "No, no. We will be worshiping you, not the other way around." He grabs my face between his hands and kisses my nose gently. "Goddesses don't have to work for their pleasure. Goddesses are given pleasure."

He looks at Marshall behind me and says, "Marshall, don't let her fall." Fall? Why would I fall? Marshall clamps around my waist, bracing against me. The sound that escapes his mouth when his body collides with mine sends a shiver of excitement down my back. His body finally pressed to mine, makes sparkles erupt from my erogenous zones. My knees go weak, and I am happy that Marshall is holding me up.

At my moan of delight, Ezra says, "Oh, sweet goddess. I'm going to make you so wet that that tight pussy can take us both. That's what you want, right?" Then to Marshall, he barks, "She comes first. Understood?" Marshall answers with one curt nod.

"Yes," I exhale, desperate for him to return his body to mine.

I lean against Marshall and turn my head so my face is at his. I kiss the side of his mouth, startling him. Once he realizes what I am trying to do, he shoves his tongue into my mouth with the desperate fumbling of someone who has never done it before. Despite his inexperience, the kiss is filled with a longing and lust that brings me pleasure. His kiss gains confidence, and I feel as if I might be fully devoured.

I break from my kiss with Marshall, and Ezra is upon me, his tongue in my mouth. His kisses are more confident but just as passionate. He's obviously kissed before, but he makes me feel like this is the best kiss of his entire life—like all kisses up to this point have been so inferior that they barely can be categorized as a kiss. I come up for air and gasp, unable to process the sheer pleasure they've already brought me. I've never once enjoyed a kiss like this, so I, too, am experiencing incomparable kisses.

Before I can fully catch my breath, Marshall returns to my mouth—tired of waiting his turn. Ezra, an obviously impatient man, lunges at my mouth as well. Our three tongues collide, and we all moan in delight. I cannot tell whose tongue is whose, whose lips are whose, and I do not care. Ezra and Marshall pull away at the exact moment, and the taste of them lingers on my tongue. They exchange a glance loaded with a lot of emotion—they realize they have been making out with each other. I worry they may start fighting and ready myself to mediate, but their intense stares soften. Marshall nods slightly. Ezra grunts and does the same. Some unspoken agreement between them just transpired, and it seems they have resolved to just let this happen.

"Keep kissing her; I've got some work to do," Ezra tells Marshall. Marshall does just that. Then Ezra repeats, "Do not let her fall," and now I wonder what he has in store for me. I open my eyes and peer at him, barely able to see him out the side of my eyes. His kisses begin working their way down my front, and, wanting to watch, I break away from Marshall so I can follow Ezra's progress with my eyes. Marshall is undeterred by my breaking away and continues his kisses to my neck and ear.

By the time Ezra gets to my nipples, I am electric with anticipation. He looks up at me with those sparkling blue eyes and mischievous grin before gently nibbling on my nipple. A guttural groan escapes my throat, and my pelvis moves on its own, lurching toward Ezra, trying to put him fully inside me. Marshall grips me tighter against himself as I buck, pushing himself into my back with soft grunts and moans of his own.

Ezra takes his time, though; my writhing does not hurry him. He places his hand firmly on my ass, slipping between my and Marshall's bodies. Marshall and I both moan in pleasure. Marshall, no longer content with stroking my back and shoulders, creeps his free hand to my breast, gently cupping the underside. He gasps out, "Perfect. So perfect," and humps me, pressing Ezra's hand into my ass.

I reach one hand upward and wrap my fingers in Marshall's silky hair. He moans and ventures to my nipple with a tentative pinch. Wanting to make sure he knows I like that, I say, "Yes!" then tug at his soft ear. He dick bounces against my back in thanks.

Ezra's smile fades slightly, a small twinge of jealousy in his eyes. I wrap my hand into his soft, fluffy hair and smile down at him. I fist the hair and give a small tug while biting my lip and pushing my pelvis harder against him. He runs his hand down my side and smirks at me, but once I move my hand to the ear atop his head, his laser focus on me breaks as he leans into my touch with his own moan of pleasure.

Composing himself, Ezra returns to his quest of kissing down my front, stopping to lick at my belly button. It tickles and makes me giggle, but it also shoots sparks through my pussy. These gentle kisses are so arousing and teasing. I want these men inside me now!

Ezra kisses around the pooch under my belly button, just above my panties—a location on my body past lovers have avoided, or if they brought attention to it, they did so in a negative way. But Ezra is making me feel like this is his favorite spot in the whole world—the universe—both our universes. "If you let me, I would stay right here, at your feet for the rest of my life—just kissing this delectable spot," Ezra whispers between kisses.

He grips the edges of my panties, inching them downward, exposing more flesh that needs the attention of his mouth. His mouth is so close to my pussy that I can feel the warmth of his breath spread between my legs. I am unable to stop myself from arching forward, attempting to put his mouth exactly where I want it.

He smirks up at me, in that mischievous way he tends to do, and barks at Marshall, "Don't let her fall," again.

Marshall tightens his grip around me, and I lean into him, leveraging his body to push toward Ezra's mouth. Marshall whispers to the top of my head, "I cannot believe I get to hold you like this. You are so perfect." He kisses the top of my head.

"I need you inside of me," I say to neither of them in particular.

"I don't think you're ready for us, babe," Ezra says, still gently kissing around the edge of my underwear—the teasing is maddening.

"Yes, yes, I am!" I rasp out.

Ezra yanks my panties down with a fluid motion and forcefully grabs my hips, positioning my pussy directly in front of his face. He stares at my pubic region, inspects it, and then strokes his chin in a mock-thinking face. "Let's see," he says, then presses his nose into my pubic hair and inhales. My clit is so swollen, and he is so close yet so far away I can feel his breath on it.

"Please," I whimper.

"You're not ready yet," Ezra says. And blows on my clit. The warmth followed by the cold this produces is mind-numbing. My knees buckle, and I am jelly. Marshall's tight grip around my waist keeps me from falling to the floor. All my weight falls back into his chest. He is heaving against me. Now I know why Ezra kept warning Marshall not to let me fall.

"I got you. Lose yourself," Marshall says in a breathy voice against my neck.

"Sit down with her," Ezra says, pointing to the couch behind us.

Marshall lifts me from the ground and brings us both downward on the couch, sitting on the edge with me in his lap.

"Lean backward. Let her lie on you," Ezra commands. And Marshall leans backward, bringing me down with him.

Ezra grabs my hips and positions me on top of Marshall so that Marshall's dick is docked between my butt cheeks. The sensation of his dick makes me wail in anticipation. His balls are directly under my pussy. Their heat emanates to me, reminding me both how close his sex is to me and how far away.

Ezra spreads my legs with a graceful motion, running his hands slowly from crotch to knees. He stares at my nakedness spread in front of him. "That's the most beautiful pussy I've ever seen," he says and licks his lips.

He moves his hands up my thighs slowly, in the opposite direction he used to spread them. I writhe in anticipation as his hands get closer to where I want them to be. He stops just before he reaches my labia, avoiding my pussy, teasing me. Driving me absolutely wild. He spreads my lips further by pulling at the skin right next to them with his thumbs—opening me further and allowing him to see even more of me. He gasps as if a warm, bright light from heaven just shone on his face when he says, "Heavenly."

I grind backward, digging into Marshall's dick, and he whimpers. Ezra looks at him, "Control yourself. You cannot come until she does," Ezra says forcefully.

"Understood," Marshall says. I turn my head to try to look at him. I can barely make out his face, but I see a look of anguish. He is using all of his willpower not to come. I smirk and push my ass harder onto his cock, grinding against him. His embrace around my waist tightens, and he groans in pleasure.

Ezra's thumbs move inward more, massaging my labia and spreading me even further open. He leans forward and blows on me again. Marshall and I both moan—the breath must also be hitting his balls.

A gentle tongue reaches out and quickly flicks at my clit. I cannot take it anymore. I'm going to come before he even really touches me. He licks around the edges of my labia, missing my clit with deliberation.

"Please," I wimper again.

"I am the one who should be begging you," Ezra says. "Marshall, move her so that your dick is between her legs."

Marshall lifts me effortlessly, causing his stiff dick to appear between my legs with a pop free from my weight against it. I reach for it, wanting to grasp it with both hands. I want to stroke it and push it into me, but Marshall grabs both of my hands, pinning them at my side. He whispers into my ear, "I would not be able to contain myself if you did that, my sweet angel. Please be patient."

Ezra gives him an approving nod and continues to massage around my pussy with one hand. "Please, I need more," I gasp, unable to take this teasing any longer.

"I will deny you nothing, my love," Ezra croons, then forcefully grabs Marshall's cock in his hand. I suspect for a moment that Marshall may come undone in that instant. Marshall moans and arches, pushing deeper into Ezra's touch, but Ezra ignores this reaction.

Ezra then positions Marshall's cock at my opening, gently grazing me with it. "Do not enter her until I say," Ezra commands. I can feel Marshall nod, but he says nothing. If I just move my body slightly… I shift my hips, trying to put it inside me, but Marshall holds me tight against himself, burying his face in my shoulder, hiding from the view, and doing everything in his power to stop me—stop himself from letting me.

Ezra leans forward and places a soft kiss on my clit. I wail. He does it again, this time longer, placing his full mouth around my clit. He sucks lightly and flicks with his tongue. I am so incredibly keyed up, so teased, I cannot remember the last time I felt such pleasure. Marshall's embrace is no longer strong enough to hold me, and I start to grind, desperate to get more of Ezra's mouth on my clit and any amount of Marshall's dick in my cunt. I wail in pleasure and need. Marshall wails as well; Ezra's mouth and my pussy so close to his dick must be driving him just as crazy as it is me.

And just when it feels like Marshall, and I can't take it anymore, Ezra whispers into my clit, "Marshall, enter her. Get her ready for me."

With a smooth movement, Marshall pushes deep into me, and I am thrown into ecstasy. Fireworks explode throughout my body as I come into Ezra's mouth and on Marshall's dick.

Marshall freezes as my walls clench around him, and I scream through my orgasm. "This is more than I could have imagined. Thank you. Thank you. All my dreams—" Marshall says into my shoulder as a tear falls from his face onto me.

Marshall's grip on my hips is steadfast as I melt into him, my body now boneless and unable to move. Ezra steps back slightly, and I close my eyes, ready to sleep.

"Oh, we're not done worshipping you yet," Ezra says, rising from his knees to stand over me. "I told you, the orgasm has to be mind-rocking, remember? You might have just come on Marshall's dick, but it's my dick that's going to send you over the edge."

He leans downward and places a hand on the couch to the right of my face, hovering over us. "I want to taste her, too," Marshall says.

Ezra rolls his eyes, annoyed at Marshall, but sighs, "I suppose you've earned it. You have helped make room for me. And you have done well not to come yet. What do you think, Adley? Has he earned it?"

"Yes," I rasp out.

Ezra reaches down and drags a finger through my slit. He slowly brings his finger to Marshall's mouth. Marshall lunges and sucks on his finger with a moan—his cock twitching inside me. Ezra exhales loudly and leans forward, placing his full weight on me. In a surprise move, he kisses Marshall on the mouth.

Marshall's grip on me tightens as he pushes one hard pump into me. I let out a gasp as his dick hits an extremely sensitive and untouched spot inside me.

Ezra pulls back, and I miss feeling his weight against me. His voice softens, no longer commanding, no longer seductive, more like caring, and he says, "I think you're ready. I'm going to enter you now. Are you ready?"

"Yes," I plead, recovering from my orgasm, already eager for more.

Back in the commanding voice, "Marshall, contain yourself just a little longer," then more softly, "Okay?" Marshall nods vigorously. "You're doing good, bro. It's almost time."

Still holding himself over us, Ezra glides over me so that his dick is at my entrance. How will this fit? Is this possible? I'm a little scared.

He puts the thumb of his free hand onto my clit and starts massaging in a circular motion. His disposition changes momentarily; it softens like he's been playing a part this whole time and is now showing me his true self. He whispers into my ear, "Tell me if it becomes too much, okay? One word is all I need, and I'll stop. Are you ready for it?"

"Yes," I breathe out, eager to see if this will work.

He enters me.

I am so stuffed with both their dicks inside me I didn't think this was possible. He glides in without any resistance, and if I hadn't been convinced this was a dream before, I would have been convinced now. There is no way this is real life. The feeling is so out of this world it is indescribable.

I cry, "Oh my god," and they freeze. They watch me and wait while I take in the feeling—process the sensation, and allow my body to adjust. Ezra's mask drops again, and he looks afraid. Afraid that he's hurt me? They're waiting for my cue. "GO!" I shout with a buck.

Ezra's calm, controlled composure sways further as he gets lost in the feeling of rocking into me. I weave my hands through their hair again, and they each lean into my touch, enjoying my petting their heads.

I arch forward, bringing my chest closer to Ezra, and he takes the cue to bring my breast into his mouth—not slowing his rhythmic pumps.

Marshall begins groping at me, circling my body as if he can't cover enough surface area fast enough. He no longer needs Ezra to tell him what to do; he follows his body's orders now. Ezra's speed quickens with each thrust. I'm lost in the pleasure and the pain of it as Ezra and Marshall grunt around me.

My body explodes from the pressure and pleasure; I come so forcefully that my whole body contracts. As if on cue, Ezra stiffens, releasing his orgasm into me. Marshall wraps his arms around me and Ezra, pulling us both closer to him, squeezing us tight, as his orgasm follows suit.

Ezra is not distracted from his mission on my clit with his thumb and begins rubbing even harder, and now, full of their seed, my orgasm continues for so long that I think my body has short-circuited, stuck in a perpetual loop of pleasure.

Eventually, the orgasm does finish, and we all melt together in a pile on the couch.

"Y'all should stay here with me… forever…," I say. "We should do this every night."

I fall asleep there with them both still inside me.

EZRA

Marshall and I silently clean sleeping Adley up and dress her. I carry her to her bed. Marshall follows behind me, keeping his distance and looking toward the ground. When I place her gently down, I marvel at her beauty. A deep sense of tranquility rushes over me. This is my mate. My fated mate. I brush her hair from her face and fluff her pillow. Then, tuck her in, ensuring she is fully engulfed in the soft blankets. She is my most precious treasure; I will protect her with my life.

Marshall moves beside me and stares down at her with me. We stay silent, not yet ready to cease worshipping her. However, his presence sullies the moment. I cannot bask in her beauty anymore—my mood now soured. "We should probably talk," I whisper to Marshall.

He nods silently. I transform into my ailo form and exit the room, implying that he should do the same and follow. At least in this form, we can speak without worrying about waking Adley. He transforms as well and slinks slowly behind me.

I stalk to the kitchen, silently brooding as my rage festers with each step and jump onto the counter, ensuring that I am higher than he is and thus have all the power in this conversation. I'm so pissed. She was going to be mine. Mine alone. Now I have to share her with this pretentious douche for eternity. And I let him enter her first. How am I supposed to be the center of her world if he's going to be there, sucking up some of her love? Taking up room in her heart and her cunt?

His body tenses as if he is going to leap next to me, but he balks and lies down on the floor. *Interesting.* My rage intensifies. I hate this fucking guy. He stole my mate. He took her first. He has shoved his way into my happily ever after and shoved his dick into my woman. Now he submits to me! *What is his game?*

Maybe I can still scare him off. Convince him to leave. Find some other woman for him to shack up with. Time to play the part of the asshole—that shouldn't be too hard. I smirk, lick my paw, and rub it over my face. The taste of her still lingers. I stand, making myself even higher, and show him my side. My tail sweeps behind me in long, fast thwacks.

Before I can say the big scary speech building up in my head, he quietly says, "Thank you."

I whip my head around and stare at him. "What?!" I say, taken aback.

"Thank you. This is all I've ever wanted," and the dude fucking starts crying. Crying! How dare he cry! Is he trying to manipulate me into feeling sorry for him? Because it's fucking working, and I fucking hate it.

I pause, unsure how to control this situation, "What do you want?"

"I want to stay with Adley."

"Me, too," I hiss out. For some reason, I am disappointed that he only mentioned wanting to be with Adley. I'm unsure why that disappoints me. I don't like this guy. I don't want to be friends. I don't want to be lovers.

The moonlight glistens off his black fur as his tail slowly sways behind him. I can see the strength in his back, and his muscles are illuminated.

I don't want to be his friend, but I also don't want to fight with him. All this bluster is for show. I hate conflict. I wish we could move on, but I don't know how to turn the dynamic in the direction I want logically. I usually have no trouble molding people's reactions to my whims, but Adley and Marshall, while obviously both enamored with me, don't seem to respond the same way as everyone else.

Maybe I can use the fact that I'm pretty sure he's secretly harboring feelings for me to my advantage. How can I use that to gain the upper hand? Why is he hiding and denying his attraction?

I stare at him, my chest still fluffed up, and he looks so… pathetic, isn't the word. Innocent. Adorable. I don't want to hurt him. Something about him makes me want to protect him. I don't want to hurt him to gain the upper hand. I won't force him to admit to his sexuality. I'll let him come to that in his own time. I won't attack him. I will not fight this. Because, as much as I may hate it, Adley wants him, too. And, as I told her, I'm just going to have to learn to live with that.

His innocence has softened my rage, and I decide to change tactics. "Well, perhaps we can both stay with her," I say in a defeated sigh.

"How do you see that working?" he says with hopeful curiosity.

"Well, we just keep doing what we did earlier tonight," I chuckle. He looks sternly at me, obviously not one for jokes.

"You mean we just live here with her?" he asks.

I clear my throat and continue in a more serious tone, "Yeah, let's make a truce that we can't fuck her alone. Isn't that the way clowders of legend used to do it?" I say.

"Yeah, basically," he says quietly. "I don't know…"

I jump down and rub against him. "Come on. It'll be fun." He shudders and hisses but doesn't swat at me or back away.

He turns and looks towards her room, reflecting on my proposal. I wait patiently while he thinks—unsure of what he will say. *I'm still willing to kick your ass, bro, so I recommend you take the deal.* He looks back at me with a newfound determination, "For her, I'd do anything." He keeps saying that: "For her." I'm unsure why I keep taking it as a passive-aggressive slight against me.

I note the chill in the air and shiver a little. "The portal brought us to a fucking winter hellscape. Let's keep her warm," I say, strutting toward the bedroom, sure he will follow.

11

ADLEY

I awake to my alarm blaring and Cheddar on my chest, sleeping soundly. I stroke his back, and he purrs loudly, slowly opening his eyes to stare at me sleepily.

"Morning, Cheddar. I mean Ezra," I coo. He stands and does a long stretch before walking to my face and nuzzling against my cheek—with his full weight on my breasts. I giggle at him, but holy crap, his paws are boring their way through my breast tissue. "As much as I love this, you feel like you weigh a million pounds on my tits," I say. He looks offended and walks off me, jumping to the ground.

I feel badly so I say, "I'm sorry, I…"

He sighs, then stretches again with a yawn before his body quickly transforms into his anthro form. He places a hand on my breast. "This better, babe?" he asks while nuzzling into my neck and kissing me.

I laugh as he gropes and kisses at me. "So, it wasn't a dream, huh? You're real."

"Sure am, babe," he says, sliding under the covers with me. He turns me to face him and sinks his hands into my flesh so that he can pull me close to his body in that way he does—like he's trying to meld our bodies together, and he just can't get close enough.

"Holy fuck, you smell so good," he says, inhaling me and licking at my neck.

I look behind me and around the room. "So, where's Marshall?"

He sighs, likely annoyed that I am asking about Marshall in this instance, and I feel kind of shitty. He responds, "He's making us breakfast."

I arc my neck so I can see the kitchen. Standing at the stove, Marshall is facing away from me. He's naked with his long black tail, slowly whipping back and forth, pink ribbons wrapped around his neck and waist. He's wearing the frilly apron I've never put on once.

"Yo, Marshall. She's awake," Ezra shouts, his voice deep and resonating in my ear—reverberating through my whole body uncomfortably. I plug my ears instinctively, which Ezra notices. I'm embarrassed by my reaction and not looking forward to explaining my sensory problems to yet another boyfriend.

Marshall turns and waves a spatula at us while saying, "It's almost done."

Ezra pushes my hair behind my ear and touches and strokes my ear gently. "Hey, sorry, I won't yell across the house like that. I can't hurt these adorable human ears." He sighs and moves forward, nibbling at my lobe. "These ears are divine."

I stroke Ezra's face and rub his ear—the human-like one on the side of his head. "I meant to ask last night, but which ear do you hear from?" I ask, running my finger around the curves. He nuzzles into my hand and kisses my palm.

"Those are vestigial," Ezra says, pointing to the ones on the side of his head. "They don't do anything. Some Ailura can hear out of them, but it's pretty rare. They're mostly sexual…"

"Oh, really," I say, stroking them further.

He laughs, lifts my shirt, and buries his face between my breasts. "Yeah, really," he says while nuzzling his face back and forth. His soft hair and ears tickle my nose, and I giggle.

"So, I got myself a ticklish mate," he says with a laugh, ready to start tickling me.

"We probably should go eat," I laugh.

"Alright, babe," he sighs, then grabs his shorts from the nightstand, slipping them on under the covers. He leaps out of the bed and kneels to stay at eye level with me. He stares lovingly at me for a long moment, grinning stupidly with his chin on his arms, before quickly pecking me on the forehead and lifting me in one swift movement.

He wraps my legs around his waist, cradling me via my ass and pecking me on the neck and cheek. "I'm just going to assume you can't walk this morning," he says as he carries me toward the kitchen. His tail sways behind him confidently as he walks me down the hall—his gate barely affected.

Marshall looks a little silly in the frilly pink apron, but it does perfectly frame his ass. "The apron looks good on you," I say as we approach Marshall from behind.

He chuckles nervously. "Thanks. I'm not sure where my shorts are. I was worried about my dick and the gas stove," he says with a blush while turning off the stove. He grabs three plates and positions them on his arms with the finesse of someone who's worked in the service industry.

Ezra drops me by the table so I can pick my seat. "Yeah, looking good, bro!" Ezra says, gently slapping Marshall's ass while he walks towards the seat at the head of the table. Marshall stiffens at the slap and flattens his ears, glaring at Ezra. Ezra only smirks back, positioning his arm on the back of the chair and crossing his ankle over his knee. It appears the animosity wasn't resolved by us all fucking. *Bummer.*

Marshall positions the plates on the table, and it looks like he made omelets. He places his hand on the small of my back, pulling me close to him, his package pressing against my belly. He looks fucking good in this apron. He smiles down, and his voice changes—less harsh, smoother. He says, "Good morning," then kisses me gently on the head. He does not release me; he just holds me against him, grinning stupidly at me. His tail wraps around my leg and tickles the edge of my buttocks up into my shorts. "And you look good in anything you wear," he says as his eyebrow raises.

"Thank you," I finally say, mesmerized by the smile and giggling at the tickle. "I'm sorry we lost your shorts; they're probably shoved in a cushion or something."

"It's not a problem," Marshall says smoothly, rubbing his face against mine. His voice is less curt than it was last night. I guess losing his virginity has loosened him a bit.

Ezra is no longer lounging arrogantly in the chair—he is leaning forward, hands on the table, watching us as if he's about to lunge at us. Arching his back in a distinctly cat-like way. He hisses, "Hey!" and growls low from deep in his belly.

Marshall hisses and releases me. Okay, so I guess they are still fighting over me a bit and aren't friends yet. Marshall pulls back a chair and motions me toward it.

"Thank you," I respond bashfully.

I sit, and he gently pushes the chair forward with me before putting a long, slow kiss on my head. Ezra is shooting eye daggers at him, hands still firm on the table. Marshall backs away from me and slinks to the chair opposite Ezra, not breaking eye contact or turning his back to him—his ears flat on his head, ready to pounce if Ezra even flinches. The tension is mounting, and I'm about to have a literal catfight on my hands. I am not in the mood. If they're going to act like cats, I'll treat them like cats.

"Hey," I say with a loud clap of my hands. They snap out of it, ears up, and stare at me. "Now this," I say, pointing back and forth at the two of them, "Isn't going to work for me. Seriously, I need you two to try to get along."

"Sorry," they mutter and lean back, eyes down, only glancing at each other.

"Marshall, thank you so much for making us breakfast," I say, bringing my hands together gratefully in front of my face.

"Yeah, thanks," Ezra says under his breath with less enthusiasm.

"Um, what is it?" I say dubiously. It looks like an omelet, but there's a slight smell that I'm not able to place.

He puts his hands between his legs on the chair and lifts in delight and excitement to tell me, "So, I made omelets. I checked your fridge and found some eggs, bell peppers, and cheese." Then, in a less sure voice, "I hope it was okay for me to look." Ezra picks up his fork and pokes at the food.

"Oh, yes, of course. Is there something else in it, though?" I ask.

"I put some of that delicious canned food you gave us yesterday in it! I thought it would pair well with the peppers," he responds proudly.

Ezra perks up—his ears high in the sky. "Oh, fuck yeah!" he says and scarfs the food down.

"Oh, um, this is so incredibly sweet of you, Marshall, but I can't really eat that canned food," I say.

"Oh, you can't? Why not?" he asks, deflating.

"Ha, umm…," I pause, considering how best to say this without insulting him, "I don't know how to say this nicely, but… umm… it's gross."

Ezra stops shoving the food in his mouth and stops his fork mid-flight. They both look at me dumbfounded. "What do you mean?" Ezra asks.

"Umm, it's… sorry, I'm not calling you cats…but…it's cat food," I say and cringe.

"Looks like I have some things to learn," Marshall laughs, but looks so sad. He stands and reaches toward my plate, attempting to take it away.

I place my hand on his, stopping him. "It's ok! I can get it. Thank you so much for making it for me, though."

"Why would you give cats something like this? It's amazing?!" Ezra asks, confused. Then, he points his fork at my plate and says with a mouthful, "Can I have that?!"

I look toward Marshall to see if he'd mind. He nods, and I say, "Sure."

Ezra leaps forward and grabs the plate. "Thanks! Marshall, it looks like you won't be completely useless around here," Ezra says, shoving the food into his mouth.

That was rude, and I'm unsure if I should meditate. I'm not their mother, but I also don't want them to be mean to each other in front of me actively. I feel like I should defend Marshall, but I don't know how to do so without seeming like I'm taking a side in all this. *Should I take sides?*

Marshall's ears flatten, and he scowls at Ezra. Instead of scolding Ezra, I'll compliment Marshall. I place my hand on his neck, and his demeanor softens as he leans into my touch. "You are not useless. Thank you, truly. Eat. I'll make something for myself a little later. Okay?" A small smile quirks the corner of his mouth, and he eats silently, staring at his plate.

=^..^= ♥ =^..^=

"What do y'all want to do today?" I ask them.

"I will do whatever you want," Marshall says very matter-of-factly.

"Well, I sent a message to work claiming to be sick, so I'm free all day. We can do whatever," I respond.

"I wouldn't mind exploring. Seeing what this world is all about," Ezra says bashfully. The look on Marshall's face tells me that's what he wants as well.

"Okay, well, first things first. I guess I should buy you two some clothes. You can't exactly walk around outside in shorts... or an apron," I respond. "If y'all are going to live here, you will need some clothes, toiletries… Oh, umm...," I stop. I recall asking them to stay with me in my drunken, sexed-up stupor. But I fell asleep almost instantly and never got a response. Do they want to live with me? Do they have anywhere else to go? Are they only hanging out with me because they are literally stuck here with nowhere else to go? Was all this "you're a goddess, you're our fated mate" stuff a ploy to find a place to shack up? This is just like me falling headfirst for some dudes and asking them to live with me after they have sex with me. Dudes I haven't even known for 24 hours! *What kind of loser does that?*

I say, "Um, I'm sorry. I've just assumed you both wanted to live here with me. I'm sorry to presume. Do you want to live with me? If not, I can help you find—"

"Absolutely," they say in unison, cutting me off before I start rambling too much. Well, I guess that answers that.

"Are you sure?" I ask tentatively.

"Babe, why wouldn't we want to live with you? You're the hottest woman on the planet, and you have this amazing food. What else could we want out of a live-in girlfriend?" Ezra says. Marshall nods as if he agrees with everything Ezra just said. "I know I should be ashamed of eating this stuff, but honestly, I can't imagine your world has anything that tastes better," he shrugs, leaning back and crossing his arms defiantly.

Let's roll back to that hottest woman on the planet thing. "You literally have no idea what other women on this planet look like," I laugh.

"Sure I do! You turned the TV on yesterday. I saw all those movie stars. The hottest woman on the planet is sitting right in front of me," he says, pointing at me.

I laugh, "Okay, but—"

"Babe, do I need to fuck you silly again to prove my devotion to you?" he says, standing from the chair.

"No, no! That's okay," I say, waving him down.

"Because I can, you know. You asked what I wanted to do today, and the answer is 'you,'" he says, leaning forward. "I just didn't think that was the kind of answer you were looking for. But, if you're going to go doubting my devotion, I might need to change my answer."

They both stare at me intently, waiting for me to say, "Okay, yeah, let's just fuck on this table," and I'm definitely tempted, but my pussy needs a little bit of a break.

"Okay, I believe you," I say quietly.

"You'll need to hear it often, won't you?" Marshall says. At first, I assume he's passing judgment on me in that statement—that he's calling me needy. That he's going to argue with me about how I should just trust him. But the look on his face implies he's asking for "purely scientific purposes." He's asking because he genuinely wants to know if that will make me happy.

"Ummm, yeah… probably," I say, ashamed.

"Noted," Marshall says.

"Sorry, I'm so—" I begin.

Ezra cuts me off, "Oh, I get that, babe. I'm a 'words of affirmation' kinda guy, too. Don't apologize. And don't worry, I'll never stop telling you how breathtakingly beautiful you are," Ezra says.

"Literal manifestation of our world's concept of a goddess—an angel," Marshall says.

"Yep, that!" Ezra says, pointing at Marshall.

"I could explain scientifically why our bodies will always consider you the most att—"

"No, that's ok. Thanks, Marsh," I laugh.

I'm uncomfortable with these compliments I was obviously fishing for, so now it's time to change the subject.

I pull out my phone and say, "Well, anyway, let's get you some clothes. Target is down the road. We can buy some stuff online, and I'll pick it up."

"What's Target?" Marshall asks.

"It's a department store. They have clothes and groceries and stuff," I respond.

"So, we're going to buy our clothes from a grocery store?" Ezra asks incredulously.

"What, will the fabric burn you if it's not designer?" Marshall says.

"Well, no," Ezra says in a way that almost sounds like a yes.

I hand Marshall my phone and say, "Here, why don't you pick out something you can wear today? Then we can all go shopping, and y'all can get more things like toiletries, extra outfits, and some food y'all will like."

"Incredible. This phone is just like mine. Our writing is the same, too. It seems the only difference is the people and the names of things," Marshall says, marveling at the phone and turning it over to inspect the back.

"Hurry up, bro, you can do your little sociology or scientific study or whatever this is after we get some pants," Ezra says.

Marshall takes a few moments to select some items then hands the phone to Ezra. Ezra looks confused as he scrolls, "Um, what should I get?"

"A pair of pants, a shirt, underwear, socks, shoes, and a coat," Marshall lists.

"Dude, stop talking to me like I'm stupid. I know that, bro. I mean, like, what's in style in this universe? I don't know what to get."

"Why does it matter?" Marshall asks.

"I can't make my debut in this universe and look like a tool," Ezra wines.

Marshall snatches the phone from him, "I'm just going to get two of everything I got."

"NOOO, you can't do that! We can't fucking match. That's so embarrassing," Ezra squeals and reaches across the table. Flopping his whole body on it with his tail in the air.

They hiss and launch at each other across the table. I lift from my seat, backing away and trying to get away from their swinging arms, afraid I'll get hit. They both notice my reaction and recede.

"I'm sorry," they both say.

"We'll try to reign this in," Marshall says, gesturing between them.

"Yeah," Ezra says. "I'm sorry. I'll just get what he got, but, like, a different color, at least," he says, giving Marshall some serious side-eye.

Ezra scrolls through the phone briefly before saying, "Dude, you know there are colors other than black, right?"

"I like black," Marshall shrugs.

"Oh, um, maybe get a hat? You might want to cover your ears," I chime in, pointing at the top of my head where my ears would be if I had them.

"Oh, yeah," Ezra says, touching his ear sadly. He scrolls around a bit more before handing me the phone.

"Here you go, babe," he says. "I added a hat in there for you, too, Marshall."

"Umm, thanks," Marshall says, blushing. Ezra smirks, and I suspect that the hat will likely be embarrassing.

"Thanks for this, Adley," Marshall says.

I look at the total. They got modest clothes. Everything was on sale. Marshall is obviously thrifty, but it's still a few hundred dollars—made more expensive by the need for winter shoes and jackets.

Suddenly, the gravity of asking two men I just met last night who literally materialized in this world yesterday to live with me hits me.

This is just one outfit for them. I have to buy them toothbrushes, underwear, socks, food, and God knows what I'm probably forgetting. I didn't expect this when I let the cats in. I didn't even think I'd be keeping the cats. How is this going to work? Are these my cats or my boyfriends? Do I take care of them, or do they get jobs? I mean, they're hot and in another dimension, but am I now obligated to take care of them just because they're in an isekai story? What about health insurance? They don't even have social security numbers. How are they going to work? They can't… can they?

Marshall must sense my internal struggle. "Don't worry. I'll figure out how to pay you back. I recognize what an imposition this is," Marshall says.

"Oh, um…," I sputter. I don't know what to say. Do I admit that I was spiraling just now?

"Yeah, babe, we'll pay you back, and not just in double-dickings," Ezra says.

12

EZRA

My excitement is visible as I bounce about the room waiting for Adley. I try to contain myself. Containing myself is something I tend to be great at—until I'm not. And this is one of those times I'm not. The fact that my movements about the room annoy Marshall probably feeds into my lack of restraint—and my skin is itching from Adley being so far away from me. The sound of the garage door opening faintly hums in the recesses of the home, triggering me to bolt to the door. Marshall, having been sitting quietly—except when he would bark at me that I should do the same—perks up as well. He doesn't want to show it, but he, too, has ached for her return.

We greet her at the door, and she seems startled by us blocking her path. She smiles wryly and asks, "Were y'all waiting at the door for me?" She laughs as she hands us bags with prominent red target symbols. I drop my shorts to the ground, ready to put these new items on, when Adley chuckles, saying, "Hey, can you let me in the house before you start dropping your drawers, Ezra?" I realize I'm still blocking her path into the house—Marshall and I are essentially pinning her at the door, and I blush at my impulsiveness.

"Oh, yeah, sorry." I yank them back up, not worrying about threading my tail through the hole and rushing to the bedroom, my asscheeks exposed. Adley must consider this action comical because she laughs as she follows me to the room. Marshall follows slowly, sorting through his bags. I drop my bags to the ground, pull more items out, and throw them to the bed.

I dress quickly, anxious to leave and anxious to put on some clothes that are hopefully more fashionable than these.

Still in that apron, Marshall states, "I missed socks," as he puts some on before anything else.

"If your feet are cold, bro, you could have just transformed," I say, confused.

"I can't talk to Adley in my ailo form. But it's not because I'm cold. I don't like how hardwood feels on my feet," he says.

"I'm sorry, Marshall, I could have given you some socks. Is it the floor crumblies?" Adley says, making a little fluttery motion with her fingers at the word "crumblies."

"Yeah," he blushes.

"Same! I can't stand them. You can ask for stuff, Marshall. I don't want you to be uncomfortable," Adley says.

"What are floor crumblies?" I ask, trying and failing to make the same motion with my fingers.

"Oh, it's like I can feel every spec of dirt, every crumb on the floor if I'm not wearing socks. It's… bothersome," Adley responds.

"Oh, okay," I say, making a mental note to keep this aspect of Adley's personality in mind.

I put on underwear and am annoyed at the feeling of it sitting below my tail, but I don't feel like dealing with it. I'll sew a tail opening later.

I inspect the pants and am confused by their design. "Huh, weird, there's a zipper," I say. I didn't notice this when we were purchasing the pants.

"What do you mean?" Adley asks.

"Oh, I see how it works. The fly is in the front! The pants back home put the opening on the back. We fasten our pants around our tails. We'd never use a zipper, though; that sounds awful," I cringe.

I climb into the pants, and my tail blocks their path up my waist. "Oh, I guess I should hide my tail," I say while shoving it down through my underwear and pants. I sinch the pants around my waist with the button and zipper and am terrified of getting my junk caught in the zipper, but luckily, the process is uneventful. I throw the shirt on and walk to the floor-length mirror to inspect my fit.

Not bad. Everything looks pretty good. Nice lines. I study my silhouette in the mirror and turn to the side to see my shape. I am horrified at the way the pants conform around my ass and tucked-in tail. *I look so dumb.* For the first time in my life, I regret having a fluffy tail. It makes my left leg look weirdly off-balance, and it definitely looks like I have a tail shoved down my pants.

"People are going to think I look weird," I say dejectedly. Maybe I should just stay here.

"That's okay. Most people won't even notice you," Adley says. Not notice me? Why wouldn't they notice me? Would people of this world find me so unappealing that they don't look at me? That's not something I really know how to handle. Can I fit into this world? I put my hat on, and my ears and hair are covered. I look like a schlep with a weird ass.

Should I even leave the house? Everyone is going to laugh at me. They'll think I'm a weirdo with a weird-shaped ass. What's the point in going if I look like shit?

Adley chuckles, "Cute hat!" at Marshall. His hat is a knit cap made to look like he has cat ears.

"Ezra, seriously?" Marshall sighs at me.

"What?! It's black!" I say, laughing to myself.

"I like it, Marshall!" Adley says. Damn. Now I wish I had gotten one for myself, too, if she's going to be gushing over it like that. My hat is just a plain winter knit cap. His hides his ears better than mine does, too. This fucking sucks. What are we going to do in the summer? Pretty much every hat looks terrible on me. Is this some kind of karmic payback? I was too hot in my universe, so I was sent to one that would take me down a few hundred pegs?

Adley hooks her finger in my belt loop and tugs my hip to get my attention. She smiles at me with that beautiful fucking face and that adorable fucking grin. "I think you look hot, Ez. But we don't have to go if you don't want to. We can buy stuff online and have it delivered. Or I can go pick it up for you." She knew exactly what I was thinking. She knows precisely how vain I am. But she doesn't seem to mind.

In direct contrast to the understanding and loving look Adley is giving me, Marshall looks at me with annoyance. I know he thinks I'm being difficult. Maybe he's ok with being ugly in public, but I'm not. I look him up and down; unfortunately, he does not look ugly. The black does look good on him. I see why he favors it. And his tail is easily concealed in his pants. *Damn him.*

I scowl at myself in the mirror, considering my options. Marshall looks hotter than me—with his easily hidden tail and weirdly cute hat. How can I get out of this without being super obvious about why I don't want to go? I don't want Marshall to know it's because he looks hot, and I look like total trash because dude would never let me live it down. I don't feel like being made fun of right now by him for being vain. And, despite Adley being understanding, I don't want to be this pathetic in front of her. Fuck. I was so excited to go out.

Adley checks out my butt and says, "It's the tail bothering you, isn't it?"

"Yeah," I pout, unable to hide my disappointment.

"Let's figure it out. There's got to be a way to make it less noticeable," she stands and stares at my ass. I can see the gears turning in her head—sexily. I'd try to fuck her if I didn't feel like an unattractive child being dressed by his mother—thoroughly emasculated.

"We could shave it," Marshall suggests with a smirk.

"No, the fuck we can't!" I snap. "You'd like that, wouldn't you, thin tail!"

"Thin tails seem to be an advantage in this world, bushy," he laughs back. *This fucking guy.* He's getting off on this, isn't he?

Adley ignores this altercation and states, "I know this probably would be uncomfortable, but we could wrap a soft bandage around it to reduce the fluff. We could even strap it down the inside of your leg to make it less noticeable and easier to stop its movement." That sounds like a decent idea which gets me a bit hopeful.

Adley jumps up and claps her hands! "Oh wait! We could do kind of what drag queens do with their junk! My roommate in college was a drag queen, and she showed me how she wrapped her package and tucked it to kind of make it look like labia. We could wrap your tail similarly, but instead, move it to the front to make it look like you have a huge… well, extra huge dick."

That sounds like as good an idea as any. "Oh, yeah, let's do that!" I say, not wanting to turn down the opportunity to have extra huge junk. I'm not jazzed about having my tail wrapped up; that sounds uncomfortable, but maybe we can figure something else out later.

Adley runs out of the room excitedly and returns shortly with gauze bandages. She hands me the bandage and asks, "Would you like me to help you?"

"Yes, please," I say. "But, um… I might come if you start wrapping my tail." Maybe having my tail wrapped won't be such a bad thing.

Marshall asks, "Can I have some of that bandage?"

"Why, bro? Your tail looks fine!" I ask.

"I wanna tuck mine forward, too," Marshall says. Oh, he's jealous of my potentially extra huge junk.

=^..^= ♥ =^..^=

Adley opens the garage door, and I was really hoping it would reveal a cool flying car or something, but like most of the tech in this world, it looks nearly identical to the cars in ours. *Lame.* Parallel worlds are fucking weird. Adley gets in on the driver's side, but Marshall and I both go to the other side and reach for the handle simultaneously. *This fucking guy.* Why does he have to challenge me with everything? We both bristle and hiss, ready to attack, when

Adley says, "Just rock paper scissors for it. Do you have that in your world?" Weirdly, we do.

We rock, paper, scissors, and the smug look on Marshall's face when he wins makes me want to clock him. Is this really what the rest of my life with Adley will be like?

The whole ride, Marshall asks Adley questions about the car and all sorts of other shit, marveling at how things work. I can barely get a word in with her. And Adley can scarcely hear me from back here. Instead of trying to compete with Dr. Dorkster for airtime, I watch the buildings pass by. Everything is so similar. The stores look almost exactly like ours, just slightly different names. Even the logos look the same. *This is so weird.* Is this what I've been reduced to? Bored in the backseat. Ignored?

I pick up Marshall and Adley's conversation mid-sentence, "…can go to the mall tomorrow if you want. Oh, let's get dinner while we're there! I've been dying for some sushi!" Adley exclaims.

"Oh, I love sushi! It's so good! I get it every year on my birthday!" I chime in.

Marshall says sadly, "I've never had sushi before!"

I scoff under my breath, "Of course you haven't."

"What does that mean?" Adley asks. Shit, I didn't want her to hear that.

"He's calling me poor and unclassed. I, like most people, can't afford a delicacy like sushi," Marshall says. Can Adley afford sushi? Based on her house and car, she's middle class. After insulting Marshall, I can't ask her now; if I ask, she'll think I'm insulting her, too.

Luckily, Adley saves me from myself by stating, "Oh, it's not the cheapest food here, but it's affordable. You don't have to be rich to eat it."

Marshall says excitedly, "That's amazing!"

Adley speaks up, looking at me through the rearview mirror, "You've had it before, Ezra. Does that mean you were rich in your world?"

I blush and break eye contact, looking out the window, "Um, yeah, kinda."

Marshall looks back at me with a confused expression on his face. "Why are you being coy?" he asks.

I maintain ignorance and respond, "What do you mean?"

"Why are you hiding that you were from one of the richest families in the world?"

"So, wait, he's rich *and* famous?" Adley asks Marshall, glancing at us and trying to keep her eyes on the road.

"Yeah, his family is 'old money.' He's essentially famous for being a layabout, rich, fuck boy who jet-sets around the world with models," he retorts. Why'd he say it like it's a bad thing? I'm fucking awesome! I fold my arms across my chest, annoyed.

"Is that so?" Adley says flatly. *This fucking guy!* He keeps throwing me under the bus.

"I'm not a layabout fuck boy! I work really hard, and I have had actual girlfriends," I pout.

"Really? What's your job exactly?" he asks in his matter-of-fact way to imply he's not judging you, but I know he totally is by the smirk he flashes me in the rearview mirror. "And how long did your previous relationship last?" Ouch, going for the kill—literally. Images of Sarah pushing me off the balcony flash in my head. *Shit.* Was she right? Am I worthless? Is my only contribution to this world to take what others make?

Fuck that. I won't let him make me get all weepy right now. I snap back, raising my voice to make sure they both can hear me, "Modeling is work! It's a job! And Sarah and I have been together for six months!"

"You mean the girlfriend who's sitting in prison for murdering you?" Marshall smirks.

"Bro! What's your fucking problem? That shit happened to me literally yesterday. Let a guy fucking process his shit before you throw it in his face." Tears well in my eyes, and I really don't want to cry because of this fucking guy.

Adley pulls into a parking spot and turns to me, "Ezra, are you okay? Do you want to talk about it?" Not with this fucking guy around, I don't! Marshall's head hangs and I'm not sure why he's looking all regretful.

I unbuckle, fling the door open. "Maybe later," I say cooly and bound out.

ADLEY

"Okay, guys, the key to today is to try not to draw too much attention to yourselves, blend in, and could you maybe not fight?" I say, wanting to have a deeper conversation with them about the constant bickering but not feeling like it's my place just yet.

Marshall seems shaken by the interaction in the car, but Ezra is back to his giddy, bouncy self. "Got it! Blend in. Don't fight," Ezra says with a salute. He moves to my side and practically skips next to me.

Marshall slinks to my other side, his movement more contained, reserved, and purposeful. They tower over me. As we approach the store, women holding their lattes and pushing their red carts full of impulse purchases all but stop and stare. A short, mediumly attractive woman, flanked by two towering, hot as fuck men. *What's to stare at, ladies?!*

"We had a store exactly like this at home!" Marshall says. Not noticing the young women by their car who say, "Oh my fucking God," and drop their keys in total confusion.

"Really?" Ezra and I both say in unison.

"Yeah, it's like a sanctuary for suburban women."

"Same here," I laugh.

"I've never been," Ezra says. "I'm kind of excited."

"I can tell," I say with a laugh. "Normally, I don't shop without a list, but since we don't have one, let's approach this methodically. We will start at the front of the store and work our way back. That should have us hit the freezer aisle of the grocery section last. Then we can stay here as long as we need, and y'all can explore as much as you want," I say, mentally mapping out the store.

"Sounds like a plan," Marshall says.

"Whatever you say, Ads," Ezra says, now actually skipping. We enter the store and the lights are significantly less blinding than the snow outside. "Oh, wow!" Ezra says. "It's huge!"

"So, you've never been to a department store before?" I ask.

"No, I never shopped for stuff like groceries. And… I always got my clothes from designers," Ezra says with a little bit of shame.

"Well, if you think this place is fun, you'll love the mall tomorrow—I'm super excited for you to see it." I beam at him. I'm not a fan of going to malls, but I can't have a fashionisto move in with me and not take him to the biggest mall in the country. That would be cruel.

In stark contrast to Ezra's exuberance, Marshall's expression remains stoic. But his eyes reveal a flicker of nervousness and fascination.

"You okay, Marshall?" I ask.

"Oh, um… sometimes, I have trouble in large spaces and around a lot of people," he says.

"Me, too," I admit and look to the ground.

"Well, I guess we'll just have to stick together then, huh?" he says, putting his arm around me.

"Oh my God! What's with these? Are these so you can get lots of stuff?" Ezra roars by the shopping carts.

Marshall removes his arm from around my waist and walks toward the cart Ezra is pointing at. "Seriously, Ezra, we have fucking shopping carts in our world. You can't be that sheltered."

"I know! I was just trying to get your hands off my girl," Ezra laughs and runs to take Marshall's place.

Marshall sighs and yanks the cart from the corral while giving Ezra an eat-shit look.

I unzip my coat, as it's getting a bit hot already. "Let's start with the clothes," I say. "We can get more at the mall, though, so don't feel like you have to get your whole wardrobe here."

Ezra breaks away from me and wanders toward the men's section, causing everyone, even a little kid, to stop and look at him. He walks with such exuberant purpose he commands the whole world's attention. Looks like blending in isn't really an option.

Marshall pushes the cart beside me and says, "Adley, are you sure about this shopping trip? It's going to be… expensive."

I beam at him, "No worries, Marshall, I've got it." I've got credit cards, which is what I really mean. Paying for this is Future Adley's problem. For now, I just want to take care of them and make them happy.

When Marshall and I get to the men's clothes section, Ezra is already holding a shirt up, inspecting it, and rubbing the fabric between his fingers. He makes a "well, okay" harrumph sound and drapes it over his arm.

Marshall wanders beside me, scanning the racks with a discerning gaze. He picks up a pair of pants and frowns. "What's wrong?" I ask him.

"Our tails. Are we going to have to strap them down all the time? Even at home?" he asks. Home? The fact he's calling my house his home warms my heart.

"Don't worry about it, bro. I'll add tail flies to all of them," Ezra says, running up toward him.

"What do you mean?" Marshall asks.

"All I gotta do is cut an opening in the back and put a button at the top. No biggie," Ezra says. "Ha, I'll put a buttonhole stitch on a hole on our butts!" he says, looking to us to join in on the laugh, but we don't. It's a bad joke, even when presented by a smoke show. I'm sure he's used to people laughing at even his bad jokes, though. Not noticing, he continues, "Adley has a sewing kit, so we're all good."

"You can sew?" I ask.

"Of course," he says, "I had to alter my clothes all the time."

"Will you show me how to do it?" Marshall asks demurely.

"Of course, bro. No problem," Ezra says, but I do hear a coldness in his voice that he's trying to hide.

"Thanks," Marshall says, blushing.

Ezra strolls off, and Marshall watches Ezra with a look that I can't quite place. I'm pretty sure it's admiration. While his attention is focused on Ezra, I sneak two pairs of grey sweatpants into the cart.

=^..^= ♥ =^..^=

I'm lost in the process of touching a soft sweater and enjoying the stimuli when I hear Ezra shout, "Which do you prefer, Adley?" I turn to see him pointing at packs of underwear. "Tighty-whities or boxers?" he says so loud everyone looks at us—well, they were already looking at him anyway. "Or perhaps, why choose when you can have them both in the form of… boxer briefs?" he laughs.

"Ezra," I say in a low tone, laughing with embarrassment, "not so loud." I look at everyone looking at us. I can feel the fire in my face as it undoubtedly lights up with embarrassment.

"Oh, sorry," he says, noticing the people around us, and then whispers, "So which do you want to see me in?"

Oh, my God. "Boxer briefs. But, um, not white," I say.

Ezra grabs a few packs, and basketball shoots them into the cart in front of Marshall a few feet away. "How'd I know you were the type who didn't want to choose?" Ezra says with a laugh.

"Grab me some, too," Marshall requests. So Ezra shoots two more into the cart.

I cover my face in embarrassment. Is this going to be my life from now on?

13

ADLEY

The squeaking of Ezra's snow boots fades in the distance as he sprints to the front of the store to get another cart. After shopping for clothes and basics like toothbrushes, which Ezra took an inordinate amount of time selecting, one cart is already full. I rest my arms on the cart's edge, exhausted, and watch Marshall as he slowly scans the modest book section.

"This is so cool," he says, grazing his fingers across their covers. "There are so many new stories. New histories. I have a whole new universe to learn about." He picks up a book about the Roman Empire because, of course he does. What is it with dudes and the Roman Empire? His face contorts as he studies it, reading the blurb on the back. He opens it gingerly, trying not to break the spine, and peeks at its innards.

"Get it," I say, wanting to make him smile. So far, this trip has been "the Ezra show." I suspect that will be true for most of our interactions. I appreciate this quiet moment with Marshall, as our temperaments seem more aligned. A small break from Ezra's boundless enthusiasm and blinding beauty is a nice respite for my senses.

"Really?" he asks. And the smile on his face makes me want to throw everything I've got at him to make him keep smiling.

"Yeah, sure. Get one of these, too," I say, holding up an e-reader.

"Really?!" He says, and I can see his ears bounce under his hat.

"Yeah, I told you, I'll get you the stuff you need."

"But I don't need this," he says, taking the e-reader from my outstretched hand and looking at it like he's looked at everything—with an eye of scientific curiosity, respect, and caution. I can almost see the calculations running in his head as he mentally compares it to familiar items.

"Sometimes wants are needs. You literally appeared in this world naked with nothing. Having some possessions will help anchor you."

"Okay," he says, slowly putting it in the cart, and I wonder if I perhaps pushed too hard. Am I showering him too much? Overcompensating for my struggles with legitimate affection by trying to buy his love?

He grips the end of the cart, looking down at the stuff within it, quietly reflecting. He seems more than lost in thought; he looks pensive. I want to connect with him but balk while searching for a valid topic. I know jack shit about the Roman Empire and next to jack shit about history in general. I could study, but that won't save me in the next thirty seconds.

We both stand silently, and it's likely he's also trying to decide what to say to me. The tension of uncertainty is overwhelming. So, I steel myself and creep around the cart to stand beside him. A shy smile cracks his face as I place my hand on his. "It's all so… overwhelming," he says, finally looking upward from the cart.

"I can't imagine," I say quietly. Trying to give him the space to open up.

"I've never—" Marshall begins but is cut off by Ezra barreling towards us on a shopping cart, his feet balanced precariously on the lower bar. Just before he reaches us, he hops off the cart and yanks it to a stop before it collides with us. The loud squeal of those noisy boots grinding to a halt makes Marshall and I cover our ears—I the side of my head, Marshall the top of his. Ezra's face is flush with the excitement of whatever adventure he is returning from. He grimaces at our reaction and exhales a "Sorry."

Recovering quickly, I ask, "Want any books, Ezra?"

"Nah, I'm good," he absentmindedly says, looking past the books towards the electronics.

"Want to go look at the electronics, Marshall?" I ask, catching Ezra's attention.

"Sure," he says, saddling up to the cart and pulling it backward to the central aisle leading us to our destination. Ezra similarly pulls his empty cart back, but once he gets to the central aisle, he jumps atop it again, pushing forward with one deep kick and riding it to the video game aisle. Abruptly stopping in front of it with another hop, at least his boots didn't squeak this time. It must be nice to feel comfortable being so extra all the time.

"I'm excited to try out some video games here. We never got around to checking out your video game collection, babe—we were going to, but then you went to the bathroom and came back begging for dick," Ezra jokes.

"I did not beg!" I say, slightly offended at the truth in his statement.

"Sure, babe," he laughs and kisses me on top of the head—teasing me with a wink.

"Which of these systems do you own?" Ezra asks, gesturing toward the aisle in general.

"Um… all of them," I say, slightly embarrassed.

"What? Really?" Ezra asks in disbelief.

"Yeah, I told you—I *really* like video games," I laugh.

"Where do you keep them, though? I didn't see them anywhere," Ezra says, eyes scanning the colorful boxes.

"Oh, that's because you haven't entered the basement yet," I say.

"You have a basement?!" Ezra asks excitedly.

"Yeah, I have a whole gaming room set up down there. I haven't been down there in a while, myself. I haven't had the energy to play lately," I say sadly. It's honestly the understatement of the year. I'm a "sit in one place for twenty-four hours and then realize she forgot to eat, maybe even forgot to pee" kind of gamer (a.k.a. an autistic hyper-focused kind). I love video games. I get lost in them, and they consume my whole world.

When Bryce moved in, he packed all my stuff up to make room for his home gym—pushing my things to a small, uncomfortable corner. At first, I thought it would be nice. I could play games while he worked out. We could be together doing the things we enjoyed. Separate but together. But, whenever I tried, he'd lecture me about how video games were a waste of time—never mind, my literal profession revolves around them. Eventually, his lectures progressed to video games not only being a waste of time but also a perfect scapegoat for him to pin the blame of all the things he didn't like about me. He said they were why I was unmotivated. He said they were why I was fat. And so, I stopped playing. When he moved out, I tried to reclaim the space and tried to play a game—get back to the Adley I was when I was happy. But… it just felt like so much work.

"Let's all play some games together when we get home!" Ezra says, bouncing over to the phones, leaving his cart with Marshall and me.

"Sure," I say with a smile, knowing I'll be too tired. I'm already too tired. I'm always too tired.

Marshall and I slowly push the carts and follow behind him.

"Oh, this is the phone you have, right, Adley?" Ezra asks, pointing at the display of phones.

I pull my phone out and show him. "Yep. I've got the pink one." I add because I can't help myself, "Which color do you want, Ezra?"

"Seriously?!" he asks.

"Yeah, y'all need phones," I say with a shrug. Trying to act nonchalantly—trying not to display the anxiety building in me. I always do this. I go too far. I do too much. I'm going overboard with this trip. Tomorrow, when we go to the mall, as I've already promised, I will go entirely into the deep end of the "buys love because she struggles with affection" pool.

"I want green!" Ezra says excitedly.

I look to Marshall as if to ask him which he wants. "Black," Marshall says perfunctorily.

I guess I'm the kind of girl that meets two mind-meltingly hot guys and gets dicked down so well that within 24 hours, she has invited them to live with her and starts a cell phone family plan with them. Honestly, how am I going to explain this to my friends? Maybe they'll get one look at Marshall and Ezra and say, "Oh, yeah, I get it. Do they have any interdimensional brothers I too can support financially?" I don't spend too much time dwelling on that thought since I don't even have any friends now that Veronica… never mind…

The phones take forever to get since I have to flag down a clerk, sign some contracts, and… it's a whole thing. But the guys are excited to have the phones working and in their pockets already. "I'll show you what apps to get later," I tell them as we finally stroll away from the electronics section.

"Adley, you are the absolute best. I was dying without a phone," Ezra says, kissing me on the cheek and pushing the less-full cart (even though most of the stuff in the other is his). "Thank you so much!"

"No problem, Ezra," I giggle.

"This has all been very kind of you," Marshall says exhaustedly, leaning on the cart he's pushing.

They follow behind me, each pushing their carts, as we walk toward the grocery section, the final stretch of our shopping trip. I am all too eager to finish up this trip. It's been fun, and I'm enjoying spending time with the guys, but the whole experience has been overstimulating. Take the already too bright, too loud, too colorful environment of the store, add two hotties who take up a lot of space, and pepper in multiple passersby whispering about those two hotties, and you have a whole-ass day, and it's barely past 2 p.m. I'm also verging on the hangry side of hungry.

Suddenly, they both stop in their tracks, causing me to do the same. Ezra bolts to an aisle to our right, and Marshall slowly follows behind him, mesmerized by something. Oh, no, I was kind of hoping they would overlook this aisle.

I enter, revealing them both standing in a wide-eyed stupor, as if they are seeing an impressive work of art in a museum in front of the wall of cat food.

Ezra's expression changes from awe to excitement. "Oh my God, babe! What kind of paradise is this fucking place? Why didn't you lead with this aisle?" He looks at Marshall as if he might hug him with excitement but changes his mind and starts darting up and down the aisle, trying to see everything it offers. "You weren't lying when you said your people love cats!"

I suppose I should have expected this. I really have to convince them this is not appropriate food. "Look how cheap everything is!" Ezra shouts, grabbing cans upon cans of what I'm guessing appears appetizing to him and rushing them to the cart.

"Marshall! Almost all of these have fish in them! Babe, how is this so cheap?" He says, not stopping his quest—that I'm now understanding—to get every flavor this store offers.

"Ummm, fish is cheap...," I say with a confused shrug. I'm pretty sure I don't have enough context to answer the question sufficiently, but I'll just wait for him to ask clarifying questions.

"How is fish cheap?!" he exclaims, taken aback. Okay, so he's not going to offer any clarification.

"Ezra, I don't know how to answer that question. Why are you asking me this? Are you trying to tell me fish is expensive in your world?" I ask. In the car, they mentioned sushi was expensive. I didn't think much about it, and the topic changed so quickly that I didn't have enough time to really register it, but now I'm realizing that fish is the delicacy—not necessarily sushi.

Marshall stands next to me, staring lovingly at a can of what looks to be tuna. "Due to overfishing, the catching and consumption of fish are highly regulated. Its difficulty to obtain has made it one of the most expensive items in our world. Unfortunately, it's highly coveted, so a black market for it has been actively thwarting conservation efforts."

"Oh, that's too bad. So, I guess you wouldn't understand the idiom, there are plenty of fish in the sea," I joke.

"I am not a fan of idioms," Marshall says.

"I'm gathering that," I respond flatly. "Fish is plentiful here, hence the idiom. Yes, there is some regulation on it and some bad actors. Still, it's not something the average consumer has to concern themselves with beyond their personal ethics and nutritional needs around how the fish are raised, collected, or whatever…," I say, trailing off. Was I really about to go into the whole spiel about the different ways in which fish are raised and caught?

"Anyway. If it's the fish y'all are excited for, why don't you put the cat food back?" I say. Ezra looks at me, aghast at the suggestion, dropping his cans into the cart. "And let's go get some fish meant to be consumed by people."

They look at each other, and even Marshall lights up, saying, "Please take us to look at the fish."

"Sure." I say, "It's this way," and proceed to the grocery section.

"Hold up," Marshall says, stopping in his tracks again. "What's that?" He crouches down and creeps to the back of the aisle. He stops at the end of the aisle and points at a fluttering feathery thing.

I giggle at him, amused at their insistence they are not cats despite the uncanny resemblance. "It's a cat toy," I say.

Marshall straightens quickly and darts his hand out so fast to grab the toy I didn't even see him do it. He holds the toy in front of his face, dead set on it. Ezra slinks next to him, and his gaze locks on the toy as he stands beside Marshall.

"Do you smell that?" Marshall asks him.

"Yeah," Ezra sighs out contentedly. "It reminds me of you, Ads," Ezra says dreamily, tilting his head at it and resting on Marshall's shoulder.

"What?! Why?" I ask. I smell like catnip?

"I dunno. I get the same feeling when I smell this that I do when I smell your cunt," Ezra says, perhaps too loudly—kind of like everything he says. An older woman walks by at that exact moment and gasps but then smiles and blushes when she notices that filth came out of something so fucking pretty. She shoots me a thumbs up. Trying not to die of embarrassment, I walk closer to them.

Marshall rubs the toy against his face, and Ezra does the same, fully invading Marshall's space and essentially rubbing cheeks with him.

"Oh, Adley. You've got to feel this," Marshall says.

"I'm alright. It doesn't do it for me, boys," I say, looking around nervously and wondering if we're about to get kicked out of this store.

"That's a shame," Ezra says dreamily. They lean against each other in a relaxed embrace, sinking to the floor. I don't know what to do.

They are on the ground, wrapped around each other, and rubbing the toy between them—their actions haven't quite reached a "get arrested" level of sexual inappropriateness. Still, it's exceeded the "get kicked out of the store for being fucking weirdos" level.

Marshall pins Ezra to the ground and proceeds to do what I can only describe as "aggressive grooming." He rips Ezra's hat off, fully exposing his ears, and runs his hands through Ezra's locks. He's now rubbing Ezra's ears and nibbling at them between his fingers. Ezra gropes at Marshall's leg, and it is officially time to break this up because I think the next step in whatever this is involves nudity.

I get closer to them and say, "Umm, guys, please," but am cut off by Ezra grabbing at me and trying to pull me down to the floor in their pile of catnip-induced lust. I escape his clutches and dart a little further away. "Guys!" I say in a panic, frantically checking for possible passersby.

"Yeah," Marshall says.

"That's catnip. Maybe let's get one and enjoy it at home, in private," I plead with them.

"Catnip!" Marshall says, startled, and throws it on Ezra. "They just sell this at the store, too?!" Ezra fully shoves his face into it now that he has control, inhaling so loudly that the moan echoes through the aisle.

"Umm, yeah," I say, waiting for him to explain why that's so startling, but I think I know the answer.

"This place is paradise," Marshall says. "This is rarer than fish in our universe."

"I've only ever had it once," Ezra says. "Even I couldn't afford to have it more frequently than that."

Marshall shakes his head. "We need to snap out of it," he says, smacking Ezra. "We can't waste away here."

"Ow, bro! But, yeah," Ezra says sadly and still a little dreamily. He stands and puts his hat back on while tossing the toy away from them.

They both adjust themselves, trying to hide their massive erections and doing that little leg shake thing guys do when their junk is all twisted up in their pants. Ezra brushes some dust off Marshall's back, and Marshall shoots him a glare, which implies he forgot what he was just doing with Ezra a few moments ago. Ezra raises his hands in surrender and walks toward me. He pulls me tightly to him and inhales my neck, then nips it slightly. I startle, and he says, "Sorry, babe, just needed to get that out of me," then jumps atop his cart, careening away. Marshall exits the aisle with significantly less je ne sais quoi, sulking after Ezra and forgetting his cart—still a little out of it.

I'm left standing alone in the cat aisle. At the bottom of the display is a pack of four cat toys that look like sushi—perfect. I grab them and the feather wand and sneak them into the cart, hiding them under the pile of clothes.

=^..^= ♥ =^..^=

The fish aisle is a whole thing. I don't know if I've ever spent so much time in this store, and that's saying something, considering there's a candle aisle, blanket aisle, and a coffee shop right at the entrance.

I'm hungry and ready to go, but I'm excited to see how eager the guys are. Even Marshall can't stop smiling after we put literally every frozen fish variety they have in the cart. When I told them there's a store just a few blocks away where we can get fresh fish of even more variety, it looked like their minds melted.

We each push one of the three stacked full shopping carts up to the cashier, and she looks incredibly annoyed until she notices the two men pushing two of the carts. Once her eyes land on Ezra and Marshall, she begins frantically straightening her hair and stands tall, sticking out her chest. I won't say the look she gave me didn't hurt my feelings, but I'm just going to pretend it was out of jealousy and not actual disgust.

Since we walked into the store, Ezra's enthusiasm has not waned. He excitedly looks at all the candies and holds them up to me as if to ask, "Can I get these?" I nod with each item. He is literally a kid in a candy store.

Marshall moves to the front of the first cart and begins methodically unloading items onto the belt, picking them out to group similar items.

"Good afternoon," the cashier says, giving her best "please notice how pretty I am" look.

Marshall is undeterred and simply nods and grunts out a "hey" as he continues to put things on the belt—a man on a mission to perfectly sort the merchandise. I try to assist in the endeavor, excited to be accompanied by someone who takes bagging groceries as seriously as I do, but there's not much room for me to stand. I can never figure out where to stand in these checkout aisles. In front of the cart and behind it always feels incorrect.

"It sure is cold outside today," the clerk says, still trying to get Marshall to interact with her. She's resorted to talking about the weather. I'd feel bad for her if it weren't for the stank eye she keeps giving me.

"Yep," he says, continuing to unload the carts, finishing up the first one, and swinging it to the area by the bags so he can start loading it.

I turn to see what Ezra is up to. He is leaning on the cart, his leg casually up on the lower rack, and playing with his new phone, not even attempting to help unload the cart. At least three other aisles are open, and the self-checkout has a minimal line, but three women and one man are lined up behind him, the man only holding a pack of gum. They're preening and whispering to each other while staring at Ezra.

One woman starts to reach out to touch his shoulder as if she's going to tap him. Unaware, he looks up at me and waves me over. "Adley, I'm looking at the app store. Come tell me what apps to download!"

Before I can go to him, I hear the clerk say, "You must love your cat," to Marshall, once again trying to talk to him when she sees all the cat food—which I really should have put back. *Sigh.*

He looks at her like she just said the most horrific thing. He sternly says, "No," and gets back to work. She looks like she might cry.

"Let me go help, Marshall," I say. Checkout aisles make me anxious. And now that Marshall is bagging, the two full carts are gnawing at me.

"Oh, I'll help too, babe," Ezra says, launching toward me.

The woman behind him who went to tap on his shoulder looks like she just lost a million dollars and may burst into tears. These dudes are breaking hearts and don't even know it.

I don't see her complete reaction because I am too busy laughing at Ezra reaching into the cart, grabbing as many things as possible in a big scoop of his arms, and plopping them on the belt.

Marshall looks at him more horrified than when the clerk tried to talk to him about his non-existent cat.

"What are you doing?!" Marshall yells.

"Helping, bro. Lighten up!" Ezra says. "Hey, how ya' doing?" he says to the clerk, flashing her that smile of his and leaning by the payment machine.

I can see her brain melting as she gapes at him. The massive pile of stuff moves toward her, hitting her arm and rebooting her brain.

"Ha... hi," she says, looking down at the merchandise. She starts frantically scanning things, moving at a speed I didn't think she was capable of. Fueled by embarrassment, fear, or lust, I don't know.

"You gotta sort them before you put them on the belt!" Marshall yells, leaning over and pointing at the pile.

"If you care so much, sort them down there. Let me do my thing, bro," Ezra says, leaning into the cart to grab more stuff.

Suddenly, he exclaims, "ADLEY! Did you sneak these in here?!" He holds up the toys I got.

"Ha, yeah," I blush.

"Marshall, look what she got," Ezra says.

Marshall's scowl rescinds, and he looks at me, "Adley! That's so sweet," his voice a whole octave higher than when he talked to Ezra or the clerk.

"Excuse me, miss, but would you be a doll and scan this for me real quick?" Ezra asks the clerk and hands her the sushi cat toys.

"Absolutely," she says, scanning the toys and returning them to him with trembling hands.

"Thanks, doll," he says sweetly and winks at her. I grimace, not liking him winking at her.

"Here," Ezra says, throwing them at Marshall and hitting him directly in the face. "Take that and chill the fuck out. This is supposed to be a good time, bro, not some weird excuse to show everyone what a control freak you are."

Marshall grabs the toys, ready to throw them back, but they do seem to have an effect on him. He puts them down on the counter in front of him and simply grunts. His movement slows, and he does actually chill the fuck out.

The clerk looks at him bewildered and like she's going to ask what all that was about, but Ezra says first, "Cold outside today, huh, Callie?"

Her attention snaps to him, and her brain melts once again. This poor girl. I hope she doesn't have a lot of student loan debt because everything she's ever learned is seeping out her ears. "How… how do you know my name?" she asks.

He leans on the counter and points at her tit. She looks pleasantly scandalized before he says, "Your name tag, doll."

"Oh, ha, duh," she says, embarrassed, and returns to her frantic scanning. My heart sinks to my stomach. Is he going to keep flirting with her? Is he trying to take another mate? Am I not enough? Are Marshall and I not enough?

Ezra turns to me and flashes a grin. He grabs the last item from the cart and hurls the cart toward the end of the checkout where Marshall is standing. As if this was a coordinated move, Marshall pushes the other cart aside, catches the cart Ezra throws, and twirls it into place before continuing his bagging. I stand there, dumbfounded at how in sync they are.

Ezra leans over, smacks my ass, and says, "Scootch, babe, I gotta get the other cart," before moving me to the side and pulling the cart into place. He grabs a massive armful of groceries from the cart like he's a grocery store UFO machine and places them in another large pile on the belt.

Once everything is on the belt, he slowly strolls to the end of the aisle with the third cart, saddles up next to Marshall, bumps him over with his hip, and begins haphazardly throwing things in bags.

Marshall looks at him, annoyed. He opens his mouth to yell but gives up with a sigh.

"You're taking too long, bro. We gotta get home; I bet Adley's hungry, we've been here all day, and you made her that shitty breakfast, so she's barely eaten," Ezra says.

Stunned, I stand by the checkout and watch this weird dance unfold further—my initial plan to help was thwarted by their shenanigans.

The clerk scans the last item, and I am terrified to see the total. She tells me a total so astronomical that I did not think spending this much money in this store was even possible. Add to it the e-reader and phones I already paid for; this is the single most expensive day of my life. I do some mental math to determine which credit card I need to whip out, but I try not to look phased. I can't make the guys feel bad, and I certainly can't lose face in front of this cashier.

I hand it to her, trying not to shake. "So, you're a sugar mama. Now it makes sense, I guess," she says, scanning me up and down with the stank face she's given me the whole time we've been here.

I guess I am a sugar mama.

14

ADLEY

"Wow, it's almost as if you've never worked a day in your life," Marshall says from the kitchen. He leans against the counter, arms crossed over his chest as his tail flicks with amusement.

"Less sarcasm, more useful advice, please," Ezra says. His ears twitch and turn back in feigned annoyance at Marshall's commentary.

Marshall grabs his phone and reads the directions on it: "Like I said, it says to sear the tuna for approximately two minutes on both sides."

"Yeah, you keep saying that, but what does 'sear' mean?" Ezra asks.

"It's searing now. What you're doing is searing," Marshall retorts.

"Oh, wow! I'm searing!" Ezra says and wiggles his butt a little in a dance.

Marshall grins at him, obviously a little frustrated but charmed. The tension between the two has dissipated somewhat. My stomach growls loudly. I missed lunch. I was going to eat when we got home from shopping, but I crashed out hard the moment we got back from the store, and the "just rest my eyes" nap turned into an over two-hour nap.

Ezra notices I've wandered into the kitchen, likely hearing my stomach. "Adley!" he exclaims, rushing toward me and leaving his food on the stove unattended. "I'm searing tuna steaks for us!" he says, emphasizing the word "searing."

"You're going to burn it! You can't just leave it like that!" Marshall barks with a scowl.

Ezra rolls his eyes, chimes "Yes, sir," and returns to his pan.

When Ezra turns his back, Marshall's face softens to a grin. Why does he do that? He won't let Ezra see him smile at him. Their bickering seems more playful than it was earlier today. Maybe we're finally through the storm?

Ezra sings, "I hope you're ready for a feast, Ads!"

"Feast might be a strong word," Marshall comments, the grin on his face widening as he teases Ezra, but only when Ezra isn't looking. Curious.

"Be nice! I'm learning. Plus, don't act like you know what you're doing just because Adley's here. Adley, he admitted to me the only thing he knows how to make is an omelet."

I look at Marshall for confirmation. "I have a limited palate," he says, folding his arms and looking to the side in embarrassment.

"I get that," I laugh. He looks at me and warms, his smile returning slightly.

"What have y'all been up to while I've been napping?" I ask.

"We played that game you said you loved—" Ezra responds.

"*Deadly Premonition*," Marshall finishes.

"Are… are all the games here like that, Adley?" Ezra asks.

"Oh, my God. Are you telling me that the first video game you played from my world was *Deadly Premonition*? If I had known you would play it, I would have talked about a better game," I say, facepalming.

"You said you loved it," Marshall says.

"I do! It's weird, quirky, and has amazing characters, but it's a cult classic game. It's not indicative of our video games as a whole. Not to mention it's, like, 15 years old!"

Well, something about playing the game seems to have warmed them to each other, so at least there's that. But I need to introduce them to something else.

"We had to stop playing because Ezra got scared," Marshall jokes.

"Bro, don't lie. You were scared, too. You made me turn on the lights," Ezra says, holding the pan high over the flames and flopping the tuna steaks onto a plate.

I peer down at the tuna steaks Ezra has plopped on the plate. "Nice work, Ez! It looks like you're a quick study!"

"I know, right!" he says, looking down comically at the steaks. He made a whole pile of them. How much does he expect us to eat?

I look around and ask, "Did you make any sides?"

"Sides? Why would we need a side?" Ezra asks me and looks at Marshall.

Marshall shrugs, "Must be a human thing."

"You don't eat side dishes? Wait. Are Ailura carnivores?" I ask incredulously.

"Are you not a carnivore?" Ezra asks.

"I'm an omnivore," I say.

"Like a rat?!" Ezra asks, surprised and making a disgusted face.

"Well, yeah, I guess like a rat," I say, feeling thoroughly insulted.

"So, you don't eat vegetables or grains or fruit? But you put peppers in the omelet. And eggs aren't meat… are they? And you said you made wine with apples. You said you eat sushi, but do you not make sushi with rice? I thought the word sushi meant vinegar r—," I ask, confused by the whole thing.

Marshall cuts me off from my spiraling rant. "Our diets are primarily animal proteins. We eat other things, but only for flavoring and special treats." Their species is fascinating.

I open the freezer and pull out a bag of frozen broccoli, "Okay, well, I'll just make this for myself then."

=^..^= ♥ =^..^=

Ezra beams as I say, "Thank you for dinner, Ezra! It was delicious!" Although the meal was simple, Ezra is as proud as if he had prepared a five-star meal—and I suppose, considering fish is a delicacy for him, he had. Watching the two of them devour their meal was funny and more pleasant to see than them eating cat food. They ate four tuna steaks each. I wondered why Ezra made so many, but now I understand. If all you're eating is meat, you need a lot.

"Thanks, Ads! Since Marshall made you breakfast, I wanted to make you dinner. Next time, I'll make a veg for you, too. Especially since all I gotta do is microwave them," he says.

"You can make non-microwaved broccoli, too, Ezra," I laugh.

"But why put forth more effort for a vegetable?" he scoffs.

"I would guess it tastes better if you put more effort into it," Marshall says matter-of-factly.

"I don't understand how you could make a vegetable taste better without putting meat in it, but I will chalk this up to a difference in taste… ha, literally!" Ezra says.

Marshall stands, grabbing the plates and taking them to the sink.

"Thanks, Marshall!" I say as he scrapes and rinses the dishes.

"I'm going to take a shower before bed," I say, standing to leave.

"The shower in that bathroom is big enough for three," Ezra says with a sly smirk, placing his chin atop his hands.

Marshall's head whips toward me expectantly—his tail thrashing behind him.

I attempt to sound seductive, but I know I am not. "Would you like to help me wash my back?"

"Desperately," Ezra says, standing and slinking toward me. Taking Ezra's cue, Marshall turns off the water and drops the dishes in the sink.

"So, I do have to bathe. Can I please wash my hair before you two start up with your funny business? I don't want to run out of hot water before I can wash my hair."

"No promises," Ezra says, kissing my neck and corralling me toward the bathroom. Marshall follows behind.

=^..^= ♥ =^..^=

I stand in front of the shower, fully dressed and an anxious mess. Steam is already building around us as they wait for me to do something—anything. The fog in the mirror doesn't entirely hide the view that jump started this debilitating anxiety—my reflection mixed in with that of two Adonises. The thump of the water and humm of the fan don't drown out the pounding of my heart. They're going to see me naked!

The cramped space, filled with steam, makes the oppressive atmosphere unbearable. It feels like the walls are closing in on me, like I'm trapped here, facing the consequences of my decisions.

Why do they want to sleep with me? ME?! They are perfect. I am not. Yes, they'd already seen me naked, but the lighting in my living room was so much more forgiving than the judgmental lights of my bathroom. The living room is soft, dim, and cozy. Whereas the light in my bathroom is bright and overhead and, oh, so revealing. Why do I have so many lightbulbs in here? What the fuck wattage are they? And, you know, I was drunk. It's so much easier to believe you're a goddess when you've got a bottle or two of wine in you.

"Does that feel okay?" I ask, stalling, not wanting to disrobe. They both reach into the water and nod. "That's good. I was worried we'd all like vastly different temperatures." I laugh nervously and eyeball the space.

Technically, the shower is large enough for the three of us, but it will be cramped. They will be close to me. They probably won't be able to see too much of my body—just the top of my head. But I have to get in the shower first. There's still the whole business of getting undressed outside the shower—where there's enough room for them to see everything I offer.

Ezra seems to have no shame in his nudity. He peels his clothing away as if it's nothing. Like nudity is second nature to him. And I suppose it is since he's always nude in his ailo form. Marshall removes his clothing, as well;

however, not in the same carefree way as Ezra.

The heat from the shower can't compete with the heat pooling in my pussy. With each article of clothing removed, a shiver of desire shoots up my spine. As they bend, the muscles of their backs ripple and flex, their flesh slick with the moisture of the air. I want to slide my body across their backs, feeling their smoothness on my nipples.

Once all their clothing is on the ground, they look at me expectantly. Ezra gives Marshall a quizzical look and then asks me, "Are we taking a shower or what?"

I am torn between my overwhelming desire to push them down, take a bite out of them, and engulf them with my pussy and the overwhelming desire to run and hide from their vastly superior beauty.

"Babe, you okay?" Ezra asks gently caressing my shoulder and, not on purpose, poking me with his erect cock.

Marshall asks, "Didn't you want to wash your hair before the water got cold? If we're going to stand here, we should turn off the water."

"Yeah, I just am. I don't know. I'm scared to get naked in front of you," I admit.

"We saw you naked yesterday," Marshall says matter-of-factly.

Ezra ignores him and asks, "Why, babe? Are you scared that I can't keep my hands to myself? I promise you no funny business until your hair is washed."

"No, I'm just embarrassed," I say. "Just look at you and look at me. It's just it's… embarrassing."

Ezra attempts to say something, but Marshall cuts him off, and it comes out as just a noise. "She needs to hear it often," Marshall says, recalling our conversation earlier.

As if the lightbulb in his head is as bright as these fucking bathroom lights, Ezra's face shows he, too, remembers the conversation. He coolly states, "Babe, since these two rock, hard dicks pointing right in your direction aren't convincing you, let me tell you explicitly: You are the most gorgeous woman I have ever laid eyes on."

They keep saying that, but I just cannot believe it. I argue, "But that can't be true. The cashier today that you were flirting with: she was so much younger and prettier than me. She wanted you so badly she could barely talk. Why would you want to look at me naked when every woman in that store would let you look at them?"

"Sure, I could look at them. In the same way, I could ignore the stars and stare at the dirt. But why would I do that? Why would I look at them when I have, standing in front of me right now, a beauty that is so ethereal, so perfect, so astronomical, that the beauty of the stars isn't even a comparable metaphor?"

I scrunch my face in utter disbelief. He can't actually mean that. He's just a wordsmith. He's a flirt. He's just trying to get me naked in the shower, and it's almost working.

Ezra looks to Marshall for support, but I'm not sure why, because Marshall is a man of few words. So, unless my naked body has some undiscovered physics theorem on it, he won't have much to say. "I'm not good with metaphors," Marshall says. Yep, that's what I thought. He continues, "Umm, I see them, yes. But they are just there. They are nothing. When I see you, I don't just see you; I feel you. I feel a warmth and contentment that I have never felt. It radiates through my whole body. And I feel an unquenching lust. It's so unquenching; I can barely think of anything other than what your tits look like under that shirt. In fact, I hate that shirt more than I've ever hated anything, except maybe those pants. Because it is the one thing that is stopping me from seeing those marvelous tits bounce when you laugh."

"Nice one, bro," Ezra whispers to him, causing him to blush. I want to argue with them.

"Perhaps, we should turn the water off," Marshall states.

"Don't rush her, bro!" Ezra snaps.

"I am not rushing her. I am simply stating a fact. We are losing hot water. If the goal is to use the hot water, we should preserve it when we are not in the shower."

My eyes burn as tears threaten to pool. No one has ever said anything that nice to me before. I want to argue with them, but I suppose, even if they don't believe those nice things, they must find some quality in me desirable—otherwise, why would they be trying so hard? I'm just going to pretend that I believe them. As Ezra stated, their dicks are pointing attention directly at me, so I know they want to have sex with me. And knowing they want to have sex with me is going to have to be enough for now because I desperately want to have sex with them and want to get the fuck out of my own way.

I steel my nerves and slowly unzip my pants. The whimper that comes out of Ezra and Marshall as my pants drop to my ankles is encouraging. I awkwardly try to pull my pants from around my feet and fall slightly. Two slick, naked bodies are on me in an instant, bracing me for the fall. The intertwining of their masculine musk washes over me, causing my clit to pulsate. I instinctively lurch toward them, a slight smack of flesh on flesh.

"We got you, babe," Ezra says, with that lustful voice that is much deeper, darker, and more focused than the light one he uses throughout the day—Marshall grunts in agreement.

Their warmth emanates, making me want to rip my clothes off. Not so that they can see me, but so I can feel them. I want them. I want to feel them. I want their wet flesh slapping and sliding against mine.

"Would you like our assistance?" Ezra asks.

"Yes, since you are clumsy, we can help," Marshall says, nodding.

"Dude, work on your game, please," Ezra pleads.

Marshall's ears rise in alertness, and his face lengthens in momentary confusion before both fall from the chastisement.

"Okay," I say.

Ezra pins me against Marshall, placing his leg between mine and allowing me something to grind my swollen clit against. He gently pulls up the edges of my t-shirt, gliding his hands up my side. I raise my arms, and he traces my body, leaning forward to kiss my exposed collarbone once my shirt raises over my head.

Marshall's hands gently brace my hips as he unsnaps my bra, exposing my breasts to Ezra, who latches himself onto my nipple while Marshall grabs at my other breast. Ezra's hands reach down the front of my panties and give one quick flick of my clit, before yanking them to the floor. He lowers himself to remove my socks and says, "God damn, I want to sink my tongue so deep into those pretty petals, but I promised no funny business until after you washed your hair." He slowly rises upward.

Marshall's hands are still exploring my breasts with gentle determination—unwilling to let go.

"I did request that, didn't I?" I sigh as my lust tingles and throbs where he touched me.

"We could just turn off the water," Marshall suggests.

I break away from Marshall's embrace and his grasp for me, wanting me to return.

I slide back the shower door, and the warmth of the steam further envelops us.

I step into the warm water and tilt my head back, letting the water cascade down my body. My nipples are so hard and erect that the water tickling against them stirs my arousal further.

I might not think I'm hot, but these two do, so I'll act as if I'm hot. I try to channel every hot woman I've watched shower in a movie. I rub my hands over my face and down the back of my hair. I open my mouth slightly and gasp at my touch, partially for show and partially because I am so aroused that the slightest touch is sending me to new heights. I run my hands down my side, making sure to outline my breasts and hips. My hands travel to my inner thighs, and I push my tits together with my arms.

"Will you boys help me wash my hair?" I ask.

Ezra tells Marshall, "Well, we can't waste any time if we're going to make her come at least twice and get her cleaned up before the water gets cold."

Their expressions change to determination, and as if perfectly in sync, they split from their positions: Marshall goes to the front of the shower, and Ezra goes to the back. In perfect unison, they slide the two shower doors to the center. This choreography is matched and so perfectly timed that it is surreal. They are like automata, built for pleasure and running on the same program.

They slide the doors closed, locking the three of us in the small space, increasing the warmth with their presence and trapping the steam. A loud hum further engulfs me; at first, I think the fan has broken. However, it is not the fan but a purr—well, two purrs. But they're so perfectly in sync that their wavelengths have combined, increasing in strength, creating what a video game nerd like me would call a "mega purr."

Marshall's tall, looming body blocks the water from hitting me, and I shiver once its presence is removed. He brings his body closer, warming me and rubbing my arms.

"Don't worry; you will be soaking wet soon," Marshall says. Since he said it, I don't know if the double entendre was intended.

Ezra inspects the line of shampoos and body washes—full now that the products he picked for himself and Marshall are mixed with mine—and selects my shampoo from the shelf.

In one fluid motion, Ezra squirts the shampoo to the ground, only for Marshall's hand to already be below it, catching it. This is the same weird synchronicity I saw with the cart at Target.

Marshall runs his fingers through my hair, massaging my head and creating a lather. Oh, okay, so they're just going to wash my hair? I did expect some funny business.

Ezra returns the bottle to the shelf and then smiles at me before dropping to his knees. Damn, this dude loves to eat pussy. He grabs my ass and guides my hips in front of his face, tantalizing my clit with a long stroke of the tongue through my folds. A torrent of need surges through my body, and I push deeper into his face.

Ezra's fingers reach into me. He hooks them within me, pulling me forward, beckoning me. I am taken off guard by the pleasure and stop myself from falling forward by bracing myself on Ezra's head and pulling on his ears. He moans loudly into my pussy, causing me to clench harder around his fingers.

Marshall is still washing my hair diligently, but he gently pulls me backward, wrapping his arm around my chest and locking it onto my breast—the same one he was sad to lose earlier.

Marshall leans to the side, letting the water rinse out the shampoo from my hair. He nibbles at my ears and shoulder before tilting my head backward from my chin and giving me a deep, tantalizing kiss.

I'm close to coming, wildly bucking on Ezra's face when he suddenly stops, stands, and steps backward. What the fuck? Why did he stop?

"It's time for conditioner," Ezra says as if answering my question. At that, as if on command, Marshall gently bends me forward and enters me with such a deep thrust I scream in pleasure as he hits the spot Ezra had been caressing with his finger.

Ezra grabs a bottle of conditioner from the back wall, his tail gently flicking in my face, and when he turns, I grab his hips and pull him forward, latching onto his cock with my mouth. Ezra is shocked and almost drops the conditioner, but he composes himself.

Marshall's thrusts into me cause my mouth to move up and down Ezra's cock in the same rhythm. Marshall still refuses to release my breast, but he puts his other hand on my clit rubbing it in a circular motion that is both in rhythm and not in rhythm with his thrusts.

Ezra runs the conditioner through my hair and lets me pleasure him with my tongue. His thighs tighten and flex with each pound as I try to take his entire length into my mouth. I grip his hips and move him deeper into me. Ezra's hands roam around my head possessively, combing through my hair.

He caresses my chin and throat and says, "Ah, babe, you're too good. You feel too good. You can't make me come first." Marshall removes his hand from my breasts and unhooks the showerhead from its perch. He gives Ezra the shower head, who now rinses my hair. Marshall's thrusts quicken, become desperate, and Ezra, who had stood sentinel up to this point, now begins to thrust into me as well.

Ezra returns the showerhead to Marshall, but he does not return it to its position; he turns it up high and points it directly at my clit. The torrential water pummels against my clit with such force that I scream out around Ezra's cock as I orgasm.

At that exact moment, Ezra and Marshall both shoot their orgasms into me. I gulp down Ezra's seed and wonder if the taste is because he's a different species or because he eats next to zero vegetables.

Marshall helps me stand, turns the pressure down on the shower head, and rinses semen running down my leg for me.

I laugh, "I thought you would make me come twice."

"Babe, all we've done is wash your hair. You've still got a whole body that needs cleaning. It's time to wash your back," Ezra says, spinning me around.

Marshall puts body wash on two luffas before he hands one to Ezra.

Ezra leans me forward slightly, bracing me against Marshall's broad chest, and gets on his knees again. Marshall's heart beats against my cheek. Combined with the purr resonating within him and the water beating on my back, I might fall asleep. However, I'm awakened when Ezra gently bites my ass as he runs the luffa up and down my leg.

"I've been waiting to bite into that peach since I first laid eyes on you," Ezra says before lurching forward and sinking his face into me.

Ezra's tongue traces the crease of my butt, sending goosebumps down the back of my thighs. He dips his tongue, circling my anus, causing me to gasp and lean further into Marshall's chest. I squirm as my arousal, which I thought was entirely spent, begins to build again as his tongue dips into an area never explored by anyone before.

He runs the warm, soapy luffa over my body, circling my trembling legs. I buckle and sit further into Ezra's face when it reaches the ticklish spot behind my knees.

Marshall washes the rest of my body with his luffa, focusing on my back and tits. I am once again driven wild with desire, chasing an orgasm moments ago I did not think was possible.

Ezra sinks his fingers back into my pussy, massaging inside me. I bite and claw at Marshall's chest, feral in my lust as Ezra causes me to quiver and moan, leaving red welts in my fingers' wakes.

Marshall begins working my clit again, and he does it so expertly, you'd think he'd been doing it his whole life. I clench around Ezra's fingers and buck as waves of pleasure once again wash over me. As I come again, I bite at Marshall's chest and grab his ass, desperate to pull him close to me. I scream so loud that I suspect I may go hoarse when this is all over.

Before I fall, Ezra stands and hooks his hands under my arms, catching me.

"Well, looks like you reached your goal," I say, exhausted and ready to sleep.

"Stretch goal?" Marshall says to Ezra standing in front of me with a suddenly hard dick. What? How is he hard again? What are these guys? Does their species have absolutely no recovery time?

"I mean, I didn't wash her face and I think maybe you only got one of her tits," Ezra says.

"No, no, no! I'm sorry, boys, I cannot go one more minute!" I genuinely don't think I can come again. I am entirely spent. I am boneless.

"No prob, babe," Ezra says, giving me another good rinse. The water starts to chill, and I am awakened from my orgasm-induced stupor.

"Bro, we forgot to wash ourselves," Ezra shouts.

"Shit," Marshall says.

MARSHALL

Adley jumps out of the shower, shivering, aggressively rubbing her arms, and scrambling for a towel. When she bends to wrap the towel around her hair, I am struck by the beauty and elegance of the movement. She then wraps a second towel around her body, shielding her beauty from me.

Ezra hands me my shampoo and then gets his own, frantically scrubbing his hair and tail. The cold has removed any semblance of an erection left in me. Ezra is back to his bouncy self, hissing and whooping at the cold exaggeratedly.

Adley sits on the toilet and rubs lotion into her body. She laughs at our yelling as we try to wash quickly, our bodies slapping against each other as we reach for our various products.

"Dude, you gotta leave your conditioner in longer than that! It says two minutes," Ezra says to me with a shiver.

"My hair will understand," I say, shaking my head under the stream.

"Mine won't," he says, rubbing his arms and trying to warm himself, counting to presumably one hundred and twenty.

"Next time, I'd like to watch y'all wash each other," Adley giggles.

I push past Ezra, and when my body glides against his, my dick threatens to rise again despite the cold water. He looks at me with a fleeting expression of recognition before saying, "Fuck, I can't take it. Adley, will you still think I'm hot with flat hair?" while jumping under the water. I wrap a free towel around my waist.

"Of course I will, Ezra," she says, putting toothpaste on her toothbrush.

I rub the towel over my arms, ready to be dry and dressed, but Ezra stops me. "Bro! You gotta pat dry! Don't rub. It messes up your skin!"

"That can't be true," I say.

"No, it is," Adley says before popping the electric toothbrush into her mouth. She continues with the brush vibrating in her mouth, "It disrupts the skin barrier or something."

"Please, pat dry. I can't have your sandpaper skin chafing us all," Ezra says, turning off the shower.

"You can't be serious," I say, looking at him in disbelief.

"I'm dead serious, bro, and while you're at it, you need to put on some lotion or body oil before drying off fully." He wraps a towel around his waist with a flick of the wrist that makes me feel like an uncoordinated nerd—which I guess I am.

"Why do I have to do it before I dry off?" I ask.

"It locks in the moisture," Adley says through her toothbrush.

"That!" Ezra says, pointing at Adley.

"That sounds like a lot of hassle," I huff as I rub the towel over my body.

"Dude, come on! I wasn't going to say it, but your hands feel like an ailo tongue," Ezra says, and Adley spit-laughs around her toothpaste. Spurred by her laughter, he continues, "Adley can't be the only one bringing the moisture when you finger bang her."

"Gross, Ez," she says, shooting down his joke.

I look to Adley, hoping she will say I don't have dry hands, but she doesn't. Instead, she removes the towel from her head, letting her hair fall to her shoulders. Her beautiful soft shoulders. I have rubbed them multiple times. Were my hands dry? Did I hurt her delicate skin with my dry hands?

"And this cold as fuck weather isn't going to do you any favors. It's just going to make you dryer," he says, sticking out his tongue in mock disgust.

"Is it cold where you are from?" Adley asks, changing the topic.

"Nah, I'm from a place that is perpetually summer. It gets colder north of where I'm from, but it never snows," Ezra says.

"It doesn't snow where I'm from either," Adley says.

"What do you mean?" I ask, pointing at the ground. "Are you not from here?"

"Oh, no, I'm from a state south of here. It's hot as fuck there," she responds.

"Is that why you're hot as fuck?" Ezra jokes and kisses her shoulder while he reaches past her to grab two bottles from the cabinet. He hands one to me. "Seriously, please don't argue with me about this. I got this for you. The smell reminded me of you. It just kind of had your vibe."

I open the bottle and take a sniff. It does smell nice.

Ezra hugs Adley's midsection, pinning her against the counter. He squeezes her tight, causing her to release air from her lungs. "Adley, will you put my lotion on for me?" he coos, pressing more gentle kisses on her back and nibbling at her ear.

"How about you, Marshall? Is it cold where you are from?" She asks, grabbing his bottle of lotion in answer to his question.

"Umm… I'm from the same city as Ezra," I say, squeezing a glob of the stuff into my hand.

"Really?!" Ezra says, "I wonder if we know any of the same people."

"We absolutely do not know any of the same people."

"Put this on your face when you're done," he says, handing me another lotion.

"I can't just put this on my face?" I ask, holding up the first bottle he gave me.

"Dude, I'm not even going to justify that question with a response." I look at the two bottles. One says body lotion, and the other says face lotion. I guess this makes sense.

"Ezra, back up if you want me to do this," Adley giggles. He's pinned her against the sink and is rubbing his face into her hair.

He backs up slightly and lets her turn, only to press himself back against her and start combing through her hair with his chin pressed against the top of her head. Jealousy boils my blood as I watch them, standing by myself as they entangle further.

"Ezra, I need some space, okay?" she says, pushing him gently away.

"Okay," he says with a pout. Then stands in front of her, grinning stupidly. She grins stupidly back, and I feel like a third wheel in their adorable love story. I suppose I kind of am.

15

MARSHALL

I hope our day at the mall will ease this crushing anxiety brewing in me. All night, I laid in my anthro form, staring at the ceiling, unable to quell this awful feeling in my heart. The only sleep I received was that fitful kind in which I dozed in and out of consciousness. My mind would finally turn off, only for me to jolt awake and check that Ezra and Adley were still there—lying next to me. Adley's beautiful face pressed against her pillow, causing her mouth to part. Ezra was curled on her back in his ailo form. It's the only time I've ever seen him perfectly still. The memory of them sleeping like that brings me both comfort and stress.

Their presence would calm me, but only momentarily. I can't quite identify the source of my anxiety. Being in an alternate dimension and a new relationship are anxiety-inducing events, yes, but I know that's not what's causing this gnawing fear. Whenever I looked at Adley and Ezra's sleeping forms, my heart would start racing—not because of my attraction to them.

It took us forever to leave for the mall. Adley and I wanted to get here much earlier, but Ezra spent so much time fussing over his hair and outfit that it was past lunch when we finally left. I hate being late. I hate making a plan and not following through on it. As each moment passed, the tightness in my chest further constricted. Just when I thought he was finally ready, he'd run back to the bedroom or bathroom to do something else.

"Dude, don't rush me because you woke up on the wrong side of the bed," he told me as he fluffed his hair in the mirror. And, while I am familiar with the idiom, there may be some truth to it. Maybe if I had curled up in my ailo form atop Adley, on the other side of the bed from mine, I would have felt better.

Ezra's lateness and rushing about seemed to stress Adley out, as well, but she's much better at suppressing her negative responses to the anxiety. While I would snap at Ezra and try to get him to move quicker, Adley simply sat at the kitchen table reading and waiting. She tried to talk to me during this time, but my bouncing leg and inability to stay seated broke any conversation she started.

After two hours of me trying to rush him, him saying, "You can't rush beauty, bro," and my complaining to her, Adley said, "I understand it's frustrating, but he's anxious about his appearance, so let's give him a little time." I hadn't considered Ezra would be anxious about his appearance. He's perfect. Why would he be nervous about it? But now, as we're walking toward the mall's entrance from the parking lot, I see a glimmer of truth in her statement. His usually confident gate is more reserved, and he fidgets with his hat, which he's lamented having to wear multiple times.

She eventually convinced him to hurry the fuck up with promises of new, "even better" clothes. But now we enter the mall entrance three hours past schedule, and I can't help but be furious with Ezra. I empathize with his anxiety, but why does his anxiety take precedence over my own? And Adley's? You'd think the anxiety of two people would outweigh the anxiety of one. I worry this will be the pattern that defines our relationship: the two of us conceding to his whims. The thought of being with Adley forever should bring me contentment. But being with Adley also means being with Ezra, and being with him for the rest of my life causes a sinking sadness that churns in the pit of my stomach, twisting into a hard block.

Instead of dwelling on that fearful feeling, I'll acknowledge that we have some communication issues to work out and try to focus on my feelings for Adley. My feelings for Ezra are for evaluating another day.

My eyes blink to adjust and I welcome the warmth that hits our faces as we enter through a pair of double doors. The entrance opens to a long, wide, white corridor. We appear to be the only people in the mall. This could be nice. I'm not a fan of crowds, and the lack of people makes me think maybe this trip will ease my anxiety. Uncomfortable from the sudden temperature shift, I unzip my coat, feeling instant relief. My tail has scrunched up against my cock irksomely, so I adjust it, and I feel instantly better. It's still unpleasant and will nag at me the rest of the day, but I do my best to ignore it. Now, if only I could take this hat off.

Ezra and I tower over Adley, flanking her sides as we march into the mall. She walks demurely between us with her hands tucked into her pockets.

Ezra's anxious fidgeting seems replaced by excited anticipation, which builds with each step. On her opposite side, he is almost vibrating with excitement.

Ezra's energy is the exact opposite of Adley's, but somehow, they match—they appear a perfect pair. And that really pisses me off. Adley notices me looking at her and smiles back up. The smile seems forced, and

I'm not sure, but maybe she is uncomfortable.

Should I ask her how she is doing? What if she is fine and thinks I'm being judgmental? Often, people interpret my questions as judgmental, and I don't know how to gauge when a question I ask will or will not be perceived as such. She removes her hands from her pockets and begins tapping her fingers together in a precise way, which I believe is a self-soothing strategy. So, I brave the question, "Are you okay?"

"Just bracing myself for the crowds, large space, and sensory overload that's about to hit me," she says. At least there don't seem to be too many people here right now.

"Ditto. But it doesn't look too crowded," I respond with a nervous edge.

"This corridor is usually pretty empty, but it will be crowded once we enter the main part of the mall," she says flatly.

As she predicted, we turn a corner, revealing the corridor opening to the enormous expanse of the mall's main walkway. My heart sinks at the sight of people jammed into every corner, and the din of their voices strengthens, reverberating in my head and dulling the sharpness of my mind. Now I see why she was nervous.

Adley and I balk at the sights, but Ezra is invigorated. His face lights up as he all but skips into the open space. He beelines to the first store he sees, leaving the two of us ambling behind. He points to the window of the first store and shouts to us, "Let's go in here!"

"Actually, I have somewhere else I think we should go first," Adley says with a sly smile.

The disappointment on Ezra's face is apparent when he says, "Oh, where?"

"It's a surprise. I promise you both will absolutely love it," she responds with a chuckle.

=^..^= ♥ =^..^=

I am so overwhelmed with excitement that I can't stop myself from pressing my hands against the cool, smooth glass. I cannot believe that this glass barrier is all that separates me from these creatures—extinct or nearly extinct in my world. In my wildest dreams, I never thought I would see a live fish, let alone this many in one place. I turn towards Adley; her radiant smile warms my already exploding, joyous heart. She was right—this is remarkable.

Ezra rushes between the tanks, pointing at fish gliding by while giddily saying, "Look at that one! And that one! And that one!" He's unable to lock his attention on one fish or even one tank, entirely losing himself to the excitement of the place.

I join in his excitement and jog toward a tank. "Oh, my God, look how big that one is!" I say. Adley giggles as Ezra and I, two grown men, run back and forth between the displays, occasionally reading the informative descriptions of the fish aloud like children on a school trip. In fact, there are children here right now, and none match our excitement.

I zip to another display and skim the contents of its informational plaque before spotting the tiny creatures with horse-like faces and tails curling around blades of grass, latching themselves in place. *They are so fucking cute.*

Ezra runs to my side and exclaims, "Woah!" before bending to read the information about them. "They're monogamous," he says with sadness. I do not need to dissect his tone; I know exactly what he's thinking because I feel the same. "Must be nice," he sighs out, and I relate so hard to the statement that I can't even be offended. Monogamy is a fate lost to us.

I look at him from the side of my eye and say, "And the males give birth."

His face crinkles, and he says, "Well, at least we don't have to do that."

"Yeah," I laugh. I watch the tiny creatures and note two curled together. They must be mates. I wonder what fate brought them together. Will he birth her children and live happily ever after with her and her alone? I break my gaze from these tiny, adorable creatures and look toward Adley, her angelic face made even more unreal by the reflection of water upon it. Does she want children? Can we even have children? Do our species share enough common traits to combine? If we could, would our children be sterile like hybrids in the wild?

Adley's beauty draws me to her. "Marshall, this is a side of you I didn't think I'd see," she says as I join her at a tank with floating bubble-like creatures.

"Adley, I can't even explain how amazing this is," I say. "It's the most beautiful thing I've ever seen. Thank you so much for bringing us here." My eyes water at the sheer fascination of the existence of this place. The plaque says they are jellyfish.

"You're welcome, Marshall," she responds. The light from the aquarium casts a blue water pattern across her face, making her so beautiful I can't even be distracted by the jellyfish. I pull out my phone and point it at her.

"Actually, this is the most beautiful thing I've ever seen," I say while taking a picture of her looking into the glass. This is the first picture I have on my new phone. She laughs nervously. She is still uncomfortable when we compliment her.

Ezra screams from far away, "Oh, my God, look at that!"

A little kid beside him giggles. "It's like Nemo!" the little kid says to him.

"I have no idea what that means, kid, but it is so cool," Ezra responds with the same excitement as the child.

He spots us and rushes to our side. "Wow! What are those?" he asks.

"Jellyfish," I respond.

"They don't even look real," Ezra says. He rounds the tank and peers in from the other side. He places his hands firmly on the glass and smushes his face against it, mesmerized by their movement. I take out my phone and take my second picture.

"Mister, you shouldn't touch the glass," the kid who followed him says.

"Oh, sorry, you're right," Ezra says and rubs at where his hand was with the sleeve of his coat.

I don't know how long we sit here, just watching the jellyfish floating, lost in their elegant beauty.

"You haven't even seen the best part of this place," Adley says, walking away from the tank.

"What?! There's better than this?" I say, thumbing at the jellyfish. I don't know how anything can top their beauty or the cuteness of the seahorses.

"Yep. This way, guys," she says. Ezra takes a picture of the jellyfish, and we reluctantly follow her, looking back at the tank as we leave.

=^..^= ♥ =^..^=

As we turn a corner, the hallway ahead gives way to something unbelievable. "Adley, is this real?" I ask, standing there, astonished.

Before she can answer, Ezra and I walk forward in absolute awe. A curved glass forms a glowing tunnel stretching out before us. The walls shimmer and ripple as the light from the water reflects off it. The blue light dances over Ezra's face—locked in wonder.

We tentatively stand at the entrance, looking upward in stunned silence, unable to believe what we see—too shocked to cross the threshold. I hadn't expected anything like this. My heart quickens as I realize its enormity—is this gigantic tank under a mall? A mall in which the floor above holds a rollercoaster. What other marvels does this place have? Adley truly lives in a world of opulence.

Cautiously, I step forward. The water surrounds me, curving up and over my head. It's as if I walked out into the ocean's center—swallowed by the sea. Gliding above my head are hundreds, thousands, of fish. Tiny, shiny ones flicker past us in a group. Bubbles rise in the distance, catching my attention, but not for long. A big, graceful fish careens above me, its body swaying majestically to propel itself forward. Others dart past so quickly my head whips sideways to keep them in sight. An instinct deep within me wants to leap forward and collide with the glass.

How thick this glass must be to hold this much water. I tilt my head back, gazing up at the glass ceiling. The water above is almost oppressive in its vastness. I can practically feel it pressing down on me. A small crack in the glass would be catastrophic. The pressure that must be pushing against it exhilarates and terrifies me.

Ezra, possibly for the first time in his life, is speechless—as am I. He meanders slowly with his hands in his pockets, silently observing the fish swimming past. "We really did go to a different universe, didn't we Marshall?" Ezra breathes out, spinning around, following a group of fish with his eyes and body. "I was struggling to believe it until now."

I feel similarly. This view is so amazing, so magical, my brain can hardly comprehend it. Now I understand why Adley wanted to call everything about our world magic…there's no other word for something your brain cannot wrap itself around.

A shadow casts over Ezra as a huge… what is that? A shark swims over his head. "Wow," Ezra says.

"Wow, is right," I hear a giggle behind me. Ezra and I are staring at the fish, but almost everyone else in the tunnel is staring at us. Why are they staring at me? I am confused by their expressions. I touch my hat, ensuring it is still on and not exposing my ears. I return my attention to the water, trying not to let my self-consciousness ruin this moment.

"Look at that one! It looks like it has a chainsaw on its face," he says in amazement. His eyes track a sleek shark, with, yes, a chainsaw on its face, as it cuts through the water with effortless grace. This creature that doesn't seem like it should exist. But it does. Would this creature exist in my world had we not been overfishing the oceans since the beginning of our existence?

Could our world have contained such beauty had we not been so shortsighted in pursuing the pleasure that eating fish brought us?

I lean forward on the faux rock wall and shed a tear. The gravity of my ancestors' actions weighs on me with the same level of pressure weighing down on the glass above me. *My people will never see this.* Ezra approaches from behind and puts his arm across my shoulders, saying, "Makes you think, doesn't it?"

"Yeah," I respond despondently.

He removes his hand from my shoulder, then turns, placing his back on the rock and looking upward. Ezra croaks out, "Can you believe these creatures used to be in our world?" His voice carries a weight of loss.

"No," I reply.

We stand, appreciating the fish for a long time, before proceeding further down the tunnel. We move together, silently weaving through the people, occasionally stopping to gape as a new species passes. It feels like it's just us and the vast ocean above us.

My eyes are drawn to a flat creature with what appear to be wings and a long whip-like tail. It glides over us slowly and gracefully, almost as if it wants us to see it.

"Beautiful," Ezra and I say simultaneously. Beautiful. Adley?

"Adley, what's that?" I ask and realize Adley is not standing next to me. Where is she?

"Ezra, where is Adley?" I ask in a panic.

"Huh?" Ezra snaps out of his stupor. "Um… I don't know." He looks around frantically.

"Adley," I shout out. Fear rips through me. The oppressive weight of the water above now feels like it's collapsing onto me. Adrenaline rushes through me with a wave as if that tiny crack I envisioned has come to fruition—flooding me and everyone in the tunnel.

I look at my phone to see if she has texted. No. I try to text her, but my phone doesn't have any signal.

Ezra grips his phone, knuckles white. "We are underground AND underwater. I guess that makes sense. Fuck," he says.

"Adley!" I yell, now fully panicked. Where is my Adley? People look at us—judge us—but I do not care. This tunnel is hundreds of feet deep; I have no idea how much further the exit is. I turn, unsure which way to run. Do I go forward? Do I double back?

She has left us. She dropped us here and left. I knew I was undeserving of a mate. The gods would never fate me to an angel—what arrogance I had to believe such a fate could be bestowed upon me. The world spins, and my vision clouds. A rush to my head makes me feel like I am falling backward.

"Marshall," I hear a small voice call from in front of me.

Ezra and I jog toward the voice. The tunnel's exit reveals itself almost instantly. We had been nearly upon it. Adley stands at the exit. The relief I experience as she is revealed to me is unparalleled. It is as if she truly is an angel, rescuing me from the depths of hell. She says excitedly, "Did you have fun?!"

I rush to her, slamming my body into hers as I pull her into a deep embrace. Ezra collides with us a mere moment later. "Thank God, Adley! I was so scared," I sob into her neck.

"What? Why?" she asks, barely able to talk as Ezra plants multiple kisses on her cheek and mouth.

"I thought I lost you. I thought you left us," I cry out.

"Oh, Marshall, no. I'm sorry. I told y'all I would wait for you at the exit, but I guess you didn't hear me. You were pretty zoned out," she says with a nervous chuckle. I pull away, wiping the tears from my face. I'm not sure why I'm crying.

She continues, "I'm sorry. I don't like the tunnel. It scares the shit out of me. I can barely go near it. But I knew you two would like it, so I thought I'd let you explore it without me."

I am embarrassed by my visceral reaction to her absence. I am a grown man—not a little boy left by his mommy. I've heard of men going crazy when their mates were not near, but I chalked it up to poor self-control. Now I understand. I told myself I would never react so emotionally if I got my own mate.

"Are you two okay?" she asks with concern, wiping a tear from Ezra's cheek—who remains latched onto her. "Oh, no, you hated it?" she says disappointed.

"No. We loved it," I say with a sniffle. Ezra nods furiously, agreeing with me.

"Okay...," Adley says as we stroll away from the tunnel and compose ourselves.

Ezra seems to reach composure quicker than I do, flipping a switch inside himself. "Thanks, babe! That was an amazing idea!" He grabs her arm and drags her away from the tunnel. "Now, let's go check out some clothes," he says cheerily, as if he weren't a blubbering mess mere seconds ago.

16

MARSHALL

We weave through the throng of shoppers until Ezra spots a store he wishes to enter. "Wanna go in here?" he asks, pointing at the window of a clothing store. I know little about fashion, but the clothes here seem on the higher end than the ones we are currently wearing.

Two girls exiting the store pause in front of Ezra. "Oh my God, look at him." I overhear their whispers before they turn crimson and flee. This seems to be the new normal—Adley and I trailing Ezra as he leaps around with exuberance, drawing the attention of those nearby. I don't mind it. I'm just glad to be with Adley, and while I find him a little annoying, he is entertaining to watch.

Adley's gaze flits to the mannequin-clad display. "Yeah, let's go," she says with feigned enthusiasm.

"Whatever," I say, keeping close to Adley as her ever-present guard. I'm still feeling the aftermath of losing her at the aquarium. I refuse to feel that way again and will remain at her side for the rest of this trip.

Adley and I meander through the store, stopping so she can look at various things. I follow her so closely that I often bump into her when she stops.

She stops at a pink sweater and softly says, "Oh, this is cute!" as I collide with her.

"Marshall, are you feeling okay?" she asks, looking up at me with beautiful grey eyes.

"Yes. Why?" I ask.

"You seem very tense," she says. Am I? I examine my body. My hands remain in my pockets, a barrier between me and the world. The tension in my neck aches deeply because my jaw is clenched. I remove my hands from my pockets and force my jaw to relax.

"Shopping isn't really my thing," I say, trying to mask the truth that I'm holding onto her tightly, fearing someone might take her away. Take her from me.

"That would look amazing on you," I say, smiling down at the sweater and attempting to change the subject.

"Really? Should I get it?" she asks.

"Definitely." I'm not lying. She would look fabulous in the soft pink. Her pale complexion flushes easily, and the pink would bring out the rose in her cheeks. It's a lower cut than anything I've seen her in, and I imagine her breasts may blush the same color. I'd love to find out.

She turns her attention to Ezra. "He'll probably buy everything in the store," she laughs. "Maybe I shouldn't get this," she says dejectedly, obviously considering the costs.

"You should get something for yourself. Don't just get him stuff."

"We're here to get you stuff, too," she says.

"I need nothing," I say sternly.

"Nonsense. I'll get this sweater, but you must also get something. Want me to help you?" She looks so eager to help me; I cannot refuse her. I will do anything to make her happy.

"That'd be great."

Ezra, in stark contrast to my and Adley's reserved meandering, is the embodiment of extroversion. He darts from one display to another, seemingly on a mission, until he is distracted by another equally important one.

"Look at this!" he exclaims, holding a sweater against himself and checking his reflection in a mirror posted next to the rack. I can't help but admire how the color looks on him. Green is his color.

"That'd look great on you," Adley chirps.

"I know, right?!" Ezra says without a hint of humility.

A group of whispering women behind Ezra catches my attention. I look around, and the hushed whispers and pointed stares indicate almost everyone in the store is looking at us. Not just Ezra—all of us—but particularly Ezra and me. Can they sense we are not human? I understand why they are looking at Ezra. He's hot and making a scene, but why me? The same thing was happening at the department store yesterday. I'm not a fan of all the eyes looking at me.

"Why is everyone looking at me?" I whisper down to Adley.

"Because you're fucking hot. You and Ezra look like supermodels," she says.

"What?" I ask in extreme surprise. My tail twitches at my junk, and I have to grab my hat to stop it from popping off as my ears threaten to push it off.

"You didn't know you were hot?" she asks with a giggle.

"I've always been… average, I guess," I shrug.

"Well, either you've had the wrong impression of yourself, or your species is way hotter than mine," she laughs. Sadness etches itself onto her face. Why is she unhappy? What just happened? What did I do? Oh, does she think she is unattractive? I should compliment her. What would Ezra say and do right now?

I push past my discomfort and pull her tight against my waist. "You are the most gorgeous creature in both my and your universes. Your inclusion in your species predicates your species must be the hotter of the two," I say, trying to be suave. She giggles at me, indicating I picked the right thing to say.

"Well, maybe the men in your species are just super hot then. I read a manhua like that before," she laughs. I don't know what a manhua is, but this is an interesting enough premise to distract me from the unknown word.

I scan the room and assess the men within. There aren't many, but every one of them is unattractive. In fact, they are downright hideous. "There may be something to that idea, Adley." However, not enough men are in this room to make a full assessment, "May I ask? Are the men in this room on the unattractive side of your species?"

She looks around, "Hmm, no. They'd all be considered on the attractive side." What?! Really?

"Interesting. I will collect more data and let you know what I determine, but I believe you are right. These men would not be considered attractive in my world."

"What about the women? Are they more attractive than the women in your world?" she asks excitedly.

"I do not know. They are all faceless blobs to me," I respond truthfully.

"Come on! I know you can see them. This is for science. You don't have to worry about my feelings. You already told me I'm the hottest in both universes. Now I just want to know if they are hotter than the women you usually see. I know your answer will be given with the parameters that they are not as hot as me," she responds.

I feel like this is a trap. I know women do not like it when you reference the attractiveness of others positively. But she answered my question about the men, and I was not offended. She did say it was for science.

I review the faces of the women in the room and confirm that the women in this room are on the more attractive side. I consider the other women I've seen since I've been here, and, yes, they are more appealing than Ailura women. I answer carefully, "Yes, the women of your species appear to have more favorable features than Ailura women."

"Wow! It is just like that manhua I read! The men in that were all ultra hot, and the women were just meh. And the men could transform into animals. Hold on. Do female Ailura have ailo forms?"

"Yes," I state.

"Bummer, so not exactly like the manhua, then. But I guess that would explain why the two of you think I'm so hot. I was the first human you saw, blew your brain, and you had no idea there was even hotter out there," she laughs and breaks away from me.

"We think you are so hot because you are so hot. There is no hotter out here," I respond.

"Okay, Romeo," she laughs, wandering over to a clothing rack. This was the name she gave me when we first met, and I know she is referencing something, but I don't know what it is exactly. Before I can ask her to define "Romeo" and "manhua" while she's at it, she holds a black sweater to my chest and asks, "How about this?"

The feel of her hands pressing against my chest reminds me of her hands on my chest in the shower last night, and I instantly get hard.

"My signature color," I laugh, put my arm around her waist, and push myself against her again.

"Dear God, get the dude something that isn't black. PLEASE. If I'm going to have to live with him, I can't have him depressing me every time I look at him," Ezra calls from across the store. Giggles erupt across the store as every woman in the room laughs at his joke—laughs at me.

"Maybe we should just let him pick for us? I bet he'd make us look nice. Nicer than I think we would," Adley says. She seems pretty excited by the idea. Ezra looks at us with excited anticipation, awaiting my response.

"Fine," I say, not hating the idea but not wanting to admit to him that I would like his assistance.

"Yes!!" he says and pumps his fist. "We're all gonna look so hot."

"Don't buy the whole fucking store," I growl back to him. God, we must look like two parents letting their kid go shopping.

"Yes, Daddy," he says with a chuckle as if he's read my mind.

"So, I guess the way to stop y'all from fighting is to let him dress you up," Adley laughs.

Adley and I spend the next hour standing to the side of the store while Ezra holds various items up to us. He chats with every person in the store, and eventually, every person who works there assists him in finding clothes for us. People are drawn to him, and they crave him. I get it. I crave him, too.

People, particularly the women, keep trying to lock Ezra into conversations, but his excitement won't keep him still long enough for them to get more than fleeting responses from him. He is friendly and flirty, though. However, I can tell he's just putting on a show for them, but he is not interested. I've watched Ezra long enough to know the difference between his authentic self and the persona he shows to the world.

The way he looks at Adley and the way he looks at them is different. However, each time a woman puts their hand on him to get his attention, each time he smiles at one or calls her "doll," Adley reacts. She doesn't know him well enough to know this is all an act.

And for his part, he is trying to signal to these women that he is not interested. Whenever he brings a clothing item to Adley, he gushes that she's the most beautiful woman in the universe, touching her with lingering fingers. He glances at the women, checking to ensure they see these interactions—hoping they get the hint. However, they don't seem to notice, and I hear multiple whispers of people trying to figure out the relationship status between the three of us.

"Adley, is your culture monogamous? Like seahorses?" I ask.

"Umm, mostly. There are exceptions, but the laws and predominant religions encourage monogamy," she responds.

"So monogamy, while not required, is the norm?" I ask.

"Yes."

"That explains the whispers. They are trying to figure out if Ezra is romantically involved with me or you or if you and I are together," I state.

"Oh," she giggles, "I suppose it is a good question."

"What do you mean?"

"I guess I'm not sure of our relationship status, either. Like, are we a throuple?" she says, trailing off. I have not heard this term before, but can assume its meaning via context clues. I consider the question. Are we? We had sex together as a group. And in my mind, that meant we are now a throuple, but was that not clear to everyone else? Am I just making assumptions about our relationship? We haven't officially marked her as our mate yet, but I thought it was clear she was our fated mate and we were in this for the long haul. Is that where the confusion lies?

Does she not want to be with us? Does she not think we're serious about her? Does she not understand the concept of fated mates, after all? Maybe it's because Ezra and I fight so much that she doesn't realize we are bonded, as well… albeit reluctantly.

This must be one of those situations where we need to tell her how we feel. Once again, I pull her to me like I've seen Ezra do multiple times. I'm getting the hang of it. "You are our fated mate. You are ours. We are yours forever," I say with as much authority as I can muster. I tilt her face toward mine, making sure she looks at me. I kiss her with such force that her knees weaken, requiring me to hold on to her.

Ezra perks at this, and he plops the enormous pile of clothes he is holding into the arms of the clerk cooing at his side, "Hold these for me, will you, doll?"

She swoons, "Whatever you need."

He stalks toward us, locking eyes with me. Fear freezes me in place as he prepares to pounce. Did I do something wrong? Is he mad at me?

His eyes do not leave mine as he approaches. "She's mine, too," he says, sending shockwaves throughout my body. He pulls her away from me and sinks another deep kiss into her, causing her knees to weaken yet again. Multiple gasps can be heard throughout the store as multiple hearts break.

He breaks from his kiss with her, and his previously fierce expression softens. Still holding onto her, he runs his hand down my jaw, making my spine shiver. He doesn't kiss me, but the touch is tender. I instinctively lean into the gesture. He whispers so that only we can hear, "Yes, we are a throuple." I do not know how to respond. We all look at each other for a long moment.

The moment passes, and his demeanor shifts entirely back to the excitable frontman he had been. Am I his, too?

He turns back to the store, to his admiring fans, and opens his arms toward the clerk. "Thanks for holding those for me, doll!" he says in that loud voice he seems to preserve for his adoring fans. The shock and sadness on her face instantly vanished now that his attention is directed at her. She giggles and stammers, "No… no problem." The blush rushes up her face.

"These women are like putty in his presence," Adley laughs.

We all are.

ADLEY

I hold back a grimace as the clerk takes the credit card from my trembling hand. An icy dread splashed over me when she stated the ultimate cost, far exceeding my estimations. I can handle it, but it hurts. Going from buying for one to buying for three is a kick in the teeth. Not to mention, I'm lavishing gifts on them as if I'm made of money—I'm definitely not.

I put the receipt into my purse, ready to run from this store and the evidence of my irresponsibility. "We have to change into these now! Let's go put them on in the dressing room," Ezra says excitedly.

"Is it okay for us to do that?" I ask, looking at the clerk who processed our transaction. The fluorescent lights buzz softly, scratching my brain with the oppressive hum. She doesn't even acknowledge my question—her eyes and attention are locked on Ezra.

Ezra returns her gaze, inciting a swoon, and says, "Sure it is, right, doll? Can we change here?"

"Whatever you want," she sighs out.

"See!" he says, dragging Marshall and me to the dressing room.

He pulls some things out of the bags and shoves them at us. Unable to resist his insistence, we go into the dressing rooms, not entirely begrudgingly.

Ezra selected jeans and a sweater for me. They are casual and comfy but significantly more stylish than anything I've ever worn. I remove my winter coat and current outfit, bundling them together in a pile on the floor. I pull on the jeans, which fit well, but they are tighter than I would have picked for myself. I don't wear jeans often. It's impossible for me to ignore their tough fabric against my body, but these aren't so bad. They fit me like a second skin, but the fabric is soft, and when I squat and bend, they dig into my gut.

I rub the sweater's fabric between my fingers, studying the texture. It feels wonderfully soft and gentle, not even a little scratchy. It seems Ezra was listening when Marshall and I told him texture was crucial to us. When I pull it over my head, I am startled by how much I'm boobing in it. My tits are spilling out in an almost pornographic way. No wonder he picked this for me. It is very low cut—way lower than anything I would typically buy for myself, and it, like the jeans, is far too tight. I think Ezra miscalculated my size. I should have tried this stuff on before buying it. "Trust me, babe. I know that body's measurements better than my own," he said. I scoff. *Sure, bro.* I leave the tags on and slowly exit the dressing room, holding the bundle of my previous outfit in front of me, hiding behind it in embarrassment. He won't believe me if I don't show him it doesn't fit.

Marshall is already done and waiting for me. He's wearing a dark blue sweater—not black, but close to it. A color compromise that resulted from a five-minute argument between him and Ezra. The way that sweater fits him is breathtaking. He's rolled the sleeves up his arms, revealing the strong sinews of his forearms. And it stretches over his chest to reveal his pectoral muscles and all the delicious divots around his collarbone and shoulder blades. His pants fit the lines of his tall, lean body, accentuating his tapered waist. And you can't even tell he has a tail stuffed in his pants—even though his package is more pronounced than it should be. If the girls thought he was hot with a winter coat on, they're going to be surprised now. Well, at least Ezra got one of our sizes right.

"I don't know if I like this outfit," I tell him.

His eyes light up at the sight of me. "You look amazing," he says. You'd think I walked out in an evening gown, the way he is reacting.

Ezra throws open the curtains of his dressing room as if to unveil himself to the world. He looks fucking fantastic. He beams as if he knows he's beautiful and struts out, allowing eyes to fall on him and appreciate the view. The jeans and sweater fit him just as well as they do Marshall, and the color suits him perfectly. My heart races when he stands beside Marshall—they are so unbelievably attractive. He looks at Marshall and says, "Nice," in a warm tone that somehow feels more like a compliment to himself than Marshall. Marshall blushes anyway and looks to the side.

"It's too bad we have to wear these fucking hats," Ezra says, placing his hand on top his head while looking at a nearby mirror. "Also, our butts look like we have a mono cheek with our tails tucked like this."

"Ezra, stop. You both look amazing," I say, knowing that he is likely fishing for compliments. He looks at me, and his smile drops. *Oh no, he thinks I look terrible.*

"Babe, why are you hiding? Do you not like it?" he asks, his voice tinged with concern.

"I think it's too small," I say and tug at the top, trying to cover more of my cleavage.

"What?!" He grabs my bundle of clothes and pushes them into Marshall's arms. He grips my shoulders and holds me at arm's length, studying me. Not studying. Devouring. His eyes devour every last inch of me, hooding with lust.

"Babe, you look so fucking hot," he says. "Right?" he asks Marshall.

Marshall also looks like he's about to drool and is, I notice, now strategically holding my clothes in front of his groin. He nods and licks his lips.

Ezra slinks toward me and puts his finger on my chin. He then traces his finger from my chin to my cleavage. My chest heaves as his touch sends fireworks to my loins. "All this outfit needs is a necklace right here," he says, stopping in the middle. I gulp.

"Um, okay," I say, caught in his sexy trap yet again.

He kisses where his hand is and reaches behind me with the other, yanking the tags off the sweater, and making me jump. Then, ripping the tags off the pants and smacking my ass—making me jump again.

"You don't know how much self-control I need right now to not rip the whole damn outfit off of you," he growls. He actually growls. "Unless your world doesn't have any public indecency laws?"

"Oh, no, we do," I say.

"That's too bad," he says, twisting his mouth as if he were thinking of what to do next.

Marshall comes up beside him and drops my clothes on the floor at his feet. "Maybe we should take her right now in the dressing room," Marshall says. *Marshall? What?*

"Excellent idea, bro," Ezra says, guiding me backward and pinning me against the floor-length mirror. "I'm going to enjoy the mirrors," he smirks. Ezra lunges at my neck, kissing me with such force I gasp. Marshall lunges at my other side. Neither of them bothered even to shut the curtain.

"Guys, I don't think we should do this here," I pant out. I close my eyes and sink into their warmth as a hand reaches into my tight jeans and flicks at my clit. Another pinches at my nipple.

"Um, excuse me," an annoyed female voice chimes behind them.

We freeze. The hand down my jeans slowly removes itself, but not before giving me one firm press. The hand at my nipple drags itself away reluctantly. Luckily, Ezra and Marshall were blocking my body from view, and I don't think whoever the voice belonged to could see what they were doing to me.

Ezra's voice changes to that showman's voice again when he says to the clerk standing at the dressing room door, "Oh, sorry, we left all our stuff out there! We were just helping her get the tags off! She looks amazing, doesn't she?!"

"Yeah, sure," she says incredulously. *Gee, thanks, lady.*

As Ezra sweet-talks the clerk, Marshall grabs our bags and stuffs our old clothes into them.

The bags look heavy, especially with our winter coats in them. "Do you need help carrying those?" I ask.

He just laughs, "No, I'm good."

Ezra has somehow managed to get the clerk to scurry away. He turns to me, and eye fucks me again before saying, "fucking perfect." He sensually licks his lips and then the fingers that were in my pants. He shudders in a way that makes him seem absolutely deranged. "Now, let's get you some accessories, babe," he says.

I thought we were shopping for them, not me.

17

ADLEY

Ezra leads the charge through the mall, walking slightly in front of Marshall and me. His confidence parts the sea of people. The crowd moves aside, letting him pass and gawking at the three of us. Marshall moves quietly, an island of calm in the retail sea beside me. His sharp jawline and new, well-fitting clothes draw surreptitious glances from passersby, and the attention he is getting now has ramped up a notch. Obviously, no one is looking at me, and that is 100% okay with me.

While Ezra is soaking up the attention lavished on him, Marshall seems unaware or, at least, uninterested in the attention he's receiving. His eyes occasionally meet mine with a reassuring smile that barely creases his stoic expression. He's enjoying himself, but his discomfort in the crowd is apparent.

The first store we stopped at was stylish yet affordable. But the store Ezra eyes now is way out of my price range—it holds high-end shoes, purses, and accessories. "The key to any outfit is accessories," Ezra says, gesturing at me with a flamboyant motion. "You can make even the most basic fit look hot if you style it."

"Really?" I ask, wondering if my standard yoga pants and video game T-shirts fit this rule.

"Yeah, well, and being hot. That always helps," he laughs. "Luckily, we've all got that on lock." *Speak for yourself.* Marshall scoffs, but blushes, obviously not used to being called "hot" so many times in one day.

Ezra glides into the store, but Marshall and I linger at the entrance, hesitant to step inside. We exchange shrugs and cross the threshold tentatively as if it's a portal into another world.

Ezra's demeanor in this store is different than in the previous store. Previously, he fluttered around, feeding off the energy of those in the room—who shared his excitement. But in this one, he has a stoic confidence, much closer to the vibe Marshall usually exudes. His movements are slow, deliberate, confident, and controlled. He looks rich even though I know he has zero dollars. I suppose he was born rich, and that's likely a vibe you maintain for life.

I realize at this moment that Ezra wears a mask for social interactions. He changes his face and voice to fit the situation. He has a different persona for each situation he finds himself in and instantly recognizes which one he needs for the occasion. It makes me think that maybe I, too, can at least pretend to have his confidence. I try to stand a little taller and fix my posture. *Be hot and confident, Adley.*

Ezra breaks away from Marshall and me and heads for a bag that catches his attention. Initially distracted and blasé, the clerk notices him, immediately perking up. "Commission and a hot guy," I'm sure she's thinking.

"Adley, I think we should get this for you," he says, holding up a black leather bag that is so out of my price range that I can tell without seeing the tag. I don't know much about designers, but I know this brand is past the tier I can generally afford. I feel like I'm splurging when I buy a mid-level brand, but this one falls squarely in the luxury brand range. The purse is gorgeous, and God, do I want it.

Before I could even muster a nod or a word, the sales clerk swoops in with a practiced smile, drawn like a moth to Ezra's charm. Her beauty is next level, and I slink back in her presence, intimidated by her. "Fantastic choice, sir," she says, angling her body towards him in a way that signals she is willing to do more than help him make a purchase. It also signals to me that I should fuck off with my poor, ugly self.

"Thank you. I think we might get it," he says, beaming at her and turning up the charm. He uses his smile as currency to get what he wants. I can see the deliberate choice to use it. It's transactional. It's calculated. Does he do this to me, too? Is it just an act when he shows me attention?

The clerk looks at us, and her eyes flit at me long enough for her to turn up her nose, but she spots Marshall, and I can see the recognition of beauty on her face.

"Oh, are the two of you out shopping for —" the clerk says to Marshall, acting as if I am not even here. *What the fuck, lady? I'm the one with the money.*

"We're looking for a bag for our girlfriend," Marshall says, putting his arm around me.

"Oh, your *girlfriends*?" she asks, accentuating the 's'. She's confused. Obviously, they couldn't be here with little ol' me. I must be the fugly sister who accompanies them and helps them pick stuff out for their supermodel girlfriends.

"Nope, *girlfriend*," Marshall says, accentuating the 'd'.

"Oh," she says and pulls away from us in disgust.

Ezra notices that his control over the situation is slipping because of Marshall's brusqueness. He places his hand on her back and glances at us as if to say, "Be cool, dorks."

We both tighten up at the sight of his hand on her back. He leans in and whispers something into her ear. She giggles uncontrollably. He whispers more. She giggles again, unable to speak, nods, and takes the bag to the counter.

"What did you say to her?" Marshall whispers in a confused tone.

"Don't worry about it, bro," he hisses. He positions himself to block me from the clerk's view and says, "Adley, can I please have your card?"

"What?! I can't afford that bag!"

He leans down and whispers, "Trust me, we'll get that bag for a steal. I just need her to think I'm buying it."

"What?!" I ask incredulously.

"Please, trust me. If you don't want it after this, we can return it. But let me work my magic."

I lean over to see the clerk. She is applying lipstick and looking in a handheld mirror.

"Are… are you going to fuck her for this bag?" Marshall asks.

"What?! No, dude! Just trust me, okay?" he says, pleading with us.

"Okay," I say and tentatively hand him my card.

"You two wait over there and watch the magic. Remember, whatever happens, it's just a facade. It's an acting gig, and I'm playing a role. I don't want her, and I will be going home with you, okay?"

I don't know if he was saying that to just me or both Marshall and me, but we both are interested in seeing this go down. So we slink to the side of the store and pretend to look at a purse, but really, we're watching him.

He glides over to the counter, and honestly, I feel like he's going to grab her and bend her over the counter. She's getting the same vibe and is so flustered I'm surprised her ass isn't up in the air already. She's fully ready to let him take her right here, right now—security cameras be damned.

He leans forward on the counter and says something to her. She fans herself, unable to stop appearing like a cliché horned-up cartoon. She giggles, and he reaches forward, brushing her chin. She pauses and looks like it is taking all her willpower not to put his thumb in her mouth.

"Damn, this is a level of swagger I have never seen in my life," Marshall says.

"It's kind of getting me all hot and bothered," I say.

"Yeah," he sighs, eyes glued to the scene.

Ezra pulls my card out of his pocket, holds it between his two fingers, points it upward, and casually hands it to her.

She rings up the purse and barely contains herself, fumbling around to wrap the bag for him.

He kisses her hand, and the move seems cliché, but it works for her. She writes something down and hands the paper to him. He nods and walks off. Hope and despair fill her face as he leaves. The moment he faces us, his face switches from the proud, mature, sexual one he's worn since we walked in back to the goofy little kid who runs around an aquarium marveling at fish.

He gives us a tiny thumbs up, hidden from her view, then runs his hand through his hair. He turns and gives her one of the waves dudes do where they raise their hands in the air but don't move their hands. Her face flushes crimson, and she leans forward, practically begging him to come back with her hanging cleavage—shit, she's made me want to go over there and lick those tits—she's almost as good at this as he is. Almost.

We rush to ask him what happened, but he says, "Be cool, not until she can't see us anymore." So we walk as cooly out as we can, following behind him—not nearly as cool as he is.

When we turn the corner out of sight, he changes back to his goofy, kid-like self and almost laughs. "She would have given you a lot more," Marshal says.

"How much did you get it for?" I ask, anxious as fuck that my entire bank account just drained.

"See for yourself," he says and hands me the receipt. His smile is bigger than I have ever seen, and his composure and coolness are gone.

"Holy shit! Are you kidding me?!" I say so loud I startle them and everyone around me.

"Shhh," Ezra says. Marshall looks at the receipt, aghast.

"Is… is this what they mean by pretty privilege?" I croak out. "How is this kind of discount even possible?"

"Employee discount, along with some other stuff," Ezra says with a shrug.

"Wow, it's too bad you can't talk to the bank that holds my student loans," I say.

"What's a student loan?" Marshall asks, but Ezra runs toward a shoe store before I can answer, waving "Come on, guys" to us.

=^..^= ♥ =^..^=

Ezra drags us toward a shoe store, where he's already chatting up giggling clerks before Marshall and I even get past the theft detectors. Every single clerk in the store has flocked to him.

Spotting Marshall, one clerk breaks off from the gaggle around Ezra and jogs to him. She must prefer the tall, dark, and handsome variety of men. I guess I must get used to being chopped liver in the presence of these two, as everyone in the store either ignores me or gives me the stink eye.

"I'm good," Marshall deflects her smoothly, stepping back to return the spotlight to Ezra.

"No, dude. You need shoes, too. Let her help you," Ezra says, plopping us down on a couch in the middle of the room.

The clerks swarm around us, abandoning all the other customers in the room and rushing from shoe to shoe to us in a flurry of excitement. Ezra's draw on people seems almost magical, and I wonder if there is a supernatural element to this. I know Marshall said there wasn't, but maybe what is science in his world is magic in ours.

After we've found a few pairs of shoes, Ezra distractedly leaves the seat next to me. He returns with a grin and a pair of heels that could be dubbed "fuck me pumps."

"Oh, no, I can't walk in shoes like that," I say, shaking my head.

"You don't have to walk. Just wear them," he says, kneeling in front of me.

"Will you at least try them on for me?" he asks with a pout that is clearly fake, but still melts my heart.

"Ah, now you're manipulating me, too, huh?" I ask, with a giggle, leaning back, ready to let him put the shoe on my foot.

"Is it working?" he asks, seductively sliding off my sock. His eyes glaze over as he looks at me, and I can tell some spicy stuff is about to go down. I'm recognizing the lust in his eyes.

Marshall, sitting at my side, shifts his focus from tying his shoes to me. His breath quickens as he angles his body in my direction, and he places one hand on the back of my neck. Cool tingles flood my neck despite the warmth of his touch. His other hand is under my knee, gently lifting my leg.

Their purrs fill the room, causing nearby people to glance around for the sound's origin. The atmosphere grows dense, and everyone around us appears slightly drowsy. Vibrations from their purrs create a heavy, sleepy ambiance, as if their soothing sounds are tangibly influencing the surrounding environment.

The sounds of the mall have gone quiet. All I can hear is their purrs, the light creak of the bench beneath me, and the panting breaths shared between us. It's as if time has stalled for everyone but us and we are the only three people in existence.

Together, they gently lean me back, lifting my leg and spreading my thighs. Ezra, with careful precision, slides the shoe onto my foot. A soft kiss lands on the exposed part of my foot and another on my knee, sending shockwaves to my core.

Marshall's lips brush against my neck, leaving a trail of soft, feathery touches. He plants tender kisses on my face and breasts, each making me gasp.

My arousal has peaked, and my senses are on overdrive—thoroughly focused on the here and now. Their masculine musks, twinged with the cologne Ezra purchased for them, perfectly mingle—filling my lungs with a pleasure akin to eating a fantastic meal. Their purr soothes me with the gentle vibration, tantalizing my body and dulling my perception of everything but them.

The seamless synchronization in which they purr, breathe, and kiss me adds to the hypnotizing effect. Every movement, every touch, and every sound harmonizes in perfect unity, heightening the sensations and stirring a deep lust within me. It's intriguing—their ability to work as a team in such perfect unison that you'd think they were one unit.

A woman nearby drops to the ground. Then another. I'm so consumed with my lust that I can barely force myself to care. When a third drops, I break slightly from my stupor and observe the room. The people who are still standing, slump as if all function has ceased within their brains. More fall.

"Stop, stop," I breathe out in confusion. "What's happening?"

In a dazed state of arousal, Marshall pauses our kiss and glances around. "Oh, wow," he exclaims, giving Ezra a playful smack to get his attention.

Ezra stops kissing my inner thigh, surprised. "Bro, what the hell?" he responds after being hit.

"Ezra, look," Marshall says, jerking his head toward the people. He releases me and hurriedly removes the shoes he was trying on, tossing them haphazardly into a box—which is uncharacteristic of him.

Ezra looks around, and when he sees the people slumping over as if hypnotized, the glaze in his eyes disappears. "Seriously?!" he says, looking at Marshall with pure joy.

"Yeah, looks like it?" Marshall responds.

"What? What's going on?" I ask, disoriented.

"We have to cool it while we're in public," Marshall says as a non-answer.

"Yeah, I'll try," Ezra says. "Come on, Adley, let's get out of here."

They help me put my shoes back on and assist me in standing. My senses slowly return to normal, and the sounds of the mall return to me. People slowly stand as everyone appears to regain consciousness. Curiously, they return to their bustling activity and act as if nothing had happened once their senses return.

Ezra leaves to return the shoes to the shelf, but Marshall stops him with, "What are you doing? We're getting those!" Ezra grins and bounces back to us with them.

"No. I can't walk in those!" I chime in.

"We'll carry you," Marshall states. Okay then. I guess that solves that problem.

=^..^= ♥ =^..^=

We exit the store, and Ezra rushes to the next; his step somehow has even more pep. I didn't even think that was possible. How he looks like he's walking down a catwalk and also skipping is a skill I will never understand. Although our number of bags seems ungodly, Marshall carries them as if they were nothing—allowing Ezra to strut unhindered. Marshall's walk is significantly less graceful because of his general vibe and all the bags in the way, but he also seems to be in a better mood than he has been—more confident somehow.

They're both acting as if a bunch of people didn't just pass out in the shoe store. Did I imagine it? Did I fall asleep? "Can y'all explain to me what happened in there?" I ask, grabbing at Ezra's arm to stop him from walking further.

"We're a clowder," Marshall says matter-of-factly—as if that explains everything.

"Yeah," Ezra says with a bounce as he continues walking.

"And what the fuck does that mean?" I ask, looking at them. I'm seriously not the crazy one right now.

"It's a rare form of fated mates. It happens when three or more Ailura purr for each other. I thought they were legends. But, essentially, they are always horny for each other and can knock out entire cities with the sound of their purring," Ezra says.

Marshall continues, "That last part is unproven. Supposedly, powerful clowders caused the falls of multiple civilizations in our history. However, historians think it is an exaggeration."

"Wait, what? Like apocalyptic fucking?!" I ask.

"Umm, I wouldn't call it apocalyptic, but the more in-sync the clowder is, the more they can control the world around them," Marshall responds.

"WHAT?!" I ask.

"Don't worry about it, babe. It's just a legend. Plus, you're not an Ailura, so it won't get that bad. You can't purr," Ezra says and walks away.

"Don't tell me not to worry about it. It's worrisome. Does this mean…," I lower my voice, "Does this mean we can't all have sex together without, like, hypnotizing people or something?"

Marshall says, "It's based on sound. So, we just have to do it privately where people can't hear us."

"See, babe, problem solved! We just can't fuck you in public. No biggy. Disappointing, but whatever," Ezra says. "Plus, the legends always focused on the three Ailura purring. Something about triangulation of sound or something: I don't know, that math shit is your and Marshall's domain. You're not Ailura, though. You cannot purr. So it's just the two of us purring. Therefore, by the transitive property, we don't have to worry."

"That is not the transitive property," I respond, palming my face.

"I told you that math shit was your domain," Ezra shrugs.

Marshall chimes in, "Well, actually, the argument you just provided was denying the antecedent. It's a logical fallacy that incorrectly assumes that—"

Ezra raises his hand, cutting Marshall off. "Bro, who knows how many of the legends are true? It'll be fine," he says with an exaggerated cavalierness.

"Is this why the two of you get a weird look on your faces and then magically work together?" I ask, holding my hand up to Marshall, stopping him from chiming in. "I know, I know. It's not magic, but some kind of science. It's just a turn of phrase."

"We do?!" Ezra asks and excitedly looks at Marshall. Marshall only shrugs.

"You seriously haven't noticed? The two of you seem to predict what the other is doing somehow. It's almost scary," I respond.

"If we did that, then yes, it could be a reason," Marshall replies.

"It'll be fine! We just can't fuck you in public, and we need to control our purrs… I think. Easy peasy," Ezra says, grinning at me.

I look at Marshall for reassurance, but he shrugs. "Yeah, if we control ourselves in public, we should be fine," he says, adjusting himself with the hand with the fewest bags.

I look at him incredulously, "Are you aroused right now?! I thought you were the voice of reason in this group."

"I am. It's my desire for you that is unreasonable," Marshall responds.

"Dude, cut it out. You're going to get me all riled up, too," Ezra says and shifts his weight, his erection already building in him. Marshall at least looks chastised and abashed. Ezra looks smugly proud.

"Are you two actually going to control yourself? You've tried to fuck me multiple times in the last hour, and you currently have raging boners," I say, pointing at their crotches, forgetting we are in a public place.

A woman walks by, giggling at us. "Need help with that, honey?" she says, brushing her hand across Marshall's back.

"Please do not touch me," he states with no emotion, but it scares her enough to make her scurry away.

"Sure we can, babe! We're men! Not teenagers who just started popping boners for girls," Ezra says while walking to another store. Marshall brusquely nods at me and follows behind Ezra. I stay standing in place, watching them walk away toward the store, and I am so overwhelmed by how hot they look strolling away that I highly doubt any of us will control ourselves.

=^..^= ♥ =^..^=

We visit many more stores as the day progresses. The first is a jewelry store, where Ezra picks out a necklace for me. Things get a bit out of hand as he stands behind me and holds the necklace in front of me, saying, "See, I told you those fabulous tits needed some diamonds." At that, he and Marshall engulf me and almost fuck me right in front of the mirror. However, when a clerk drops to the floor, we snap out of it, cash out, and get out of there wondering if the cameras are monitored and if someone will think we're some sexually deviant group that knocks people out when they make out—which, let's face it, we are.

Our last stop is a skincare store. Ezra fusses over Marshall and tells him how to better care for his skin. As with the previous stores, clerks hover around them, agreeing with everything Ezra says. I stand back, totally overstimulated at this point, and just watch. I am so ready to go home, but Ezra is having so much fun, and I don't want to spoil this for him.

Marshall also seems to be at his last stretch because he mostly nods and grunts at Ezra. An avalanche of shopping bags sits at his feet, and he leans against a wall with glazed eyes and a dower expression.

When Ezra is done, I gape as the transaction unfolds; the clerk applies discounts with a flourish and gushes over Ezra's choices. I don't even want to know how much money I spent today. Guilt twinges at my heart over the excessive consumerism of the day. Each heavy bag is a tangible measure of Ezra's excitement. Designer clothes and high-end skincare products are all things I never thought I would purchase or even desire, but his enthusiasm fueled me. Whenever he tossed a "thank you" over his shoulder to a heartbroken clerk, I felt a curious mixture of satisfaction and anxiety. I had something they did not. I had him. So, while my bank account is undoubtedly depleted, I feel a sense of pride to have been able to do this for him.

We exit the last store. The number of bags is now too much for just Marshall to carry, and we all have arms covered in bags. The weight drags at me and further shows how much we indulged. My shoulders ache under the strain. A small price to pay for the light in Ezra's eyes and Marshall's more subdued but evident gratitude.

"Thanks for this, Adley," Ezra says, grinning ear to ear. "This was probably the best day of my life."

"I actually had fun, too," Marshall adds, his voice low and sincere, a shy smile pulling at the corners of his mouth.

"Actually? Dude, you gotta watch those passive-aggressive

compliments," Ezra says, hitting his bags with Marshalls.

"Oh, sorry, I didn't mean it," Marshall says.

"I know," I say with a grin, and I'm not lying. I'm constantly called passive-aggressive and never have any idea what I said that would be considered as such.

Ezra wraps his arm around me. A bag almost smacks me in the face. "Ah, sorry, babe!" he says, kissing me multiple times where it nearly hit me.

"How are you so lively?! I'm exhausted," I say with a slight yawn.

Marshall grunts in return, as if to agree with me.

"I don't know. I get energy from this. I guess we're classic introverts versus extroverts, huh?"

"I recall there was talk of sushi," Marshall says slyly, eyeing us.

"Oh yeah! Do you still wanna?!" Ezra asks, looking at me with a renewed bounce in his step.

"Sure, let's put the bags in the car first." I don't dare look at the receipts yet. I know Ezra got me some extreme discounts, but this will still hurt. I don't want to know how much yet.

We make our way towards the exit. I'm exhausted and overstimulated, but I find comfort in the rhythm of their steps. The three of us navigate the waves of people together. My two extremely tall, extremely sexy shields. Their proximity makes me feel like a slight edge of the world is worn down. As we enter the desolate corridor to the parking garage, the relief I feel from the lowered noise and stimulation is palpable.

I look at the two of them flanking me and feel blanketed in their presence. I feel incredibly blessed to be among them. This was really fun.

18

EZRA

I lift the small cup to my lips, inhaling the scent of the sake Adley insisted I try. This is my third cup of the night, and the way it accentuates the pleasurable experience of the night has made it hard for me to stop—but I know my limit is three drinks, so I will savor this cup as it is my last. A faint aroma of maybe pear, melon, or some fruit exclusive to this world, whispers across my nose and into my throat. The smooth liquid slides over my tongue, carrying a gentle weight of comfort that makes me sink into my chair, lost in the taste and the sensations.

Sake is not available in my world, but Adley informed me that while it is called "rice wine," it's not considered a wine and is made of rice, not grapes. Seeing her get animated and tell me all the random facts she knew about it was pretty cute. She and Marshall both do that—start rambling about a thing they know, their personality changing shape with each word, getting more animated. She is fucking adorable, and I'm jealous of all the random stuff they seem to know and are passionate about.

When they do it—reveal some new subject they randomly know a shit ton about—it makes me feel flat. Like I'm a flat character in their 3D world. I am energized when Adley does it, as if she's adding depth to me. She's sharing her knowledge and making me better. But when Marshall does it, I feel like he's flattening me further—drawing attention to my flaws. And, I'm not sure if there's a difference in their method—or if it's shaped purely by my feelings for them.

As the flavors of the sake unfold slowly, dispersing themselves throughout my body, I watch the two of them. There's a mild sweetness at first, balanced by a light acidity that causes a tantalizing burn that tingles just enough to wake up my palate. And it feels like I'm swallowing both Adley's sweetness and Marshall's acerbity.

A subtle umami depth follows, like a warm embrace, grounding the experience. And it makes me think of them embracing me in a pile of naked flesh after we've all come. It's not overpowering—just a delicate, harmonious blend that lingers lightly, inviting me to savor the moment.

I'm not usually a poetic man, but I reflect on how my relationship with them compares to the experience of drinking sake. That if I just let it happen, if I just swallow it down, it too can leave a soft warmth throughout my body that calms me, energizes me, and makes me feel like I can take on the fucking world.

My fingers brush the cool surface of the porcelain plate, holding a delicate array of sushi artfully arranged on it. I glance up to find Marshall's gaze fixed on the food. His deep-set eyes have an inscrutable look, making him appear even more enigmatic. The soft lighting of the sushi restaurant plays along the sharp angles of his face, casting shadows that highlight his high cheekbones and the slight furrow between his brows. He's not unattractive. Today has made him more attractive to me; maybe being stuck with him won't be that bad.

"Try the salmon nigiri, Marshall," Adley says with excitement. Her energy has shifted significantly since we entered the restaurant. She enjoys introducing us to the sushi and has been plopping pieces in our mouths, giddy every time we moan around her fingers or chopsticks.

Marshall's enthusiasm for sushi has been almost childlike, starkly contrasting from the grace and allure he usually exudes effortlessly. I'm happy I can be here with him at this moment. In our world, eating sushi is a treasured experience, a rare pleasure to be savored with every one of my senses. I reflect on the last few times I had it at home. I didn't enjoy it the way I should have. I didn't recognize what a gift it was to have access to it. What a privilege it was! How did I become so jaded to it? I am almost jealous he is having this experience. Don't get me wrong, this whole thing is fucking erotic as hell, and I'm enjoying it, but I wish I could enjoy it for the first time like he is.

I'm sitting on the other side of Adley. Despite her protests that it would be weird if we all jammed into a single booth. I have to lean forward to see his reaction, but I need to see it. The way he eats food is quite amusing. Marshall says in his low, steady voice, "This is exceptional." He pushes back, eyes closed, to savor the food—letting it take over his body and drop his guard. A look of contentment graces his face that rivals his orgasms. Heat rushes into my face as I picture him in the shower last night, making that same face as we both released into Adley.

I laugh at this, accidentally drawing nearby diners' attention. I get a bit self-conscious. Are we being annoying? Are we being weird? Does my hat make me look ugly? I touch my hat and wish I could release my ears. My confidence wanes momentarily, but I decide to do what I always do: lean into it. I laugh harder and watch out of the corner of my eye as more people look toward me. They all make that same face. That face that shifts from an initial annoyance that is quelled the moment they lay eyes on me. I am relieved to see I have the same effect on people here as I do in my world.

Adley's eyes sparkle as I mischievously reach over and pluck a piece of tuna sashimi from Marshall's plate while his eyes are closed. I pop it into my mouth with delight. She giggles at me and takes a sip of her wine. I kiss her cheek, still chewing, inciting another giggle in that ticklish way she does.

I still feel the familiar tug of my and Marshall's competition. However, there is also a gentle push and pull of affection between the three of us, exaggerated by the sensations brought on by delicious food and alcohol. I take a slow sip of my sake and reflect on this day.

"Marshall may favor the salmon, but this tuna is divine," I declare loud enough for my audience to hear. I grin at Adley with a warmth that I hope invites her to share in my joy. "You must taste it for yourself, babe."

She looks at me with that loose expression of a happily drunk woman. She is so fucking cute. I love this look on her. She's been on edge all day. I can tell that the mall experience is a bit too much for her. I am grateful she put up with it for my benefit. Marshall, too, although he didn't hold in his complaints quite like she did. I suppose I'm also grateful for his complaints, since his grumbling made me aware Adley was struggling. I need to do everything I can to ensure she isn't uncomfortable just for me. I must be more attentive. I must watch more closely for the subtle signs that she is uncomfortable despite her mask. One day, maybe she won't feel she needs to hide her feelings from me—she doesn't have to wear the mask. Maybe one day, I won't feel like I need to wear mine for her.

I pick up a piece of sushi between chopsticks. "Open up," I whisper, so only Adley and Marshall can hear. I place my hand on her thigh and squeeze, willing myself not to drift my hand further. As if he senses my impending arousal, Marshall leans forward and looks toward me. I think there is something to Adley's observation that he and I are syncing. We seem to be on the same wavelength as if our arousal is linked. And multiple times today, our movements have been in sync, too.

My senses tingle, and I want to take both of them right now. My erection is raging, and I do my best to stifle a purr as Adley opens her delicate mouth, and I gently place the sushi on her tongue. I don't want Adley to get mad at me. She seems freaked out by the whole clowder thing. I didn't think she would be. Any woman in my world would be overjoyed to find out she was in a clowder. It's like the number one sexual fantasy of my people. But this is another example of how Adley isn't as I expect her to be because of our differences in species. What other things will she surprise me with?

Marshall's smile is serene as he basks in her beauty and the sensation of the moment, expressing deep adoration. I lean closer, unable to resist the pull toward them any longer. Their energy wraps around me like a warm embrace. Their reservations and quiet nature are the perfect complement to me. They are perfect for me.

"Both are exquisite," Adley agrees, her voice threading a careful balance between me and Marshall. "I couldn't possibly choose."

"Are you still talking about sushi?" Marshall almost growls.

At first, I don't understand what he's referencing, but it dawns on me when Adley speaks up. "Oh," she giggles and hiccups, "you got the metaphor?"

I catch the subtle shift in Marshall's demeanor, the way his shoulders relax—a sign that her diplomatic answer has pleased him. I, too, am happy with her response and soften into a tender, almost sleepy disposition.

Marshall places his hand on the table in front of Adley—forming a shield around her with his body. I make eye contact with Marshall and place my hand on his. The sake has made me brave. I hope this small signal is enough to indicate that I want a truce between us. Maybe it's the sake's pull on me, but I am ready for us to be a team—a clowder.

Adley sees this and places her hands on both of ours. We both lean toward her and take a deep breath, inhaling each other's scents. They're all intermingled and almost indistinguishable.

At this moment, I am content. In the intimate triangle of our table, surrounded by the hum of the restaurant and the scent of lust, seaweed, and fresh fish, the three of us exist in a world of our own creation. A cozy cocoon where the only thing that matters is the three of us. *We will be a clowder of legend.*

MARSHALL

This trip to the mall has warmed Ezra to me. I'm sure his and Adley's indulgence in alcohol has also contributed to this. I have wanted him for a long time—since I was a kid. If only he knew what a fanboy I was… am. Maybe I should just tell him.

I don't know if I am ready to fully drop my guard to him. But the two of us working together brings Adley great pleasure, so, for now, I will trust him… for her.

I am willing to let my guard down for at least this moment. I place my head on Adley's shoulder and lean into the group hug.

EZRA

Our server interrupts the moment of pure bliss we are experiencing. A quiet purr was building up between Marshall and me. If her timing had been just a little slower, everyone in this restaurant would be passed out right now while we fucked on this table.

"Can I bring you anything else?" she asks from my side. She always approaches from my side and has been way too attentive. It's obvious she wants to ingratiate herself to me. I lift my head from our embrace, my eyes blurry in bliss and lust and sleepiness, and I scowl. Before turning to her, I turn on the smile.

"Hmm, I think we're okay. Do you guys need anything? Adley, more wine? Marshall more water?" I respond, trying not to twinge my voice with my annoyance.

"Yes, please," Adley hiccups, and I wonder if we should cut her off. But who am I not to indulge her? She is my mate, and she's paying so she can have whatever she wants.

Marshall looks at his water and says, "Yeah, maybe get her some more water, too?" He points at Adley's empty water glass and looks at her with concern.

I look back at the server and say with my winningest smile, "Could you bring the lady another glass of wine? And another round of water for the table?"

"Of course," she says, lingering as if she wants me to say something else. *Lady, I'm not into you. I'm sorry. You literally walked in on me, embraced by my mates. What the fuck do you want from me? A compliment?*

"And please, give our compliments to the chef. This is the best meal I've ever had," I say, my arm still wrapped around Adley, but I position myself toward the server more.

"Yes, compliments to the chef!!" Adley says with a squeak and raises her glass.

"Absolutely. The best meal I've ever had, as well," Marshall says with his deep, smooth voice. The server forgets about me momentarily, with her eyes buried deep in his—lost in his unassuming charm. *Back off, bitch, I will scratch you.*

I raise my eyebrows to her, tired of her lingering and afraid I'll be rude, but I'm losing my patience.

"Thanks, doll," I smile, trying to dismiss her. I want to get back to cuddling, eating sushi, and sipping the last bit of my sake.

"Oh, yes, okay," she stammers. *I get it. I'm gorgeous. He's gorgeous.* The feeling of sexual tension and lust is permeable and probably affecting her as well, but *go away, please.*

"Um, may I ask, do you have Instagram?" she asks me.

"Huh? What?" I ask, taken aback.

"You're a model, right? What's your Instagram handle?" she asks, pulling out her phone.

"Oh, actually, I don't have one of those. What is that? Should I have one?" I ask.

"Yep, definitely. You're so hot; you should have one," Adley hiccups. I glance at her and then back at the server.

"I don't have one, but I guess I should get one," I shrug. She looks disappointed and puts her phone back in her pocket. "Well, if you ever get one, follow me, okay? Here's my info." She hands me a piece of paper. It has her name, a username following an @, a phone number, a heart, and a note that says, "Meet me in the bathroom in ten minutes, and I'll suck your brains out of your dick."

I look back at her with a smile. "Thanks, doll," I say with a wink—*no thanks, more like it.*

ADLEY

My heart sinks when I read the note in Ezra's hands. He's looking at her with such admiration. Does he look at me that way? Of course, he wants to be with her. Why would Ezra want me when he could have whoever he wants? Same with Marshall. They're just stuck with me. They feel obligated to do so because they showed up in my backyard, and I bought them stuff.

My face burns with the threat of tears, and I struggle to breathe. It's fine. I'm fine. I knew this was too good to be true. Look at him. Look at me. This was never going to work out. No amount of clothes will buy his love. "Do you need to go to the bathroom?" I ask Ezra.

"What? No? Why? Do you?" he asks, confused.

I gesture down to the paper, and Marshall arches his neck to read it. "Classy," Marshall says with a scoff.

"This? No. Absolutely not," Ezra says and crumples up the paper, sending it across the table, where it lands in a bowl of soy sauce.

"Then why did you wink at her and say, 'Thanks, doll' to her?" I ask.

EZRA

Marshall looks at me as if he wants an answer, too. "That's… that's just the persona. I have to do that," I say.

"Why do you have to do that?" Marshall asks.

Because the idea of anyone not loving me kills me. Because I'm worthless except for my smile and my body. "Um, because you gotta give the people what they want to get what you want… you know?" I don't know how to articulate it. My brain is foggy from the sake and the food. Are we about to fight? I don't want to fight. *Let's just forget the waitress, and let's get back to hugging.*

"You mean like a prostitute?" Adley hiccups.

"What?! No! It's not like that. You wouldn't get it, babe," I say, frustrated and trying to get her to drop it.

"Because I'm too ugly to get it? Is that what you mean?" she says, a tear rolling down her cheek. My heart sinks to my throat. *No, please, don't cry. I can't do this with you, too, Adley.*

"What?! No, where is this coming from? Why are you twisting my words?" I say, panicked. *Please drop it. Please, just look at my dazzling smile and remember the times I've made you come.*

"You can just go to the bathroom with her. I don't own you," she says dejectedly.

This always happens. Women I'm with never seem to get it. If someone doesn't love me, they might as well hate me. If people aren't looking at me, I don't exist—I have no purpose. It's always been like that. Either I'm beautiful and smiling, or I'm fucking nothing.

I've had this fight hundreds of times—with every woman I've ever been with. Usually, I'd get mad at this point. I'd be frustrated that my loyalty is being challenged. I'd tell her, "Fine, if you want me to go fuck that woman in the bathroom, then I will. Then you'll regret this and be sorry you said that." Then we'd break up, I'd go fuck the woman in the bathroom, and the cycle would start up all over with the next girl.

Because I need to be in a relationship. Being single is something I've never been able to do. So, I bounce from one woman to the next. But… I don't want to do that with Adley. I don't want to mess this up. I want to be with her… them… forever. They're my clowder. I stammer, unsure of what to say. Confusion and fear all swirl in my head.

Rage boils in me as I cannot face the fear or process the situation. My mind can't focus on a solution. I don't know what to do. *Fuck, I shouldn't have drank so much.* Maybe I could do this if I hadn't had that third cup.

"Do you want to go?" Marshall asks with his eyebrow raised. So now he's going to nag me about it, too? This fucking guy. *Don't you start with me, too! I can't fucking win.*

But he doesn't seem mad. Or like he's judging me. He's being matter-of-fact the way he always is. He's simply asking me a question. It's not a question wrapped around a presumption meant to trap me. It's almost like he's trying to guide me through this moment—a shining lighthouse through the fog of Adley's insecurities… through the fog of my own.

I look at him with my mouth agape. He knows I don't want to go. What should I do? He says, "Tell Adley what you want." He nods in a nudging way as if to say, "Go on."

Oh, I see what he's doing. He is trying to help me. My mind calms slightly. Clarity. The rage subsides, replaced by a cloying affection for them and a hint of despair. I stammer out, tears building in my eyes, "I…I don't want to go with her. I want to stay here with the two of you and eat sushi. I want to forget that woman ever existed and drown myself in the softness of your curves. I want to breathe you in to fill not just my lungs but my entire being, ripping away my consciousness so that all I am is the feeling of love." I get self-conscious about my inability to wax poetic and tack on, "I want to go back to being 'no thoughts, just vibes' with you… if that makes sense."

Marshall smiles at me and slightly nods as if to say, "Good job."

Adley grabs her napkin and dabs at her eyes. "Really?" she chokes out, her voice tinted with sweetness again.

Marshall lifts his hand on the bench behind her head and gives me a thumbs up before resting his hand back on her shoulders. I look at him dumbfounded and chuckle. *That was so weird.* He just smirks at me.

"Adley, we're fated mates. There will never, ever be anyone who causes our eyes to stray. Ezra's a flirt because it gets him things, but I see how he looks at you. He doesn't look at anyone else like that," Marshall says, stroking her chin.

This fucking guy saved me. I smile at him, thanking him for the assist, and I'm pretty sure there's one other person I could look at like that: him.

19

MARSHALL

"It's fine. I can drive," I say, staring at the car door. Adley is on my back, her arms draped over my shoulders. I can feel the warmth of her pussy against me and the swell of her breasts against me. I have to use every ounce of willpower not to throw her on the ground and take her.

The sun has set, and we've been out all day. I'm looking forward to getting home, ravishing Adley, and sleeping. I hope to make up for the hours of sleep I lost last night.

"I'm sorry. I forgot y'all can't drive," Adley says with a sad hiccup. "I'm used to my boyfriend always driving me home from dinner out. I shouldn't have drank." She makes a pouting hmm noise at my neck, sending a shiver down my spine. I grip her knees tighter, pulling her further into my back.

"You mean that tool, Bryce?" Ezra asks.

"Yeah," she says dreamily behind me, and I try not to read any sexuality in that tone, but the way she sighs makes my body tense. I imagine what they might have done together. I picture Adley on his lap; her legs spread wide as she bucks atop him, her nails digging into his shoulders. Telling him she loved him.

Ezra growls, a bit too drunk to handle himself, obviously thinking the same thoughts. Pulling myself back to the present, I shift my focus to Adley's body pressed against mine. Her fingers trace down my shoulder and arm, making the hairs stand on end. She pulls my hat from my head and casually strokes my ear. I look around to see if anyone can see me, but there's no one around. Lust builds within me as she grinds on my back slightly. I need to get her home so I can fuck her.

I say, "I can drive," emphasizing "can." "Cars seem like they work the same as the ones back home. But if a cop stops us, I'm fucked." Ezra gives me that cute side-tilted look he does when he's confused.

"Because I don't have a license," I say.

"Oooo," he says as if he's forgotten the events of the last three days and is just now recalling them.

"Maybe it'll be a lady cop, and Ezra can smile her away," Adley laughs. "Or we could order an Uber. But that'll take forever and cost so much money. I don't think I have any more money." She laughs with a slight air of sadness.

Guilt rips through me, and my heart sinks. I don't even want to know how much of Adley's money we've spent over the last two days.

"It's not that far. I can drive carefully. If I get pulled over, will you turn up the charm for me, Ezra?" I ask—knowing this is a stupid as fuck plan but throwing him a bone.

"You're asking for my help?" he says, pointing at his chest, stumbling a little from the sake he drank a bit too much of.

"Yes," I huff.

He looks way too excited by this tiny amount of praise. "Aye, aye, captain," he says and salutes me.

"That was so cheesy, Ezra," Adley says from behind my back.

"That's why you called me Cheddar," he says with a grin, sticking his tongue out the side of his mouth.

"I called you Cheddar because you're orange," Adley hiccups.

"I'm not orange!" Ezra says, offended.

I roll my eyes at him. "Will you open the back door for me so I can put her in?"

I'm a little annoyed by how drunk he is. I really wanted to try the sake, but I was too nervous that if we all got drunk, we wouldn't be able to contain ourselves. Plus, Adley and Ezra just started drinking without asking me what I wanted and without considering how we would get home. I've watched Adley drive the last two days, so I'm pretty sure I know how it works. Some street signs are slightly different, but their intent is easy to assume.

Ezra opens the door, and I gently place her in the back seat and buckle her in. She leans back, content and dozing off a bit. I tried to cut her off, but Ezra kept ordering her more drinks. They were having fun, so I didn't want to complain, but now I'm dealing with the consequences of their actions. I brush her hair out of her face and look into her eyes. She's not too drunk, is she?

"You okay, Adley?" I ask.

"Oh, yeah, I only drank about a bottle. I normally drink way more than this—and on an empty stomach," she responds, buckling in.

Ezra stumbles to the front of the car and sits on the passenger side.

Adley leans forward, pulling on his sleeve. "Ezra, can you sit in the back with me?" she pleads. "I'm going to be lonely," she says, biting her lip. Damn it, this is going to be a challenging ride, isn't it?

"Are you going to puke on me?" Ezra asks as he exits the car, planning to sit with her regardless of her answer.

She responds when he opens the back door, "Umm, probably not." He grimaces and gets in. "Maybe don't shove anything in my mouth, though," she says flirtily.

"Bummer," Ezra says, "After last night, all I can think about when I look at that pretty mouth is it wrapped around my cock." The memory of her bent in front of me, sucking his dick, stirs memories of pleasure and jealousy. I've never had a blowjob before, and I think I would very much like it. I've also never eaten pussy before, and I think I will very much like that, too. I suppose I can't be too jealous. I have felt the warm embrace of her tight cunt around my cock. And I got to do it before he did both times we've had sex.

I get into the driver's seat and examine the console. It's familiar. I do what I think will start the car, and it works. Adley leans forward and says, "Oh, plug this in," handing me her phone. "There," she points at a cord by the cupholder.

"That'll tell you how to get home. It's in there as home," she says, pointing at the center console, newly lit with information from her phone.

"Thank you," I say and tap away at the settings until the smooth voice of a man tells me to turn left on American Boulevard.

"Oh, it talks?" I ask and slowly pull out of the parking garage.

"Yeah, that's my boyfriend, Samuel. Sexy Samuel. He makes sure I never get lost," Adley jokes.

Ezra is only half paying attention and perks up, saying, "Wait? Who the fuck is Samuel?!"

"No one, Extra, I was just making a terrible joke. But he sounds hot, though, doesn't he?" Adley says.

I do not comment and am ashamed of my jealousy of an obviously robotic voice.

"Extra?" Ezra asks, confused.

"Oh, yeah, because your name is Ezra. Get it? Extra?" Adley says.

"But… it doesn't rhyme or sound anything like my name. You're just saying weird drunk stuff," he says, shaking his head.

"No, I'm not! Extra and Ezra are super close…spelling-wise. And you know, you're super..." I can see her waving her hands in large circles in his direction in the rearview mirror. "Extra," she says pointedly. "So, you're

Extra. It's official. You can't do anything about it. Nicknames choose you, not the other way around."

"Extra?!" he says in mock offense. "No one has ever said such a thing about me."

"Really?! That's surprising," Adley says.

"I'm being sarcastic," he says with a chuckle.

"Oh, I'm too drunk to get sarcasm," she says matter-of-factly. I feel a weird sense of pride at the fact that I got the joke.

Following Sexy Samuel's directions makes getting on the highway easy. The console says it'll be fifteen minutes until we arrive home. I think I can drive safely in that amount of time.

The windows fog, and a moan comes from the back seat. *Shit.*

"Can you drive faster? I'm so fucking horny," Adley says. I can't see what she's doing, but her face contorts in pleasure in the mirror. "It was so hard not being able to fuck the two of you all day. And then that sushi slut interrupted us in the restaurant."

I glance in the rearview at Ezra. He is watching her with the intensity of a man possessed.

"I will drive as fast as possible while remaining safe," I groan. I desperately want to speed, but everything I care about in this new world is in this car, and I will not endanger them.

"Don't worry, babe. The car said we'll be home soon," Ezra responds. "Oooh, fuck, that's so hot," he adds. A jolt of anger bolts through me. Is he touching her? We're supposed to only sleep with her together. The pact was his idea. I glance back at the rearview mirror, trying hard to see what is happening and desperately trying to drive well. I want to floor it, get home, and fuck them, but I can't risk getting pulled over.

"Do you enjoy watching me, Ezra?" Adley says.

"Very much," he responds. No longer able to stop myself, I turn to get a quick look at them. They're both leaning against their respective doors, watching each other. Ezra is slowly stroking his cock while Adley has her hand deep in her pants.

"Eyes on the road, bro!" Ezra shouts at me, and I return my attention to the road.

My knuckles whiten as I grip the wheel tighter. I want to watch her, too. I want to watch them both. My cock strains painfully against my zipper. With my tail tucked the way it is, the discomfort is exaggerated.

"Want me to describe what's happening to you, bro?" Ezra asks me.

"Yes!" I respond. And press my palm into my crotch, desperate to free my cock from its cage.

"Um, Adley's new jeans, the ones that hug her so tight they make you want to fight them in jealousy, are fully unzipped, and her hand is in her panties, rubbing at her clit."

I glance back in the mirror and can only see their faces. Her eyes are closed in pleasure. His are wide in lust.

"I'm going to help her out," Ezra responds. A moment passes, and Adley moans louder. "She's so wet. I've got two fingers in her, pumping upwards while she rubs at her clit with her palm. Oh, yeah, baby, let's make you come."

I can feel my heart pounding as I listen to the sounds of their pleasure growing louder with each passing moment. It's a mix of mental and physical torture—listening to them while knowing I can't have them, yet needing all of them at the same time. I want to feel her wrapped around my cock. I can smell the intoxicating scent of their shared lust, and I push down harder on the accelerator despite my better judgment.

I look at the console. Five minutes. I can wait for five minutes.

"She's bucking upward now, her ass is fully lifting off the seat, I think she's going to come," Ezra says.

"Does she still have her seatbelt on?!" I ask.

"Haha, yeah, don't worry, bro," He responds.

"I want you both inside me so bad," Adley moans out.

I turn to see, and Ezra yells, "Bro! Eyes on the road!"

"Sorry," I say, snapping my head back and jolting the car slightly.

Sexy Samuel says, "In 0.1 miles, take the next right at Lakeview Boulevard." That's our exit. I need to get out of this car and into Adley right now.

=^..^= ♥ =^..^=

The car screeches to a halt as I pull into the garage. Ezra leaps from the car before I've even turned it off. I press the button to close the garage door and exit the vehicle, removing my clothes as I do so.

The freezing air hits the bare skin of my chest when my sweater comes off. I almost regret removing my coat. Almost.

I watch them through the car window. Adley's legs are now across the seat as Ezra frantically pulls her pants and underwear off, tossing them into the front seat. He lunges for her pussy, causing her to scream out in delight. The echo of it in the cold, empty garage makes my cock even harder.

The door is still slightly open when my last piece of clothing hits the ground. Someone may see me, but I do not care. I unstrap my tail and throw the bandage that held it in place on top of my pile of discarded clothes.

My cock and tail spring to life when freed of their restraints. My cock aches to be in Adley, and my tail whips behind me, almost as if it has a mind of its own. The cold air on them is arousing and refreshing compared to the stifling heat they've been subjected to. I worry the cold will shrivel me, but my cock stands tall, defiant against the air's bitter bite.

Fully naked now, I fling open the backdoor, and Adley almost falls out of the car when I open the door. "Oh, Adley, are you okay?" I ask, as her head hangs out the side of the vehicle.

Ezra is at the other end, door open, ass out the door, face buried deep into Adley's crotch. He's always eating her pussy. I never get to. I try to focus on Adley and pet her face, checking her hanging head for injury.

She reaches toward me and grabs my ass cheeks tight, pulling me toward her and slipping my dick into her mouth. *Oh, so that's what her mouth feels like. She is a fucking angel. This is heaven.* I melt into her as she sucks hard.

ADLEY

Marshall startles at my mouth, suddenly wrapped around his cock. I suck as hard as I can, wondering if I can make him come in one suck. He buckles forward, overwhelmed by the sensation and unable to stand. His face falls to my chest as he moans out and twitches above me clutching at my sides. He lifts my shirt and bra to bring my nipple into his mouth. He almost imperceptibly pumps into me. Rocking only slightly.

His cock slides easily down my throat from this angle, and I resolve only ever to suck dick upside down from this moment on. *This is so easy!*

As I suck hard on Marshall's dick, Ezra sucks hard on my clit, sending a moan through me. I buck hard against his face. An orgasm rips through me, and I have to push Marshall away to catch my breath as I scream into the orgasm. I grab Ezra's ears and buck furiously into his face. Watching that fluffy hair sway with each pump of my hips. His eyes crinkle as he smiles up at me.

Unable to receive any more pleasure, I push his head away and lie back, boneless. "No more," I say and lazily sink into the seat. My heart pounds in my ears, and I place my hand on my chest, feeling my breath and heart as my vitals return to normal.

I look at them, and they have their eyes locked on me. Each smirks, as if satisfied with what has happened. But they both are still rock hard. The fact they seem content to not come is touching. I've never had a boyfriend who was okay with not coming. They were okay with me not coming, though.

They both pull away from the car. "Don't leave!" I sit up in the center of the seat. "I want you both to come," I say as I pat the seats next to me, pulling my shirt and bra off over my head.

Still fully clothed, Ezra quickly removes his clothes and bandages, tossing them into the front seat with my clothes. Marshall is already naked and sits next to me. Still a little too tired to do much else, I stroke his cock. When Ezra sits beside me, I stroke him as well.

"Please shut the doors, it is so cold," I say with a shiver. Now that I've come, my body notices the cold it ignored a moment ago. They pull the doors closed in unison. I close my eyes, still basking from my orgasm, as I pump their dicks at my side.

They each kiss at my neck and grip at my thighs. I open my eyes with a devious smile.

"Rock paper scissors, boys," I say.

"Huh?" they both ask.

"I want you to rock paper scissors," I respond, refusing to elaborate.

They look confused, but do it, anyway. Ezra throws rock, and Marshall throws scissors.

"Marshall, I want you to stroke your dick while I fuck Ezra. Is that okay with you?" Marshall nods with a grunt, and I swing my legs over Ezra's hips. In a smooth movement, I sink onto his standing erection. It slides into me so effortlessly, but I can still feel the rim of his head scraping into me as I take his full length.

Ezra groans out and leans his head back in pleasure. "You got me extra wet, Extra. Does it feel good?" I ask.

"Oh my god, yes," he says and grips my hips close to him, sinking even deeper into me. He hits that spot that so few men can, sending a pleasurable pain through my pelvis and lower back that causes my walls to clench around him. I grind down in a circle and watch his face as he loses himself to the pleasure of being inside me. He is so fucking beautiful. It feels like it's just him and me in the entire world for a moment. I kiss him deeply and remember that we are not the only ones in the world.

My gaze travels to Marshall, and I expect him to appear sad, but he doesn't. He angles toward us, slowly stroking his enormous cock and smiling dumbly at us.

"You like what you see, Marsh?" I ask and make my tits bounce in Ezra's face. Ezra sinks his head into my chest and chuckles in delight.

"Yes," Marshall says with deep strokes.

"Oh, Adley, you feel so good," Ezra says as I bounce harder. He smacks my ass, making it jiggle just a little. This seems to spur Marshall on as he strokes faster. His face reveals nothing but pleasure and desire.

Ezra's abs tense under me, and the leverage I get on my clit is even better. But I feel a little guilty that Marshall is alone, so I say, "Hurry and come for me, Ezzy. It's Marshall's turn." I bounce even harder, trying to make him come.

"No," Ezra says softly into my breasts.

I stop. "Huh?"

"We have to come at the same time," Ezra says while rubbing his nose over my nipple.

"What? Why?" I stop grinding.

"I… I don't know. It just feels wrong," Ezra says, leaning his head back in defeat.

"Wrong like you physically can't or wrong like… ethically?" I ask.

"I don't know. I'm… I'm still a little drunk. I just… ethically, I guess," Ezra says, stroking my sides and looking lovingly at my tits.

I look at Marshall. The surprise on his face is apparent, and he has stopped stroking his cock. "Do you feel the same way, Marshall?" I ask.

He contemplates this question momentarily before saying, "Yes. I think so."

"Well, that's a lot of pressure on me. How am I supposed to ensure you both always come simultaneously?" I ask. Ezra is still inside me, twitching but not moving.

"It just feels wrong to try to come without him," Ezra says. "If we don't, that's okay, but I just… I feel like I should try to do it at the same time. I'm sorry, this doesn't make sense. I don't understand it either." He sighs in frustration with himself.

"Okay..." I say, and look at both of them.

"Do not worry, Adley. I will come. You may continue," Marshall says.

"It's like a… cum-radery," Ezra says while giggling into my neck.

"Ezra, that was awful," I say with a laugh because his puns are getting next-level bad.

"We are cum-rades in arms," Marshall says and strokes his cock again, now faster.

"Not you, too," I sigh out at Marshall. Ezra pumps into me, and a shudder of pleasure fits through my body.

"Our shared mission is to make you come," Ezra jokes.

"Okay, let's stop with the joke if you want to achieve that mission," I say as I grind on Ezra in a circular motion.

He doesn't respond, just moans. The moan morphs into a purr, and Marshall follows suit. The small space makes the sound vibrate throughout my body, and I get the same dreamy feeling I got in the shoe store. The sound tingles my whole body, and I shutter around Ezra's cock.

Marshall's hand is stroking harder and faster as he approaches his orgasm, and I think maybe they will come at the same time.

I circle faster on Ezra's dick, my pleasure plateauing, and I feel my orgasm is eminent.

"Marshall, come on me," I say.

"On us," Ezra breathes out into my chest, tensing as his orgasm builds into me.

Marshall lifts to his knees and leans forward to release into the space between me and Ezra. His tail whips behind him, hitting back and forth between the seats.

Ezra leans his head backward, "Oooh, fuck!" he says and lifts his hips into me. This slight change in angle sends my orgasm over the edge. I fist Ezra's hair and ears as I release with them.

MARSHALL

We slowly climb out of the car, collecting our clothes and redressing.

"Dude, hopefully, those new clothes didn't get stained on the floor," Ezra chastises me as he hands Adley her pants.

"I think they're okay," I say, inspecting them.

I pull them up to my tail. "Fuck," I say. And sigh, defeated by my inability to pull my pants up fully. I just leave them unbuttoned—I don't feel like dealing with this.

"Don't worry, bro. I'll put a tail fly on them for you," Ezra says. "The buttons Adley ordered should be delivered on Monday."

"Thanks," I say as we both go to the back of the car to get all the bags. Adley's still getting dressed inside the vehicle. She got a deep chill and didn't want to get dressed outside of it.

"No prob, bro," he says.

I reach for the button to pop the hood of the truck's hatch when Ezra says, "Thanks for letting me win."

I look at him in surprise. He continues, "Rock paper scissors. You always win. I'm assuming that science brain of yours knows some fancy probability algorithm that lets you keep winning. But you lost just now."

I blush because he is partially correct. I did let him win. But I don't have a fancy algorithm. Ezra just always picks rock. I wanted to let him enter her first this time. I don't know why it just felt like the right thing to do.

"No prob, bro," I parrot with a slight smile, recalling how beautiful they both looked as I came all over their chests.

20

MARSHALL

Adley and Ezra are still asleep, but I'm up, anxious to start the day and prove my usefulness. Eager to pay back Adley for the exorbitant amount of money she spent on us the last two days. I've been quietly sneaking around the house for about an hour, cleaning whatever I can. The task is more complicated than expected because I don't want to wake up Adley or Ezra. I hope Adley's not hung over. She drank a lot last night—actually, she's drank a lot every night since we've been here. I haven't seen her hungover yet, so perhaps alcohol doesn't affect her in that way. I don't know if that's something I should be worried about.

I stand, staring at the litter box, laughing that it's still here. I contemplate throwing it away, but somehow, that feels disrespectful. I am stuck in indecision when I hear the bedroom door open. Ezra walks out, scratching his head, and sees me in the bathroom. "Dude, you know you don't have to shit in that, right?" he laughs.

I groan and snap back. "I know! I was considering what to do with it."

"Wow, bite my head off, why don't you? I was just joking," he says sadly, deflated. His bravado is gone.

"I'm sorry. I'm just feeling guilty right now."

"For what? For only giving Adley two orgasms instead of three?"

"No…," I say.

"Cumming on her tits? She asked for that!" he says excitedly.

"No!" I snap again.

I sigh. I don't want to be mean to him, but he's frustrating me. "She spent a lot of money on us the last two days. I feel like we're taking advantage of her."

"Nah, dude. Don't think like that. It was her idea. Plus, we got everything at the mall for a fantastic price."

"Yeah, but I don't know if she had the money to get it."

"What'd you mean? Obviously, she had it. The cards didn't get declined. Do cards work differently here?"

"Never mind," I say. He will not get it.

Adley walks out, her hair a mess atop her head.

"Why are y'all arguing over the litter box? You know you can just use the toilet. Also, there's another bathroom."

I look at her to argue that we're not arguing over the litter box, but her grin implies she's joking.

"We can just throw that out. Or dump it out and put it in the garage just in case I ever get a pet cat," she says.

We both look at her, appalled. A pet cat? She flinches, realizing what she said.

She responds, "Okay, scratch that—no pet cats. We can just throw it out, then. But y'all have to promise to sit in my lap in your ailo form sometimes, okay?"

"Oh, babe, nothing was going to stop me from doing that," Ezra says, winking at me. I wonder if Adley knows how risque it is in our world for him to sit in her lap in his ailo form.

Adley swings open the closet doors, revealing the space she'd cleared for my and Ezra's stuff. Sunlight filters through the window. A warm, voluminous beam of light casts on the piles of clothes on the bed. Instinct draws me to the spot, causing a deep desire to curl up the pile of clothes and bask in the sun.

"Will all our stuff fit?" Ezra asks, ever the accidental passive-aggressive. We share that in common.

"Of course, it will fit," I say, smacking him lightly with the back of my hand. He looks appropriately chastised.

"I've also cleared out some drawers for you two. This was harder, but I'm going to get rid of some stuff so you can put your things in here," she says as she gestures to a large trash bag in the room's corner. "I'm sure I'll have a lot more to donate in the coming days as we make more room."

I feel guilty that she's removing her items to make room for us. "Are you sure you don't mind getting rid of things?" I ask, looking toward the bag.

"Yeah, it's fine," she says with a shrug. "I needed to do a purge, anyway. This was an acceptable excuse. Normally I don't also get dicked down for donating, so this was nice," she says with a chuckle. She frowns slightly and continues, "It wasn't too hard. This used to be where Bryce kept all his stuff before moving out.

This Bryce guy comes up quite a lot. She must not be over him. I want to ask her, but it doesn't seem appropriate somehow. She'll tell us when she's ready. We've forced ourselves on her as she rebounds, which doesn't feel too great. I try to repress the visions of the memory of him bending her over in the hallway, ready to enter her and slapping her ass. If I ever see that guy again, I will scratch his eyes out.

I look at the empty drawer and feel a twinge of anger, thinking about how my clothes will now sit where his clothes once were. Ezra glides around the room excitedly, moving his clothing from his bags to the closet. Playful winks and flirtatious grins aimed at Adley punctuate his movements.

He is way too exuberant all the time, but it is a little cute. With every shirt he tucks into a drawer, he compliments her, making her blush.

Seeing all our stuff on the bed puts the amount we accumulated in the last two days into perspective. I'm panicking at the sheer volume of it.

"Oh, my god, I can't wait to see you in this," Ezra says, his voice light and teasing as he holds one of the shirts he picked out for her up to her chest. "Wanna go ahead and put it on? Or, just take off your shirt?" he says, draping his arm around her and kissing her neck.

"Must you always flirt?" I ask from behind. I hope my tone conveys a hint of jest rather than reproach, but Ezra seems hurt by my words. I try to save it by adding, "We have a lot to do right now. We don't have time to fuck," I laugh.

"Come on. Cheer up, Romeo," he says and comes up to me, slapping my ass. "It's Sunday. We could fuck all day if we wanted to. You know, Adley, in our world, Sunday is earmarked specifically to be a 'day for fucking.'"

"Really?" she asks, still unable to tell when he's joking.

"No, not really," I say.

"Dude?! Why are you cockblocking me… and by the transitive property of our relationship yourself?! Did I use it right that time?" he jokes.

"Yep," Adley laughs, folding a sweater.

I've been quiet throughout the morning, taking silent note of the tags still attached to the toiletries and clothes Adley has paid for us over the last few days. Guilt gnaws at me, weighing me down. I don't know if I could get it up in this mood, anyway.

"I'd like to get all this stuff put away first," I say, and I try to put some clothes in the closet.

Ezra swats me away. "Dude, you can't hang it like that! It'll crease! Just let me do it!"

Ezra is taking his sweet time putting our clothes away. He admires each piece as if he's never seen it before and ensures it goes in the closet just right. He seems to have some obsessive tendencies when caring for his stuff. Each thing must be cared for and placed very specifically. He's even rearranging my stuff and Adley's. I consider giving him a hard time about it, the way he gave me a hard time about the groceries, but I'm not in the mood to tease him right now.

As Ezra fills the space with his energy, I back out, feeling like there's not enough room for me. The oppressive weight of his presence and my guilt make me feel claustrophobic.

I stand at the door, watching him bounce off the walls while Adley sits on the bed chatting.

Bryce said he came from work. He has a job. I wonder how much money he makes. Adley mentioned he paid half the bills when he lived here. Even he was able to help Adley. I cannot.

I feel a mounting anxiety about my uselessness and inconvenience. I'm taking up too much space and must make room for the others, so I leave them in search of cleaning supplies. Now that they are awake, I can continue my morning tasks without worrying about waking them. Hopefully, I will find some semblance of self-worth in usefulness.

Under the kitchen sink are the various cleaning supplies. I find what I am searching for: a cloth and dust spray. I grab the cloth. It feels like it grabs hold of every molecule in my skin and rips them away simultaneously. I drop it immediately. *What devil cloth is this?*

Adley enters the kitchen and refills her water bottle. "Adley, do you have a different cloth for wiping surfaces? The texture of this is… unpleasant."

"Oh, yeah, microfiber. I hate it, too. Um, I have regular washcloths, but unfortunately, that's the best for getting dust. I usually spray the stuff on the cloth and only hold it where it's wet. That helps...," she trails off. "But Marshall, you don't have to do that. I know you've been cleaning all morning," Adley says softly, approaching me from behind and wrapping her arms around my midsection as I pick up the cloth, trying to touch it with as little of my hand as possible.

"I like to be useful," I say without turning, "Plus, I umm… don't like mess." Adley pulls back but maintains her grip on me. I continue, "Not that your house is messy! I just… I like to clean."

"You don't have to be useful, Marshall," she says.

Ezra's humming and fiddling stop in the bedroom, and I can tell he's listening to our conversation. "I enjoy doing it. I enjoy having something to do. And since Ezra is putting away the clothes, I'll do this."

"Dude, why don't you bask in the sun and keep us company while I put away the clothes? I saw you eyeing that sunspot!" Ezra says, bouncing into the kitchen, obviously spying on us. He cannot keep up the ruse that he's not listening up.

I just can't shake the feeling that she's not candid about how much of a burden we've been. "I've got to pay Adley back somehow for everything."

She grimaces at me, "Marshall, you don't—"

"I want to," I insist, offering her a smile. I squirm from her embrace and move into the living room. I spray the cloth and then the surface. "Oh, yeah, it is much nicer wet!" I say, smiling to myself, happy to have something different to concentrate on.

"Just like Adley," Ezra chuckles and wraps his arm around her, kissing her neck.

"Gross, Ez," Adley says, but laughs.

"It's because your skin is so dry. If you listened to me and moisturized, it wouldn't feel so gross," he says, and I don't know why I don't want to use the lotion. It's stubbornness that I'm not able to dissect just yet.

"Okay, well, we'll leave you to it, I guess," Adley says, disappointment in her voice. "But I'd like us all to spend a little time together today, okay?"

"Yep," I say, not looking up from the spot where I'm wiping.

"Come on, babe. Want me to model my new clothes for you?" Ezra says, pulling her into one of his crotch-first hugs.

"Uh, I guess," she says.

"What? You have more interesting things to look at than me in a state of undress," Ezra says in mock offense.

Adley laughs. "I hoped to finish reading my book today, but I'll have time later. Show me your outfits, Ezzy."

"Why don't you read it to me while I try on clothes?" he responds.

"Oh, yeah, that'll be fun! Do you like cozy murder...," her voice trails off as they leave the room together. Adley giggles. That same giggle she makes when he fawns affection on her. I grimace at the sound and stop scrubbing. I try to will myself to follow. I want to lie on the bed with her, watching him change his clothes, too. But I can't move. The storm in my head is raging.

"Useless. Burden. A waste of money," a familiar voice screams in my head, a ghostly amalgamation of my father and my own.

I shake my head, trying to clear the screaming from within and continue scrubbing.

=^..^= ♥ =^..^=

Adley and Ezra enter the living room where I've been cleaning surfaces for a while. I've been scrubbing the same spot on an end table, lost in my racing thoughts.

"Dude, I think you got it," Ezra says from behind me. I startle at his voice.

"Marshall, do you mind if we sit in here? I want to light a fire, get a glass of wine, and curl up with my book," Adley says as she slowly enters the room.

Ezra, a stark contrast to Adley's demure sensibilities, leaps over the couch and flops onto it. He puts his arms behind his head and closes his eyes, content.

"Oh, no, that's fine, Adley," I say with a small smile to her. "I was going to vacuum now. I can do another room if you want to be in here. Um, where's the vacuum?"

"It's in the hall closet. But why don't you sit with me and read that book you got?" she says coyly.

You mean the one you got me? The one I need to pay you back for?

I stand frozen in indecision, looking at them. I want to sit with them and cuddle by the fire. Ezra is looking at me, waiting to hear what I say. His smile is bright and beautiful.

"Ummm… after I vacuum?" I say as a question.

"Okay, sure…," Adley says, and the disappointment in her eyes makes me want to hug her and tell her I'm sorry. Instead, I go to the hall closet.

=^..^= ♥ =^..^=

Adley is whispering, reading from an e-reader out loud, while Ezra rests with his head on her lap. The fire roars behind them, and they look like such a perfect couple. She strokes his hair, and he purrs contently. The sound of his purr triggers my instinct to purr, too, but I repress it. I need to finish this first, and then I can be with them.

I've been lugging the vacuum around the house for a long time. The sun is setting outside the open window, but the illumination of the setting sun and fire on their faces is beautiful. It gets dark so early here. What is this fucking place? Why would anyone choose to live somewhere so dark and cold?

I have attacked every dust bunny in this house, real or perceived. The only room left is this one. My anxiety is mounting. If I can just finish this one room, I can relax. They've made a bit of a mess in the room. Some of Ezra's stuff is thrown on the couch. There's a drink on the coffee table—not under a coaster.

I enter the room so Adley can see me, and she smiles. "Hey, Marshall! Are you done now?" she asks hopefully.

Ezra dreamily lifts his head and looks at me, his eyes hooded in contentment.

"Um, almost," I say and hurriedly tidy up the space—placing the drink on a coaster.

"I just… need to do this room."

"Oh," Adley says dejectedly. "Um, I guess we can go into the other room. But after, will you hang out with us?"

"Yes," I say, standing stiffly.

"Okay, umm, let me just put out this fire real quick," Adley says, standing. Ezra rubs the sleep from his eyes and sits cross-legged on the couch. He rubs his hands over his ears a few times, waking himself up.

I rush to Adley and stop her as she opens the fireplace. "Let me get that for you," I say.

"Um, okay," she says and reluctantly moves out of the way.

"After this, I'll make everyone dinner! How about salmon tonight!"

"That sounds nice, Marshall. But really, I can do some of this. You should relax, too. I'd like to spend some time together."

"No, no, it's okay! You have to work tomorrow. I don't! You should get all the rest you can today," I say and push her gently, indicating that she should go into the other room and rest.

I put out the fire and rush to the vacuum in the hall while I wait for the embers to cool. I lug it into the room. Ezra stands sleepily from his spot. Adley is gathering her things.

"Let's go into the bedroom, Ezra," Adley says softly.

"Oh, yeah," he says, ears perking up. "You coming, Marshall?"

"No, I have to finish this up," I say, leaning over to plug it in and not looking back. This is my way of contributing and showing gratitude without finding the right words. I've never been great with people and never been great with words. But I am good at getting shit done.

"I put all your clothes away. The bed's cleared off now," Ezra says, standing still and looking at me. What does he want? He's in my way. I can't do my work if he's standing there.

"Uh, thanks," I say. Why is he telling me this?

"Do you want to come lay with us, Marshall?" he asks.

"I need to finish this up. Then I'm going to make dinner," I say and avert my eyes, not wanting to look at him. I'm a little taller than he, but it feels like he's towering over me as he stands there.

Adley holds her wine and e-reader in her hand and looks like she wants to say something but doesn't.

"Dude, relax. Come lay with us." Ezra reaches for the vacuum as if to take it from me.

"Don't!" I yell and hiss, my ears back. Snatching it backward.

He pauses in shock. His tail bushes up behind him in a way that accentuates its beauty. He's so beautiful, but right now, his beauty infuriates me.

"Just because you are okay with being a fucking useless mooch doesn't mean I am okay with it! We have to pay her back," I say, wrapping the vacuum cord in my hand.

"Fuck you, Marshall," Ezra says and walks out of the room.

I follow him, wanting to apologize but not sure how to.

He turns into his ailo form and leaps on the bed. He begins pumping at the bed, picking the fabric with his claws.

His clothes lay in a pile on the floor outside the bedroom door. He is so messy. He's left stuff all over the house all day. "You are so messy! I'm going to be cleaning up after you the rest of our fucking lives?" I yell to him. He whips his attention to me.

"Dude, you're the one who's assigned that role to yourself. Don't blame me for how you chose to deal with your anxiety!"

"It's not like you'd fucking do it! All you're good for is to look at and fuck. Just because you're only able to pay her back with your dick and your smile doesn't mean I can't be more useful," I say.

Adley gasps behind me. She couldn't hear Ezra's side of the conversation, but she could hear mine. And it's not like he said anything to merit that from me.

Ezra looks at me long and hard. His eyes squint, and it seems like he may attack me. Instead, he gracefully glides to the floor, silently transforms into his anthro form, and walks toward me. Is he going to hit me? When he gets to the door, he stops and slams it, blocking my view of him. Adley yelps at the noise, and I am startled, as well.

Why did I say that? I can't believe I said that. It's unfair of me to use what I know about him—what I know will hurt him—to hurt him. He doesn't even know that I know his greatest insecurities.

Adley looks to the ground and sniffles. Is she crying? A tear rolls down her cheek as she clenches and unclenches her fists. She says meekly, "I don't know what to say. I'm sorry that buying you things has made you feel so stressed, but... please don't project your feelings onto Ezra. What you said to him was cruel and untrue. I got those things for the two of you because I wanted to. It made me happy to help you."

"I don't want your help," I snap. Adley jumps at the sound of my voice. Fuck, I scared her. I can't believe I'm yelling at my mate. My beautiful, sensitive mate. More tears escape her eyes. "I... I didn't mean it like that. I'm sorry, that was—" I say, reaching towards her.

She cuts me off and moves away from me, avoiding my touch. She doesn't look at me when she says, "I'm going to rest with Ezra. Once you've calmed down, feel free to join us." She cracks the bedroom door and slides into the room.

21

ADLEY

I gently close the door behind me. Ezra is nowhere to be found. I scan the room. "Ezra?" I know he came in here. Where'd he go?

Still sniffling, I look in the closet. "Ezra?" I hear a tiny "mew" from under the bed.

I get on my knees and spot him hunched under the bed. "Oh, hi. Are you okay?"

"Mew," he responds.

"That sounds like a no."

He slinks out from under the bed and leaps on top of it. He transforms into his anthro form, naked, and pulls a blanket over himself. He's not one to typically cover himself, so he must be feeling horrible.

"You okay?" I ask.

"Yeah, what he said just really hit a nerve."

I sit next to him with only a little space between us. I want to place my hand on his leg, but I'm unsure if that's the right thing to do at this moment. "Yeah, it was really cruel. To be clear. I don't think of you like that, Ezra."

He looks at me, the sadness in his eyes still glistening, but a small smirk tugs at the corner of his mouth. "Thanks," he mumbles. We sit quietly for a moment. I'm not sure what to do or say. "Um, can I have a hug?" he asks.

"Of course," I say. I go to hug him, but he beats me to it. He grabs me and pulls me close to him. The hug is awkward and clumsy, so we fall over. For the first time, Ezra does not get hard against me. We just lay like this, hugging silently.

"Being only good for my looks… for sex. That just hits my deepest insecurities," he mumbles into my chest.

I pull back to look at him while he continues, "I'm sure you figured it out by now, and Marshall has said as much, but yeah, my family is extremely well off." He pauses and thinks about what to say next. "My parents were…" He pauses and gets choked up. Anguish contorts his face, and my heart sinks for him. I don't want him to tell me if it will hurt him.

"You don't have to tell me. It's okay, Ezra," I say, wiping the hair from his eyes.

He smiles that sad smile I'm learning he wears when he's not putting on a show. "They weren't cruel, exactly, but they were extremely absent. I was always alone. With only staff taking care of me. The staff wasn't allowed to hug or talk to me about anything other than 'essential functions.'"

"Oh, Ezra," I say and pet his ear the way I have seen him do to himself when he appears anxious and doesn't know anyone is looking.

His face melts as he nuzzles into my hand. "I was so lonely. I only ever saw them on TV or in magazines. They were constantly photographed attending parties and fundraisers or awards shows, so that's how I knew them. Whenever my parents did come home, I would get so excited. I'd have all my school papers on the dining room table and ready to show them. When they were gone, I'd study really hard. I learned different hobbies I thought would make them proud. I'd have all my work laid out, waiting for them. They would barely stop to look at it. They'd barely look at me. They'd just flit to their room, get a change of clothes, and run right out the door."

"I've always been...," he pauses, "attractive." He sounds as if he's ashamed of his looks, which is the exact opposite of what I'd expect of him. Is his appreciation of his looks a facade, too?

"The only thing my mom would ever compliment me on was 'my beautiful tail.' Long hair is kind of rare—a genetic mutation. Neither of my parents has it. Sometimes, my mom would stop, look at me, really look at me, and say, 'We gotta get you into modeling. That tail is beautiful.'" He pulls his tail to his chest, hugging it.

"I realized the only thing I'd ever be good for was to look at."

"Oh, Ezra. That's not true. It's just not," I say, tears building in my eyes.

"One hobby I got really into was making clothes. I was sewing. And knitting. And crocheting. I started by altering my clothes. If looking good was all I was good for, I'd ensure I always looked my best. My dad discouraged it. He said it made me a pussy. I still hoped my mom might find a reason to appreciate me since she showed some interest in my modeling career—a model herself. She got me an agent and seemed genuinely proud when she introduced me to her modeling contacts. It was the first time my mom had ever done anything with me. We were starting to feel like an actual family. At least, I thought we were."

He sighs. "When I was about seventeen, I was watching an interview with my mother, who was dazzling at a fundraiser. She was wearing a scarf I had crocheted. I don't know how she got it. For the first time, I felt like my mom would be proud of me for something other than my looks. I've never felt like that before. I was so proud to see her wear it. Then… the interviewer asked her where she got the scarf. She said," he gulps. "'Oh, this old thing? I don't know. I just found it lying around the house. I think it's a Seybon,' and she laughed." He wipes his face on the bed. "Anyway, that's when I knew I'd never be good enough for my mother. I moved out that day. They never even called to find out where I had gone." His tears stream faster now.

"Oh, Ezra," I grab his head and hold it to my chest.

"So, for him to say that… it's just so…," his shoulders shake as the tears come more freely.

"I tried to get the world to love me. It wasn't hard. I just put on the face they wanted. I have a knack for figuring out what version of myself people want. So, I found love from my fans. I know they don't love the real me—the me who likes puns and crocheting despite it being a girly thing. I know as long as I'm pretty and as long as I say what they want to hear, they'll love me."

That explains the constant personality change in the mall.

"Ezra, you don't have to do that for me. You can let your guard down. The puns are cheesy sometimes, but I like them," I laugh.

He laughs, "Thanks, Adley."

"There… there's something else I should probably tell you. This is hard. Marshall wasn't lying when he called me a fuckboy. I have been. I use sex to make women fall in love with me. I know I do it. As Marshall already told you, my girlfriend, Sarah, tried to kill me. And…"

He's stammering, struggling to spit this out. I know he wants to talk about it, but I can tell it's hard, "Ezra, it's okay. You can tell me whatever you need to," I pet his head, and he nuzzles into my neck.

"Adley, thank you for not pushing me to talk about why she pushed me. I've had to think about it the last few days and have been avoiding it, but I… I need to tell you. I never cheated on her. I promise you, I've never cheated on a girlfriend, but she was mad at me for flirting with other women," he hugs his tail tighter and moves closer to me, hiding his face from mine. His breath warms my chest as he lies there silently. I wait for him to continue because he doesn't seem done, especially when the sobs get harder.

"I loved her. I loved her so much. She wasn't my fated mate or anything, but I thought she was the one I could commit myself to. She just couldn't understand my desire to make everyone like me. And I don't know how else to make them. I've got nothing else that anyone wants from me. To be fair, I never… I never told her this stuff… I never told her about my parents or how I need people to love me."

More sobs. I know the memory of his attempted murder is painful for him, "Right before she pushed me, she said the world didn't need any more roses—pretty to look at but painful to love. I know she and Marshall are right. All I have to offer this world is my face and body. It's painful to love me—because I need too much attention, I will desperately try to get it however I can.

"But, Adley, I promise, I talk to other women but don't even see them. The only woman I see is you. My eyes, my heart, my body, they belong to you. And if you want me to change. If you want me to be more serious, less extra, to be… anything. I'll do it. I'll do it for you. I'll do whatever I gotta do to make you keep looking at me. To keep hugging me. I think your adoration will be enough for me."

I hug him close to me, unsure what to say. Uncertain if there is anything to say. I go with wordplay because I think he'll like it, "I promise to help you see how much I adore-ley you." I cringe because I thought that would sound a lot better.

"Did you just combine your name with the word adore?" he asks, stunned at how an educated woman can say something so stupid.

"Yeah, I know you're more of a pun guy, but I thought maybe you'd enjoy any kind of wordplay," I respond cringing.

"I mean, I would have maybe gone with Adl-oration," he quips, "but, yeah, it doesn't roll off the tongue."

"I'm sorry, your Ez-ellence. Not all of us were gifted with a portmanteau-y name," I respond, kissing the top of his head.

"Oh, I like that one. You're Adl-orable," he sniffles and laughs, his tears drying up.

"I've got a whole bunch, Ez-uberance, Ez-traordinary, pretty much any word that starts with e-x I've got in my back pocket just waiting to throw at you," I laugh.

He laughs and wipes his tears. He then goes to kiss me on the lips, but I turn my face, so the kiss lands on my cheek. He looks at me, hurt.

"Um, while we're revealing things about ourselves. I… I don't like being kissed on the mouth. It grosses me out. I… I like it if I'm really horny or drunk, but I don't like it usually. I also… I also don't like to be touched too much and generally prefer to sit by myself. I like hugging, but after a while, it gets to be too much, and I need to get away. Only my cat could touch me for prolonged periods. I don't know why that was okay."

He looks at me, and I know where this is going. He's going to tell me I'm crazy. Tell me I need to let him touch me and kiss me the way he wants to touch and kiss me that I need to get over it.

But instead, he says, "Okay, I understand."

I'm shocked. He didn't take it personally.

"You don't mind?" I ask in complete shock.

He responds, "I mean, I like kissing on the mouth—a lot. But, as long as I can still do it when we're having sex, I can live without it. I'm a touchy guy, and I won't be perfect at upholding this boundary, but please let me know if I'm bothering you, and I'll stop."

"You, you don't take it personally?" I ask.

"Why would I? I've been watching you, and I can tell you have sensory issues. That's not about me. It's about you. If I want to be with you, I have to interact with you in a way that's comfortable to you. Do people normally take it personally?"

"Yeah, they kind of do…," I say, trailing off. He looks angry that anyone would do such a thing. But doesn't say anything. It just looks like he's reflecting for a minute. His ears tilt to the side, deep in thought.

He startles, ears facing me, and perks up. "Shit. You have problems with loud noises!"

"Yeah…"

"Oh, Adley. I'm sorry I slammed the door. I won't do that again. I'll be Ez-tra careful," he says, nuzzling into my chest, and purring.

I'm dumbfounded. How did he know exactly what to say? How is he so perfect? Bryce would slam every door and cabinet in the house. We wouldn't even be fighting, and he'd just slam things shut. Always. He'd try to say it was because his muscles couldn't be gentle or some other stupid excuse. Or he'd say I was being crazy. I was being super sensitive. Or that he wasn't slamming the doors. And I needed to stop using my autism and sensory issues as an excuse to try to make him feel bad. I've spent so much time blaming myself, thinking something was wrong with me. It was my fault for not being able to adjust myself to meet others. I never thought they might do a little of the same for me.

"Thank you, Ezra," I say with a smile. "It's nice to be… accommodated."

He looks at me like that's a weird thing to say. "Of course I'm going to ad-ccommodate you—sorry, that's the last one. You're my mate. I will do anything for you."

MARSHALL

It's been a while. I put my ear against the door, and it sounds like they're watching TV now. Maybe I can go in.

I knock on the bedroom door, and Adley is under the blankets, leaning against the headboard. Ezra is in his ailo form, curled up in her lap. They're watching some animation. I stop and stare at it. On the TV, a young man with orange hair and a young girl with brown hair are talking. She touches him, and he transforms into an ailo! No, a cat. She freaks out and picks him up.

"What is this?!" I ask.

"*Fruits Basket*," Adley says.

Ezra responds, "It's my favorite show here."

"What did he say?" Adley asks.

"That it's his favorite show."

Adley, excited, begins to rant, "Oh, really?! I love it, too. It's why I had that shirt I gave you. This is the original version of the show. It doesn't actually finish the manga. There's a new version, though, that does."

Ezra looks at her and transforms. "Wait, what? There's another version. There's a manga?"

"Yeah, and a movie too. I've got them all. I actually have the collector's editions of the show on Blu-ray."

Ezra looks at me as if he wants to say something. Like he wants to share his excitement with me and joke with me, but he remembers he's mad at me, deflates, and tells Adley, "That's awesome." He grabs his clothes from the floor by his feet and starts putting them on.

I swallow. "Ezra, I'm sorry. That was really shitty of me. I shouldn't have said that."

He looks at me, his lips pursed. "It was shitty."

"I get… anxious."

"No shit."

"I have never lived with anyone before. I don't know how to act. I'm not good with people. I tend to lash out when I'm anxious."

He just stares at me, arms crossed.

"I will work on it. I promise," I say and look down.

"Okay," he says.

"And Adley, I'm sorry to you, too. I see how yelling and loud noises bother you. I will be better."

"Thank you, Marshall," she says quietly. "Would you like to watch this with us?" she asks.

"Um, what's happening?" I ask.

Adley begins, pointing at the girl on the screen, "Well, Toru is an orphaned girl who—"

"Babe, sorry to interrupt, but let's just start the series over for him," Ezra says.

"You sure?" she asks. "I don't mind. I've seen it a million times already."

"Yeah, that's fine," he says with a smirk. Then, he jumps into bed in his ailo form, leaving his clothes back in the same heap.

"I'll pick those up later," he tells me in his ailo form.

"Oh, uh, okay," I say and walk to the other side of the bed.

"And the next time you yell at Adley, you will be fucking sorry, bro. So get your shit together." Adley strokes his head, unaware of the threat he just said to me.

22

EZRA

Adley's alarm blares, and I instantly wake, leaping from her chest and transforming into my anthro form. I get on my knees so my face is next to hers and shout, "Wake up, beautiful!" kissing her on the cheek multiple times.

"So, you're a morning person?" she says, rubbing her eyes.

"Not really. I'm just excited to see you work!"

"Ezra, you can't, like, watch me work all day," Adley says.

"Sure I can!" I say. And kiss her again. She grimaces. "Is it my breath?" I say, breathing into my hand.

"Ha, no, it's just a lot to wake up to, is all."

"Oh, am I being extra?" I ask.

"Yeah, but it's okay. I just need some coffee."

"Already on it," I hear from behind me. Marshall is holding a tray of food and wearing the frilly pink apron.

"Dude, why are you wearing that apron again?"

"I don't want to mess up these nice clothes you picked out for me," he says with decidedly less acid than he usually speaks to me. I look at him incredulously, why's he being nice? He strolls in and puts the tray table in front of Adley. "Breakfast in bed? A girl can get used to this," she says, reaching for the coffee and sipping it gently. "Thank you so much, Marshall."

I stand and face him. He looks… good. Fully groomed. Fully dressed. Did he actually use that lotion I've been nagging him about? "How long have you been awake?" I ask him.

"A while. I don't sleep well," he says with a shrug. Interesting. I hadn't really noticed. Every night he has gotten into bed opposite Adley at arm's length from us and in his anthro form. I'm one of those "falls asleep as soon as his head hits the pillow" (in this case, Adley's tits or ass) kind of guys. But does he lie next to us, stiff as a board, trying to sleep each night?

Adley brings a forkful of omelets to her mouth before pausing. It really is all he can make, huh? "There's no cat food in it this time," Marshall says.

"Thanks, Marshall!" she says and slowly places it in her mouth. The way she eats is adorable—tiny tentative bites, as if she's scared whatever she's eating is going to turn on her at any minute. Unless she's drunk. When she's drunk she shovels food into her mouth the same way Marshall and I do, as if she's experiencing the food for the first time and letting the sensation fully take over.

Marshall leans on the doorframe, arms crossed with a level of casualness I don't think I've ever seen in him. What's up with this fucking guy? His personality is as inconsistent as mine when I'm schmoozing at a party. He did seem last night like he resolved to relax a bit. Maybe this is him trying to relax.

Well, if that's the case, it's working. He looks relaxed and cool and kinda hot. It's fucking annoying. I consider how I must look comparatively. I can't have Marshall strutting around all day showing me up. I need to go get cleaned up and dressed.

"I made one for you. It's on the kitchen table. It does have cat food in it," he says with a smirk.

"Really?!" I say excitedly. "Fuck yeah," And start for the kitchen.

"Ezra, don't you want to put on some clothes?" Adley asks.

"Why? No one's here," I shout back halfway down the hallway.

"The idea of you sitting on everything, bare-assed, is…" Adley says.

"But it's okay in my ailo form?" I ask.

"Please don't ask me philosophical questions this early in the morning," Adley laughs.

I don't particularly understand what she's talking about, and I assume that will be the case with our conversations quite often. Let's face it, she's way smarter than me. And she comes from a completely different world than I do. I don't know if this request is because she's a human or because she's got her own unique hangups, but I won't argue with her. "Alright, babe," I respond. Whatever my mate wants my mate will get.

I open the closet and check out my new outfits. I have to pick something nice just in case one of Adley's coworkers catches a glimpse of me. I look back at Marshall. I also gotta look better than that dude.

"So, what are y'all up to today?" Adley asks, taking a bite of her eggs. Oh, was she serious about me not watching her work all day? I guess I could find something to do.

"I was thinking of doing some things around the house…" Marshall says, but before Adley can protest, he says, "But I was also thinking of doing some research. I'd really like to learn more about this world. Is there a library near here I could walk to?"

"Well, you could maybe walk to the library. It's kinda far, and it's super cold outside. I could take you after work. Or, you could borrow the car," she says with a glint in her eye, obviously recalling the last time Marshall drove.

"I don't know if I feel comfortable driving without someone who has a license," Marshall says, "I'll just look for stuff online."

Not to be shown up, I respond, "I'm going to do some research, too. I was planning to watch some TV, start checking out the various fashion sites, and learn about what's cool here. Get that Instagram thing…"

ADLEY

"Babe, you have too many serums. This is going to kill your moisture barrier," Ezra says, looking at the various items I have laid on the counter. He picks them up individually and inspects them, shaking his head.

"Oh?" I say through the buzzing of the toothbrush in my mouth.

"Yeah," he says, looking a little confused. He gets in my face and asks, "How old are you?"

Why is he asking me this? I pop the toothbrush out and turn it off and it gently sprays us in the face. "Sorry. Um, I'm 34. Why? Do I look old?"

"What?! Absolutely not! I was just wondering why you thought you needed these things. Your skin looks fantastic," he responds, but the way he scrutinizes my face makes me think he doesn't think my skin looks fantastic. Is the honeymoon phase of this whole fated mate attraction wearing off already?

I look at the line of admittedly too many products, ready to justify every overpriced purchase. "Well, that one is for pores, that one is for blemishes, that one is for texture, that one is for wrinkles, that one is for discoloration, and then these are for hydration."

"And what about all the stuff in the cabinet?"

"Umm, that's my night routine."

"I haven't seen you do any of this since I've been here," he asks, confused.

"Oh, well, yeah, I was too tired." Fuck. I've missed a few days of the routine—too tired from all the fucking to spend the time necessary to complete all the steps. My skin is just going to look like shit now. I frown and inspect my face in the mirror. He moves his face next to mine and continues to look at me in the mirror. To say his skin is flawless would be an understatement. Does his body fucking rebuild every skin cell with each transformation? Do Ailura men even have pores?!

"So you do all these in the morning," he says, motioning to the lineup on the counter, "and all these at night?" he continues, motioning to the open cabinet.

"Yeah…"

"Adley! You're putting three different retinoids on your face and combining a retinoid with vitamin C. And you don't have sunscreen in the lot?!" He looks at me like I've lost my mind. Have I?

"What? I only have one retinol—"

"Retinoid, babes. This acne cream is vitamin A—it's a retinoid. Also, AHA is a retinoid. Then, there's this retinol, which is obviously a retinoid. Oh my gosh, this has retinol in it, too," he says, gesturing to each product.

"They are?!" He looked at these bottles for 30 seconds before spotting all the conflicting ingredients. What is he, a fucking face chemist? Maybe that's why his face looks flawless.

"This is terrible. I can't believe you have any skin left on your face. How long have you been doing this?" he says, getting even more in my face and peering at it with one eye closed. He thinks I'm gross, doesn't he? He's finding every clogged pore, line, and spot.

"Um, not long. I've been adding things gradually. Bryce told me I—"

He cuts me off. "Well, we all know he's an asshat, so let's not concern ourselves with whatever he said… let me guess. You started doing this one, and your skin got dry, so you added this one. Then your texture probably got wonky, so you added this one, then you needed some more moisture," he says, pointing at the different products, "and with each product you added, you'd look great for a few weeks only to find a new thing to fix?"

I guess it did happen that way. Have I really been sabotaging my skin? That can't be. My skin was shit before I started all this. It looks better now! "Yeah…" I say dejected, not sure if I'm buying my own bullshit at this point but not ready to cave, "My skin is just really problematic, and I'm getting so old—"

"Ads, babe, you don't need all this stuff," he says, gently stroking my face. He doesn't honestly believe that. He's just saying this to be nice.

"But…I have wrinkles and this sunspot here, and my pores are large…" I say with tears building in my eyes. *I'm hideous. Why is he saying all this to me?*

"None of those things are true," he says, wiping the tear from my eye with his thumb.

"Because I use all these products," I say, still reluctant to admit he's right.

"Babe, trust me. I know this stuff. All you need is this and this: a cleanser and a moisturizer. You are so beautiful, and you have good skin—it's just a little dehydrated from all this stuff. I cannot let you treat this beautiful face like this a moment longer. Trust me. Do just these for a week, and you'll see that all this stuff is drying you out."

I let the tears fall to my face. Do tears moisturize because that's been a part of my skincare routine for a long time? "Do you truly think so?"

"Well, technically, we need one more thing?" he responds. Here it comes; he will point out a flaw and tell me how to fix it. *Brace yourself, Adley.* I tense, ready for him to rip into me.

"We need to get you sunscreen. We need to protect that beautiful face, not harm it. You can use mine today." He grabs a bottle from the cabinet, pushes my bottles to the side, and sets it in their place.

What? Why would I need sunscreen? "But I don't go outside…"

"I hate to break it to you, babe, but you need sunscreen indoors."

"That can't be true," I say incredulously. Why the fuck would I need to protect myself from the sun inside?

"Babe, that computer you stare at all day is putting harmful light on your face," he says with a kiss on the tip of my nose.

"Oh, I almost forgot this," I say, laughing and reaching for my birth control.

"What's that?" Ezra asks.

"It's birth control. I have no idea if you two can knock me up, and I don't really want to find out right now. That's a conversation for a much later date. Besides, I get super bad periods if I'm not on this, and my PMS is terrible."

"Babe, I have no idea what the fuck you're talking about," he says, looking at me like I grew a second head.

"Um, you don't know what birth control is?"

"No," he responds as flatly as Marshall would.

"It stops you from getting pregnant," I respond.

"Why would you need that?"

"So I don't get pregnant," I state, knowing that I am not giving sufficient information but also lost on how to.

"But…," he screws up his face, "it's the winter."

"So…," I respond, hoping he will elaborate.

"You can get pregnant during the winter?!" he exclaims, backing away from me as if he could be accidentally impregnating me right now.

"I can get pregnant pretty much any time. Well, specifically, there's a window each month, but —"

"Each month?!" he doubles over as if I kicked him in the balls.

"Yeah, um…"

"Your mating season is every month?!"

"You have a mating season?"

"Yeah," he says incredulously.

Instead of continuing this weird game of misunderstanding, I'll just ask him, "Can you explain mating season to me—like the way you'd explain it to a kid?"

"Well, when a man and a woman love eac—"

"Not like that, goof! Explain it mechanically."

"Um…I think I need an assist with this one…," he says, then shouts, "Marshall!" his voice reverberates in my ears, and I cup them even though it accomplishes nothing.

"Fuck, sorry, babe. I'll get better at this."

Marshall appears in the doorway, "What?"

"Can you explain our mating season to her?" Ezra asks.

"Why?" Marshall asks, looking between the two of us.

"Long story short: we found ourselves a mate who can get pregnant year-round and doesn't have a mating season," Ezra says.

"WHAT?!" Marshall's tail sticks up right behind him. "Are you pregnant right now?" he asks me.

"No, I take these," I say, waving my pills at him.

"What are those?!" Marshall asks.

I sigh, really not wanting to explain this again, but knowing I have to anyway, "They stop me from getting pregnant. I'll explain how my stuff works, but first, I want to learn how yours works."

"Well, February is the only month we can procreate. The ovulation of female Ailura can only be induced during that time," Marshall responds.

"What do you mean, induced? How is it induced?" I ask.

"By orgasm," Marshall responds.

"So, I'm guessing Ailura doesn't have periods then, huh?"

"I do not know what that means. We have punctuation if that's what you're asking, but based on context, I do not think it is," Marshall answers.

I groan loudly, feeling utterly defeated by what I must do now. "Fuck, y'all are not gonna like what I have to tell you about my reproductive system…"

=^..^= ♥ =^..^=

After explaining the basics to them and giving them some words to look up on the internet, we leave the bathroom. Marshall quietly strolls to his couch, picking up his turned-over Roman Empire book. I'm happy to see he's been reading it. Ezra leaps over the back of the other couch, flopping onto it. He pulls out his phone and holds it over his head while he taps away at it—probably googling menstruation. Even though Marshall is on the opposite couch, he's thoroughly jostled by the entrance.

"Hey, babe! Why do they call it Google?" Ezra asks.

"Um, I don't know, you should Google it," I laugh. "I'm guessing you don't have Google…"

"No, we have Purruse," Marshall says, "Works the same, though. Even has the same color scheme."

"I have to log into work in about fifteen minutes. I need a few quiet minutes to prepare myself for the day, so I'm going to go into my office. Do y'all need anything from me?" I ask.

Ezra is making kissy faces and victory signs at the camera of his phone, obviously taking selfies and appreciating the effect of gravity on his jawline while he lies on the couch—his head on the same frilly pillow that once covered his dick.

"Um… could I use your laptop?" Marshall asks.

"Oh, yeah, just a sec," I grab my pink laptop bag from under the side table and hand it to Marshall. "You can use these. The password is 1234."

"Really, babe?" Ezra asks, "I thought you were, like, a computer nerd. You should know better. Wait! Unless cyber security isn't a thing here!"

"One: I am not a computer nerd. I am a code nerd. A video game code nerd, to be precise. We don't necessarily care about cybersecurity or even how computers work. Two: I don't take that thing anywhere; it stays here. So, who am I trying to secure it against?"

"Okay, babe, whatever you say," he laughs at me.

"Here's the remote," I say as I toss the TV controller to him. It hits him in the gut. He exaggerates the damage it does to him.

"Babe, don't go throwing stuff at me just because you have no concern for your own data protection," he laughs.

"Anyway. I'll have lunch at twelve. Let's all eat together, okay?"

"Oh, yeah, that will be nice," Marshall smiles at me.

"I'll see you at noon!" I say.

"Have a good day, babe!" Ezra shouts as I retreat to my office, closing the door behind me and dreading the day a little less than usual.

=^..^= ♥ =^..^=

I close the door behind me and attempt to mentally prepare myself for the shit show that tends to be my workday.

My office has two desks: my personal desk and my work desk. My work desk has two monitors and a shitty laptop forced upon me by my company's cyber security team—so they can spy on me between the hours of 9 to 5. I guess they gotta make sure I'm not dicking around, getting paid to do my laundry or something. It's also a way to ensure I can't disseminate the company secrets no one actually wants.

I grimace at the desk next to it. It's shrouded in darkness, just like my hopes and dreams. *Symbolic.* When in use, the three monitors and drawing tablet illuminate the space. The desktop tower next to the monitors has clear glass that exposes the various RGB-lit components. Even the keyboard, mouse, and speakers light up. When it's on, it looks like a unicorn has blown its bright, sparkly rainbow load all over it. Now, it's just the carcass of a unicorn; its horn sawed off, and all the color drained from it.

I use that desk to work on my personal projects. Its powerful processor and graphics card make the resource-intensive part of game development much more bearable. Unlike my shitty work laptop that makes me sit and watch it chug as it melts my desk's surface and sounds like a vibrator working overtime. Whatever. If they want to pay me to sit and watch the game development equivalent of paint drying—compiling—that's their prerogative.

Despite the darkness in which my desktop computer sits, from this angle, the light hits it just right, revealing the word "Fuck" written in cursive in the layer of dust on the drawing tablet. This was a result of my getting drunk and considering turning the machine on one night. Instead, I got overwhelmed, laid on the ground, and cried. At least the word looks pretty. And people say cursive writing is a useless skill.

Figures from all my favorite anime and video games litter the pink-painted room in what could probably be described as girly otaku dopamine decor. Each figure smiles at me, trying to bring just a little bit of joy to my bleak existence. Unfortunately, they are unsuccessful in their quests.

I fling open the curtains for a few minutes of sunshine before I eventually darken the room again. The crystals hanging from my window sway back and forth. Maybe I'll leave the window open today. Let them catch the sun in the afternoon. I touch my face, acknowledging the sunscreen Ezra slathered on it. I suppose he was right that I get some sun during the day. I laugh as I recall the way he pinned me against the counter and insisted on applying it for me while he ground against my leg.

I pop my AirPods into my ears and open my "Bad Bitch Energy" playlist on Spotify. It primarily features strong, sexually empowered female rappers. I let their words of feminine world domination and sexual freedom seep into my body. This ritual is necessary to hype myself up enough to sit down and log into my work computer. Otherwise, the dread will fully set in.

I sway to the music and mumble the lyrics. I hope Megan Thee Stallion is out there having the best fucking day because her music is often the only thing that can get me through mine. She is a true gift to this world and my muse. I close my eyes, try to internalize her lyrics, and attempt to convince myself I am even marginally as hot and powerful as she is.

My inner boss bitch channeled; I sit at my work desk and remove my AirPods. I need absolute quiet to work.

I enter my password that is entirely too fucking long, thanks to the company's excessive security concerns. I really give zero fucks about cyber security. I know, I know it's important, but I can't bring myself to add it to the ever-expanding list of things I care about.

My impatience swells as the machine takes forever to boot up—slowed not just by its own inefficiency but by the millions of background tasks needed to let my company monitor every keystroke. If my personal desk is the carcass of a unicorn, my work desk is the cage the unicorn was held in until its brutal demise. And I know I'm overextending the metaphor here, but this shitty fucking laptop was probably the saw that took off the unicorn's horn.

I have no drawing tablet at this desk because all I do at work is code—I gotta stay in my lane—and don't get the opportunity to be even remotely creative or "arty." Which is fine, I guess; it's not like I'm artistically talented or anything. Nope, my skills lie in my ability to see the intricate weaving of systems and code. My work towards this game lies on the "backend" spectrum. I make the foundation that allows the rest of the game to work. I do the lame shit that most people think is automatic, but it actually takes a fuck-ton of work—like save systems. When a character in a game I've worked on does something cool, I likely had nothing to do with that. But, if his save data boots up correctly, I probably had something to do with that.

John Carmack, who transitioned from the aerospace industry to the gaming one, claimed that making games is more challenging than rocket science. I don't know about that, but sometimes I think about that quote and wonder if maybe I should have been a rocket scientist instead. More prestige and less brain work? Yes, please. But my code only has the ability to accidentally bleep a video game character out of existence. I don't know if I could handle the pressure of writing code that could determine if a billion-dollar rocket (possibly containing humans) blew up.

My computer is finally functional and done chugging through its multitude of startup processes. So, it's time to get to work and reach the intense level of compartmentalization necessary to achieve any task. I spend the first thirty minutes of the day replying to emails, reviewing my calendar and tasks, and trying not to cry.

I've got thirty minutes until my first meeting: daily standup. I open the game engine and code editor, ready to tackle today's task. A boisterous laughter booms from the other side of the door, distracting me. *Ezra.* I refocus and get back into the groove, only to hear the boom of two male voices and the banging of pots. *What the fuck are they doing?*

"Focus, Adley," I mutter and retrace my mental steps, shifting back to the appropriate context. A message pings on Slack, snapping my attention to my other monitor. I groan and check the message. It's nothing, just a coworker making a joke about something I don't even get. As one of the only fully remote team members, I don't understand most of their inside jokes. Another alert chimes, letting me know I only have five minutes until my meetings. Fuck, I've been so distracted I haven't accomplished anything.

I shut the curtains, enveloping the room back in the darkness. Every day, I consider leaving these curtains open, and every day I don't. The relative inner peace I achieved before logging into my computer is gone, and I need to reduce as many stimuli as possible. So, that means bye-bye, bright light. Bye-bye, vitamin D. I go to the restroom across the hall and check out my face while I wash my hands. *Hmm, my skin does look better.*

I wander into the kitchen to refill my water. There is a soft rustling of pages from the living room, where Marshall has surrounded himself with various books and gadgets. He sits bolt upright with a semicircle of academic-appearing paraphernalia surrounding him. It covers the couch and the tables. He is completely absorbed, with a scholarly concentration. In direct contrast, as everything they do seems to be, Ezra sits on the opposite couch, lazily looking at his phone. Ezra spots me and leaps up from his languid position, "Babes! Are you done for the day?"

"Of course, she's not. It's only been an hour," Marshall says, annoyed.

"Oh," Ezra says sadly. He peps up, jumping from his seat. "Check this out, Ads!" he says, dashing toward me, holding out his phone. My water bottle is almost full. I check my watch. I have two minutes. I need to get back into my office.

"I'm sorry, Ez, but I have a meeting I need to get to," I say.

"Well, this will only take a minute."

Panic sets in. The idea of being late gnaws at me and pulls me toward my office door. "I'm sorry, I have to go. Show me later, okay?" I say and slink back to the office, shutting the door pretty much in his face. I imagine him sitting at my door, sad and rejected. I feel bad but don't know what I can do about it in this instance. So I sit at my desk and log back into my computer with this obnoxiously long password.

=^..^= ♥ =^..^=

I put on my heavy, pink, cat-eared headset and connect to the Zoom meeting. The camera shows a nearly empty conference room with only two men. However, more are piling in. While most of my coworkers live near the office, many work from home occasionally or attend meetings at their desks. So, only part of the team sits at the large conference table. Unsurprisingly, the few members of my team who aren't white, cisgender men all either work remotely or call in from their desks.

We have this meeting every morning. The whole team is involved, and the first ten minutes, while supposedly "social time," usually involves the few loudest voices on the team holding the rest of us hostage while we listen to them banter and make their dumb dude jokes.

The men in the room chitchat like always, but today, they break from their self-involved bubble and ask me about the weather here. *Huh, why are they talking to me? Did I draw attention to myself somehow?* They're in California and get a sick pleasure comparing my usually snowy weather to their perpetually sunny one. The only things they know about me are that I live in Minnesota and write code. "Oh, it's snowing pretty badly today. Good thing I don't have to drive into an office because the roads haven't been plowed today yet."

Chuck snickers at the end of the conference table and says, "Well, have you been plowed yet today?" Uproarious frat boy laughter ensues—my boss included.

"Uh, okay. Someone's going to call HR on you, Chuck," Mike, another in-office co-worker chortles. Those of us online simply sit in silence.

"Again?!" Chuck shouts while slapping the table, unable to contain his self-congratulating laughter. *Fucking pricks.*

Chuck is probably the biggest douche on the team—even more so than my boss, Daniel. He's also Daniel's best friend, which means he gets away with near-murder. When I started the team, I did my best to be friendly with all of them. I'd do the various social hangouts and even sparked a casual friendship with Chuck. When I thought he was my friend and a nice guy, I got on a Zoom call with him one Friday night. He ended up getting super drunk and sobbing about how women aren't into him. It ended with him slipping out his dick and begging to see my tits.

I was tempted to show him. I hadn't started dating Bryce yet, and I was desperately single. But something about the whole thing felt wrong, so I politely refused. The next day, he said, "I can't believe I did that! I'm a nice guy! I just had too much wine. I was so sad." I let it go, decided he was having a bad night, and tried to maintain a friendship. However, any time we would chat off a work-sanctioned device, he'd get sexually aggressive and kinda mean. My dumbass still tried to forgive his behavior for months and did honestly consider a romantic relationship with him.

Our friendship finally ended when I learned he gave a presentation about my work at an online conference and didn't credit me. Why it took all of that for me to realize what a prick he was, I will never know. That's not true—I know. I was lonely, and all the red flags look purple when you're feeling blue. Now, he's like a little boy rejected on the playground, taking every opportunity to be cruel to me. I wonder how many other women who work here have been down this same path with him.

Jason, in charge of ensuring our meetings stick to the agenda, unmutes and quickly changes the subject, "Okay, let's get into the standup, everyone." He's a nice enough guy. He does a good job of changing the subject when they get like this, but he doesn't do the gentlemanly thing, which would be calling them out on their shit. *You're not an ally if you sit on the sidelines, buddy.* But what can he do? He's a subordinate, just like me. He needs the check and can't throw it away, either.

I turn off my camera and ensure my mic is muted. I need to hide my face right now. I must not say anything. I don't need to be dubbed the "office bitch." This is a title I have gained in the past by simply being a woman in a man's world who occasionally expresses emotions. Nothing makes a man madder than a frowning woman. I place my face in my hands, and my arms shake. *Fuck this job. Fuck these dudes.* I'm so tired of this bullshit happening over and over and over.

I squirt the lotion I keep at my desk into my hands and slowly rub it in. It's a trick my therapist suggested. Since I can't stand the way my hands feel typing with lotion, I can stop myself from sending rage messages by putting the lotion on my hands when I'm most angry. And sending a message to my boss that says, "Fuck you, I quit, douchebag," is something I have to actively avoid in this moment. I try to let the calming scent enter me and take me to a place far away from here—a lavender field—adorned with the spiked heads of these assholes.

I take a deep breath and let out a long, deep, guttural howl. I guess I focused too much on those heads on a spike because my heart rate isn't lowering. *Okay, Ads, just chill the fuck out.* Jason calls my name. *Fuck, it's my turn.*

I scramble to turn my camera and mic back on. *Just give your status update. That's all you gotta do. They won't be paying attention anyway.* "Yesterday, I worked on creating an algorithm that will allow the monetization team to enter the in-app purchase data into a spreadsheet online. It will automatically populate the data in the game—"

I'm cut off by the sound of my door popping open. Ezra stands behind me, fully visible from the camera, shirtless—hot as fuck with a look of deep concern on his face. "Adley, are you okay? I heard you yell." He notices my headset and says, "Aww, babe, those are cute!" pointing at the lit-up ears.

I snap my attention back to the screen and continue, "Today, I plan to update the layout of the game's UI to accommodate various icon sizes for the items. No blockers."

Ezra leans down and waves at my team, cheesing hard. "Hi guys," he says, and I don't know if my headset picked up his voice because they all stare at him dumbfounded. I quickly turn off the camera and mute my mic.

"Wooahoo, it looks like Adley was getting plowed," I hear Mike say in my headphones.

"No way. Did you see that guy? That's a brother or something. There's no way he'd be into her," Chuck says. Tears pool in my eyes. *This cannot be happening right now.*

"Ezra, please leave," I say sternly.

His face, still concerned but now also sad, stays focused on me as I usher him out. "Alright, but are you okay?"

"I'm fine. Please leave. Do not bother me again," I say, closing the door behind him.

The voices of my coworkers still joking about me are in surround sound thanks to the excellent audio quality of this headset. I settle myself as best I can before quickly returning to my seat and turning my camera back on.

"Who was that, Adley?" Daniel, my boss, asks.

"Oh, um…" Who is he to me? My cat? Someone I thought was a cat but is actually an Ailura and can transform into a hot dude who loves to eat pussy? My mate? My boyfriend? One of my boyfriends?

"Um, that's my boyfriend," I say nervously, biting my lip.

"Fucking bullshit," Chuck says, "No need to lie to us, Adley. We have eyes." He laughs maniacally at me for the second time today. *Oh, I'm ugly, am I? Not what you said when you were begging me to tell you what a big dick you had.*

My heart drops. Is this a reaction I'll get whenever I tell people about Ezra? "Yeah, you got me. He's just a friend visiting," I say with a slight chuckle.

"See, told you!" Chuck says.

"I find it hard to believe you'd have a friend that looks like that, but that's definitely more believable. Is he gay?" Daniel asks with a level of lust in his voice.

"Hey!" his boyfriend, James, exclaims.

"What! I'm asking for a friend," Daniel responds, obviously not asking for a friend.

Images of Ezra's face buried in my crotch flash through my mind, as well as images of him kissing Marshall. Maybe sexually fluid, but not gay. I hadn't asked about his orientation. Should I ask? "Um…no," I say, shaking my head and going with the answer I hope will move the conversation away from Ezra as fast as possible.

Jason, ever the subject changer, interrupts with, "Chuck, what's your update?" and everyone moves on. The rest of my team provides their updates—stating what they did yesterday, what they'll do today, and whether or not anything is blocking their progress. I don't listen to their updates, just like they didn't listen to mine.

I turn my back to the computer and try unsuccessfully to incorporate the various breathing exercises the numerous therapists I've had in my life have taught me. I spin my chair to check that I am muted, tilt my head back, and scream at the top of my lungs.

I'm lucky. I'm lucky. I have to keep reminding myself I'm lucky. I'm making the salary of someone living in Silicon Valley, and I don't have to live there. I can live here in my significantly cheaper home and don't have to commute to work. I have a job. I have a 401k. I have health insurance. I need to be grateful for what I have.

Once this meeting is over, I can just turn off Zoom and get heads-down on my work. I like the work. I like the pay. I hate the people. But at least I don't have to sit next to them. At least I can just sit here in the comfort of my own home, turn on my aromatherapy machine and ignore all these assholes. And then, at 5:00 p.m. on the dot, I can go into the living room, snuggle with Marshall and Ezra, and pretend like I don't have this fucking job.

It dawns on me that I just yelled so loud I probably freaked the guys out. I pull out my phone and start a group text thread with them. "Sorry for yelling. Nothing to be alarmed about. I'm okay. Work just sucks. See y'all at lunch." Ezra replies immediately with a GIF of an animated cat hugging another with tons of hearts popping out. He responded pretty quickly with that. I wonder if that's what he wanted to show me earlier. Marshall responds shortly after with just a thumbs-up reaction.

"Have a good day, everyone," Jason chirps, signaling I can sign out of the call.

Okay, now I don't have to deal with those douches anymore. Thank god it's the only meeting I have today. I can get some work done.

I'm still reeling from the meeting. I hate this job so fucking much. Why do I let them talk to me like that?

I press my palms into my eye sockets, which causes a small amount of pain. The feeling is not enough to knock me out of this downward spiral of self-hatred, so I slap myself in the face—it's not a full-stop slap, but it's not gentle either. "Suck it up, Adley! Just do the work. They're assholes. It will be fine. Just ignore them."

"You okay, Ads?" a Slack message from Madelyn—my one friend on this team—pops on my screen. She's a remote texture artist, and the two of us have bonded over how shitty most of our coworkers are.

"I'm fine," I type back, trying to keep it short and sweet. I don't want to brush her off, but I must stop thinking about it and get to work. I cannot dwell on this all day, and bitching about it with her, no matter how cathartic, will just rile me up again.

"I've been worried I haven't heard from you all weekend. The last I heard from you, you said something about finding a dying cat. Is the cat okay? And who the fuck was that shirtless hottie?!" she responds.

Well, shit. What do I tell her?

"Oh, um, the cat is alive! That guy was the owner. He was pretty grateful for my help, and he's been staying here with me the last few days—repaying my kindness," I respond with a suggestive, winky-faced emoji.

"OMFG, girl! What a meet-cute!" she responds. *Ha, you have no idea.*

She barrages me excitedly with more messages, each new sentence punctuated by my computer making a ping noise, "That's so awesome. He was stunning! I hope you're getting that jerk Bryce out of your system."

"Yeah. I gotta get started on this UI stuff. I promise to tell you all about it!" It's not that I don't want to talk to her. I do. I'm just still frustrated and need a moment to myself. I also have to figure out how to talk about Marshall and Ezra to her.

"Wine and Zoom this weekend?! I need that tea!" but instead of tea, it's a teacup emoji.

"Maybe. I've got a lot of work on my side project this weekend." That's a lie. And I send one final message, "TTYL, Mads!" before changing my status to "Focus Mode." She responds with a heart reaction, and I close Slack out completely.

I'm frustrated with myself for not calling Mads all weekend. *Fuck, I'm a lousy friend.* I'm so fucking self-involved. She's the only good fucking thing about this job, and I'm doing what I always do—chasing dick and neglecting my friends.

I sit up in my chair. Wipe my face and open the game project. *Okay, just focus on the work.* Luckily, once I get started with a task, it is pretty easy for me to get fully absorbed in it—as long as I don't have any distractions.

Before I know it, I've finished the work. I commit my code with the message, "UI in-game now displays the in-app purchases via online API call =^..^=." The commit posts at 2:13 p.m. *Fuck.* I told the guys I would eat lunch with them at noon.

23

ADLEY

I set my status to "Lunch" and lock my computer. When I exit, my feet hit against something. There are a few different baubles at the base of my door: the cat toys I bought for the guys, a few balls of paper, a bottle cap, and a straw. Did they put these here for me? Mittens used to scatter random items at my office door when it was closed.

The living room window is open, and the harsh light stings my eyes as they adjust. I should start doing that thing where you occasionally look away from the screen.

"I told him you'd come out eventually," Marshall says.

Ezra curls on the couch, lying on his side, facing its back. He does not turn to greet me, "Ezra, are you okay?"

"Yeah," Ezra says, still not turning around.

"Well, he's done nothing but complain about how you yelled at him, will never love him, and you're embarrassed by him—for the past four hours," Marshall says, not looking up from his papers.

Ezra launches himself around, "Bro!"

"What? It's true," Marshall says. He looks up from his papers and notices the betrayal on Ezra's face. He quickly says, "Oh, um. Sorry," before looking back down at the documents. I suppose I'm not the only one who gets engrossed in work.

"Ezra, I'm sorry. I'm not embarrassed by you. When you came in, they were saying some mean things in my ear. I… I got overwhelmed and didn't react well. I'm sorry."

His ears perk up, and he looks at me, his face no longer showing sadness but now concern. "What did they say?"

I really don't want to tell him they were joking about my getting plowed and that I was too ugly to get plowed by him. "Oh, it was nothing," I say with a shrug, trying to brush it off.

Marshall stands. "I made you a sandwich for lunch. Let me go get it." He walks toward the exit, but stops in front of me, grabs me in a hug, and squeezes me hard, inhaling.

"I missed you. Can you take lunch on time tomorrow?" he says, his voice softening as he looks at me.

"Yes, I promise I will," I say.

"Good," he says, kissing me on the top of his head and proceeding to the kitchen.

"I helped with your lunch," Ezra says, sitting cross-legged with his hands between his legs and looking at me out the side of his eye.

I recognize this face. It translates to "Look how cute I am, praise me," so I oblige. "Oh, yeah?" I say and sit next to him. "What'd you make?"

"You'll see," he says and leaps on me, nuzzling his face into my neck with a hug.

Marshall returns with a plate containing a sandwich and a tangerine sliced and arranged to look like a goldfish. "I did that!" Ezra says, pointing at the art.

"Wow, Ez! That's cute. Thanks so much!" I say.

"I saw someone doing it on Instagram and thought you would like it," he beams.

"Oh, and I saw my gifts at the door," I say, unsure if that's what they were.

"Oh, um… I was feeling anxious," he says and scratches behind his head.

Marshall hovers, and I realize I am neglecting him. "Sit with me, Marshall," I say, patting the couch on my side opposite Ezra. He slowly sits, his back so straight he might have a pole down his shirt.

"Thank you so much for making me lunch. What have y'all been up to all day?" I ask.

They both light up and verbally stumble over each other to tell me what they learned—both info dumping on me in their decidedly different ways about their decidedly different areas of interest.

Marshall's more reserved style changes slightly as he discusses how he's been learning about the history and technology of my world—cataloging the differences and color-coding them in a spreadsheet he's put together. His speech is faster, more animated, and happier, and I appreciate seeing this side of him.

Ezra fights for my attention by explaining what he's learned about pop culture and fashion. He's also excited about the technology, but from a consumer perspective rather than a technical one. The best part of the conversation is when their info dump topics intersect. Instead of competing to talk, pushing and pulling the conversation in opposite directions, fighting to take over the air space with their little information, they work together to flesh out the topic thoroughly. It is a fascinating, coordinated rhythm: a team effort to understand and teach the subject more thoroughly. It has almost the same mesmerizing effect as their coordinated sex sessions.

Unfortunately, after approximately fifty minutes of them telling me what they've learned, I have to return to work.

EZRA

Adley's returned to work, and now I'm stuck out here alone with this fucking guy. I'm not sure what's going on with him. His tolerance of me ebbs and flows for reasons I can't figure out. He's currently regarding me with indifference, which I suppose is better than the disdain I've gotten from him.

There were times when we were chatting with Adley that he would warm to me. He would talk to me, with me, instead of over me. But then the subject would change, and he would return to acting as if he wished I would just shut up.

I guess I need to find common ground with him. The other day, we had fun playing video games together. "Hey, Marshall! Wanna play video games with me?" I ask, standing to go downstairs.

"No," he says curtly, not even looking up at me, continuing to scroll through whatever he's looking at on the tablet and bouncing between it and the laptop.

"Um, okay…" I say, slinking off. Maybe if I appeal to his desire to compare our worlds, he'll hang out with me. Let me try again. "Are you sure? It could be fun to see if we find any games similar to ours at home," I say, thumbing towards the basement, where Adley keeps her collection.

He breaks his intense focus to stare at me blankly. His face scrunches momentarily before he says, "No, thank you." He returns his attention to his work. *What the fuck was with that face?*

"Alright," I say. I live with two people, but I feel so isolated. Maybe Adley will hang out with me. No, she doesn't want me to bother her. It's only another hour. I can make it another hour. But what if she gets off work late, just like she took lunch late? I don't feel like playing video games. So, I'll just go lie in bed and scroll Instagram while I wait for her to get off work. Maybe take a nap. Once she gets off work, I'll feel better.

I'll leave Adley another token. I grab a blank piece of paper from the table near Marshall and ball it up. I wander away from him toward Adley's office.

The tokens I've left throughout the day lay at her doorstep, but not exactly where I left them. They're pushed to the side of the door—a path cleared. She just pushed them aside?

A sharp ache starts in my chest and spreads through my body. Why would she do that? Does she not want me to be her mate? My heart races as I consider everything I've done in the last twenty-four hours. I recall every interaction, but each one leaves me with more unanswered questions. I feel like I can't trust my memory. Was she smiling? Did she lean into the hug? If she was, was she faking it? But why would she do that? I try to rationalize each moment, but self-doubt pushes back on all logic—offering an alternate opinion of me in her eyes. Each moment has infinite possible mistakes—each amplifies the sting in my chest.

I try to convince myself her smiles were genuine and that she would tell me if I upset her. She said she wasn't mad at me; she was just having a bad day. But the sight of the tokens pushed aside, along with my inner demons, is stronger evidence. I toss the balled-up paper into the pile and stare at the door.

I sink into the void of rejection. A mew escapes me—a noise I hadn't made in my anthro form since I was a kid. I haven't felt this way since I was a kid. I thought having a fated mate would be, I dunno, less lonely.

MARSHALL

Ezra spent most of the day trying to get me to interact with him, but this only increased my discomfort around him. I want to spend time with him but don't know how to talk to him. Everything I say seems to upset him, and I am scared to talk to him. He misunderstands me. He hears a "no" as a judgment rather than a fact. To avoid future conflict, maybe it is best that I just don't talk to him.

I know I could try harder. I could soften my tone and be "friendlier." He seems to enjoy teasing banter, but I struggle to tell when my banter crosses the line from teasing to aggressive. That anxiety makes talking to him in such a way terrifying. I've hurt his feelings many times when I didn't mean to, and it's only been a few days. The version of me he likes doesn't come naturally to me. It requires a lot of effort and is uncomfortable—it's scary because I don't know if I'm doing it right.

It's made even more difficult by my conflicting feelings about him. I don't want to hate him, but sometimes I do. There are moments when I care less about accidentally hurting his feelings. In fact, sometimes I want to hurt him, and I am glad when I do. My jealousy and anger make me lash out when I see him with Adley. So, instead of dealing with all that, I will immerse myself in this research.

But… he mewed when he left the room. It was quiet, but its impact made it feel like a scream ripping through my chest. I felt his intense sadness at that moment, even though I didn't know why he was sad. Perhaps I should have just played video games with him. I stand up, resolved to go to him.

But if I talk to him, I will just say something that upsets him. I'm just going to fuck it up like I've fucked everything else up. It's best to sit here by myself and do what I know I'm good at—research. I sit back down and pick up my papers.

No, Marshall. Try. Don't let your fear block a relationship with them. I stand; my knees shake. We can be friends. Maybe even more. I just have to stop being such a pussy.

I can do this. I just go in there and say, "Hey, actually, let's play a game." *That's all you have to say. Smile. Don't cross your arms; that makes you look mad. Where should I put them? At my side?*

I usually take my cues from him. I let him set the tone of the conversation with Adley. His body language tells me how I should set my face and stand, but it's harder when it's just the two of us talking—I can't copy how he interacts with himself.

On my way to the basement, my eye catches a pile of stuff at the door to Adley's office. Ezra obviously left these here for her. Tokens of affection. Bids for attention. Physical manifestations of longing—of desire—of devotion. Further down the hall, Ezra lies on the bed in his ailo form, soaking up the sun. But instead of content, he seems sad, lonely, and disheartened. What happened? This isn't because I didn't want to play video games with him.

I study the tokens. They're pushed to the side instead of spread purposefully in front of the door. No doubt Adley has pushed them aside. Ezra would not have arranged them this way. Does she understand what this small gesture means? Pushing tokens aside like this symbolizes a non-reciprocation of feelings. If she felt the same way he does for her, she would have taken them in or returned them to him. To push them aside is the ultimate refusal. To leave them would have been preferred to… to this.

Why would Adley do such a thing? She did not indicate that she was upset with him during lunch. I don't recall any moments when her demeanor shifted from affection.

Hold on. Is this a custom with her people? I open the search engine on my phone. I search "tokens of affection," "love tokens," and as many search terms as possible. Nothing shows up. People here give gifts, but there is no "ritual of leaving." He must know that she is not saying anything by this, right?

I must talk to him. There appears to be a misunderstanding, and I will clear it up. I can fix this. I approach the door and consider where to put my hands. *Pockets. That's neutral.* "Hey, Ezra."

He lifts his head and says sadly, "What do you want?"

I need to explain to him that this meant nothing to Adley. "I saw your tokens of affection in the hall had been pushed aside," I say, gesturing to the door.

He stands, arches his back, and hisses at me, "What of it?! Are you here to gloat?! To tell me how fucking unlovable I am?"

"No, that's not—"

"Fuck off, Marshall. I don't want to fucking hear anything you have to fucking say."

"I'm trying to—"

He launches at me. This is not like him. Why is he attacking me?

"Ezra, listen!" I say, stepping back. My foot crunches a piece of balled paper, flattening it under me.

"I will kill you!" he howls. "This is your fault. I finally found a woman who will love me unconditionally, and you got in the fucking way!"

I can't fight him off like this. I transform into my ailo form, leaving my clothing in a pile atop his tokens.

"If you'd just listen to me instead of being crazy," I say. We roll around in a pile of flying fur, screaming at each other. I sprint to the living room and try to avoid his attacks.

I jump on top of my bookshelf, knowing he cannot get up. The fur pads of his paws cause him to slide on hard surfaces, ensuring such a move would be too dangerous for him. I yell to him, "I'm trying to tell you that Adley does not understand the ritual of leaving. They do not have tokens of affection here."

"What?!" Ezra says, looking at the door. "But she said she saw them."

"She misunderstood. She knew you left them and probably thought they were presents, but didn't know pushing them aside meant anything," I yell. My tail flicks wildly behind me, sending a vase flying to the floor. It crashes beside him.

"What the fuck, dude?!" he says.

"I didn't mean to!" I howl, desperate for him to listen to me.

"What is going on?!" Adley yells from the door to her office.

24

ADLEY

"What are you two doing? Why are you fighting?" I ask.

Marshall and Ezra are in their ailo forms. Marshall rarely enters this form, so I almost forgot what he looks like. He is on top of the tall bookshelf, and Ezra is on the ground below him, a shattered vase beside him.

Marshall jumps down, transforming. Ezra transforms as well.

"Just a misunderstanding, babes," Ezra says.

"About what?" I ask. They both look abashed. Why don't they want to tell me? "Please tell me. Was it about me?" I ask.

"Um… yeah," Ezra says, "I thought you had rejected me. And I thought Marshall was making fun of me, rubbing it in. But he was trying to explain that I misunderstood. So… I overreacted."

"Why did you think I rejected you?"

"You pushed aside my tokens," Ezra says, looking at the pile of stuff at my door. "When you brought them up at lunch, I thought you were confirming your culture does the ritual of leaving, too. So when I saw them pushed to the side, I thought you didn't want me. I thought you didn't love me."

"Oh, Ezra, no. No," I say and put my hands on his face. "I was just moving them so I wouldn't step on them."

"I'm sorry, Adley. I acknowledge I've got some… attachment issues. Some mommy issues. I know. But, when I thought you rejected me. I lost it. I love you so fucking much, and I don't know how to deal with this. And the thought of you not loving me kills me. Every second I am not touching you, kills me."

"And so today, my being away was upsetting, huh?" I ask.

"Yes," he says and looks to the side, ashamed.

"You can stay with me tomorrow, okay? You can sit in my lap all day. You just have to let me work, alright?" I say, still stroking his face and hair.

"Really?" He says, sniffling.

"Yes. But we need to figure out a way for you to be away from me. It's not healthy for either of us." I say and wipe the tear from his eye. This big, beautiful man is a blubbering baby for me. It's incredibly touching.

"I know," he says and sniffles. "I love you so much, Adley." He's sitting here, baring his soul to me, telling me he loves me, practically begging me to tell him I love him, but… I am scared to say it back. I care for him, I do. But I'm not ready to say it back. I know it's selfish, but with Ezra's current mental state, I don't know if lying to him would be helpful. Fuck, that may be even more selfish. I don't know what to do in this situation.

I look into his eyes and kiss him hard on the mouth. I hope he knows I care about him. I've told him how I feel about kissing, so maybe this is enough for now.

Ezra turns to Marshall, "I'm sorry, bro. I lost my cool."

"It's okay," Marshall says.

"We probably should apologize to Adley for breaking that vase, though."

"Oh, it's okay, it's just some old vase I had," I say.

"No, Adley. We broke your vase! You are extremely upset with us, and we must make it up to you. How can we convince you how truly sorry we are?" Ezra says with that suave smirk, his dick digging into my hip. "Right, Marshall, we have to make it up to her somehow," he says, smacking at him slightly and lifting his eyebrow.

Marshall startles upward, pulled out of the stupor of watching the two of us talk. I get what Ezra is hinting at, but Marshall isn't as quick to the uptake.

"Marshall, Ezra is saying that the two of you were bad boys and need to convince me to forgive you," I say. "Really, really, bad boys!" His eyes squint before recognition finally shows in his eyes. I nudge Ezra away from me.

"How dare the two of you break my most favorite vase? I don't know if I can forgive you," I say. I poke my lower lip out as far as I can and fold my arms under my tits to push them upward.

EZRA

Marshall stammers, "Yes, we have been very bad boys." I can tell this kind of roleplaying stuff is challenging for him, but he's giving it his best shot, and damn if this guy isn't a trooper when it comes to fucking.

I turn on the charm and lean into Marshall, putting my arm on his shoulder. He catches the vibe and subtly adjusts his posture, mirroring my casual seduction. He always takes my lead, and I appreciate it.

I thought his clear sexual inexperience and struggles with social cues would make his presence a hindrance during these sessions. But these fuck-sessions have been damn near acrobatic, and having a second pair of strong arms to help with various positions has been invaluable. Not to mention, he and I keep getting into this unspoken rhythmic sync. I didn't notice it at first, but now that Adley has brought it to my attention, I look forward to those moments when we embrace our clowder sync.

"What can we do to make it up to you?" I say.

"Beg," she says. "Get on your knees and beg me to let you enter me."

Marshall doesn't skip a beat and immediately gets on his knees. This guy likes to submit. I quickly do as well because obviously. My cock aches to be inside her, and before I can say anything, Marshall says, "Please. Let me enter you. I'll be such a good boy."

I've been shown up with the groveling. Adley looks at me expectantly. "Please let me enter you," I plead.

Adley giggles and teases, "Oh, I don't know," walking away from us toward the bedroom, removing clothing with each step. "I'm not sure if y'all really want it." She stops in the doorway, naked but for some panties, her silhouette perfectly framed by the glow of the lighting. The spot above her ass, where her tail should be but isn't, is so fucking sexy. My cock jerks, and my breath catches at the sight of it. If I hadn't already been on the ground, I probably would have fallen to it.

Marshall says loud enough for only me to hear, "I get to taste her this time." I simply grunt, my words lost to me.

"Follow me," she commands and disappears into the bedroom.

We scramble to our feet and fall over ourselves, hurrying to the bedroom. There, we find her sitting on the edge of the bed with her legs crossed.

"Kneel," she orders with such force that my body obeys without hesitation. "To prove that you want me, you must go on a quest—a journey, if you will. Your quest starts at my toes and ends right here," she says, pointing at her forehead. "You must travel by mouth. And once you reach your destination, if my pussy is sufficiently wet, I will consider letting you enter me."

Oh, I guess I will get to play a game with Marshall today, after all.

"My pussy will be sufficiently wet once I have soaked through these panties," she spreads her legs wide, running her hands down her thighs. "But there is one caveat. You cannot touch it. I don't want you to even look at it because I don't want you to neglect your quest and rush to the end boss. Will you accept this quest?"

Her panties would not be considered sexy in the standard sense—just pink cotton. But they cling to her lips, revealing a slight crease between her thighs. Her wetness is already seeping through them, revealing a small, dark spot. I vow to have them completely soaked by the time I get there.

"Yes," we say in unison.

"The fate of your desires rests in your hands. I wish you well on your journey," she smirks.

Without further instructions, we embark on our quest and kiss at the tips of her toes.

She reclines on the bed, supported by her elbows, watching us intently. "That's it. Good boys," she moans, parting her legs further. My eyes have remained locked on the small spot pooling on the pink panties. She notices my stare and bites her lip seductively. "Are you looking at my wet pussy, Ezra?"

"Yes," I admit with a gasp.

"I thought I told you that was against the rules," she playfully scolds and gently tugs at her erect nipple. At that, I place her big toe into my mouth and suck—hard. She laughs and leans back, breaking eye contact. Marshall takes a gentler approach—stroking her ankles and placing delicate kisses on her foot.

I release her toe from my mouth and cradle her foot. My tongue traces the tip of her toe and drags slowly upward, tracing her body. I know she's ticklish, and I want to watch her squirm. All that matters is that I reach her forehead and sink myself deep into her.

As I work my way up her leg, Marshall works up the other. While I lick, he kisses. When we reach her knee, the damp spot on her panties has doubled in size. The material clings to her, perfectly outlining her form and leaving just enough to the imagination that mine runs wild. I imagine those velvety-soft lips curling around my shaft while her pillowy mound pounds against my abdomen.

"Ezra, you naughty boy, you just can't take your eyes off my cunt, can you?" she scolds, looking at me.

"No, I'm sorry. I am weak and pathetic," I concede, holding her gaze.

With her middle finger, she gently pushes the panties aside, revealing her glistening lips. "This is what you want?" she inquires provocatively.

We both moan in delight and kiss our way toward it. I want to taste it. I pull back to admire it, ready to devour it, but she releases the panties, snapping the fabric back into place.

"No, no, you greedy boy. I told you. You must get here first before you can enter me," she says, while tapping her forehead with her moistened fingers. I will lick the arousal from her forehead.

"Marshall, you are such a good boy. You follow orders so well. If Ezra keeps this up, you might be the only one who gets to fuck me." She knows precisely how to manipulate me—pit me against him. *Challenge accepted, my love.* With renewed focus, I continue my journey up her body with my tongue.

By the time my tongue reaches her upper thigh, my resolve to stay away from her pussy has wavered significantly. The temptation is too difficult to resist, and I squeeze my eyes tight, trying not to look. I navigate to her hip bones and sink my fingers into the soft flesh of her thigh.

Past the danger zone, I lavish attention on her hips and stomach. She giggles and lifts in response to my touch. By the time we reach her breasts, her hand is in her panties. I want to press my body against hers. I want to feel her soft flesh against my chest. The desire to do so is almost painful, but I remain obedient.

I suck gently on her nipple and tease it between my teeth, causing her breaths to hasten. She's so vigorously rubbing herself that I worry she'll come before we get to her forehead. But even if she does, Marshall and I are so attuned to her pleasure that I do not doubt our ability to bring her to climax again.

As I explore the crevices of her neck, her heart beats on my tongue. I lick up towards her chin, and she tilts her head back. Marshall has kept pace with me and is on the other side. I put my hand under her ear, gently pressing my thumb into her jaw.

She rises to her feet, and we stand taller—locked onto her. I'm finally standing enough that I can press myself against her. I do so with such force that she knocks into Marshall. She lets out a sound that first makes me afraid I hurt her, but she grabs each of our asses, pulling us into her.

"My good boys," she exhales.

I nibble her ear, then lick toward her temple. Finally, I am at her forehead. I lap at the delicate skin at the exact moment Marshall kisses it. My tongue intersects with his lips, and a shockwave sends through me. Our eyes meet for a moment as we both purr in delight.

ADLEY

The desire in their eyes is apparent. Each time their lips meet hesitantly, there is a hunger in their eyes that I don't think they're ready to explore. I wish they would start making out. *That would be so hot.* I can see that they're still unsure about exploring this part of their sexuality, so I don't push them. As much as I want to request they make out, I will not. I don't want to pressure them to explore the part of their sexuality they are not yet ready to face. Instead, I will silently watch them navigate their hunger for each other.

"You've reached the end of your journey," I say to Marshall with a teasing smile. "Marshall, you've played by the rules, and now it's time for your reward. What do you choose?"

A fervent look crosses Marshall's face. "Please let me taste you," he begs, eyes glued on the floor. I'm loving his commitment to the bit.

"And what of Ezra? What will he do?" I ask.

"He will sit on the bed, inside you, while I make you drip on his balls," he says. I'm startled by his direct request.

I glance at Ezra to gauge his reaction, but he's already behind me. His lips press against my neck in a mix of gentle and heated kisses as he moves down my back.

"As you wish," I agree.

And once again, they are in sync. They move in tandem, lowering themselves down my body like it's a pre-choreographed dance. Ezra kisses down my back until he sits behind me. His breath is fast and hot against my back as he pulls me close, nuzzling his face against me. He gently rubs the spot above my buttocks, clearly enamored by the novelty of my human form.

Marshall returns to his knees in front of me and grips my hips. He marvels at my pussy for a moment before saying, "It is beautiful." He hesitates, and his eyes flick to Ezra behind me. I cannot see Ezra's response, but he must give Marshall some sort of direction because Marshall nods slightly and then leans forward. He draws my clit into his mouth, swirling his tongue expertly against the sensitive bud.

Ezra reaches around, holding me open for Marshall and enhancing the intensity of the sensations coursing through me.

Ezra whispers into my back, "Are you ready for me?" His hot breath sends shivers to my core.

"Yes," I breathe out, anticipation flooding my veins.

As one, they guide me to a seated position right onto Ezra's erect cock. The familiarity of this position reminds me of the first time we slept together—except they've switched roles. Ezra even said something about me dripping onto Marshall's balls. It's kind of cute how much he relies on Ezra for coaching.

Ezra secures his feet around my ankles and then spreads me even wider. He wraps his arms around me, leaving tender kisses along my spine. He nuzzles his face against me as he thrusts deeper inside me, hitting every pleasure zone with precision.

My fingers reach Marshall's ears, tugging gently at the sensitive tips. His moan vibrates against my clit as waves of pleasure crash over me. I come for what I know will only be the first time tonight—locking Marshall's head between my thighs and refusing to let go until the pleasure subsides.

Marshall looks up at me with such pride that it's almost endearing. Maybe he didn't think he could make me come like that.

"I want both of you inside me," I say breathlessly, guiding him to standing with a gentle tug of his ears.

Marshall holds out his hand to help me stand, and I take it—not that I need it because Ezra lifts me off his cock and onto my feet between them.

Marshall grips my ass and hoists me up. "Wrap your legs around me, angel," he instructs softly.

I do as I'm told. He fills me up as I sink deep onto his shaft. My fears of being dropped are quickly put to rest when Ezra stands behind me and braces my back against his chest—pinning me between them.

In one fluid motion, Ezra aligns himself with my entrance and whispers against my neck, "Ready, babe?"

He pushes in alongside Marshall at my eager nod, stretching me farther than before. I wrap my hands tightly around Marshall's neck and brace myself for what comes next.

"Fuck me!" I cry out.

The two move in perfect rhythm as they drive into me, each thrust more powerful than the last. I can barely hold on as they pound into me, sending so much pleasure through my body my grip falters. Ezra guides my head back onto his shoulder. I close my eyes, surrendering to the whirlwind of pleasure. Each thrust is so perfectly timed that when one pulls back, the other pushes inward. Their relentless pace only takes seconds to send me over the edge. My orgasm leaves me breathless, weak, and boneless in their arms. Their purrs vibrate through my vaginal walls as their seed fills me.

As the last tremors of our twitching bodies subside, we collapse onto the bed in a tangled mess of flesh and gasping breaths. They drag themselves out of me as we all regain strength and shift to find more comfortable positions amidst our intertwined bodies.

I rest my head on Marshall's chest, and Ezra presses his cheek against my lower back. The strong, steady beat of Marshall's heart and the hum of their waning purrs lull me into a peaceful doze.

Before unconsciousness completely overtakes me, I hear their hushed voices above my head. "Marshall, we can't keep doing this. Fighting. Crying. Fucking," Ezra murmurs sadly.

"I know," Marshall agrees softly.

"How can we fix this thing between us?" Ezra asks.

Marshall's voice is heavy with resignation as he replies, "I don't know." And with that haunting admission hanging in the air, I drift off to sleep between them.

25

ADLEY

The guys have lived with me for a few weeks, and the dynamic has still not evened itself out. Tension seems to be escalating, and I feel the pressure of trying to get these two to get along.

It's been a fucking rollercoaster. One minute, everyone is in sync and we enjoy each other's company. The next, they're fighting. With each conflict, Marshall pulls further away, and Ezra pulls me closer. I like Marshall, I do. When Marshall is sweet, he's really sweet. But it's almost like he can't let things get too comfortable. The moment we start to vibe, he starts to sulk.

I awoke today, sensing it was going to be tough. Everything feels too loud, too scratchy, too bright, just too much. I showered, requesting it be alone so I could have some time to myself and try to regulate my keyed-up nervous system. Neither seemed too happy with the idea that I was behind a closed door without them—naked. Their cat-like qualities show up in the strangest of ways. I half expected to see little black and gold paws under the door while I dried off.

Despite my and Ezra's initial discussions about him only spending the first few days with me, he's always here. I try to get him to spend time with Marshall, but that's a no-go. The fact that I spend at least eight extra hours a day with Ezra than I do with Marshall has further created the divide between us all. The first few days of us living together, I asked Marshall if he wanted to spend time with us. He always declined—saying he wanted to clean or research. Eventually, I stopped asking. I need to try to have some time with just him. Because that's a nut I won't be able to crack as long as Ezra is around.

Every day, I have to remind Ezra I need quiet. Today, I'm feeling particularly on edge and annoyed with him. This is my first luteal phase with them around, and my body is not coping well with all the added sensory inputs of their presence.

"Okay, Ezra. You can sit here with me, but please, I need you to be as quiet as a mouse."

"Gross," he says with a bleh sound.

"Huh?"

"Mice are gross," he says.

"It's an idiom," I say flatly.

"Yeah, I got it. I'm not Marshall," he says and laughs. I squint at him because I don't like when he mocks Marshall, especially since he's mocking Marshall for things others have mocked me for in the past. He looks chastised before proceeding, "But just because I got it doesn't mean I don't think it's gross."

"Noted," I say. "But, anyway, it's always tough for me to get into focus while at my job. And anything that pulls me out means I gotta go through this whole cycle of trying to get back into the zone."

"I know, babe. I've been with you for the last few weeks."

"But I'm PMSing really hard, and everything is just…" I wave my hands in the air, trying to indicate I'm overwhelmed. I've explained PMS and PMDD, but honestly, I don't think they'll fully get it with their extremely limited understanding.

"Extra?"

"Uh, yeah… no offense," I say with a cringe.

"None taken, babe. I will be quiet."

"Thanks," I say, relieved he gets it. At this point, I think he probably knows more about menstruation than men of my species do.

"I still can't believe you're fertile in the winter. That is so weird," he laughs. "Anyway, I'll stay in my ailo form. Can I sit in your lap today?"

"I would like that. It helps when my coworkers are being assholes to have you with me."

"Babe, why do you have this job? You don't really talk about it, but it seems like you hate this job," he asks.

I sigh. "I'll have to get into that some other time. I'm sorry. It's not that I don't want to tell you. I just… I just know if I start talking about it now, I'll get all worked up and unable to make it through the day."

"Okay," he says, a bit saddened.

"For now, it's time for bad bitch energy."

"Watching you dance and sing about having a wet pussy is my favorite part of the day, babe," he says, leaning back in the chair, ready for the show.

=^..^= ♥ =^..^=

Today has been so busy. I had to work through lunch. At noon, I got a group text from Ezra to Marshall and me. "She's having a tough day and will need to work through lunch. Sorry, bro!" he texted.

Marshall texted back with, "Okay. I will bring lunch."

Marshall quietly came in, laid a plate next to me, and kissed me on the top of my head. He also gave Ezra a plate, but no kiss on the top of the head—not so much as a side glance, actually.

The first half of the day was okay. Ezra sat in my lap during my morning meetings, which really made it more tolerable. However, since lunch, it's like he forgot the whole "be quiet" request. He's moved to the recliner I have at the back of my office and is surfing the internet. To be fair, he is not talking. He's fidgeting. His fidgeting paired with Marshall banging around and vacuuming makes me feel like the walls are closing in on me.

I am feeling incredibly claustrophobic. The sensory overload of the noise is getting to me. I have turned on my AirPods' noise cancellation, but it only helps so much. As soon as I feel like I can get some quiet, Ezra will start touching me, or I'll get a ping from the Slack channel at work.

I need some fucking air. I stand, and Ezra does, too. His clinginess is a bit too much today. I enjoy having him around, but I need some space right now. "Um, I'm just going to go to the bathroom. You stay here, okay?"

"Um, yeah, sure," he says and sits back on the couch.

I close the door behind me and stand in the hall momentarily. *Breath. Breath. You can do this, Adley. You just need to power through.* Marshall shuts a door in the kitchen. He doesn't slam it, but it feels like he does. The whole sound reverberates from my skull down my spine. I shiver.

I go into the bathroom and shut the door quietly, wriggling my AirPods to ensure a secure seal. The light is so bright. I turn the light off and sit on the toilet, my head in my hands, begging everything to just leave me the fuck alone.

Stop it, Adley. You have everything you ever wanted. You just have to suck it up.

A vacuum hums behind the door, breaking through the silence I am trying to foster. Followed by Ezra's laughter. *Motherfuckers. Can I have one fucking moment of quiet?!*

Calm down. Calm down. Don't go out there yelling. Be sweet, kind, calm, and understanding Adley. They're not trying to upset you. You're just having a moment.

Calm down, Adley. Marshall is helping. Ezra isn't trying to be annoying. There is no reason you should be angry right now. Then why do I feel like my skin is crawling and I'm about to physically explode?

EZRA

Adley's mood has shifted drastically. She was in the bathroom for a long time, and I desperately wanted to ask if she was okay, but I'm trying this new thing called "boundaries." Trying and failing, but trying nonetheless. She explained PMS to me, and it sounds like a fucking nightmare. Apparently, it sucks for her whole species, but Adley is one of the unlucky few who gets an extra bad version called PMDD.

Even more baffling to me than the reproductive system of her people is how they make those who suffer from it just… deal with it. They don't get time off or anything, and it's considered uncouth for her to talk about it. Hopefully, those a-holes she works with don't do anything to set her off.

Adley makes a loud groaning noise from her computer, followed by a short burst of energy, as if trying to release whatever has frustrated her.

I've spent most of my days laying in her lap or on the chair behind her, quietly tapping away at Instagram or watching videos. But mostly, I watch her.

She has made this noise and done that energy burst thing multiple times over the last few weeks—usually after her computer pings, presumably with some message from her coworkers. Usually, she does it one or two times a day—max. She's already done it seven times today. I was in her lap the first time she did it, and she startled me awake. The second time, she pushed me off her lap. So, I took that as a cue that she was getting overloaded to the point that even my adorable ailo form was causing her stress. I suspect her coworkers are giving her a hard time and that the whole PMS thing is making it harder for her.

From what I've observed, the people she works with are dickheads. I can't fully hear their side of the conversations because she has headphones when she calls into the meetings, but I can tell what's happening. I hear her side of the conversation and read the text on the screen when they message her.

She seems extremely smart. I don't know much about what she's doing, but I've watched her write code with passion and fervor that only someone who knew what they were doing would exhibit. It's apparent she loves the work, at least on the micro level—on the task level. But she hates the people and doesn't seem passionate about the project.

She stands, and I'm hopeful she'll acknowledge me. She stretches her arms and taps her cheeks a few times. She stiffens with her hands balled into fists at her side and says aloud, "It's OKAY, Adley. They are just jerks. They do not matter. You are smart. You are capable. A sexist pig does not determine your worth." She moves her fist closer to her chest and stomps her feet three times in another quick burst of energy.

I've seen her do one of these small pep talks, followed by energy bursts twice. She must repeat some intricate coping ritual to allow herself to get through the day. It is childlike and adorable. I feel bad for thinking such a thing. For infantilizing her. For finding her moment of stress so fucking cute. I wonder if she has done this in front of her previous boyfriends or if she hides it from them. Am I the first man lucky enough to see this? Have others seen this and made fun of her? What of the men she works with? The men who outwardly objectify her in such a demeaning way? In a way that diminishes her power and brilliance?

The fact that she has performed two stress-coping rituals in the last few minutes does not bode well. I have never seen her do them both with such frequency, and I know it means she is having a rough time. As much as I want to comfort her, I know that is not what she wants. She wants me to stay here and will tell me if she needs help.

She plops back down on her chair and exhales loudly for a long time. Then, as if a switch has flipped in her she begins typing again as if this slight detour never happened. She has instantly regained her focus and state of flow. She begins to hum softly to herself, seemingly content in her work.

She has mastered a level of compartmentalization that I could never achieve myself. It is truly admirable. This woman is a machine for work, and if she could work at a place that appreciated her, she could do great things for that company. The men who work with her are too blinded by their sexism, both overt and subconscious, to truly see the fucking amazing tool she could be.

ADLEY

Ezra is lounging on the couch in my office, legs reaching toward the ceiling, iPad in the air, kicking his feet. I am struggling to concentrate on my work. He would be distraught if I asked him to leave—so I don't ask.

Slack is pinging nonstop, and I feel my anxiety mounting. There's a bug in the game that has zero to do with any of the systems I've worked on, but I'm getting blamed for it. I know nothing about the system that's failing. But since it happens at the beginning of the game when most of my systems load up, it's assumed to be my fault. I'm trying to explain on Slack I am not responsible for that system, but they're not hearing me. According to them, everything is my fault. Everything is my responsibility.

Get it together, Adley. I stand to get away from the computer for a moment. I look at my watch, and it's 4 p.m.—the day is almost over. I just need to make it one more hour. Then I can sign off and pretend my phone died or something.

Often, I work late into the night, fixing their mistakes or working on bugs that aren't my responsibility. The in-office employees are supposed to take their laptops home with them, but they leave them in the office—making me the one able to fix the mistakes when the live version of the game goes down. I bet they'll fucking make me work over the holiday.

The pings are chiming at a constant rate. *Sunshine. Sunshine will help.* The sun hasn't set yet. Maybe I can get some sunshine before it sets at the ungodly early hour of 4:30 p.m.

I go to the window, and Ezra stops what he is doing to watch me. I slide the curtains open and try to feel the sunlight on my face. The light comes in at just the right angle, and the sun catchers pick up the light. Hundreds of tiny rainbows transform my room, making it beautiful. This is nice. I should do this every day.

Ezra's head whips to the side, eyes locking in on one of them. Oh, no. His ears turn back, and he leaps from the chair, turning into his ailo form and launching onto my chair—causing it to spin uncontrollably and knock over my water bottle with a loud metallic clang. I plug my ears as my heart races in response.

My computer rings; someone is video-calling me from Slack. *Fuck.* What do they want?

Ezra leaps joyfully around the room, chasing the rainbow lights. I close the curtains, and he transforms into his anthro form, sighing, "Babe, why'd you do that?"

"I'm getting on a call. Be quiet. Put some clothes on," I snap. He picks up his clothes with a pout. *God, he can be such a baby sometimes. He's a fucking grown man.*

I rush to my chair, and my socks instantly soak from the water, which I didn't realize was there. "FUUCK!" I sit in my chair and put my AirPods in. Fuck, my Airpods are dead. So are my backup headphones. *Where is my headset?* I can't find it, but the ringing pesters and rushes me. "My headphones are dead, Ezra, so please be super quiet."

He gives me a thumbs up while he bounces into his shorts, dick swinging.

I answer the call, but leave my video off, not wanting my boss to glimpse Ezra.

"What's up, Daniel?" I ask.

"Why is your camera off? Turn your camera on."

I position the computer so that it doesn't pick up Ezra. I have a background filter on, but occasionally, it will pick him up in the background. Luckily, people rarely pay attention to me in our group meetings and don't notice the half-naked cat man behind me most days. But, on a one-on-one call, I can't take any chances.

I turn on the camera and say, "What's up?"

"Why haven't you fixed that bug I've been messaging you about?"

"Well, I am working on something with a pretty strict deadline. Jason and Chuck handle that system. They should look into it. They'd be able to better identify the problem. I do not have enough knowledge to determine the bug's source quickly."

"Adley, don't give me that shit. You haven't written a single line of code all day, and now I'm asking you to fix a single fucking high prio bug. Everyone else is busy, Adley. What the fuck have you been doing all day, Adley?"

"I've written code. I just haven't committed it to the repo. It's a big change, and I don't want to commit it until it's fully stable."

"Stop passing the buck, Adley. This bug happens at the beginning of the game—it's your responsibility."

"Actually, it's not. Like I said, it's a system that I don't know anything about. Multiple systems run during startup. I am only responsible for some of them."

"Adley, I do not want to argue with you about this," he says, annoyed with me.

"I'm not trying to argue. I'm trying to explain. I really would not be the best person for this. It really would be quicker if James or Chuck looked into the bug. Since they built the system, they understand it. I don't know enough about it to—"

"Adley, you're a programmer. You should be able to look at this and figure it out. When we hired you, you said you had all that experience and education, but I do not see evidence of that," he responds. Ezra growls and fidgets behind me, hearing the whole conversation. "Maybe if you didn't spend all day eye fucking that guy who's obviously pity-fucking you, you'd be better at your fucking job."

"Um… that's… that's not what… you can't… I do understand code… I, it's just, I can't just hand you a novel and tell you to find the one typo in it—even if I told you the Chapter, you have to read the whole—" I respond.

"I'm so tired of you not being a team player. And don't fucking blame your autism on this. You're just not collaborative," he says.

My blood begins to boil. My hands shake at my side. This is all so fucking unfair. I cannot take this shit anymore. Why am I always the villain? Why am I always blamed for everything? Why does no one seem to hear me when I talk? Why can't they fucking just listen? What am I doing wrong?

"Fuck you. I quit," I say flatly. And slam my computer closed. I am in a rage, shaking. My phone starts ringing, obviously work. I hang up the call. *It's all too much. Fuck them. Fuck this job.*

Tears roll down my face. *Fuck Adley. Fuck. You are so fucking stupid. Why did you do that?* I slam my fists on my desk. I slam my fists on my knees.

Ezra moves to my side and kneels in front of me. He rubs my leg and touches my face. "It's okay, it's okay. Just calm down." He grabs my hands, trying to hold them down—to stop them from swinging up and back down on my knees again.

Why does this always happen to me? Why can't I control this? Why? I don't understand. I don't understand. I don't understand.

"DON'T FUCKING TELL ME TO CALM DOWN," I scream. I let out a howl of pure pain and anger. It is so loud and long that I feel like the muscles in my neck and temples will snap against the rage.

Ezra stumbles back, having never seen this side of me.

"GET THE FUCK OUT!" I yell.

I rock back and forth. A guttural groan vibrates in the back of my throat. It soothes me slightly, but not enough. My closed fist flies to my cheek. I wail in agony. Not agony from the hit, agony from the swirling awful emotions storming in me that feels like they're trying to break out. They rage against my skin and nervous system—punishing me for pushing them back and trying to ignore them for so long. I feel like a balloon about to pop. Static electricity shoots out of every pore.

I need silence. I rock and rock and rock. *Calm down, Adley. It's okay. It's okay.*

"Adley, don't hit yourself," Ezra says and tries to hug me.

My phone rings again, and I need it to stop. Too much. It's all too much. I pick it up and hurl it to the ground. It smashes into pieces at my feet.

I need him to leave. I need to be by myself. I cannot have him near me. The last semblance of my awareness recognizes that I do not want to hurt Ezra. I cannot control myself, and I don't want to hurt him. He must leave. Now!

"DON'T FUCKING TOUCH ME! GET OUT, GET OUT, GET OUT, GET OUT!" I chant.

EZRA

Marshall runs through the door aghast—as unsure as I am what to do.

Fuck, this is all my fault. I pushed her. I annoyed her. She was having a hard time, and instead of reducing her stress, I focused on my insecurities and stayed around. I should have left when I noticed she was stressing.

I say, "Okay, okay. I'm sorry," I say scrambling backward.

"AAAAAAAAH!" she screams. It's like a storm is exploding out of her. The floodgates of her nose open, letting the blood pour out with her rage.

Marshall grabs me. "What the fuck did you do? Did you hit her?" he yells in my face.

"It wasn't me, bro. Her fucking asshole coworker. She quit her job. She's melting down. Fuck, I'm so stupid," I say.

"She's what? Is this a human thing? Is this a PMS?" Marshall asks.

"SHUT THE FUCK UP AND GET OUT!" she screams.

We fall out the door and close it tight, the wails of my mate resonating through the walls.

26

MARSHALL

Her screams transform into sobs. The sound makes me want to go to her, to open the door, and hold her. I approach the door, and Ezra stops me. "No, dude, we gotta leave her alone." I feel powerless. I want to argue with him, push him out of the way, and rush to her. But the look on his face seems sterner than usual. I will trust him on this.

I go to the living room and sit with my thoughts on the couch. The sounds of her wailing fill the house, and I cover my ears—elbows on knees. I tremble. I do not know what to do. What should I do? What can I do? I cannot go to Adley. I cannot go to Ezra. I must just wait and sit with this. Sitting with my feelings has never been something I could do.

I want to clean. I want to do something. But I feel like making too much noise would be a decidedly bad idea right now. So, I'll do what brings me comfort when I feel out of control. I'll learn. My hands shake as I grab the laptop and type the word "meltdown" into the search engine.

Almost all the results bring up autism. So, I guess the meltdown is likely related to Adley having autism. She's mentioned it a few times casually, usually when she's trying to apologize for something. For example, when something bothers her that she thinks shouldn't.

I've never asked her about it—never asked her what it means. It's not a word I've ever heard, but I never asked her to define it. Why? Why didn't I? Normally, my curiosity about things can't stop me from asking questions—from over-exploring. I rarely stop until I fully understand something. Not knowing, not understanding, is my most significant source of anxiety. It makes me feel out of control. Why didn't I ask?

Instead of reflecting on why that is, because I don't have time to dissect my feelings, I'll try to learn about Adley—I don't want to feel them, anyway.

Many of these supposed symptoms are confusing to me. Adley can make eye contact and doesn't have difficulty with touch, right?

Apparently, the symptoms of autism are on a spectrum. Some need a significant level of support. Some cannot speak. Adley isn't at this position on the spectrum. She lives by herself. She's highly educated. She has a full-time job. Had a full-time job. Does that mean autism doesn't really affect her life that much? That it's not that difficult for her? If that were true, then why the meltdown?

I am struggling to find any helpful information. Most articles are about how to help children, and there is no advice on what to do if your romantic partner is experiencing a meltdown. Based on what I have learned about children, I think giving her space is the solution. However, we are supposed to ensure she is safe and cannot hurt herself. We've already failed that task.

I break from my focus to notice the sobs have stopped. How long have they stopped? Now, it's just silence. I rise from the couch and approach the door slowly—afraid to do anything more than place my ear to it.

Ezra approaches. "Has she calmed?" he asks. His face is unreadable.

"I think so," I say. What should we do? I resolve to open the door, afraid that the moment the door opens, she will launch at me with curse words and screams—or worse. I peek my head in. She is quiet and unmoving, lying on the floor, her face in a pool of blood and likely tears. She looks dead. And my heart sinks.

"Adley, are you okay? Do you need anything?" I ask. There is no response. I am terrified of crossing the threshold. The air is repressive.

Ezra pushes past me and slowly creeps into the room. He kneels in front of Adley.

"Adley, can I pick you up and put you in bed?" She just stares blankly at him. The spark in her eyes is gone, but she's aware of him. Her eyes look toward him, even though they look through him. "Can you nod or blink for me if that's okay, babe?"

She almost imperceptibly nods, her eyes closing as she does so. "Alright, babe."

"Do you need my help?" I ask him. I am frustrated he figured out a way to communicate with her.

"No," he says curtly and scoops her up, carrying her over the threshold across his arms. "Move," he says, as I still stand in the doorway watching him. I shift out of the way and follow them down the hall.

He stops at the bed, and I rush to pull back the covers so he can lay her down. There's a towel over the pillow. He must have placed this here earlier. For her nose?

"Get her weighted blanket," he says, laying her down and tucking her in.

"The blood," I say.

"We have to leave it. We can't touch her too much," he whispers. Now I understand why the towel is there.

He whispers to her while I get the weighted blanket, "Can I put in your earplugs? Okay. Can I put on your eye mask? Okay." He gently raises her head while he puts on her earplugs and night mask. After I drape the blanket across her body, he ushers me out of the room and tiptoes behind me, turning the lights off as we leave and quietly closing the door.

"Should we, like, try to contact her job for her?" Ezra asks.

"Did she really quit?" I ask.

"Well, she told someone she quit. I don't know if it was official or anything. But that job sucks so fucking much. I'm happy she did it. Not happy it came to this, but—"

"You're so fucking out of touch. She needs that job. She has bills to pay. Not everyone gets to be a spoiled little rich boy supported by Daddy. She was your fucking meal ticket, and now she doesn't have a job. Say goodbye to your pretty clothes," I snap.

Ezra just looks at the ground. "Dude, I don't know why you always act like I'm your enemy." He walks away from me, but I follow.

I grab his arm, stopping him. I hate that he always does this. He always walks away when I'm trying to talk to him. "How'd you know what to do just now?" I ask.

"She told me," he responds and turns to leave again.

"What? What do you mean?"

"The other day, she told me about her meltdowns. She explained what to do." He goes to leave again, and I am getting incredibly frustrated.

"Don't fucking leave. Explain!" I say, grabbing his arm again.

He shrugs my hand off and shouts, "Stop grabbing me!"

"Please explain," I plead. I wish he would just do what I want. This is so frustrating.

He sighs, exasperated with me. "She said she rarely has meltdowns, but when she does, it's like her brain is a nuclear reactor melting down. Just like a nuclear reactor, it's best if everyone just gets the fuck out of dodge until it's over.

"Then, if it's really bad, she might have a shutdown. That's when she's not able to talk or move. I'm guessing that's what's happening now. She said we can just leave her there. Eventually, her brain and body will boot back up. She just needs to be removed from all stimulation for a while and given time to get back up and running.

"But if we talk to her, we must ask only yes or no questions. She might be able to nod or blink in response. She can think; her brain is racing, but too many things are happening. She can't make her brain make her body do anything. She can't latch onto a response. And the more stuff we throw at her, the more questions we ask her, the worse it will get.

"Unfortunately, I didn't recognize it soon enough when she started melting down. I feel bad. I made it worse." He looks at the ground, lost in thought.

"Why didn't she tell me?" I ask, confused.

"You didn't ask," Ezra says.

An arrow pierces through my heart at the truth of that statement.

I'm such an asshole.

I haven't tried to learn anything about Adley at all. She's asked me so much about me. She's even asked me about my work. She asks me about me whenever we're alone, but I've never asked her about herself past the superficial.

I incorrectly assumed that because we were fated mates, it would all be okay, and eventually it would all click. I thought the problems we were having connecting were because we hadn't mate-bonded yet. And I blamed Ezra. I told myself his presence was stopping me from fully loving her and her from fully loving me.

I think back on all the times she waited until Ezra was gone to snuggle up to me. To talk to me about myself. I convinced myself it was because she would rather talk to him than me. But that's not it at all. She noticed. She saw. She knows my feelings for him are more than I have said. She knows I won't talk when he's around.

At this moment, I realize we haven't connected because I haven't let us. I've been a shitty boyfriend. I can purr for her and make her come, but I don't know how to talk to her.

I need to fix this. I need to fix how I communicate with her, and I need to fix how I communicate with Ezra. I need to be better. "Ezra, I—" I mumble.

"Dude, I don't feel like being lashed out at right now. This was emotionally draining, and now I also need to decompress." He walks away from me.

"No, I'm… I'm sorry. I've been a fucking asshole," I say.

"Yeah…" he says and continues to walk away.

ADLEY

I awake to a fluffy, purring cat on my chest. I stroke Ezra, and he purrs, nuzzling my chin. He jumps down and transforms into his anthro form, peeking at me from the side of the bed.

"You verbal yet, babe?"

"Yeah," I say with a sigh.

"Did I do good?"

"Yes, you did," I say, rubbing his head and ears. He leans into them and purrs. He looks at me with one eye raised expectantly. "You're such a good boy," I giggle. He grins and kisses me sharply on the forehead. "I'm so sorry if I scared you, Ezra," I say as tears pool in my eyes.

His happy, teasing demeanor drops, and his face droops. He swallows hard. He's getting choked up. "I'm sorry I didn't realize you were building up. I could tell something was wrong, but I thought if I were super quiet, it would be okay."

"It's not your fault, Ezra."

"I was annoying you," he says.

"Yeah, but… it's not your fault. My senses just overload sometimes. I suck at recognizing it, too. I didn't realize it was coming. Or… maybe I did. I just didn't want to admit it."

"Can I get in bed with you and cuddle?" he asks.

"Yes," I say and raise the blanket, allowing him to jump in. "No funny business, though."

"Well, I'm naked and hard as a rock, but that's about as 'funny' as I'll get," he says, making air quotes with funny.

"Alright," I say and laugh as he gets beside me and pulls me close. I bury my face in his chest. His purr vibrates through me, causing a deep sense of relaxation. He wraps his arms around me and hugs my head.

"You okay, babe? Do you wanna talk about it?"

"Yeah, and not really."

"No probs, babe, I'm here if you need me." He places his head atop mine, and I nuzzle my nose in the little hole under his Adam's apple created by his collarbone. No one, not even my parents, understood this part of me. I didn't even understand it until I was diagnosed with autism a few years ago. For years, I was told I had "anger issues."

"I love this spot right here," I say as his heart beats against my nose, causing me to feel a deep sense of warmth and comfort.

"Yeah, you love that spot?" he says. I don't sense any sadness or ulterior motive in this statement, but I know him and what he wants me to say right now. And I'm ready to say it.

"Yeah. I love all your spots," I say.

"I think I'm more striped than spotted," he laughs.

"I love all your stripes, too. I love all of you. I love you, Ezra." I say, nuzzling into him the way he nuzzles into me.

"Thank you, babes. I love you, too," he says and hugs my head tighter.

We lay like this for a long time.

I lose consciousness and drift asleep, soothed by his warmth and purr. I jolt awake when I realize something is missing in this perfect moment. "Where's Marshall?"

"I don't know," Ezra says with a sad sigh.

27

ADLEY

I emerge from the bedroom, ready to face reality. Everything is still. Quiet. Where are the guys? I wander into the kitchen and open the refrigerator, looking for what? The secrets to the universe? I don't even know.

Ezra bursts into the room, speaking in a tone of annoyance only ever reserved for Marshall, "You can say the PhD stands for pretty huge dick…" he stops at the sight of me, and his voice changes to that of someone addressing a crying child. Which, I suppose, I am. "Hey, you. You've come out of the bedroom," he says.

The sound of measured footsteps approaches from behind Ezra, and Marshall appears, startled to see me. His presence is a stark counterpoint to Ezra's frivolous charm.

Ezra slides beside me with the grace of a man who can weave through the world untouched and hovers his hand at the small of my back. "Can I touch you?" he asks in a low tone.

"Yeah," I say with a shy smile, "I'm feeling much better. Thank you."

"Excellent," he says, embracing me in a caring and sensual way. He inhales and says, "I'm so happy you're feeling better, babe."

Marshall looks at me pitifully. "Hey," he says, walking toward me with a different grace than Ezra.

"Hey," I say, pulling him into a group hug with Ezra and me. Ezra buries his face in my neck as he always does, and Marshall rests his chin on my head. We stay like this for quite some time. It's nice. Usually, Marshall or I have pulled away by now.

"What are y'all up to?" I ask, pointing at the laptop Marshall holds at his side.

Marshall pulls from the embrace and plops the laptop onto the nearby kitchen table with a soft thud. "We're looking for jobs," he says. "But it's proving difficult."

Marshall clicks the laptop to life, and the backlight casts a glow on his face, bringing out his features and making him appear gentler. I am in awe of him momentarily before I notice the screen.

He has a spreadsheet with multiple information tabs that he's been diligently compiling. "What is this?" I bend down to examine the sheet. His brow furrows, and he says, "Well, as you know, we aren't exactly cleared to work in the United States. Or anywhere." I must look confused because he says, "You know, because there is no record of our existence. So, I've been trying to determine how we can work without things like a birth certificate or driver's license or what was it called?" he asks himself. Then he asks me, "Security something number?"

"Social security number," Ezra responds, lounging on the countertop across the room—his usual whimsical expression replaced with quiet contemplation. We look at him in surprise, and he straightens up. "What? I pay attention sometimes." He shrugs in embarrassment.

"Anyway, I've been searching the internet to figure out how Ezra or I could get a job. We need to make money through… alternative means," Marshall says.

Ezra chimes in, "I told Marshall he should start an OnlyFans account, but he wasn't interested."

"I have a PhD in Theoretical Physics. I'd prefer not to resort to sex work," he says.

"You can make substantial money with it. My Instagram followers always tell me they'd pay tons of money if I created an account, but it's not in line with my brand. You, on the other hand, have no brand. Start an account. You're considered hot here," he says to Marshall. Marshall growls at Ezra's obviously underhanded comment.

"Wait a minute," I say. "You have Instagram followers?"

Ezra blushes, putting a hand behind his head, and says, "Oh yeah. I've got five million followers." He grins ear to ear.

"What?! That's amazing, Ezra!" I say.

"I was focusing on growing my TikTok account, but I guess it's getting banned next month or something. I've only got about one-million on there. I wanted to stream myself playing games or just chatting, but I'll have to look at a different platform," Ezra says.

MARSHALL

I whip to the open laptop, dismissing my disheartening spreadsheet of unattainable opportunities. My jaw clenches at the amount of work I put into it. So stupid.

I navigate to Instagram. "What's your handle?" Ezra strolls to the adjoining living room and leaps over the back of the couch, plopping onto it with a thud. He lounges on it, stretching across the entire surface, feet up, and whips out his phone, holding it over his face—like he always does.

"Why, you gonna follow me? Download the app on your phone, dude. No one looks at it on their computer. The formatting is all wonky."

Adley follows him to the living room, and I follow her. He sits up to make space for her to sit with him. I sit on the other couch.

"I wanna see, Ezra," Adley says with more excitement than I've heard from her in a while. He sits up quickly, eager to please her. He wraps his leg around her, placing her in his lap so he can hold his phone in front of her face and his. He rests his chin on her shoulder and grins when she says, "Wow, Ezra! You took all these pictures in the house? They look so professional."

"It's all about the lighting, babe," he says, kissing her shoulder and nibbling at her ear.

I desperately want to see it. I pull out my phone. "The handle?"

"EzraFromAnotherWorld. No spaces," he says absentmindedly to me while he flicks at the screen for Adley. "This was last weekend right after we did it in the backyard. I liked how my cheeks were rosy from the cold, and my hair was all tussled from Marshall pulling it."

I try to maintain my excitement as I type in the handle. The pictures are beautiful. I scroll, mesmerized, for quite some time.

"You've been busy," Adley says. "How long have you been doing this?"

"I opened it after that sushi chick brought it up."

"Why didn't you tell us?" Adley asks.

"I dunno. It's not a big deal."

"Five million followers is a big deal, Ezra!" Adley says.

"Nah, at home, I had a billion followers on Purrdy. So, it's not that big a deal."

I stop scrolling. "Hey, what's this?!" I ask and point my phone at Ezra.

He laughs with a jovial charm that can have me on my knees. "What? You looked so cute. Adley took that one," he says. It's a picture of me, in my ailo form, curled up on his bare chest—a rare moment of vulnerability. He's asleep, and the light from the bedroom window falls voluminously on me, making him look like an angel. I don't even remember this moment. Why was I transformed? The draw to lie in the light must have disarmed me.

Adley grins. "I love that picture!"

"That's my most liked one, babe! It got me a bunch of followers. You've got an eye," he says, kissing her neck and making her giggle.

The effortless charm that practically oozes from Ezra's pores is so magnetic that I can barely contain the wry smile that tugs at the corner of my mouth.

"Oh, look, Ezra! You actually have six million followers!" Adley exclaims. She's bubbling with excitement, and Ezra is trying to be nonchalant, but he is eating up all the attention.

The digital realm has always been Ezra's domain. He was the king of social media in our world.

"I started a YouTube channel last week," Ezra says. "I'm not sure if I want to focus my attention there, though. It's a lot more effort. I think I might just automate my Insta and TikTok lives over there. But, since TikTok might go away… I dunno… maybe I'll focus on it more."

I scroll to the top of the page, finding the links to his other pages. I click on YouTube. "Oh, you're doing vlogs. Just like you used to," I say.

Ezra's interest piques, and he peers at me. "How do you know I used to do vlogs? That was like fifteen years ago." *Actually, for me, it was 25.*

I look up, caught red-handed. "Um..."

"Wait a minute. Were you an Ezronie?"

"What's an Ezronie?" Adley asks curiously.

"A fan," Ezra says with a sly smile.

"I… I may have followed you," I say, clearing my throat.

"WAIT WHAT?!" Ezra jumps up, perching on the back of the couch, eyes laser-focused on me. "Bro, are you serious?!"

I say nothing. I just continue to scroll on my phone.

He jumps over to me and gets in my face, "Adley, look at this tsundere mother fucker. He's obsessed with me!"

"I was NOT obsessed." I drop my phone, scrambling backward, trying to escape him.

"Oh? I bet you used to touch yourself while looking at my pictures. All alone in that lab, thinking about alternate dimensions and me, huh?" *Bingo.* Except I didn't work in a lab.

"No," I say as the heat rushes to my face.

"Did you have that black and white K. Caprice photo hanging over your bed? You know the one where I was like this?" He stands, pulling his shirt up with one hand and his shorts down with the other, revealing just a hint of the area under his v-cut. He turns his head to the side and makes… the face.

My mouth hangs open. Because, yes, I had that picture. And now I'm seeing it right here in person.

He instantly translates the look that must be plastered on my face. His exuberance fades. "Bro, what the fuck? If you were a fan, why are you such a dick?"

I look at Adley.

"She's not going to save you. Just answer me. Why have you constantly pushed me away?"

My gaze fixes on the ground. I'm unsure of what to say. "I don't know," I croak out.

"Don't give me that shit. You know. You just won't admit it. I haven't pushed you. I've tried to let you come to me on your own, but this is getting really fucking old, bro," he says. "What? Am I not good enough in person or something?"

"No, that's… that's not it."

"Then what is it?" he demands.

"You… make me feel like a piece of shit," I stammer out.

"Oh, Marshall. Why?" Adley asks, bringing her hand to her face in surprise.

"Isn't it fucking obvious? Look at him! Look at me! He's fucking perfect," I say, my voice gaining volume and traction.

"I'm not perfect," Ezra says bashfully, knowing full well I'm not buying this humble shit.

How dare he act like he doesn't know he's perfect? "Yeah, like you fucking believe that. I don't need your pity, Ezra. Everyone loves you. You can talk to anyone. You never get mad. You know how to make her come. You make her smile. Look at your fucking tail! Everything about you is everything I am not. You have everything, and I have nothing!" Hot, steamy tears roll down my face.

"I HAVE EVERYTHING?!" he shouts, his voice deep and disarming. I've never heard him speak like this before, not even during the token misunderstanding. "EVERYONE LOVES ME? Huh? Well, I guess you aren't really an Ezronie, because if you were, you'd know that isn't fucking true."

He storms off into the other room. Just like he always does. He gets the last word and leaves. Not that I am much better.

28

MARSHALL

"What was that about?" Adley asks, approaching me with a box of tissues. I yank one out and wipe my nose as masculinely as I can.

I stare at the door Ezra exited through. Realization dawns on me, and I instantly feel like an even more enormous prick than I thought I was. "That was a shitty thing for me to say," I respond.

She raises her eyebrow at me questioningly.

I sigh and sit down. My face in my hands. Adley sits next to me and waits patiently for me to continue.

"For me, it was twenty-five years ago… Ezra was still a teen. He was a good bit older than I was back then," I laugh. The fact that I'm older than him now still bothers me. He feels like a walking corpse to me sometimes. Frozen in time on the day he supposedly died ten years ago. "He had a vlog series in which he chronicled his life. It was before he was famous, but not before he was hot. He's always been hot. He was this cool older kid, and I… I looked up to him," I laugh, trying to dissipate the feeling in my chest.

"I was a dedicated follower. I watched it every day. It got me through some tough times. I felt like… like he was my friend. He was so personable and easy to like. His videos were raw and real. This was before he learned about production value and got a genuine sense of his brand," I say while air-quoting "his brand."

I continue, "Anyway, it showed a lot of his personal life. A lot more than he let the world see once he got famous. And there were lots of videos of him crying over his parents."

Adley's expression is pained when she mumbles, "He's told me about them. I get it now—why saying everyone loved him made him react that way…" she trails off.

"He went through a dark time where he considered taking his own life. I related to those videos because I was going through something similar…" I stop and stare at my shaking hands, unable to meet her gaze. I tap my leg, trying to soothe the intense ache in my chest.

"Your parents didn't make you feel loved?" she asks, breaking the silence.

"I just had a dad. He didn't make me feel unloved; he made me feel hated.

He was… abusive. My mom died giving birth to me, and he never wanted me. He told me daily I was useless—a waste of space and resources."

"Oh, Marshall," Adley says gently, placing her hand on my non-tapping thigh. The warmth of the gesture makes my other leg stop. She's not trying to make me stop; she's trying to comfort me. And, uncharacteristically, I am comforted. I'm not pulling away; I lean into it.

"I'm sorry, Adley. I've been an asshole. Can I be alone for a bit? I need to calm down and work through some stuff. Plus, he probably needs you. Being alone will just make him spiral."

"Okay," she says and silently follows Ezra.

I suppose it's time I finally face it. Since I've been here, I've spent a lot of time reflecting. I've been trying to sit with my feelings and understand myself.

I've been researching myself as much as I have researched this world. I've learned a lot about myself. But my fear has prevented me from doing much about it—I've been afraid to admit these things to myself. I suppose it's time I tell them what I've learned.

A sense of inadequacy gnaws at me. The nagging thought that I bring so little to the table, I have to remind myself that these are just thoughts, not facts. I have to give Adley and Ezra my honest self.

EZRA

Adley leans down and peers at me. I've done this enough—hidden under the bed—for her to know to look for me here first. "Wanna talk about it?" she asks.

"No," I say.

"Well, seeing as I can't understand you, I'll take that sad-sounding meow as a no. I'm going to lie down. If you wanna talk, I'll be here, okay?"

"Okay," I say. She smiles at me like she does when I'm being stupid, but she doesn't want to say I'm being stupid. I know she can't understand me, but I want to stay like this for a while. We've done this dance before. Marshall hurts my feelings, I hide, and she comforts me.

The bed above me creaks as she sits on it. Her presence in the room is enough to comfort me. A long time passes before I emerge from under the bed. Adley is reading a book on her Kindle.

I jump onto the bed and curl up on her chest, my head on her breasts.

My favorite pillow. She strokes my back in those long strokes she does and continues to read. I tap my hand on the book, a signal she knows well.

She explains the plot up to this point and then reads to me. It's a cozy mystery about a woman and her dog solving murders. Usually, I'd protest her reading a book with a dog in it, but I don't have the energy to do so at the moment.

A content purr escapes me, and I feel safe and happy with Adley. I nuzzle my face under her chin and breathe her in. The heartbeat in her throat against my nose is comforting and reassuring.

After many moments, she stops reading and says, "Marshall explained why you were upset."

I can't talk to her like this, and I can't transform on her chest, so I slink off her and snuggle next to her under the blankets. I transform a bit slower than usual, stinted by my lack of energy, and respond, "Oh, yeah."

"He said you used to have an extremely personal blog in which the dynamic of your relationship with your parents was apparent."

"So he is an Ezronie," I say with a chuckle.

"Are you deflecting?"

"Probably."

"Anyway, I think the two of you need to have a heart-to-heart and be honest with each other," she says.

I rise to look at her with incredulity.

"I know, I know. He's the one who probably has to do some work in the honesty department. But you also need to let him talk. Listen. Don't deflect. Don't get defensive. No quips. Don't say a cutting comment and then just walk away," she says.

I sigh. I know she's right. Yeah, he's holding back, but I haven't given him the space to open up. He's just so frustrating.

"Believe me, I know it's easier said than done. But this clowder won't work until the two of you start breaking down your walls. You have to trust each other—fully. You have to trust me, too," she says, putting her hand on my face.

I purr at the warm feeling against my skin until there is a knock at the door.

"Should we let him in?" Adley asks.

"Yeah," I say softly. I sit up cross-legged, covering my junk with the blanket.

"You can come in," Adley says. "Should I leave?" she asks Marshall, but looks at me, too.

"No, you can stay," Marshall says.

I just nod.

He sits on the edge of the bed and doesn't look at me when he says, "You were right. I was an Ezronie. And I did have that picture. It wasn't over my bed, though; it was under it… hidden."

A twinge of happiness flits through me at being right and the fact that he was a fan. I was joking previously, but to know it's true is an interesting feeling. It's confusing, actually. I've strongly suspected he was attracted to me from the first day we met. I catch him looking at me occasionally—and honestly, I don't know why I finally decided to try to push it out of him today.

"I've always been a fan…" he stops talking, trembling. I want to make a joke. I want to say something to remove this tense moment from our lives, but Adley's right about it being a wall I need to knock down. I'll give him time and let him talk. He continues, "My dad. He was abusive—angry that he was stuck with me. Whenever things got really bad, I'd watch your videos. They made me feel… less alone.

"Then when I got older, I… umm… had a crush on you. That photo of you: I drew it. I drew myself lying next to you. I kept the picture and drawing hidden under my bed. When my dad found them, it was the worst beating I ever got. It just affirmed to him that I was even more of what he hated. I was a burden. I was useless. I was gay… He destroyed them, obviously." He takes a long, deep breath, and I hold mine.

He continues, "I have always struggled with my sexuality. I never had any sexual attraction to anyone… except you. So, I thought, 'Maybe I'm not gay?' Maybe he was just special. Who wasn't attracted to the guy voted the sexiest man alive—twice? Right?" He laughs at himself, shaking his head.

"I resolved that night that I would only be with girls and I would give up art. I tried to date a girl who had a crush on me in high school. She became my best friend. I loved her, and after we were together for a while, I became sexually attracted to her, too. We were planning to lose our virginities to each other. But I ruined it…

"I still harbored my feelings for you. She saw me looking at a picture of you in a magazine, and I guess I was looking a little too hard. She confronted me about it. I thought she would understand. She didn't understand. I tried to explain, but I didn't really understand it either. She got so… mad. She hit me and screamed that I was using her to hide the fact that I was gay. But, she used a much worse word… she told the whole school I was gay and… back then… well, you know how kids were about that stuff. I imagine it's the same in this world.

"I've been doing some soul-searching since I got here. I've done some research. Trying to understand why I act and react the way I do. Trying to evaluate my feelings for you and Adley. And then Adley had a meltdown, and I… I couldn't help. It made me realize trying so hard to deny these things about myself hurts my relationship with her. It made me realize I needed to figure myself out before I could be a good mate."

He pauses, and his leg starts tapping. He doesn't want to say what's next. Adley places her hand on his, and the tapping stops. "Marshall, it's okay. Take all the time you need," she says. I stare at him blankly, not knowing what will happen next.

He smiles sadly. "I've realized I'm demisexual. I only form an attraction with a close bond. I didn't even know that was an option. And I have a lot of internalized homophobia.

"I've spent my entire adult life trying to hide that part of myself. I've closed myself off from relationships. I don't let myself get close to someone. And I realize now I don't let myself get close to someone because I'm scared to develop that sexual attraction to them. Your death… in a way, it was freeing for me. The one person I still wanted didn't exist anymore… I didn't need to worry about whether or not I was gay.

"But when I came here and immediately purred for Adley, I was so excited! I was so excited that my fated mate was a woman. I was excited to have instant sexual and emotional attraction to a woman. My deepest wish was fulfilled.

"Then, almost instantly, you showed up. Not fucking dead. All the feelings I've been trying to forget for the last ten years… to see you in the moment I was purring for her… it felt… I couldn't stop being attracted to you, too. I didn't want her to hate me because of it. I also couldn't stand the idea of you taking her from me.

"So, all the feelings I've worked hard to repress, to avoid, to deny—everything I thought I had grown from and moved on from—it has all been stirred back up. I'm just that kid being kicked by his dad for being useless and drawing gay stuff again."

I sit stunned, unsure of what to say.

"I couldn't repress the secret hope that we could be a full clowder. And I wouldn't admit it to myself, but I hoped maybe you and I could have something, too, Ezra. But I know you're only in this for Adley. And that's okay. I understand you're not attracted to me. I will try to stop resenting you for that."

I don't even know what to say. There is way more depth to Marshall than I thought. I look at him for a long moment—studying his face. I finally say, "Yeah, I'm sorry. I'm not attracted to men. I never have been… at least."

Marshall tries to hide a reaction, but his already dour expression sours further. I know he wants me to say I am attracted to him. I wish I could say that. I feel like shit that I can't say that to him.

I find him to be pleasing to look at. I don't mind fooling around with him. I appreciate his assistance with pleasing Adley, but I just don't find myself drawn to him sexually. I'm definitely not repulsed by him or the idea of being with him on some level, but is that enough? I don't know. I need to say something else, anything else, something to soften the blow. "But… I do feel… something for you. Maybe I just need a bit more time to figure out what that is."

"Okay," Marshall says, defeated.

I want us to be a full clowder, too. But can we be if I can't love him like that? Is friendship enough? Do I also need to be sexually attracted to him? There's no way for us to research it in this world—not that there would be a lot of information about it, even in ours.

I continue, "For now, just know that I enjoy sex with you and Adley. I like having you around. I want this relationship to continue, and I'm willing to explore this further with you to see where it goes."

Marshall's smile is tight. Maybe hopeful. I guess we'll see where this goes.

29

ADLEY

I always knew there was something between Marshall and Ezra, but I never could put my finger on it. I'm happy Marshall has been doing the work to analyze his feelings. Ezra has been trying to work through his emotions, too, and I've assisted him as much as possible. But maybe they can start opening up to each other a bit more.

Don't get me wrong, I want to be there for them. But the emotional labor of dealing with my shit and being the only one to help them navigate theirs is a lot. Maybe when I get a job again and health insurance, they can sign up for therapy. There are lots of telehealth options out there now. So they wouldn't have to hide their ears and tails from anyone. Maybe we could do some couples counseling. Is throuples counseling a thing? But wait? I won't be able to get them health insurance. This is all so frustrating. We must figure out how to exist in this country when you technically don't exist. Maybe we should move.

Ezra snaps a picture of me, pulling me from my stupor.

"Let me see," I ask. He turns the photo to me, and I look… nice. No one ever takes good pictures of me. I usually look like a sleepy potato. "You're good at taking pictures, Ez."

"Thanks," he says and beams at me, tapping away at his phone.

"I can't believe you are a secret social media star. How did you find the time? How did you do this without us noticing?" I ask.

"I'm not a star. Not yet, anyway," he says with a glint in his eyes. "No offense, babe, but you don't notice a lot happening around you when you get in the zone." He chuckles sadly, and maybe even if he didn't mean any offense by it, it does hurt him. "Same with him," he throws a thumb at Marshall, and Marshall startles at being referenced.

I must make a face because he says, "No, babe! Don't do that! I'm serious. No offense. I think it's cute how tuned in you get. I wish I could focus the way the two of you do. I would have done way better in school, then maybe…" I know what he's thinking—then maybe his parents would have been proud.

"Anyway, this stuff doesn't take too long. I'd just record the videos when you were in the shower or sleeping or something," he says with a shrug. I know the "or something" references my being depressed in bed, but I try not to focus on it.

Marshall bolts upright, an idea suddenly dawning on him, "Ezra! Are your accounts monetized?" Marshall asks.

Ezra rolls his eyes and responds, "Umm, no, I don't have a bank account, so—"

"Adley does!" Marshall exclaims.

EZRA

"Okay, so I started an LLC called 'Whispering Whiskers Media' in Adley's name. If anyone asks, she is your 'manager'. I created a business checking account owned by Adley. All your earnings will be funneled through there. I set up a business email for Adley, but I'll monitor it and respond to inquiries. I'll let you know if any good offers come in. I think I have a pretty good sense of your brand," Marshall says with a smirk, seemingly happy to reveal his fanboy-ness finally.

"Oh, really? What's my brand then?" I playfully challenge him.

"Himbo, fuck boy with a heart of gold," he says with a laugh, and I mock offense.

"Nailed it!" Adley says.

"Et tu, Adley," I say, rhyming Adley with Brute.

"Wait a minute! Do y'all have Shakespeare in your world?" Adley asks excitedly.

"What's Shakespeare?" I ask, confused.

"Never mind," she giggles.

Marshall, undeterred by my banter, continues, "I also opened up a PO Box for you so that you can receive fan mail, gifts, and products to endorse without anyone learning your real address. I recalled that being a real problem for you in our world, and since we don't have the same level of security your rich parents could afford you, this will have to do. Luckily, your lack of a paper trail will prove useful for us. Fewer stalkers."

I bite my lip, realizing I've fucked up.

"What?" Marshall looks at me concerned.

"So, I did give some people this address," I say.

Marshall looks at me like he's going to berate me. I cringe, ready for him to lay into me. He flinches and turns back to his laptop. "Well, there's nothing we can do about it now. Just don't give anyone else our address, okay?" Wow! This "trying not to be a dick due to his past trauma and insecurities, Marshall" is great!

"Thanks for doing all of this for me, bro!" I say and put my arm around his shoulder. He looks at my hand and then back at my face. He blushes and returns his gaze to the computer.

"So, what are you doing now?" I ask.

"Still looking for jobs for myself," he says dejectedly.

"How's that going?"

"Well, that OnlyFans idea is looking more and more appealing," he says sadly.

"Well, if you need help with lighting and camera angles, you know where to find me," I joke. I should probably say something more encouraging. I should try not to make everything a joke.

I open my mouth to tell him I have faith in him, but before I can, he excitedly tells me, "I did find some jobs for Adley, though! I sent out her resume, and she's already lined up a few interviews. She's nervous. Apparently, tech interviews as a woman are brutal. But she's kind of a big deal. I can't believe how badly that company treated her."

Adley rushes into the room with her phone. "You're at 10 million Instagram followers, Ezra! This is so awesome. I'm so proud of you, Ezzy!" The pride in Adley's voice is apparent and ignites a sense of resolve in me.

"You ain't seen nothing yet, babe! Just wait. I bet the endorsement deals will be rolling in any minute," I say, lifting her into a hug, squeezing her ass.

"The endorsement deals have already been rolling in," Marshall says in his smug, perfunctory tone.

"Ezra, put me down," Adley laughs and slaps softly at me.

"Oh, yeah?" I say to Marshall, feigning nonchalance.

"Yep," he says, "I've already filtered them and have about ten that I thought you'd be interested in." He turns his laptop to me, and a spreadsheet shines on my face.

"Dude, what's with you and spreadsheets?" I ask.

"They're the best way to present a significant amount of data," Adley says for him.

"What she said," Marshall says, pointing at her.

"Alright, data nerds, I'll teach you about infographics some other day, but

I won't derail. What am I looking at?" I respond.

"All the ones in red are those I didn't think you'd be interested in. The ones in green are the ones that seem on brand," he says.

"What's with the gradient?" I ask.

"Highest paying to lowest paying based on time commitment."

I peer down at the sheet and honestly have no sense of whether these are good deals.

"Um, Adley, can you look at this for me? I don't really…"

"OMG, Ezra! That top one would make you more money than I made in a month at my job just for a single video!" Adley responds.

"Should I do it?" I ask.

"I don't see why not," she says in a way that both does and does not answer my question. She never wants to tell me exactly what to do—even though I just wish she would.

I look to Marshall and ask, "Marsh? What do you think?"

"I highlighted it green, didn't I?" It's another non-committal answer, but I think they're both saying I should.

"Alright, well, I guess I'm gonna do it. Do I just email them to confirm or something?" I ask.

"I'll handle it," Marshall says, clacking away at the keyboard with a speed and fury I couldn't muster.

"Wow, are you like my secretary?" I tease.

"Administrative assistant. I take a 75% cut," he laughs, not looking up from the computer and continuing to work.

"What do I get for being the CEO of this company?" Adley jokes.

I lift and twirl her around, "the other 25%."

"That's it?" she says with a pout that I know has a sexual undertone. That pout is usually followed by a "classic Adley honey trap," which I have lovingly dubbed her overt flirting attempts.

Eager to please and encourage whatever she's got up her sleeve, I respond to the apparent bid for attention. I put her down and say with a smirk, "Well, what else would you like?"

ADLEY

"Well, if you recall, our very first morning together, you mentioned paying me in double-dicking," I tease. I place my hands on the back of the chair

Marshall sits in and stick my ass out to Ezra.

"I think I can afford that," he says while rubbing the flat area on my lower back that he's obsessed with. He wraps his arms around me and pushes his hard cock against my ass. The motion pushes me into the chair and nudges Marshall's chair forward, but he's too focused on his work to notice.

"God, I love this ass," Ezra says before leaning down and biting my cheek over my yoga pants. He pumps against me, grouping at my tits.

I put my hands on Marshall's shoulders and whisper, "Can you afford it, Marshall?"

"Huh? Sorry, angel, just a minute," he responds, ignoring me.

I stand up, causing Ezra to stop grinding against me as I turn to look at him. "I'm not this focused, am I?" I ask.

"Yeah, you kind of are," Ezra laughs.

"I've got an idea," I say with a devious smile. "Stay right here. I'll be back." Ezra looks at me curiously as I rush to my office. I frantically riffle through the drawers until I find a laser pointer. *Score!*

When I return, Marshall is showing Ezra something on the laptop. Perfect; they're not looking this way. I hide in the doorway, hoping they won't notice me, and point the laser pointer at the laptop screen.

"What's that!" Ezra says, pointing at the dot.

"Some graphical error," Marshall says, swiping at it.

I migrate the laser pointer to the keyboard, and Marshall stands in surprise. "What the fuck?"

I trail the laser off the laptop and onto Ezra's chest. Ezra smacks at his chest only to find the dot on his hand. They lock eyes, and Marshall smacks at it.

I double over laughing, unable to contain myself, causing the laser pointer to turn off. Now noticing me, Ezra asks, "Babe, what are you up to?"

"I just wanted to see if this would get Marshall's attention," I respond, still laughing.

"Well, it worked," Marshall responds.

I stand in the doorway, leaning seductively against the frame. "I was thinking we could use this laser pointer to show each other what to do?" I suggest, aiming the red dot at my chest. They both lunge at me, groping and squeezing at my breasts. I laugh and turn it off. "I guess that means you like the idea."

Marshall demands, "Give me that thing."

"Um, okay," I reply, hesitantly handing him the laser pointer. Ezra glances at Marshall, a knowing smirk forming on his lips. Low, sensual purrs vibrate out of them. Ezra pushes me against the wall, pressing himself into me as Marshall steps back. Ezra buries his face in the crook of my neck, sucking and nibbling while grinding against my leg. My body tenses with anticipation, both lulled and stimulated by their purrs. Ezra pins my hands above my head against the wall, flattening me against it. He playfully bites on my earlobe before whispering, "Stay right there, babes." His hand locked on my wrists, he angles his body slightly, exposing me to Marshall—then he waits.

Marshall supports himself against the counter. The anticipation of his next move builds in me. Ezra and I both squirm, ready to unleash our lust on each other but awaiting Marshall's cue. An expression of exultant joy crosses Marshall's face before he directs the laser pointer at my neck. Ezra dives towards it, planting a heated kiss on the spot where the red dot lingers. The sensation makes my body lurch forward, but Ezra guides me back into place—a gentle palm against my pelvis. He strums his fingers teasingly just above my pussy.

With one hand gripping the laser pointer, Marshall uses the other to release his erect cock from his pants. He strokes it slowly as he moves the laser pointer down to the hem of my shirt. Ezra takes this as his cue to lift my shirt over my head and past my extended arms before tossing it aside.

The red dot targets my bra. Ezra's skilled fingers unclasp it easily and discard it onto the floor at Marshall's feet. Ezra takes one nipple into his mouth while teasing the other between his fingers—giving them both gentle pinches and tender nibbles that make me let out involuntary moans.

Marshall adjusts his aim to the edge of my pants. Ezra releases me and drops to his knees in front of me. He hooks his fingers into the waistband and pulls my yoga pants down along with my panties. With quick precision, Marshall traces circles around my throbbing clit with the laser pointer. Ezra lurches toward the dot, pressing his tongue against my sensitive flesh, sending waves of pleasure through me.

Marshall's hand flies faster on his hard cock, and his eyes never leave the two of us—laser-focused on Ezra's wet mouth, lapping at my slick folds—drinking us in. The sensation of Ezra's hot mouth against me makes my toes curl, and I bite down on my lower lip—muffling my moan and bending forward—gripping his hair and using his ears to pull him closer to me.

Marshall saunters over to us, still stroking his cock as he approaches from the side. The intensity of their synchronized purrs escalates as Marshall aims the laser pointer toward the front of Ezra's pants. Not removing his mouth from me, Ezra unveils his throbbing erection. His hand encircles the head before moving up and down his shaft in the same rhythmic motion as Marshall's.

While maintaining his grip on his own cock, Marshall leans forward and nips gently at my erect nipple, sending shivers down my spine. I push his hand away so that I can grasp his length. I pump, trying to maintain the same rhythm. Marshall gasps, breaking away from my swollen nipple. His hand, now free, he grips Ezra's head and pushes it against my cunt. Marshall slips his tongue into my mouth, exploring it with a fervor that he only does when extremely aroused. Marshall thrusts into my hand, hitting my hip with the tip of his cock.

I bite Marshall's lower lip, startling him and causing his grip on the laser pointer to loosen. It falls to the ground between my feet. Seizing the opportunity, Ezra plucks the pointer from the ground and stands beside us. He sucks my lower lip into his mouth and bites my lip before aiming the laser pointer at my aching clit, directing Marshall to take his place between my folds. Marshall lowers himself before me and starts lapping at my soaked flesh.

Marshall's hand moves deftly up and down his engorged member, his eyes unyielding as he watches Ezra glide his tongue across my chest. Marshall slides two fingers inside me, crooking them to find that spot that always sends me over the edge. Ezra silences my cries of pleasure by claiming my mouth once more in a searing kiss that leaves us all breathless.

Marshall doesn't relent, his tongue swirling around my swollen bud as I whimper. Ezra's fingers from his free hand circle around my nipple, plucking it between his thumb and forefinger before giving it a delicious pinch. The pleasure-pain cocktail rocks through me, sending me into a spiral of sensations I can barely process.

Ezra's hand grips the base of his own stiff cock. His breathing against my chest mirroring the pounding rhythm of my heart against my rib cage. A glint of mischief enters Ezra's eye as he directs the laser pointer to his own cock. Marshall doesn't hesitate before gripping Ezra's rigid cock and pumping his fist along the length. His other hand still curls two fingers deep inside me, his mouth still suckling earnestly at my clit.

Ezra watches Marshall's hand glide along his length, lust clouding his gaze. He pushes Marshall's head deeper into my cunt, just as Marshall did to him earlier. Ezra leans into me; his moans muffled against my breastbone as he kisses across my chest and nips at me. Marshall must be doing a good job because Ezra is breathing as if he's about to climax.

Marshall's tongue flicks and darts over my clit, and my orgasm builds inside me, ready to break at any moment. It's too much—but not enough—I need more! I keel over the edge with a strangled cry that only serves to spur him on further; he doesn't slow down until I see stars behind my closed eyelids. My orgasm washes over me as I breathe out, "Marshall, Ezra, oh my God!"

But before I can go entirely boneless and slide down the wall, Ezra points the laser pointer above my pubic area to get Marshall's attention—then directs it at the space above my head. Although I'm unsure of its meaning, Marshall seems to comprehend it. He stands and guides me against the wall, pinning my wrists above my head again.

Marshall thrusts his throbbing cock inside my drenched center, driving into me with a fierce determination. Ezra smacks Marshall's ass, saying, "Stretch goal. Don't slow down. Make her come again." Then he leaves. Where is he going?

Marshall pushes into me with renewed vigor. He lifts my knee, hooking it under his arm while still holding my hands captive above me. The depth of his penetration feels impossibly deep and sends shivers down my spine. He kisses my jaw, then pulls back so he can watch his dick plow into me while my tits bounce above it.

Marshall pounds into me relentlessly. My moans grow louder with each thrust until I climax yet again. As the last echoes of my pleasure fade away, Ezra materializes with a bottle of lube in hand. He leans close to whisper, "Sorry I was gone so long. I trust you were in excellent hands."

I bite my lip and nod languidly.

Then he whispers, "Babe, can I fuck that perfect ass?"

"Yes," I breathe out. I'm not sure if I can come again, but I might as well let them try that stretch goal they're always going on about.

Smearing lube along his shaft with practiced motions, Ezra prepares himself for his new exploration. Marshall remains inside me; his movements are now slower but retaining their strength—his hot breath coats my neck.

Ezra smacks Marshall's ass again, causing Marshall to step back slightly, releasing me from the wall. He drives deeper within me as he shifts my weight from the wall onto him, lifting my knee even further. He angles my body just right so that Ezra can approach my ass. Ezra rubs my lower back in a circle—obsessed with the area. "God, this spot drives me so fucking crazy, babe." He doesn't move his hand from that spot as he drags the lubed finger around my back entrance. He teasingly places the tip of his finger in, causing me to bend forward onto Marshall's chest, lifting my ass further for him. Ezra takes his place behind me, and after dragging his dick across his favorite spot, he pushes past the tight resistance of my puckered asshole. He glides in and out of me with a slow, steady pace that perfectly contrasts with Marshall's ongoing brutal rhythm.

"Oh, babe," Ezra groans. "You feel like heaven." He reaches forward to grope at my breasts and bites at my ear. His movements are no longer controlled and suave but desperate and almost fumbley as he loses himself to the pleasure of being inside a place within me he's never been before.

With the same piercing focus he approaches research, Marshall continues driving into me, watching his favorite spot—my bouncing tits over his thrusting cock. He breaks his concentration only when Ezra cups the vestigial ear on the side of his face, rubbing his thumb tenderly over it. As our bodies move in unison, Ezra leans forward to capture Marshall's lips in a searing kiss, followed by a passionate exchange between himself and me. Marshall then joins in, pressing his mouth against mine with equal fervor.

In this moment of fiery connection, we share a blissful release—moaning in harmony as our climaxes intertwine and we achieve the sweetest sense of ecstasy together.

30

ADLEY

Ezra's fame is taking off at breakneck speed, thanks to Marshall's help. Offers pour in for various endorsement deals, and his follower count on all platforms is growing at alarming rates.

Frustratingly, there are quite a few things Ezra can't do, since he has to hide his ears and tail, and some of the best offers he's received are in-person modeling gigs or commercials.

At home, we can deal with the ears and tail. Either we take the pictures and videos from an angle that doesn't reveal them, or we digitally remove them. I taught Marshall how to do photo editing using Photoshop, and he instantly got the hang of it. He's mentioned his past artistic ability, so I'm not surprised. I encourage him to start digital drawing, but he's always "too busy" for stuff like that. Occasionally, we'll take pictures of Ezra outside, and since it's still cold, wearing a hat and a long coat isn't all that weird.

Marshall's confidence is taking shape, having a new purpose: helping Ezra. But having to hide his ears and tail gets to Ezra. It seems to get to Marshall, too. Whenever I suggest we go somewhere fun, they often both opt to stay home rather than deal with trying to hide their features.

Marshall, now over his fear of being caught driving without a license, visits the post office every day. Originally, he walked to the post office to empty the PO box, but now the gifts are coming much more readily, and he needs the car to bring all the stuff home.

"Record-breaking batch today, Ezra!" Marshall says, walking in the door holding a bunch of boxes.

"Oh, wow. That's a lot!" I say.

"This isn't even half of it. It's going to take a few more trips," he says.

"Seriously?!" Ezra says, running to the garage to check out his haul.

"I think the postal workers might think I'm a drug dealer or other nefarious thing," Marshall laughs.

"Well, you are driving without a license. So, they're not too far off," I say while kissing him hello.

"Yep, I'm a hardened criminal," Marshall says.

"Look at this one, Adley!" Ezra says, running in with a box so big it's half his height. His arms barely reach around the sides. "I wonder what's in here?!" he says, throwing the box on the ground and ripping at it.

"Hey, let's get the rest of the stuff first! Also, don't tear the shipping label. We need to catalog who it's from," Marshall scolds, but Ezra does not listen.

Ezra reaches into the box and performs the "whole arm scoop" maneuver he does at the grocery store, pulling everything out of the box and putting it on the ground.

In a single leap, jumping higher than is humanly possible (because, well, he's not a human), he leaps over the ledge of the box and lands right in it. He dips down into the box and giggles to himself. The tops of his ears are still visible. *If it fits, it sits, I suppose.*

Marshall looks annoyed, but then his face lights up. He transforms into his ailo form, something he rarely does, and leaps into the box with Ezra. "Claws, bro!" Ezra yelps.

I approach the box and peer into it. Ezra is sitting cross-legged, grinning like a madman, and Marshall is crouched down in his lap. "Found you," I say, laughing at how adorable this is.

Ezra stands and tries to pull me in with them. "I can't fit in there, too!" I say and run away from them. He leaps out and gently tackles me onto the couch. Nuzzling me on the neck.

Marshall meows loudly. Ezra's ears snap toward Marshall, distracting him from his nuzzling. "Seriously, bro?!"

"What did he say?" I ask.

Marshall transforms and stands in the box, which is not quite high enough to cover his junk. The sight is absolutely hilarious. I can't help but giggle.

"I said that Ezra's first check cleared today," Marshall says as he slowly removes himself from the box.

"No wonder you're in such a good mood, Marsh," I laugh. "Let's celebrate! We should get sushi! There's a place in the next town over that's getting rave reviews."

"Can we get it delivered?" Ezra asks. He hasn't left the house in a few weeks, and I'm getting a bit worried about him. But he seems incredibly happy right now, so I won't push it.

"Alright, well, if we're eating in, we're getting drunk," I say.

"Marshall, let's get you some of that sake you keep crying about," Ezra says.

"I have not cried. I have simply stated that I wish I had tried it," he says curtly.

"Simply stated? Bro, you talk about it aaaaall the time. You might as well be crying," Ezra teases.

I pull out my phone and open the delivery app, searching for the word "sushi." The restaurant I have been hearing about is the first hit, and it has a 4.75 star rating.

"Here it is," I say, handing the guys the phone. They huddle over it, clicking incessantly.

"How many things are you ordering?!" I ask.

"We're getting it all," Ezra says, grinning.

"What? Don't do that! If we don't eat it all, it will go to waste. I think we have to eat sushi within like 12 hours!"

"Don't worry, babe. We can definitely eat it all," Ezra smirks, handing me the phone. "Here you go, babe. Add what you want."

"Are you serious? You got all of this just for the two of you? I can't have any?"

"No, you can. It's just I know you'll want some vegetables or something. Like that edamame stuff you like," he says, making a mock vomit face.

"Oh, no, they don't have sake on their delivery menu," I say, and Marshall looks positively dejected.

"Wait. The wine store down the street uses this app, too! We can place a second order," I say with a little dance.

"It's okay. We don't have to do a separate order just for me," Marshall says.

"Nonsense, bro," Ezra says with a playful pat on his ass. And with the comedic timing he is known for, "It's not just for you!"

=^..^= ♥ =^..^=

The liquor store is nearby so the delivery person arrives with the sake first. Since it's alcohol, I have to open the door—which I hate. Typically, I ask them to leave deliveries on the porch.

I look at the doorbell camera, and it's a man. Gah! I look down at my outfit, and, not wearing a bra, my nipples are in full force. *Fuck*. I should have put on something else. When I open the door to the cold, it will be worse. The guys get out of the way, not wanting to be seen, and I open the door.

"Adley? I've got your order right here. Just need to see your ID," the man says.

"Okay," I say, handing him my ID and crossing my arms in front of my chest. I'm trying not to look annoyed while I cover my nipples, which are now hard as rock due to the frigid air.

He looks at the ID and says, "Is this really you?"

"Yes, of course it's me," I say.

"I'm not sure. You don't look 35," he says. I'm not sure if he's hitting on me or calling me old. I can never tell when someone is hitting on me.

So, instead of trying to figure it out, I respond, "That's because I'm 34."

"Oh, yeah, you've got a birthday coming up soon, huh?" he asks.

"Yep. Can I have my ID back, please? And the sake?"

He continues to hold the ID in one hand and the bag of alcohol in the other, down at his side. He leans in slightly, trying to look into my home. "You drinking all this sake by yourself?"

"Nope," I say.

"You seem alone."

"Well, I'm not."

"Want company?" he says, staring at my tits and licking his lips.

"As I said, I have company already," I respond. His face shifts from lust to fear, and he looks above my head. I turn to see Marshall and Ezra standing behind me.

"Those are our tits you're drooling over, bro," Ezra responds.

"And our sake," Marshall says, reaching forward and grabbing the bag and ID from the stunned driver.

"Thanks, bro. Have a good night," Ezra smiles, then slams the door shut hard.

I jump at the door slamming shut. "Ah, fuck, babe. I'm sorry. I was trying to be scary and just scared you."

"I'm pretty sure you scared him. And that was insanely hot," I say.

=^..^= ♥ =^..^=

The sushi delivery is significantly less eventful. It took much longer because the restaurant is further away, and the chefs had to prepare literally their entire menu for one order. By the time the driver leaves it at the door, Marshall is two sheets to the wind. When the doorbell rings, he pushes me gently back to the couch, saying with a giggle, "Nah, babe, those headlights will wake up the whole neighborhood."

Ezra laughs uproariously. "So, all it took was some sake to get some metaphors out of you, bro?!"

We spread the sushi on the kitchen counter, almost covering the whole surface.

"There's no way we're eating all this," I sigh.

Marshall sneaks up behind me, wrapping his arms around my waist and pressing me against the counter.

"Hey, what's up with you?" I ask, surprised.

"You're so fucking hot," he says, uncharacteristically aggressive. *Not complaining.* He gently nuzzles my neck before firmly caressing my breasts with both hands and causing goosebumps to run down my skin.

"You're drunk," I laugh, feeling the warmth of his breath against my skin.

"And horny," he states, spinning me around and planting a fervent kiss on my lips.

"Well, um… I guess the sushi can wait," I say, my heart pounding in anticipation.

He effortlessly lifts me, wrapping my legs around his waist as he walks me to the table. "We eat at the table," he reminds me gruffly. He then carefully lays me down before expertly sliding off my pants and underwear in one fluid motion.

Ezra appears behind him and comments appreciatively, "That looks delicious."

Overcome with desire, Marshall lets out a low growl and declares, "These tits have been tempting me all night. I'm going to savor you until I am full. Then I'll thrust inside you so hard that you see stars." *Dang, sake-drinking Marshall has game.*

Without hesitation, Marshall dives towards me and trails his tongue from my back entrance to the sensitive nub above. The unexpected sensation causes a pleasure-induced moan to escape my lips. He smirks at me as he realizes how much I enjoy it. "Oh, you like that?" he questions playfully before repeating his actions. "You taste delicious."

"Alright, bro, time to share," Ezra interjects while nudging Marshall aside so that they both are positioned between my legs. Together, they tease and lick me. I grip their heads between my thighs, running my fingers through their hair and up to the tips of their ears. Their skilled fingers explore every part of me, simultaneously thrusting into my core and my most hidden entrance, causing my vision to blur with ecstasy.

The overwhelming combination of sensations quickly becomes too much to handle. My body reacts with a powerful climax that leaves me breathless and spent. I come more quickly than I think I ever have with them.

"Damn, bro, we broke two records today," Ezra says and they high-five.

"Are you two high-fiving over my naked pussy?" I ask. *This is the price you pay to live with two dudes.*

"Yeah, it's that cum-radery thing," Marshall says with a grin slicked with my juices. Then, distracted, he says, "Hold on, I need to try something," leaving Ezra and me at the table. He inspects the spread of food on the counter before selecting a salmon nigiri and sinking it into his mouth. He moans in delight and says, grinning stupidly, "Yes, they should sell your pussy as a condiment because it pairs nicely with this."

Gross. Please, please, don't compare me to fish. That is not sexy. Luckily, he does not. He inspects the various pieces and grabs another, bringing it to Ezra. "I believe you said the tuna was your favorite," he says, handing it to him.

"Aww, bro, you remembered?"

"Of course," he says, walking away again.

Ezra puts the piece of tuna nigiri in his mouth, and his ears and tail shoot up in pleasure. He does a little dance before sitting next to me on the table.

"Um… didn't you say you were going to fuck me?" I ask Marshall, "If you'd rather eat…"

"Oh, no, babe, I'm going to fuck you. But Ezra and I are going to feed each other sushi while we fuck you," Marshall says absentmindedly. He's intensely focused on selecting various pieces and putting them on the two plates he has. Then he breaks from his focus and says, "Um… if that's okay with you two."

"Sure, bro, you're in charge," Ezra grins. He shoulders at me and says, "Let's just let him have his moment, yeah?"

"That's fine, Marshall. We'll wait," I say, giggling at Ezra and placing my head on his shoulder.

"He seems so happy," I laugh.

"We should have gotten the sake months ago," Ezra laughs.

"I know, right?" I respond. Wow, have they been with me for months now? The fact that I live in a perpetual winter makes it hard to tell the passage of time sometimes, but I suppose it is starting to warm up.

"But hurry up, bro! I know you got some amazing plan, but my balls are starting to ache over here," Ezra says.

"Sorry, sorry, I've got this… this whole plan," Marshall says, frantically placing more sushi on the plates. He walks toward us only to realize he forgot something, carefully selects another piece, and then hurriedly tiptoes back to us. He giggles as he places the two plates on the ends of the table.

"Marshall, I don't know if I've ever seen you giggle before," I say with my own giggle.

"Oh, do you like Silly Marshall?" he says, pulling me to the table's edge and wrapping my legs around him.

"I do," I say, lacing my fingers around his neck.

"That's too bad. I was planning to be Alpha Marshall for you tonight. But I can be Silly Marshall if that's what you desire," he says.

Intrigued, I respond, "Oh, um, I bet I would like Alpha Marshall, too." Ezra raises his eyebrows, his curiosity also getting the best of him.

"I read a bit of that book you were reading the other day. The one you read before you came storming into the bedroom and insisted on sitting on Ezra's face. You know which I'm referencing?" he says.

"Oh, yes, I know," I say.

"Which book?" Ezra says, leaning toward us.

"Shh," Marshall says, placing a finger on Ezra's lips.

"Alright, Alpha Marshall," Ezra chuckles and leans back.

"Would you like me to do those things to you?" he asks.

"Um… that depends. How far did you get?" I ask because I definitely have a line.

"Chapter five," he responds.

Oh, ok. The line is at chapter 10. "Yes, you may do all those things," I say, my breath hitching in anticipation.

"Can I play, too, bro?" Ezra asks, unable to stay out of the conversation for long.

"Yes, you are the pathetic Beta, though," Marshall says, not breaking eye contact with me.

"Ouch, alright. I guess I can do that. Are you going to be fucking me, too?" Ezra asks with a laugh.

Marshall breaks eye contact with me and says with a smoldering, severe intensity, "If you want me to, I will."

Ezra's ears and tail perk up, and he whimpers slightly—as the blush covers his face, I think he might say he does want Marshall to fuck him. Marshall and I do not break our gaze from Ezra as we hold our breath, awaiting his response. "Um, no thanks. Not tonight, bro," Ezra says.

Marshall puts his hand on Ezra's chin, lifting his face to his, and says, "That response implies that the answer will be 'yes' some other night. In which case, I will fuck that fluffy little ass whenever you let me."

Ezra sputters, unsure how to respond to this version of Marshall, "Um… okay." I gape at them as they stare into each other's eyes.

Marshall's not done yet, "However, I think I might prefer you to fuck me. I do not know. Perhaps we can find out." Ezra's eyes open wider, and I bite back a giggle. Ezra is never going to let Marshall live down sake-Alpha Marshall.

"Anyway, back to you," Marshall says, returning his attention to me, "So, I can do everything up through chapter five?"

"Uh, huh!" I say, nodding, excited for him to let some of this alpha out on me.

He lifts me to my feet, kissing me deeply, his tongue forcing its way into my mouth, making our teeth knock from the force. He turns me to face the table, kissing the back of my neck and raising my hair gently. Suddenly, he grips my hair and pulls my head back, saying, "You want my cock, don't you? Have you been a good girl? Do you deserve it?" His voice is low and rough.

I gasp in surprise. The sound of his voice makes me weak in the knees. And I quickly find myself arching my back and raising my ass instinctively to him. I nod my head eagerly as I peer back at him, ass rising higher.

He backs away and roughly tears off his clothes, revealing his throbbing cock. Ezra, struggling to maintain the role, says, "Daaamn, bro," while sitting beside me on the table.

Marshall glares at him, and Ezra says, "Sorry." He then jumps off the table and backs over to the other side.

"Go over there and watch me fuck your girl, Beta. Wait until you are called on," Marshall says, pointing at the other side of the table.

Ezra doesn't cower. Instead, he says, "Sure thing, Alpha. Can I stroke my cock while you rail that pussy?"

Marshall falters for a minute, unsure how to maintain the role, then says, "If you keep that smart mouth shut."

"Nice save, bro!" Ezra says with an excited thumbs up. Marshall tilts his head at him, annoyed and exasperated. Ezra whispers, "Sorry."

Marshall turns back to me. "Say it," he commands. He grabs my chin forcefully, turning my face toward him while pressing his cock against my ass. He smacks my ass, not as hard as he could, then says, "Tell me how much you want it."

My lips part in a silent plea for release from the agony of anticipation renewed after the little Abbot and Costello bit the two of them were doing. "Desperately. I need your cock," I whisper, my voice trembling with desire. "Please, I've never wanted anything more."

He growls low in his throat. He grabs my hips before slamming into my wet pussy with one powerful thrust. I scream out against the pleasure mixed with oh-so-delectable pain. He relentlessly fucks into me, hard against the table. I cling to the surface, desperate to find a handhold against the assault at my back. His long, solid dick hammers against my g-spot as his hand slides up to my throat possessively. "This is my pussy. Mine!" he says. His cock overwhelming every square inch of me.

"Do you hear that, Beta?!" He yells to Ezra. I look to Ezra, who stands wide-eyed, watching, stroking his cock as furiously as Marshall pounds into me and nodding in response. I try to match Marshall's intensity but can only manage whimpers and moans as he fucks me harder still. My body is no longer mine; it belongs to him entirely. Every thrust sends shockwaves of pleasure through my core while his hand at my throat squeezes just enough to make me feel like I am fully his.

He pulls out sharply, removing his whole length from me, then plunges back into my depths again, hitting that perfect spot deep within that makes me see stars. My nails dig into the table as I howl, clenching around his dick and coming so fucking hard. "Oh, my God!" I wail and twitch and convulse as his relentless pounding continues. Marshall pulls my hips closer to himself and grabs at my tits while he twitches his orgasm into me. Ezra releases his orgasm into his hand, catching it before it hits the table.

"No more," I breathe out, and Marshall removes himself from me, grinning.

As I come down from my orgasm, I'm not sure what to think. It was terrific but also unexpected. Marshall leans over me, kissing my back. His breath is hot against my skin, sending shivers down my spine.

"Did you like that, angel?" Marshall asks, the bite removed from his voice.

"Oh, my God, yes, Marshall! That was just like the book! Thank you!"

"Damn, what is this book?!" Ezra asks.

"But what was with all the sushi? You didn't use any of it?" I laugh.

"Oh, that part wasn't for you! The sushi is for us. That's the next part of my plan," Marshall responds.

"What? There's more? Oh, Marshall, you fucked the hell out of me. I don't think I can do it anymore," I sigh.

"Oh… okay… well, I guess we can just eat the sushi, then…" Marshall says, shrugging.

Ezra chuckles and licks his lips. He pats Marshall's back while saying, "Good job, bro. That was quite the show. Now let's eat."

31

EZRA

"I cannot believe y'all are still playing this game," Adley says as she plops onto the couch between me and Marshall. She rests her head on my shoulder, and I plant a kiss on it, wrapping my arm around her.

"You were right, Adley. It is an unassuming masterpiece," Marshall says. He's leaning forward on the couch, controller in hand, guiding the main character, York, through the door of Milk Barn, the quirky town of Greenvale's general store. The screen transitions to a slightly angled third-person view, giving Marshall control of York's movements again.

Marshall and I have been chipping away at *Deadly Premonition* for weeks. Our progress has been slow because it scares the crap out of us—a fact we try to hide from Adley. "This game makes me think I should start drinking coffee," I say. "York makes it sound so delicious."

"Ezra, I don't think you need any more energy," Marshall deadpans with a side eye.

"Have you gotten to the part with the giant dog yet?" Adley asks.

Marshall pauses the game and looks at her wide-eyed. "What?" he asks.

"Yeah, I don't remember when it happens, but at night, you drive around, and a giant dog chases you. It's super scary," she says, pulling her knees to her chest and leaning into me further.

"Um, maybe we should play something else for now," Marshall says, looking at me with pleading eyes.

I nod to him. He guides York to the black rotary phone sitting on a nearby table. He presses the interaction button, and the screen transitions to the save menu. Marshall saves the game and promptly turns off the console.

"I wonder why the save menu has a type-writer sound effect, but you access it from a phone," Marshall says.

"One of the many mysteries of design decisions around this game, Marsh," Adley says with a laugh.

"Have you tried *Like a Dragon* yet?" Adley asks.

"Oh, yeah! We're maybe 30 hours into it. Let's play that, Marshall!" I say. He hands me the controller and leans back on the couch. I remove my arm from Adley's shoulders to hold the controller in both hands. Turn the console back on and navigate to the game.

We wait for it to load, I chuckle to Adley, "You like some weird games, Ads."

"I like games that try something different," she shrugs.

"You seem to gravitate toward games with interesting, loveable characters," I state.

She sighs, "Yeah… I've always had trouble making and keeping friends, so video games have just been… my friends. If a game has lovable characters, I fall in love with the game. Sometimes when I finish a game, it hurts just as badly as a breakup."

She rests her head in my lap and puts her feet on Marshall's. Marshall and I discuss what to do next in the game while Adley quietly watches us play. He rubs her feet absently, and I occasionally stroke her hair. Moments like these are what I've been waiting for—moments where we can just enjoy each other's company with no drama. As much as I enjoy having sex with them, this is what I crave from them.

I lean against the couch, trying to get comfortable, but my eyes drift down to Adley. Her expression is unreadable, and something about it feels... off.

For a long moment, the only sound is the rhythmic clatter of my controller's buttons as I guide Ichiban Kasuga through the bustling streets of Yokohama. Adley pulls the blanket off the back of the couch to cover herself. Marshall and I adjust it around her, tucking her in as she bundles it close to her face. She looks so adorable. I squeeze her shoulder and smile down at her. She looks back up at me, and for a moment, she seems like she may cry. But before I can ask her what's wrong, she smiles at me and looks back at the game.

"Adley? Wanna play for a bit?" I ask, holding the controller over her.

"No thanks," she says, but her words feel hollow.

I glance to my right, meeting Marshall's gaze. I nod slightly down toward Adley, silently asking him if he knows if something's wrong with her. He looks at her, then back at me, shrugging. *It must just be in my head. Everything's perfect.*

MARSHALL

I rub Adley's soft feet resting on my legs, relishing in the feel of them against my thigh. Their heat and proximity threaten to arouse me, but Adley's sadness permeates the room. She loves this game. Whenever she talks about it, she radiates excitement. So, for her to watch us play and show no emotion at all…

Ezra seems unaware of her mood and says, "You were right about this game, Ads. It's hilarious."

"Yeah," she sighs out, but there's no enthusiasm. Her head rests on Ezra's lap, and she has the blanket tucked around her so tightly that all I can see is her face. She's not smiling like usual when discussing a game she loves. It makes me uneasy, but I don't know if I should press her to tell us what's wrong. She would tell us if something was wrong, wouldn't she?

"I know this game has been around awhile, but I think I might stream playing it," Ezra says, laughing. "Hey, Marsh, I thought we should edit the live stream archives to some snappy clips and then upload them on YouTube. Do you think you could make thumbnails for the videos for me? Something with flashy text and colors that pop?" he says, accentuating the word pop with an explosion of his hand.

"Oh, yeah, I could do that!" I say excitedly. He keeps finding ways for me to help, and I appreciate the gesture. I know he can do many of the things he's asked me to do himself, but the fact he's included me in this endeavor with him has given me a sense of purpose that I lacked. I feel like I'm contributing to the success of our little clowder.

"I think I'm ready to tackle this quest," Ezra says, his character still wandering around town as we postpone the next story beat.

Adley shifts again. I can feel it now—she's not with us. She's here physically but not emotionally. It's like there's a wall between her and us—the light of the game dances across her angelic features, accentuating the slack expression on her face.

"I think you probably should level up a bit more…," I say to Ezra while watching Adley.

"Yeah, I think I need better weapons, too," Ezra says, making Ichiban fast travel to the blacksmith to upgrade his weapons.

"Hey, babe, imagine if the bat you swung at us the night we met was like this," Ezra laughs while scrolling possible baseball bats for Ichiban to craft. The one he is referencing is wrapped in razor wire and lighting. Adley doesn't laugh at the joke. She doesn't even seem to react. She always laughs when she thinks about the time she tried to murder us with her bat.

I should probably check in with her. She stares at the screen, her expression blank, like she's watching but not seeing. I don't know if she even processed what Ezra just said or what she's seeing on the screen.

I squeeze the center of her foot, catching her attention. She looks at me blankly. I furl my eyebrows and lean toward her, rubbing her leg.

"Adley, is something wrong?" I ask, feeling a twinge of concern I've been ignoring.

Ezra stops playing and looks at her, waiting for her response.

She doesn't immediately respond, and I think I hear her voice choke when she says, "I'm fine. I'm just... tired."

"You sure you're good, babe?" Ezra asks, "You don't seem into it tonight."

There's an awkward silence that hangs between us. My mind whirls—maybe she's just exhausted from all the interviews, or maybe there's something else going on.

She looks up at us, offering a small, forced smile that doesn't feel like her. "Yeah, I'm fine," she says softly, though the words don't convince me. "I'm going to bed. Y'all keep playing. I knew you'd love this game," she says while standing, the blanket still wrapped around her. She wanders up the stairs slowly without even looking back.

Our eyes don't leave the stairs even after she's gone. "Bro, do you know what that was about?" Ezra asks.

"Maybe she is just tired. I know the interviews are mentally and physically exhausting," I say.

"I don't know… this seems… different…" Ezra says, trailing off, his face scrunched in thought. "I don't want to be 'that guy,' but… umm… when was the last time we had sex?"

I think for a long moment, struggling to remember.

"I think it's been… no, that can't be right. Three weeks?" I say.

"Yeah, that's what I thought, too," Ezra says, "Like, I know horniness cools in relationships, but this seems… different… like it's a symptom of something else."

I look at my hands while I think about the last few weeks. Ezra and I have gotten along well, so it can't be about our fighting. But we've also been spending a lot of time together without Adley. She isolates herself in the bedroom whenever she's not interviewing. She's said multiple times that she prefers to be alone mostly—so we've let her be alone. But was that the right choice?

Ezra, seeming to come to the same conclusion as me, responds, "I think the job search is getting to her, and she's isolating herself—which is probably making it worse."

I think about his words for a long moment. He's right. Her interviews have not been going well, but she has mostly refused to discuss them. I will make sure to talk to her about the next one.

"Yeah, I think you're right," I say as I reflect on the uncomfortable feeling that I've failed her builds within me.

Never one to feel comfortable in silence, Ezra says, "I think we should put in a bit more effort to do things with her, bro. I think maybe we got too comfortable and stopped worshipping her like we promised her we always would."

"Yeah," I say, looking back at the TV and staring through it. The smiling face of Ichiban beams back at me—his bat draped over his shoulder.

"We got this, bro. We just gotta work together," Ezra says, tapping my knee and resuming the game. I assume he's talking about Adley and not the game. If only life were as easy as video games.

32

ADLEY

"Fuck!" I shout as I slam my laptop shut.

Marshall leans into the door of my office. "What happened?"

"He asked me about a sorting algorithm, and I fucking forgot. It's such a basic fucking question. I literally taught it to my students when I was a professor. It's honestly insulting that he'd ask me. It's something you ask a recent graduate. Not a fucking woman with 15 years of experience and a goddamn doctorate. Fuck." My rage and frustration waffle between hating myself and hating that guy whose smirk is burned into my brain.

Marshall pulls me into an embrace, cradling my head against his chest when he says, "That's bullshit."

"It's embarrassing. I know it! I do! I was just… so nervous, and I was too focused on smiling." I feel so fucking stupid. *How could I have messed up so badly? What is wrong with me?* A bitter, aching feeling builds in my chest as I rub my face against Marshall's chest.

"That's understandable," he says, petting my head.

"But! It's not even something you fucking need to have memorized! You can just google it, for fuck's sake! The hard part of the job isn't stupid fucking sorting algorithms; it's understanding the intricacies of a system… so, to completely disregard all my experience and everything else I can do because I failed his stupid pop quiz…"

"It's shortsighted of him."

"It is! And then he fucking made this joke about how my school must just hand out degrees." *Maybe he was right; perhaps I am stupid.*

"You don't want to work with a tool like that, anyway," Marshall says, rubbing my arms.

"Yeah, you're right," I sigh. "I just… this is so hard. I have never been unemployed this long before."

"Well, Ezra's making enough money—"

"That's not the point," I interrupt, my voice quivering as the tears fall—my rage replaced with bitter despair.

"I know, angel," he says, thumbing a tear from my cheek.

"I'm just… I feel so…" I croak, trembling in his arms.

"Useless?" he asks.

"Yeah," I say, burying my face further into his chest, trying to find comfort in his warmth. I unleash a wailing cry as I pull at his soft black t-shirt. He doesn't tell me to calm down. He doesn't tell me I'm overreacting. He doesn't even tell me it will be alright. He just lets me cry and pats my head with a tenderness that conveys unspoken reassurance. This is precisely what I needed: someone who would let me rage and hold me as I sputtered out.

"Marsh! Where'd you go?" Ezra calls from the hall. Shirtless and wearing the grey sweatpants I love, Ezra stops at the door when he spots us. "Oh, shit. Did it not go well?"

"Nope," I say through snotted tears.

"Want me to play their game on stream and talk shit about it?" he asks, joining in on the embrace and nuzzling into my neck.

"Kinda," I whisper.

"Babe, I could ask people on live if they need a brilliant hot-as-fuck programmer," Ezra asks.

"Don't do that. If it resulted in me getting a job, I'd get harassed for not deserving it," I sigh and bury myself between them—the soft fabric of Marshall's shirt on one side of my face, the baby-smooth skin of Ezra's chest on the other—their steady synchronized hearts thump against my cheeks.

"Can y'all purr for me?" I ask, pulling my arms to my chest and sinking further between them.

A low purr engulfs me without a response, making me drowsy and content. It's different from their lustful purr—quieter, soothing, and soft. Their warmth and vibration reassure me that I am safe and loved. Maybe the rest of the world is against me, but they aren't.

I pull away, resolved not to wallow, wiping my tears from my face now.

"It's fine. I'll do better next time," I say with a forced grin—willing myself to get it together and do something more productive.

A bolt of bright green fabric sits against my doorframe. Marshall placed it there when he came in.

"What are y'all up to?" I ask, pointing at the fabric.

"Oh, well, Marshall and I were decking out my new streaming area," he says.

"Oh, really? I want to see."

=^..^= ♥ =^..^=

I am blown away by their accomplishments when I reach the bottom of the stairs. The basement corner that used to hold Bryce's weights is being converted to Ezra's recording area. Textured foam panels adorn the walls, simulating a high-tech look. In the middle of the floor is a desk with multiple monitors stacked atop it and a decked-out gaming PC—only one monitor appears to be hooked up.

"We've still got a lot to do around the desk area, but we're finishing up the stage area now. We just needed a little more fabric," Ezra says, running to the other side of the room and standing in what I presume is the stage area.

Bright green fabric covers the walls, and multiple flood lights illuminate the area. A mic hangs from the ceiling, and a large, expensive-looking camera on a tripod points at it.

"So, Marshall had this idea: to use this fabric on the walls, and then I can cover my ears and tail with the same fabric. That way, we can green screen them out!" Ezra says. "I'm going to sew some little ear and tail sleeves!"

"Oh, that's a great idea!" I exclaim, knowing Ezra wants to do more live videos without hiding his body or wearing his "stupid hat," as he calls it.

"I know, right?! And check it out," Ezra says. "Marshall, put this pedal here so I can tap it with my foot. Once we hook it up, it will turn the camera and mic on and off." He points to the floor pedal that resembles something a guitarist might have and taps it with his toe. I inspect it further and note that it contains two pedals, each with a sharpie drawing on them: one of a camera and one of a mic.

"You draw those, Marshall?" I ask, pointing down at the device.

"Ha, yeah…" he says bashfully, and I smile at the response. He is so talented.

"Oh, he also made me this!" Ezra says, running to the desk and picking up a box with a bunch of black buttons on it. "Hold on, let me wake up the computer to show you." He wiggles the mouse, and the computer and monitor light up. The panel's buttons alight, revealing a bunch of animated doodles of icons.

"Oh, wow, Marshall! You made those?!"

"Yeah, I figured out how to do basic frame animation in Photoshop," he blushes, then bends to pick up a cable. His black t-shirt stretches over his shoulders, revealing the rippling muscles underneath. Poking out from sweatpants that match Ezra's, his black tail sways languidly—the way it sways when he's embarrassed—behind him. These pants were the first that Ezra equipped with the tail fly since he knew how much I liked them. They wear these pants so often now they'll be threadbare in no time. Marshall turns, noticing me lusting after him, and blushes again when my eyes land on his package. I don't know Jack about color theory, but I am curious what it is about the color grey that perfectly outlines cocks.

Ezra continues showing me the panel: "Each runs different functions in this software I use called OBS. All I have to do is hit one of these buttons, and my different panels will pop up on the feed. It will also switch cameras from the one at the desk to the one at the stage area so that I can control everything all by myself. Isn't that awesome, Adley?!"

"Yeah, that's super cool, Ezra. Nice work, guys," I say, legitimately impressed.

"Man, I wish I had known keeping a brainy dude like him around would be so useful back in the day. If I had, maybe I would have picked one up years ago," he laughs. Marshall's ears rotate on his head in embarrassment as he returns to wrapping the cable he holds around his hand and elbow.

"Oh, and over here! Behind the desk, we've got all these lights," he says, pointing at a pile of lights and lighted panels by Marshall's feet. "Marshall has this whole idea of how to put them on the wall. Then I can hit a button, and it'll feel like I'm underwater. Like at the aquarium!"

"Oh, neat, I'm excited to see it," I grin.

"Wanna help us finish setting the stuff up?" Ezra asks, obviously excited to get back to his work. Marshall has ceased wrapping the cable and is now unpacking the boxes of lighted panels. They both look happier than ever. I'm so glad they're finally getting along and seem to have a shared purpose… other than fucking me. As much as I want to hang out and watch their dicks sway in those pants as they huff and puff, hanging stuff on the wall, I don't want to bring down their vibe.

"Um, would you mind if I lay down instead? I'm kind of drained from the interview," I sigh.

"Oh, yeah, of course, babe. Do you want some alone time? Or we could watch *Fruits Basket*!" he says excitedly, running back to the stage area and unfurling the bolt of fabric.

"I think I'll just take a nap. So, alone time. Y'all have fun," I say.

"Alright, babe. Rest well," Ezra says.

Marshall stops me from leaving with a hand on my back. He says, "You sure you're okay?"

"Yeah," I say.

As my foot hits the bottom stairs, I hear, "Umm, Marshall, why's that camera light on? I thought you hadn't hooked it up yet."

"No, I did it right before I went upstairs…"

"Shit," Ezra says, grabbing at his ears in realization and then leaping out from in front of it.

I get an alert on my phone. The streaming app has alerted me that someone I follow is streaming. "Ezra is streaming now!" it says.

"Shit," I say.

=^..^= ♥ =^..^=

"Wow, Ez. I knew women liked cats, but damn," I say, watching yet another YouTube video where an online journalist describes the moment Ezra accidentally streamed himself without covering his head and tail. Behind her is a video of Ezra excitedly bounding around smiling beautifully, only to look at the camera, point at it, then cover his ears and leap out of the frame. Ezra's follower count has nearly doubled overnight, which is saying something considering how many he already had.

"Damn, we had this whole plan to get you to fuck us in front of that green screen," Ezra says. "It's a good thing the sweatpants bait didn't work, huh? I would have been banned for life." He laughs at himself.

I look to Marshall, "Y'all were conspiring to fuck me on camera?"

"Yep," he says. Not expanding. Not denying.

"With your consent, of course, babe," Ezra says. I look at him incredulously. Trying to save himself, he says, "We weren't going to show anyone. We were just hoping to have a memento. Something to watch when we're old and can't get it up anymore. We were maybe going to green screen us on a beach or something."

"Most people seem to think it was a stunt," Marshall says, looking at his phone. "That his ears and tail are animatronic. There's also talk that he's teasing a promotion to some movie he's going to be in."

"So, they think my ears are fake?" Ezra says, touching his ear.

"Yeah," Marshall says.

"I can work with this!" he says and gets up excitedly, rushing toward the basement.

"What are you going to do?" I ask.

"What I always do, babe. Lean into it!" he sings, turning and skipping away.

33

MARSHALL

I watch the birds from the living room window, suppressing a slight growl that builds in my chest. They flit back and forth across the ground, excited the snow has melted, revealing the worms under the soggy soil. Adley sits behind me on the couch, reading. The late morning sun streams into the room, casting warm, golden light onto her lap—she always looks like an angel. *Just go to her, Marshall.* I give the birds one last glare and sit next to her. I rest my head in her lap, letting the warm light bathe on my face. I lavish the warmth and nuzzle her legs, spreading my scent on her. *Mine.*

She seems surprised by this affection from me, but it is part of the master plan Ezra and I have come up with: lavish her with love. "You're starting to live up to that Romeo name," she says, and I understand the reference, having researched it weeks ago. I'm ashamed I did not show her such affection in the past. This seems like a surprising gesture from me. This is how I've always wanted to be with her. But now that Ezra and I are getting along, sharing her is no longer a fight, and I feel much more comfortable expressing my feelings to her.

Arousal lifts my pants, and it's taking every ounce of my willpower not to ravish her. But that is not part of the plan. The plan is to show her that we appreciate and worship her and that she means more to us than just someone to sleep with.

Like most quiet moments, this one is interrupted by Ezra, but it doesn't bother me anymore. He rushes into the room, holding two shirts against his chest. "Which of these do you guys like?"

"Green," Adley says at the exact moment I say, "Blue."

"Well, fuck!" Ezra says, rushing back to the bedroom for a different shirt.

"Maybe next time, only one of us should respond," Adley giggles and pets my head.

I purr into her lap and say, "Good idea."

Ezra returns with two shirts that look the same to me. "The left one," Adley says.

Ezra asks, "Marshall?"

I want to respond that I can't tell the difference, but I know that will make us even later. "Yes, left. Left is best." He looks at me as if he knows I can't tell the difference but doesn't argue with me before scurrying away, hopefully, to put it on.

I sigh into her lap and say, "We'll be going to dinner at this rate, not lunch. Perhaps I should make lunch?"

"We honestly should have known he'd do this," Adley says with a resigned giggle.

"I'm going to see if I can help speed things up," I say.

"Ha! Good luck," she says. I kiss her thigh, inciting a giggle, and look at her face. She seems content and happier; perhaps our plan is working. I launch at her and give her a tickling nibble on her ear and a kiss on the cheek before leaving her to find Ezra rushing between the bedroom and the bathroom.

"Ezra, seriously?" I lean against the doorframe to our bedroom; my tone hovers between amused and exasperated.

"You can't rush art, bro," Ezra responds, a hint of defensiveness in his tone mingled with playful self-awareness. "And this"—he pauses for dramatic effect—"is art." I'm better at reading his tone now, and I know that this means he is nervous and deflecting his anxiety with humor and feigned grandiosity.

As I walk closer to him, I say, "I know you're nervous, but you've never looked bad in your life. It's just lunch. It's just a little café, not some red-carpet event. We're not even going into the city."

"I know, bro," he sighs, annoyed with himself, "I'm scared. What if they realize the ears aren't fake? What if they think they're weird?"

I shrug. "Then we come home and never leave the house without a hat again," I say.

"Bro, that's not helpful," he says with a clip in his voice.

"Sorry, I wasn't trying to be dismissive. I just meant, then we go back to how things are. It's not the whole world, just a few people in a tiny café. Are you sure you want me to wear my hat? I can do this with you."

"No, I think… since people know what I look like… I should try," he says.

I follow him to the bathroom. He inspects his reflection. Scrutinizing his face and hair—adjusting the angle of his jawline, tilting his head slightly to the left, then to the right. His thick, blond hair is styled meticulously, each strand in its rightful place, his ears perched atop his fluffy hair, turning nervously. He's wearing a fitted shirt that accentuates his athletic build and designer jeans that cling just right. His tail sways behind him—out the fly he sewed into the pants—perfectly coiffed. Not a tangle in sight. His shoes, immaculately clean sneakers, squeak against the tile as he turns to look at himself.

I smack his ass in the same way he always smacks mine, and he looks at me positively scandalized, clutching his pearls. "Well, hurry up, bro," I say with a playful wink, "you look perfect… seriously."

"Perfect isn't enough," he shoots back. "I need… flawless."

I stifle an eye roll. "Adley, I need help," I say, leaning back.

She approaches and looks him up and down, "flawless," she says.

"You're cheating," he laughs. "You heard what I said!"

"Maybe. Maybe not," she shrugs.

"Ezra, seriously. There will maybe be three people in the whole place," I say, trying to assure him.

Adley leans on me, her lips curving into a knowing smile, "He's just nervous," she says.

"Insufferable is the word," I mutter, and Ezra looks at me, feigning offense, knowing from my grin that I am affectionately teasing him.

She intertwines her fingers with his and says playfully, "Perhaps we drag him out?"

"Oh, I might like that," Ezra says, slamming his body into hers and nuzzling her neck.

"Five more minutes," Adley says decisively, putting his face between her hands and kissing him deeply. "Then we're dragging you out by the tail," she says with a devious smile.

"Okay, okay, okay," he says and rushes to the bedroom to finish his masterpiece. He applies a subtle hint of cologne, ensuring the scent is noticeable and not overpowering. He straightens his posture, practices a disarming smile in the mirror, fluffs his tail and ears, and finally deems himself ready.

He stands in the bedroom doorway and poses seductively. I choke back a laugh at the theatrical display. He struts away from us, swaying his ass and tail with the air of a man stepping onto a red carpet—except significantly more exaggerated.

"Well?" he asks, spreading his arms wide. "Am I not… stunning?" We clap, knowing if we just play along, this will speed up.

Adley's expression is a mix of genuine admiration and playful exasperation. "You look amazing, as always. Now, can we please go?"

I cannot resist a jab. "You look… exactly the same as you did an hour ago. But sure, let's call it stunning."

"Bro, I know you want this. Don't be coy," he says, then poses as he had in that picture I used to love.

"Yes, and I wanted it an hour ago; nothing has changed," I say, and the fake bravado drains out of him as his face floods with blood, and he shifts to a shy stance. He always does this when I hit on him.

EZRA

The wind against my ears and tail is exhilarating as we step outside. I nervously glance around, trying to spot prying eyes, but I don't see anyone. Our destination is a small café just a few blocks away—Adley's favorite spot.

I stop on the driveway's edge and grab my tail nervously, pulling it to my chest for comfort. Adley approaches me and says, "Time to be extra." I know what she means: it's time to pretend I'm not scared and just fucking do this thing.

I lead the way, head held high, tail swishing behind me, and attempt to radiate an aura of self-assuredness. I wear a light jacket and am happy it's finally warming up. I place my hands in my pockets, trying to hide the trembling in my fingers.

Marshall and Adley trail behind me. Adley has that sweater I picked for her on our first mall trip. Marshall has his hat on and tail tucked, and I wish I hadn't protested his joining me in the exhibitionist adventure of "tail and ears out."

"So, what's the plan for the rest of the day?" Adley asks, her tone light and conversational.

Marshall responds, "I was thinking we could hit the park after lunch. Maybe sit in the sun and watch the baby ducks at the lake. It's too nice a day to stay inside."

I wrinkle my nose, "The park? Really? Grass stains and bugs? I just got ready."

"And you look fabulous," Marshalls says with exaggerated sincerity. "And we could bask in your beauty all day, but I'd also like to bask in the sun. Adley?"

Adley nods, her eyes twinkling with amusement. "It could be fun, Ezzy. We can bring a blanket and lounge by the lake. No one will ask you to roll around in the grass… but rolling in the grass together does sound fun." *The honey traps are back!*

"Oh, um, that sounds like something worth getting grass stained for," I say with an added pep. It's been so long since we've had sex, and I like the idea of doing it outside. It seems my and Marshall's plan is working. We share a knowing look.

=^..^= ♥ =^..^=

The café is bustling when we arrive. The hum of chatter and the clinking of dishes sets me on edge. There are way more patrons than we expected. People notice me and whisper when we enter, but our entrance is uneventful. I don't know if I'm relieved or disappointed.

We seat ourselves. Marshall picks a table by the large window where warm sunlight pours onto the table—because, of course, he does. This fucking guy loves the sun. I make sure to position myself so I can see anyone who comes in. Adley sits beside me, and Marshall sits across from her.

As we review the menu, my eyes dart around the room, subtly checking out my reflection in the glass surfaces and ensuring I look good. Adley puts her hand on my knee and simply smiles at me before returning her gaze to the menu.

ADLEY

The air is heavy with the scent of freshly brewed coffee, cinnamon, Ezra's cologne, and the faint sweetness of pastries that tempt me despite my lack of appetite. The smells combined with the clatter have my senses on the verge of overloading. While nervous when we first arrived, Ezra now has an impossibly bright smile—his phone buzzing incessantly on the table as he desperately tries to ignore it. Marshall sits across from me. I try to calm the whirlwind of thoughts as I focus on his quiet, steady presence. He really is beautiful.

It was their idea to bring me here today. They had been conspiring for days, whispering plans over breakfast or exchanging knowing glances while they thought I wasn't paying attention. They claimed it was to let Ezra test the theory that he could now go out in public, but I know they have an ulterior motive. Finding the note, "*Operation Cheer Adley Up*," written on a piece of paper on Ezra's desk, all but confirmed my suspicions.

"You'll love it," Ezra had declared this morning, his enthusiasm radiating like sunlight through storm clouds. "Just a little outing to get you out of the house." I tried to muster a smile then and I try to muster a smile now. I'm trying because they are. I don't know how to explain to them that it's not them, it's me, without sounding cliche. So, since they think their actions have merited my down mood, I'll do my best to mask it around them.

Ezra, unable to resist his phone, scrolls through it, occasionally tilting it toward us to show a meme or a comment from one of his fans. "This one's good," he says, laughter bubbling.

Marshall leans in to look, his arm brushing mine. He keeps doing this, trying to touch me casually and show affection. I know it's all part of the big thing they've orchestrated. So, I play along and smile at his touch—just like I smile at the memes.

"It's funny," Marshall says, his tone warm and steady. Lately, he always knows exactly what to say to Ezra to make him feel seen. He's really figured us both out, and he's turned into the perfect boyfriend. He also seems to have figured out exactly what to say to me, but today, I feel like an unsolvable equation, my sadness too complicated to unravel. The crushing failure I feel permeates my entire being, and even Marshall's well-planned compliments and Ezra's radiant smile can't pull me out of my darkness. I stare at the wall above Marshall's head, and feel like I'm being swallowed by the weight of my own failure. I've thought about telling them how I feel, but the words tangle in my throat every time I try. So here we are, at a café that I used to love, on a day when I barely have the energy to pretend.

Ezra waves to the waitress, a young woman with pastel hair and a piercing above her lip. She grins back, cheeks flushing as she recognizes him and rushes to our table. "Oh my God, Ezra? Are you Ezra from another world?"

His face lights up with the practiced charm of someone who'd been answering that question his whole life. "Guilty as charged, doll," he says, his voice as smooth as honey. She squeals softly and leans across the table, invading his space and chattering excitedly about how much she loves his latest videos. He squeezes my knee under the table, reassuring me that he is mine.

I watch him perform the way he always does. He's so good with people—

effortless, magnetic. I should be happy this is going well. I should be proud of him for breaking through his anxiety and finally being able to be his true self in public, and somewhere deep down, I am. But mostly, I feel like I am watching someone who belongs to the world, not me. He's like the bright light Marshall loves to bask in. It slips through my fingers—uncatchable. Eventually, it will leave because why should it stay with me? I'm just a perpetual bummer that hasn't even put out in weeks. What reason do they have to stay with me? I don't even have a fucking job.

"You're amazing," the server gushes, tucking a strand of hair behind her ear. "I mean, seriously. My friends and I talk about you all the time."

Ezra glances back at us with a quick wink before returning to her. "That means a lot. Thank you."

I try to suppress the pang of jealousy that rises in my chest. I know Ezra's heart belongs to us, just as ours belongs to him. *I know it. I know it. He's proven it.* But at this moment, I feel so small. Unseen. I stare at the table, blinking back the tears that threaten to escape my burning eyes.

Marshall nudges me gently with his foot and asks, "You okay?"

I nod quickly, forcing a smile. "Of course. It's so nice to be out!"

He doesn't look convinced, but he doesn't press. Instead, he squeezes my hand, his touch grounding me in a way words can't.

When the waitress finally leaves the table, Ezra nudges me with his elbow and flashes me an apologetic grin, "Sorry about that. She was sweet."

"She seemed nice," I say, keeping my tone light, "looks like the plan is working." They look at each other, nervous. I wasn't referencing the plan to re-woo me. "No one seems to care about the ears and tail," I add to ensure they don't think their plan has been spoiled.

"It does!" Ezra replies, leaning in to kiss my cheek. His lips are warm, a reminder that I am his focus now.

Their attention is almost overwhelming, their combined warmth like a spotlight I didn't feel ready to stand under. I want to appreciate it. I want to be the kind of woman who can soak up their love and reflect it back to them. Instead, I feel like a cracked mirror, unable to show them anything but fractured pieces.

The server brings our coffee first, and we sip our drinks.

"Agent York was right about coffee," Ezra says, sipping, "It took me a while to warm up to it, but it is… let me see if I can imitate him, 'the dark liquid drips down to my soul, embracing ever molecule of my… umm…

essence. What do you think, Zach?" Ezra jokes to Marshall, imitating the titular character of *Deadly Premonition*. It's actually quite a good impression.

"Did y'all finish the game?" I ask.

"No, not yet. Marshall makes me play whenever the dog shows up," Ezra laughs.

"Well, you made me play all the other times, so we're even," Marshall retorts.

"You're so much better at those wonky controls!" Ezra chortles.

The conversation continues as we receive our food. They get two sandwiches piled high with meat, and I laugh at how silly and unbalanced they look. Ezra tells a story about filming a particularly chaotic video last week, his hands animated as he describes the mess they'd made in the process. Marshall chimes in with his usual dry humor, his sarcasm perfectly balanced against Ezra's exuberance. They laugh together, and I try to join in, but my laughter feels hollow in my chest.

A group of women at a nearby table keep glancing over, their whispers not quite hushed enough to ignore. "Isn't that…?" one of them says, her gaze lingering on Ezra. Another woman's eyes flick to Marshall, her interest obvious.

It doesn't take long for them to muster the courage to approach our table. A tall, gorgeous woman with sleek, black hair says, "Hi. Sorry to interrupt! We couldn't help but notice…"

Ezra breaks his conversation with us to greet her, turning on his charm with that switch he easily manipulates within himself. Marshall barely acknowledges them but offers a polite nod. Instead, he stares at the spot on the table in front of him—not appreciating the attention but trying to remain a rock for Ezra. The women flirt openly, their intentions clear, and while Ezra and Marshall are polite, they deflect every advance with ease, their focus returning to me at every opportunity.

"You're lucky," one of the women says to me, her tone half-joking, half-serious. "They're both incredible."

I force another smile, nodding as though I agree. And I do, objectively. But her words remind me how much I don't deserve them.

After the women finally leave, Ezra turns to me, his expression softening. "Sorry about that." I must be making a face because he seems taken aback and says, "Are you okay?"

"I'm fine," I lie.

Marshall tilts his head, studying me with those steady green eyes that always seem to see right through me. "You'd tell us if you weren't, right?"

"Of course," I say, and for a moment, I almost believe it.

=^..^= ♥ =^..^=

We exit the café, and Ezra beams brightly. He puts his designer sunglasses on and faces the sun. They both look pretty happy. They think the day has gone well. I can see it in their smiles and how they exchange triumphant looks as we walk down the sidewalk.

I desperately want them to be right. But as I walk between them, their laughter filling my ears, I can't shake the heavy weight in my chest. I can't tell them how much effort it took just to keep breathing and pretending. I can barely hear the conversation over the voice in my head that keeps screaming, "You're not enough!"

Ezra beams at me and says, "See? A little fresh air was just what you needed."

I nod, letting him believe it—letting both of them believe it. They triumphantly wrap their arms around me as we walk—their warmth pressing against me. I say with all the enthusiasm I can muster, "Thank you. Today has been great!"

Ezra pulls away and walks backward, his hands in his pockets, looking at me over his sunglasses, "I recall there being mention of rolling in the grass together?"

"And ducks! I want to see the ducks!" Marshall says with a level of excitement I didn't expect from him.

And it breaks my heart to say, "Um, my stomach is hurting a bit from the food. Raincheck?"

"Bummer, babe. Yeah, let's go home," Ezra says, turning to walk away from me. I don't know if he believes me.

34

EZRA

"It's a good thing you no longer have to wear your hat. Your head has gotten a lot bigger. I don't know if it will fit," Marshall says, walking towards me with a laptop. I turn off the computer monitor and place my headset on the desk.

"Woah, bro, have you been planning that one out for a while?" I ask with a smirk as I turn in my chair.

"Kinda," he says, with an honesty I love about him. He picks up the headset and puts it on the stand.

"Well, keep working on it," I say, walking past him and slapping his ass—a gesture he loves.

"I have some new contracts for you to look at," he responds, blushing and opening the laptop.

I look at my watch—an expensive gift from a fan. "Can it wait until tomorrow? I've been holding it in all day, but I have a surprise planned. It's time for phase two of *Operation Cheer Adley Up*!"

"A surprise? Why didn't you tell me about this?"

"Because it's a surprise for you, too, bro!" I say with a wink.

His tail shoots behind him, "Um… for me, too?"

"Yep!" I say, brimming with so much excitement I can't believe I contained it all day. I've been planning this for a few days.

"Come on!" I say, rushing up the stairs to get this party started. Marshall gently places the laptop down and follows behind me.

I rush into the bedroom where Adley is lying down, reading. "Okay, Ads! It's time for us to go on our second date. I know I've been dicking you down so good I don't need to woo you anymore, but it's time for some wooing. Oh, and Marshall's gonna come, too."

"Oh, yeah?" she asks. "Marshall, are you going to woo me?"

"Wooo," he says, making a meek cheering gesture. What a damn dork. I laugh so hard my belly hurts.

"These are the kind of jokes you should stick to, Marsh. I picked out your outfit already, bro. It's hanging in the closet. Go change." I say to him pushing him toward the bedroom. He resists but only slightly. He always just does what I tell him to.

"Babe, tonight is going to be magical," I say and slide up to her. "I got you an outfit, too."

"Yeah?" she says with a forced smile that doesn't reach her eyes. I study her face momentarily, about to lay some hardcore compliments on her when she suddenly starts crying.

I pull back and hold her at arm's length. "Hey," I whisper. "Adley, what's up?" I lean over so that my face is at her height.

"I'm just… I'm feeling really… I don't know, Ezra. I don't feel like going out tonight. I'm sorry. I'll get it together. I know you've got something all planned out. I'll suck it up," she says, wiping the tears from her eyes in fast sweeping motions.

The jarring one-eighty from thinking I was going to have a magical weekend with my mate, my mates, to her crying is shocking. I don't quite know what to do or say. I'd been looking forward to this all day. We were going to get all dressed up and go to that restaurant with the private booths. Marshall could sit with his ears and tail out without worrying. We were going to eat fondue. I was going to get the tuna and shrimp. Then we were going to go to a hotel room and fuck each other's brains out. I was going to let Marshall… well, it doesn't matter now.

I look at her face, red with tears. I consider insisting. Maybe she can overcome this just long enough to get out the door. Then, the magical evening will make her forget all of these tears. But I don't want her to force herself. I want her to want to go. The tears stream down her face as she can't contain them any longer. What happened? I knew she was sad, but I thought it was getting better.

"Babes, we don't have to go anywhere. I can woo you right here," I say and hug her. "What do you want to do instead?" I ask her.

"Can we just get in bed and watch rom-coms?"

"Of course, babe," I say, and we walk toward the bedroom. Nothing I've done has helped. Marshall and I have been working so hard the last few weeks to try to make her feel special, but now she won't even let me do this.

Marshall comes strutting out, looking like a million bucks and fiddling with the sleeves of his shirt.

"Oh, Marshall, I'm sorry, but—" Adley starts saying.

"We're staying home?" he asks.

"Yeah," she says apologetically.

"Okay," he says and turns around, betraying no feeling about the matter one way or another.

"Where are you going?" I ask.

"I can take this off, right?" he asks.

"You don't like it? You look amazing, bro!"

"It's itchy."

I sigh, "Yeah, you can take it off." I forgot he's like Adley about textures. *Shit.*

"Ok," he says and turns around.

"Marshall, you do look amazing," she says. I am sad she won't see me in my outfit. I also feel a pang of jealousy I hadn't felt in months—jealous that she saw him and that he looked so good. *Fuck. This sucks.*

"Raincheck?" she asks. I hate that fucking word. She says it quite a lot lately. "I want to see these outfits sometime."

"Yeah, babe, no problem," I say with a tight grin, rubbing her back and letting her cry into my chest.

MARSHALL

I enter the bedroom, popcorn buckets in hand. I give one to Ezra, and he takes it without a smile or a word. Popcorn is one of the few non-animal product snacks he likes. Did he not want any? I just assumed he would. Is he mad at me?

I get in on the other side of the bed. The air is heavy—I've never seen Ezra like this before. "What are we watching?" I ask.

"*Hitch.* it's my favorite romantic comedy," Adley says without a significant amount of emotion in her voice. I miss how she lit up when she talked about the things she loves. I haven't heard her do that in so long that it almost feels like I made up that part of her personality.

I look over at Ezra, and he is practically scowling. What's with him? I suppose he did have a whole plan for the night. I'm not a big fan of surprises, but it was nice for him to think of something. But why is he so upset?

I grab a handful of popcorn and watch the two of them. What did I miss? Is *Operation Cheer Up Adley* now *Operation Cheer Up Ezra*, too? Did I upset him when I didn't like the outfit? I should make sure to tell him I liked it.

Adley raises the remote, points it at the TV, and lowers it back down without hitting play. She sighs loudly. "Adley, are you okay?" I ask.

Ezra looks at her, and the scowl on his face softens—no longer lost in whatever his mind was swirling in.

"Actually, I don't really want to watch TV right now," she says.

Ezra lights up, "Oh, yeah? Wanna play with the present I got us? I was thinking we could handcuff Mar—"

"No, I just want to go to sleep," she says, cutting him off and laying down, pulling the blanket over her head.

As much as I want to hear where that was going, I am worried about Adley. I know reaching out and touching her right now has a 50/50 chance of either being the right move or the absolute wrong one. So, I do what I always do: wait for Ezra to do something.

"Babe, please talk to us. Did we do something wrong?" Ezra says.

"No, I'm just depressed."

"Why?" he asks with a plea. "Have we not been worshiping you enough?"

"Job searching is really depressing me," she says. Her sentences are getting shorter, and I'm worried she might shut down.

"Babe, you don't need a job. I'm making more than enough money," Ezra says. I sit here and watch the conversation unfold, ever the third wheel.

"It's not about the money. I just… I feel purposeless," she says. "I feel powerless."

Ezra stares ahead for a long time; his face lost in thought as he considers what to say next. "Can't you just…" he gets choked up. "Can't you just let me take care of you?" A tear rolls down his cheek.

I wasn't expecting that. Ezra has seemed so happy lately, but maybe that was a ruse. All he's talked about lately is *Operation Cheer Adley Up*. We haven't played a game together in a while, and… shit. How did I miss this?

"I'm sorry, Ezra… I just need to be able to take care of myself," she says, snuggling her face into her pillow.

Ezra looks at me expectantly. I think he wants me to help him. To take his side. But I'm on both their sides. I understand why she is sad. She wants to feel like she is contributing. Like she is important. Like her life has a purpose. Ezra's found his purpose: making people happy and helping Adley. I've found mine: helping him help her. But what is hers? Maybe for a while, she thought it might be taking care of us.

I don't respond. I don't know what to say.

"Okay, babes," he says, getting out of bed and taking his popcorn.

So now he's walking away from her, too?

I put my popcorn on the nightstand and pull my knees up to my chest. *What do I do? I hate this.*

My phone chimes, and I check the notification. "Ezra is streaming now!" it says. He didn't have a stream scheduled.

Adley lays next to me, her back to me, and I see the silent shaking of her sobs. I place my hand on her shoulder, unsure if she will welcome my touch, but not knowing what else to do in this moment.

She shrugs her shoulder from under my hand and sobs hard enough now that I can hear her. What would Ezra do to make her feel better? I look at the hand that touched her and realize the hand is the problem, not the comfort. I enter my ailo form and walk across her pillow.

"May I hug you?" I ask, knowing she will not understand me.

"Oh, Marshall," she says with a wail. *Fuck, this was the wrong move, too.* I should just leave her alone. Before I can turn, however, her hand strokes my back, and she lifts the blanket, inviting me into her cocoon. I let her hug me to her chest, sobbing onto my forehead. I force myself to purr. It's hard because I am not happy right now, but I know it brings her comfort—and I will do anything for my mate, even be like this.

=^..^= ♥ =^..^=

It's been an hour. Adley's sobs have stopped, but Ezra still hasn't come back to bed.

"Marshall?" her soft voice says into my head. "Will you talk with me?"

I don't want to remove myself from her warmth, but I move over to my side of the bed and enter my anthro form.

She turns and buries herself into my chest, crying once again. I pet her hair with the same rhythm she pets me and wait for her to speak.

"Say some nice things to me," she says.

Her sadness centers mostly on her inability to find a job, so I will focus on her academic and professional qualities. "You're so talented. You're so smart. I've seen your code; it's elegant and clean, and you've done some amazing things. Your resume is so impressive."

What would Ezra say? "Also, I don't know if you're looking for these kinds of compliments, but you're the hottest woman on the planet."

She laughs. Oh, ok, that's working—more sexy compliments.

"And your pussy tastes like ambrosia." I cringe the moment it leaves my mouth. That was gross.

She lifts her head and looks at me with a disapproving face.

"Too much?" I ask.

"Ambrosia?"

"Yeah, like the nectar of the gods," I say, embarrassed. God, I suck at this.

She squints at me. "And how is a God-nectar-flavored pussy supposed to help me get a job?"

I look at the ceiling, unable to make eye contact with her, especially as she stares me down with that expression. God, I need Ezra's help right now. What would he do?

I try to take a page from Ezra's book and double down. "I don't know. Maybe you could put it on your resume. Feel free to leave Ezra and me as references," I say with a wry smile, trying to make it very clear I am joking.

She laughs. "That is NOT funny." *Oh, shit, it's working.*

"Then why are you laughing?" I say with a smirk.

"Because it's so not funny, it's almost funny." She chuckles more and wipes her eyes. She puts her ear to my chest and stares blankly at the ceiling, lost in thought. I can see the angst on her face as her brain whips through various topics, unable to focus on one.

"What are you thinking about?" I ask.

"Just that, I fucking hate interviewing. I don't even want to work for any of these companies. It's just a bunch of ex-triple-A douche bros who got a bunch of money to start some indie company. And the only reason they got it was because they're white men. I know so many talented women, talented people of color, hustling, not getting funding, and these douchebags just skateboard into a meeting with nothing but an idea and get a huge check. I want... never mind."

"No, tell me. What do you want?"

"I want my own indie company! I want to start a company that hires marginalized devs—that doesn't sexually harass the team. That makes cozy games. That makes games that aren't just for men. Makes games explicitly for women. Makes games that are different, that say something. That bring joy—silly, weird games. I want… I want to not have to rely on these fucking dudes or their fucking investors. I want my own thing I control. That no one can take away from me. I want to work on my game that I fucking started and never finished."

"Then do that," I say flatly.

"I can't do that."

"Why not?"

"Because after all these fucking interviews, I'm fucking drained. I don't have the energy to put into my own thing. And then, once I get the job, I'll be just as drained. It's an endless cycle."

"Well, what if you didn't do as many interviews? Could you do it then?"

"Marshall, you know as well as I do that I can't do that."

"Why not?"

"Because… because I have to get a job."

"Why?"

"To make money."

"But WHY? Ezra is making decent money right now. The bills are covered. Maybe you take a break from job searching and work on your game."

"That's not fair to Ezra."

"Ask him. I know he would be ok with it. He wants to support you and help you. All he cares about is making you happy. He loves you." The words catch in my throat. *He loves her. I love her. She loves him.*

"Even if Ezra were ok with me slowing my job search so I could focus on making my game, it wouldn't matter."

"Why not?"

"Because I still wouldn't have character art. I can't draw characters, and I can't afford to hire an artist. The whole game is about the fucking characters. The stupid code won't sell it."

"Oh…" I say. "Well, let's at least talk to Ezra, okay?"

"Maybe…" she says.

=^..^= ♥ =^..^=

I can't sleep. Adley lies beside me, face down on the pillow, with Ezra curled up on her back. He came to bed after she was already asleep. He simply said goodnight to me and went to bed. I wish he would have talked to me.

They've been asleep for hours, but I just lay here wrestling with my thoughts. I want to do something—anything—to help.

The look in Adley's eyes when she said she wanted to finish her game and her reluctance to rely on Ezra is burned in my brain. She said, "I can't draw characters, and I can't afford to hire an artist. The whole game is the fucking characters."

I haven't drawn in years—decades. Not seriously, anyway. I've done a few doodles here and there, but… maybe I can do this for her. The idea nags at me.

I'm not going to fall asleep anytime soon. I should do something productive. I slip out of bed, careful not to wake them.

I walk down the hall and stop at the door to her office. The multicolored lights, which are always on, cast an eerie glow on the various action figures and plushies she has throughout.

She used to live in this room, but since she quit her job, she has avoided it at all costs, only entering to do video interviews, which are becoming increasingly rare.

All of her favorite things are in here—abandoned.

The desk where her work laptop once sat remains empty and covered in a thin layer of dust. The large gaming PC on the adjacent desk sits dark—waiting for Adley to return and wake it from its slumber.

I press the button on the casing. It glows as its various internal components come to life. One monitor illuminates and I enter 1234. I shake my head as the powerful machine whirls slightly louder, and the other three monitors light up. *Why does she even have a password on it?* I laugh to myself.

Adley hates cluttered computer desktops, as evidenced by the laptop she carries for personal use. This desktop, whose sole purpose is to build video games, is no different. There's one folder on the desktop: a shortcut to a folder labeled "HHH." I click it and look over my shoulder, realizing I've left the office door ajar. The light of the monitors illuminates the hall. I quietly close the door and return to the computer.

I open the "HHH" folder and find a document labeled "GDD." I am unsure of the meaning, but I open it. Apparently, "GDD" stands for "Game Design Document." It details the design vision for the video game called Harem Hex Healer. I scan through it, learning the concept of the game. Astrid is a character transported to another world. Astrid must defeat an evil king. To do so, she must cure seven monsters from a hex put on them. When she does so, she collects them as a harem of lovers who bestow their powers on her when she makes love to them. I read through the physical description of Astrid, and I find she is extremely similar to Adley.

Now, Adley, I know I can draw.

I search the room for paper and a pencil. Once I find them, I sit at the empty desk, paper in front of me. I stare at the blank page momentarily—scared to start. Afraid that what I do will be terrible. I tentatively draw a circle. This is going to be bad.

I close my eyes and think of the time I lovingly drew Erza. I want to have that feeling again—of doing something so effortlessly. Just drawing. Drawing for the love of it. Drawing for the fun of it. The pencil glides across the paper in a more directed, controlled way. Yet, it's smoother, easier, more fluid.

The lines come shaky at first. The pencil is both familiar and foreign. The lead scratches across the paper, wobbling like a toddler trying to walk for the first time. I start with simple sketches, trying to capture Adley's general vibe.

I don't even draw a complete character, just various pieces of her as they flash in my head. I sketch the gentle curves of her body. The slight upturn of her nose. The crook in the corner of her mouth when she half-smiles at me. The swell of her breasts under a t-shirt. I spend a few seconds on each part, the feel of the pencil becoming more familiar. The gentle scratching against the paper soothes me. I stare down at the sketches of my lover, and a purr vibrates through me, making the grip on my pencil harder to steady.

I don't know much about character design, but I've seen some art books accompanying the video games I've played with Ezra. I painstakingly sketch Adley from various angles and poses. I draw her in poses of sadness and happiness. My sketches get more detailed as I proceed. Some nude, some clothed. I draw her, holding weapons and wearing armor. I envision her with different hairstyles. I draw her with a cat resting on her back. I draw her naked, wrapped in the embrace of a man. I stop and stare at the picture, realizing I've drawn Ezra. His form flows easily from me, as I've drawn it many times. It came so naturally that I barely noticed I drew him. It's second nature. After each sketch, I fling the paper aside, replacing it with another.

I draw them hand in hand, braced to fight some unseen evil. I sketch them celebrating a victory. I draw her standing tall and strong, a leader, a warrior. I draw him following her, supporting her. Before I know it, I have so many papers scattered on the desk I cannot even count them. I have no idea how long I have been sitting here. I don't want to stop. I'm drunk on the power I get from rendering my lovers in any scenario my imagination can conjure.

The floor outside the office creaks. "Marshall, why are you in here?"

Adley says, as she opens the door. I blink at her. The sun is filtering in through the cracks in the curtains.

"What time is it?" I ask, confused.

"It's 8 am."

I've been here for six hours.

She approaches me, still bleary-eyed, rubbing her eyes and yawning. "What are you up to, Marshall?" she says, placing her hand on my shoulder while peeking over it at my work.

"Oh my God, Marshall," she says softly, bringing her hand to her mouth.

She's mad. She's going to yell at me. She's going to rip them up. She's going to force me into my ailo form and kick me again. *No… Adley wouldn't do that. That's not Adley, you're remembering.*

I look down at my work; the desk is covered in paper. Hundreds of sketches of her—small, large, low res, detailed—blanket the surface. She picks up the one closest to her, which happens to be the one with more detail.

"You drew these?" she asks.

"Um, yeah," I say, embarrassed—scared. I look like an obsessive freak. *Please don't be mad.*

"Marshall," she says, confusion in her eyes and voice. "Are these me? Why did you draw these?"

Explain yourself. Maybe she will forgive you if you apologize. "I… I'm sorry, but I looked through your computer and found the game design document for Harem Hex Healer. I… I read the description of Astrid, and she reminded me of you. I thought, maybe, since you can't afford a character artist, maybe I could do it. Be your character artist."

"Are you serious?" she says blankly.

"I'm sorry. It was stupid. I'm not that good. You wouldn't want to make the game with me," I say as I gather all the pages and pile them into a stack.

She places her hand on mine, stopping me. "Marshall, they're beautiful. I didn't realize… I didn't realize you could do this. You're amazing!" she says with awe in her voice and eyes. *Wait, what?*

"How long did all this take you?" she asks.

"Um… about six hours," I reply.

"Only six hours! That's incredible, Marshall!"

She grabs the stack and starts sifting through it, oohing and aahing at each item as she passes it.

She says things like, "You're like… a prodigy! You really haven't drawn since you were a kid?! Oh my God, imagine if you had been permitted to keep drawing!" My heart swells with each compliment. My mate is pleased with me.

I should say it. I should tell her how I feel.

"It's easy for me to draw you, because I love you so much, Adley. I'm sorry I don't say it more."

"I love you, too, Marshall. You say it enough."

"But Ezra tells you every day. I…"

"Marshall, you're not Ezra. You tell me. You tell me every single day."

I squint at her confused, because I know that's not true. I think it every day but I don't say it as much as I should.

"Marshall, you're not a words guy. That's not how you tell me you love me. You show me. You do things like this," she says gesturing to all the drawings. "You take care of me. You check in on me. You sit with me. You research things to make me happy. That's how you tell me. As long as you say it during important moments, I'm okay with you not saying it every day."

She continues to look through my drawings and pulls out one in which she stands facing forward, drenched in armor similar to ones I've seen another video game character wear. "Marshall, this is her. This is Astrid. This is exactly how I pictured her. I can use this in my game." *She can use it? My art is useful?*

"Let's make this fucking game, Marshall!" she says, hopping in place—a look of determination I've never seen in her eyes.

35

EZRA

I awake to an empty bed—which has literally never happened before.

"Adley! Marshall!" I panic. I leap from the bed and transform, grabbing some shorts as I stumble out of the bedroom. *I was being an asshole. I shouldn't have stayed downstairs so late last night.*

"Adley! Marshall!" I nearly shout.

"In here, Ezzy!" Adley says and pokes her head out of her office. Waving me in excitedly. *Ezzy*? She hasn't called me that in a while. She must be feeling better.

"What are you doing, babe?" I ask as I turn the corner into her office. Marshall is tidying up her old work desk and positioning various papers and things. Adley is at her desktop! Is she interviewing? No, Marshall is in here. She's got that program she uses to make games open and is looking at code. "What's going on?"

Adley leaps from her chair. "Oh, Ezra, look at this!" she says, grabbing a piece of paper from her desk.

It's a drawing of Adley, looking hot as fuck—which, she always does—but she's wearing armor. She looks powerful. She looks amazing. "What is this?" I ask, confused.

"That's Astrid! She's the main character of my game!"

"Wait, what?" I ask, confused.

"Marshall drew her for me. We're going to make my game together!"

"No shit?" I say dumbfounded. The first day I met her, I sat in her lap and she tried to work on the game. She cried over it. She mentions it occasionally, how she feels like a failure having not finished it.

I look at the drawing again. "Marshall, you really drew this?"

"Yep," he says and continues tidying the desk. My chest swells with admiration. Jealousy?

"Woah, bro, calm down. No need to brag," I say.

He just rolls his eyes and sits in the seat, pulling himself toward the desk. "Oh, so… you're making the game right now?" I ask.

"Yes, we're just so excited," Adley says and sits at her desk, eager to turn around and get to work.

I go over to Marshall's desk, and he has a bunch of papers spread out and grouped. I look at them and hear Adley typing away behind me.

Marshall is hunched over, drawing on a piece of paper. One of the papers catches my eye and I shift the one on top of it over just a smidge so I can fully see it. It's a beautifully drawn image of Adley and I embracing, naked, looking at each other longingly. I'm speechless. It's beautiful. It's delicate. It's like he took a picture right from his memory and translated it onto the page. Also, I must admit, I look pretty hot. *Is this like the picture he drew when he was a kid? The one his dad tore up? Why isn't he in the picture?*

"Marshall, you drew this?" I ask, knowing the answer but being literally too stunned to say anything else.

"Yeah," he says, looking at me and then getting back to drawing. He's drawing Adley in many different fighting forms from different angles, trying out different clothes and experimenting with how they would fall. I scan the other drawings, trying not to disrupt him or make a mess because I know it will annoy him. This is the talent he has been hiding? How traumatic the experience must have been if it made him stop doing this.

I am mesmerized as I watch his hand move across the paper. I place my hand on the back of his chair and watch. He looks up at me with that blank face of concentration and smiles faintly when his eyes meet mine, blushing.

His pencil breaks and the magic of the moment breaks with it. He huffs and leans back to reach a shelf beside him, grabbing a pencil sharpener, the likes of which I haven't seen since I was a child. I pull myself off the back of the chair, and he angrily sharpens the pencil. Seeing the way the muscles in his neck tense with each thrust reminds me of kissing his neck while he thrusts into Adley. A pencil and paper? Why is he using a pencil and paper? Adley has a drawing tablet on her desk.

"Why aren't you using the tablet thing?" I ask, pointing at the one in front of Adley. "Don't you need these to be digital for the game?"

"Oh, well, Adley needs that computer to code the part she's working on. We've got a schedule all planned out. I'm going to work on paper for now. When she works on the laptop, we'll trade. This is fine," he says, gesturing at the table and returning to his work, lifting his shoulders in determination. I've come to learn Marshall's mannerisms, and that shoulder shrug means it is decidedly not fine, but he's willing to put up with it. Because, as I'm coming to notice, Marshall will always go with whatever flow Adley and I set—for better or for worse.

"Alright," I say and give him a squeeze on the shoulder goodbye. He nods goodbye in return. Adley is sitting bolt upright, not even leaning against the back of the chair. I put my hand on the small of her back between her and the chair. She looks at me with a smile. I have never, not once, seen her smile like this. This is a smile I want to preserve for all time. "Have fun, babes," I say and kiss her on the top of the head before leaving.

"Well, this won't do," I say, exiting the room. Now it's my turn to take care of them. I got this. I got this so fucking hard.

=^..^= ♥ =^..^=

Those smiles are burned in my brain: Marshall's small smile and Adley's huge one. I want to make them smile forever. I must support them in any way I can. I will be there for them emotionally and financially.

I pull up the app for the store where we bought all my studio equipment. What do they need?

Marshall needs a computer that is powerful enough to run the software.

He also needs his own drawing tablet. I find one even bigger than the one Adley has.

Um, and a monitor. No, two monitors.

Oh, and I need to upgrade Adley to a better graphics card. I'll get the best one they have.

A mouse and keyboard.

RAM. Even more RAM. Adley probably needs some, too.

I imagine Marshall sitting in bed, watching *Fruits Basket* with Adley and me while sketching on a tablet, so I buy him a new iPad and pencil.

I recall the way he was hunched over the desk and find a nice desk chair for him. I might as well get Adley one, too, because her chair sucks.

I think about Adley when I would watch her work. She would get distracted by lots of noise. It was the one thing that would break her from her intense focus. Marshall does, too. So, I put two over-the-ear noise-canceling headphones—black and pink—in the cart. I make sure to get ones that Marshall could position over his ears.

It's all in stock.

This will be even better than the hotel room surprise.

I look at the office door and consider showing them what I'm doing. Asking them what they need. Asking them what they want. But I don't want to distract them further. Plus, I want to see the smiles they have when they see what I get them.

If they need more stuff, we can just order more stuff.

I pay extra to have it delivered today.

=^..^= ♥ =^..^=

Well, I didn't think this through. I sign for the delivery and look at the massive pile of stuff. I can't bring all this inside on my own. *Shit.* I wanted to surprise them, but I need Marshall to help me bring it in. *Damn it.* I was hoping to ride in there, a knight in shining armor saving the day with gaming PCs. So much for *Operation Surprise my Mates and Direct their Smiles at Me.*

I don't want to bother them. I have never seen Adley this excited. Ever. I've seen Marshall reach that level of focus, but I've never seen him smile while doing it.

Maybe I can at least get it in the house by myself. I prop the door open and drag the large items over the threshold. I'm sweating by the time I am done. *What the fuck did I buy? A home gym?*

I'm finally able to shut the door, and I sit on one of the large boxes, panting a little. *Okay.*

I spend the next thirty minutes arranging the items aesthetically by the door and in the living room. I want to present this to them. I can't wait to see their faces when they see what I've done for them.

I look at my watch. It's almost five o'clock. I'll make them a snack, call them in, and they'll see the stuff.

This is going to be perfect. "Oh, Ezra, what a great boyfriend you are," they'll say simultaneously and kiss me on the cheek. Probably also tell me I'm hot. Then we'll all fuck and live happily ever after. *Yeah, this is going to be perfect.*

=^..^= ♥ =^..^=

"Babe! Marsh! I've got a surprise for you!" I say excitedly at the door to Adley's office—their office. They don't look up. This happens sometimes. They are both easily distracted and hard to distract. A dichotomy of their personality that I try not to take personally when not in my favor.

"Babes! Marsh! I've got a surprise for you!" I say again. Their brains exit their current function, and they look at me bleary-eyed; I give them a moment to let their cognition switch gears. It's cute when it finally does. When they notice something is happening other than what is right in front of them, I can almost see a little railroad switchman in their brain, turning the train from the game track to the Ezra track.

As the recognition dawns on them, their faces etch—a picture of surprise. "Oh, yeah?" Adley says.

"Yeah, come see!" I say, grabbing her hand and pulling her from the computer.

"Well, okay," she says and gets up less enthusiastically than I would prefer. Marshall stays in his chair, unmoving.

"Come the fuck on, dude! It'll only take a second," I say, turning his chair and literally dumping him out of it.

"Hey," he says, as I help him up.

"Come on!" I exclaim, waving them to follow after me.

I lead them into the living room and run toward the pile of stuff. I leap onto one of the chairs and spin around in it. *Check me out, my mates.*

"I got you some stuff to help make your game!" I say, opening my hands wide, gesturing at the items. *Okay, now adore me. Thank me profusely. I wouldn't mind some hugs, kisses, oral sex, maybe.*

They both stand at the door, flabbergasted, obviously overwhelmed by my generosity. So, I will show them what I got.

"Check this out," I continue, grabbing the tablet box and running it toward Marshall. "It's bigger than the one Adley has! I also got you this computer and the best graphics card. So, you can go ahead and start doing all your art digitally. I got both of you new chairs because, babe, as much as I love putting my hand on the small of your back, you need more support. That is unless you'd like me to support your back all day. I guess I could do that… but Marshall also needed a chair, so…"

Marshall holds the tablet in his hands, studying the box. A grin unfurls on his face, cracking into the general stoic vibe and morphing into gratitude and astonishment. "Thank you, Ezra. This is very kind," he says.

"You're welcome, bro! Only the best for my clowder," I say with a big grin. My heart sores at the fact that I made him smile.

Adley has been decidedly quiet. I turn to Adley, eager to drink in her response, awaiting my praise, but it does not come. I tilt my head in that way she always finds adorable, but she just keeps looking at the pile of stuff. Her brow is slightly furrowed, a small wrinkle in the otherwise perfect moment.

Her hand at her side trembles slightly. She opens and closes it in that way she does when she's masking her overwhelm. *Oh, fuck. What did I do?*

"Adley, you okay?" I ask, rushing toward her. Marshall stands next to her, agape and seemingly also confused. I reach for her hand, but she flinches at my touch.

An uncomfortable weight hits me in the chest as I watch her face contort to that fake smile she puts on. Not the good one from earlier. The tight, fake smile can fool anyone but me. "Thank you, Ezra," she says, her voice slightly higher than usual and then more strained, "You... you shouldn't have."

My smile falters. I'm confused. *Why is she mad? She's mad, right?* "But I wanted to. Marshall needed a tablet, and okay, I got a little carried away, but—"

"It's not about what we need," Adley cuts me off, her voice sharp. "It's about…" she trails off, continuing to look at the stuff—contemplating what to say.

Why isn't she fucking happy? What do I have to do to make her happy? "What is it about, Adley?" I request. I don't yell, but my voice is harsher than it ever has been with her. It's the tone I reserve only for Marshall. Adley looks taken aback. Even Marshall appears startled by my indignant tone.

She looks at me with those beautiful grey eyes, filling slightly with tears, "It's about doing it ourselves. It's about proving we can do it. It's about having something we can call our own. It's about not having to rely on…" she trails off, biting her lip, her gaze dropping to the floor.

"Not relying on who, Adley?" I say, my voice raising, "Me? But it's okay to rely on Marshall?"

"That's different… he's doing the art?" Adley says with apprehension.

"So why can he help and I can't? What the fuck, Adley?! Why won't you let me be a part of this? We're supposed to be a team. The three of us."

"I can't be indebted to you. I can't owe you. I can't do this only because a man gave me money. I just… you don't understand…"

"You're right, I don't fucking understand. You bought me stuff. You said that was to help me. How is this different? I thought you'd be happy. That this would be a relief. That I'd be taking some of the pressure off you."

Her lip trembles and her hand opens and closes at her side; her voice is low, almost a whisper, "This is my baby, Ezra. I can't have you taking it from me. I can't let you take it. I can't have you leave me and take my game with you…"

"Leave you? Who said anything about leaving you?"

"You all fucking leave. That's all you ever fucking do. You find someone hotter, someone that doesn't get sad, someone nuero-fucking-typical, someone younger, someone thinner, and you fucking leave me!"

"Who's 'you all?' Not fucking me! That's not fucking me, Adley. That's them! That's other guys! You're my goddamn fated mate! I can't leave you!"

Her voice raises now, yelling, "And that's the only reason you're here! Because of some weird fucking not-magic-science-hormone-pheromone-purring thing, not because you actually fucking want to be with me!"

"Babe, that's not true at all! Why are you saying this? I just want to help you. Please stop comparing me to those assholes from your past."

"You don't fucking love me. You just want to fuck me!"

"Ha, that's rich! I haven't gotten laid in forever! If I only cared about fucking you, I would have left weeks ago! I haven't gone this long without getting laid—ever! And I have two fucking fated mates. But because of Marshall and I's pact, I can't even fuck him if you're not putting out."

"Ezra! Don't you—" Marshall hisses.

"I'm sorry… that's not how I meant that. Babe, I don't want to fuck anyone but you two, I promise. And that's not even important. I want to be with you. All of you. Tears and all. I'm not going to leave."

Adley's still not ready to back down from this fight. She's not ready to accept my words. I watch her face as the thoughts she's been holding swirl, trying to release themselves. Her hands shake at her side; that brilliant fucking brain is thinking of a million ways to eviscerate me. She can't latch on one yet, but when she does, I'm fucked.

She settles on something and explodes at me, "Do you have any idea how fucking hard it is to be a woman in this industry? Every goddamn thing I do is questioned. If someone found out, I only could do this because you paid for it. I'd never be respected for my contribution. It would be 'Ezra's game' not 'Adley's game,' and you wouldn't have even fucking done any of the work! All you would have done was fork over money! Money that you didn't even earn! They just hand it to you because you have a huge dick and a pretty face and get everything fucking handed to you because of it." She stops her tirade, still seething with rage.

The room shrinks around me.

She gasps and puts her hand to her mouth. "Ezra, I'm… I'm sorry. I didn't mean that."

"You did mean it, Adley. You said it," I say, stunned. Is this how she's always viewed me? I need to get out of here. I can't be here right now.

The air is repressive, and I can't fucking look at her, fated mate or not. I storm toward the door, but Marshall grabs my arm. *This fucking guy is always grabbing me.*

"Do not walk away from this, Ezra," he says flatly.

"Don't fucking tell me what to do, Marshall. Let go," I growl.

"No, you need to stay."

"Why, so you can tell me how I don't deserve anything I've worked for? Tell me that the two of you are so fucking smart and talented. Apparently, some fucking artistic savant on top of a genius, and I'm what? I'm just a pretty face? I swear to fucking god, daddy issues, if you don't let me go right this minute..." I growl lower, ready to hit him.

He softens his voice and gets close to me, like he might kiss me. "Listen to me, mommy issues," he says with a smirk. Did he just call me mommy issues? *Bro is always copying me.* "That is not true. You are not just a pretty face…" He pauses, looking me up and down. "You also have a huge dick, you forgot she said that part."

"Wha…?" I say, confused. Did he really just say that to me?

"I was making a joke to ease the tension. Did it not work?" he says, sighing.

"Bro, that was a zinger. Good job," I say, dejected. Because it was a good joke, but it was at my expense, and I still feel like shit, but I would laugh at any other time.

Marshall continues, "Adley needs to apologize to you for what she said. She was wrong. You are more than that."

"I get it; you already said the joke; I also have a huge dick, har har."

"No. You are kind. You are loyal. You are giving. You may have mommy issues, but you want to protect us. You want to make us happy. And you would never, ever steal Adley's thunder…" he stops and thinks for a moment. "Because you are the sunshine, and we are the dark rain clouds, your light pierces," he says, gesturing at himself and Adley. "She may make thunder, and I may make rain, but together, with your sunshine, we all make rainbows."

I jerk back, stunned, "Wow, Marshall. You're really having a day, huh? First, the joke, and now an idiom? And was that your first metaphor? That was really sweet. Cheesy but sweet."

"Ezra, I'm sorry. I really don't think that of you. Yes, I'm jealous of your pretty privilege, and I'm jealous of the fact that you get to be a man in the patriarchy, but he's right. You are all those things," Adley says.

"Damn it," Marshall says.

"What?" I ask.

"Technically, you don't need thunder to make rainbows. And I'm the more thunderous one—since I yell more. And she's the rain since she cries… I retract my metaphor. I will think of a better one. Maybe I should say that we are refraction, dispersion, and reflection…" he says.

"It's okay, Marshall. Metaphors don't have to make perfect sense," I say. Despite Marshall's stellar attempt at a romcom speech and Adley's apology, the tension still hangs heavy in the air.

MARSHALL

"Adley, Ezra," they both turn towards me, their expressions a tableau of frustration and hurt, "This isn't about who pays for what. It's about supporting each other's strengths, balancing them so they shine brighter together."

Maybe it's time to drop the metaphor. Apparently, once I get started, I can't stop.

Adley's shoulders, previously squared for battle, drop ever so slightly, her stance softening.

"Both of you have valid points," I continue, putting the tablet down. "Ezra, your heart is in the right place, but Adley needs to feel ownership over this. That ownership is what's been missing for her."

I turn to Adley, "There's no shame in accepting help that is given in love. Just like I had to accept your help when we first got here—and still accept your help every day, in smaller, more subtle ways, but the help is still there. Ezra isn't trying to overshadow our efforts. He's not trying to steal anything from us. He's trying to lift us up and relieve our burden. What's the saying about tides and ships?"

"It's okay, Marshall, you can drop the metaphors, we get it." Ezra's hands, which had been clenched at his sides, relax and he continues, "Adley, I'm really sorry. I did not consider the fact that my helping would put my name on this and essentially, due to my pretty face and dick, would cause people to attribute any success it may have to me… not to you."

Adley's eyes flicker with a mix of emotions, her internal turmoil visible beneath the surface. I place my hand on each of their shoulders, and suggest, "We'll set clear boundaries on contributions and ensure everyone's comfortable with how we move forward. Together."

ADLEY

Marshall looms over the two of us, a dark, gentle presence smoothing over the jagged edges of the argument. My anger has dissipated, and I try to make sense of my feelings.

I finally speak up, "I'm sorry, Ezra. I am not used to people wanting to help me without ulterior motives… I'm sorry."

Ezra leans in and places his hand on my elbow, not yet embracing me, waiting for further signals from me.

I take a deep breath and surrender to Marshall's reasoning, no longer wishing to fight.

"I've not had good relationships with men. My whole life, I've been a thing. First, I was a little girl who should be seen, not heard. Then overnight, I was something to look at. To fuck. But, never something of value beyond that… Men have used me. They've stolen my work and claimed it as their own. They've hit me. They've cheated on me. They've called me a fat cunt. They've blamed me for their own failings. They've torn me down to lift themselves up. And they've reduced me time and time again to the value my body brings to them. They take what they want from me, and then they leave me in the gutter.

"And, in a way, I saw this game as something I could do to free myself from the cycle of getting a job and relying on 'the man,' the metaphorical one and the literal one that sits at the top of the company. The ones I rely on to give me jobs that I need to pay my bills. Free myself from the men who use my body for sex and companies that use my mind for work. So, to need help from a man… it was… whatever the feminine version of emasculating is…

"I just wanted not to feel so fucking powerless all the time. And the ridiculous thing is I would dream of getting help. I dreamed of some investor discovering my work and giving me a boatload of money to help. And being able to quit my job and focus on my passion projects…"

I relax my shoulders not realizing they were pulled upward.

Ezra leans back on the nearby table, folding his arms in deep contemplation. "I can't say I did this for purely unselfish reasons… I wanted to be the thing that made the two of you so happy. I wanted to be part of what made you so happy. And I was probably jealous that the focus was on the game and not me."

"Probably?" Marshall asks.

"That's enough jokes out of you for one night, okay, bro?" he says, laughing and putting his hand up.

"I'm sorry. I should have consulted you before going off and doing my own thing, and I promise that I will not do something like that again. But, Adley, I swear, I really just wanted to help you… and Marshall. I saw you both so happy. I've never seen either of you like that. And when Marshall's pencil broke, I just… I saw a problem that I could solve. I wanted to do everything I could to make sure the two of you could make this game. Because I don't know if you noticed, but the main character, she's fucking hot, and I'm really looking forward to playing with her," he says with a chagrin half-smile.

God, he always has to joke. But it always fucking works.

"And when you leave," I say, tears rolling down my face, "I can't look at this game and think I owe it all to you, the one who broke my heart."

"Baaabe," he says, pulling me close. "I'm all in on you. I'm not going anywhere."

I sob in his arms as he holds me. Marshall stands to the side, a sentinel. I feel bad about moments like this—when Ezra and I are making him feel like he needs to hang back.

"I think Adley should take a break from interviewing, and she should focus fully on this game," Marshall speaks up.

I cut him a glance because we talked about this, and I told him I was reticent about that. I wasn't fully honest about why, though.

Ezra says, "How about this, babe? You go where your energy leads you? If it's around this game, then do that. If you want to interview, you do that. But I'm here to take care of you regardless of what you do. And that's okay because, as Marshall said, you take care of us, too. We're a family. We're a clowder."

I sigh. "Are you sure?"

"Of fucking course, babe."

36

ADLEY

It's strange how a fight clings to the edges of your thoughts, even when you're supposed to be moving past it. I glance at Ezra as he smooths out the picnic blanket with exaggerated panache, the corner whipping theatrically in the breeze. His blond hair catches the sunlight like a halo, and his grin is cocky, self-assured—almost as if he's already forgetting the tension between us.

The fight was a few days ago, and while the storm has theoretically passed, none of us can seem to let it go. We've had multiple mature, thoughtful conversations about it, but we have also casually dropped little bombs on each other throughout our conversations—little quips and side comments. Indicating none of us are fully ready to move on from it—except maybe Marshall.

"You sure this spot is okay?" Marshall's voice is low, measured. He kneels with careful deliberation, tucking the other corner of the blanket under a heavy wicker basket while he scans the park as if the perfect patch of grass might appear if he stares long enough.

The shadow cast over his eyes by his baseball cap makes him look mysterious and handsome. Despite Ezra feeling okay with leaving the house with his ears and tail unmasked, Marshall isn't quite comfortable with it yet. He claims his lack of notoriety will stop people from casually ignoring it the way they seem to with Ezra. We've tried to explain that his proximity to Ezra would probably convince others he's doing whatever schtick Ezra is doing, but he wants to draw as little attention to himself as possible.

"It's perfect," I say, forcing more enthusiasm into my tone than usual. It isn't that I don't feel it; I'm just not great at showing it. But today feels different. Lighter. Maybe it's the sun, the fresh breeze, or the fact that we all agree to set the tension aside for the day. But I'm going to put in the effort to get out of my own head and appreciate the moment with them.

Marshall's gaze lingers on ducks waddling along the pond's edge nearby, the water shimmering in the sun. Does he want to sit closer to the ducks?

Before I get a chance to ask Marshall if he wants to move, Ezra flops down onto the blanket, leaning back on his elbows. "See, Adley gets it. This spot has the perfect blend of shade and view," he says, gesturing to the tree at our backs and the water toward our feet. "What more could you want?" Families mill about, and others walk, run, or ride on the path on the other side of our tree.

"There's just a lot of dogs on that path," Marshall says, cringing, settling beside me with his cat-like grace. His gaze flicks toward me, softening for just a moment before he looks away.

"Don't worry, bro! I'll protect you," Ezra says, leaning forward to give him a playful punch on the shoulder.

"How? You're scared of them, too!" Marshall snaps.

"I'll fake it till I make it, bro. Have you met me?" Ezra laughs.

"This is a really nice view of the ducks," Marshall says, distracting himself from the yelps of a nearby dog and staring out toward the lake.

I pull my laptop bag closer, opening it to peer in. "Adley, you brought your laptop?" Ezra's voice breaks through my thoughts, teasing but with a thread of exasperation.

"I'm not going to work, though!" I say, pulling out a paperback. "I'm here to read and relax! I'm going to be present as fuck! I'm not even going to look at my phone!"

"That's a first," Marshall murmurs, though there is no bite to his words. He's still staring out at the ducks, the shadow casting over his eyes. He catches me looking at him and playfully leans his shoulder into me.

"Alright, babe. Remember, rest is productive! You gotta recharge those beautiful, brainy batteries," Ezra says, giving me a peck on the cheek. While my feelings of angst around the fight we had haven't subsided, I am feeling better and trying to lean into his affection. I open the paperback book on my lap, ready to start reading.

Ezra pushes himself up with a flourish. "Come on, Marshall. Frisbee time." And he whips off his shirt, glancing down at us, ensuring we are looking, and flexing. He thinks he's so slick, but he's pretty obvious most of the time. The muscles in his chest and back ripple and flex in the sun in a way that sends crashing waves of lust to my core.

The morning sunlight filters through the trees, casting a golden glow over his body. The lighting is so perfect I suspect he chose this spot for reasons other than the shade. It's been a while since we've all had sex. I hadn't realized it until Ezra brought it up during our fight. And as I watch him move, I wonder why it is we haven't. I imagine those strong arms gripping my hips as I ride his face.

I stretch out on the blanket. I am trying to relieve the tension building between my legs, pretending to be engrossed in my book, but my focus is on Ezra, now bending over on all fours and rummaging through the picnic basket. His tail sways lazily behind him, playfully grazing over Marshall and me. Marshall's focus is equally distracted, and he lazily places his hand on my thigh, his hand drifting a bit higher than it probably should in public.

Looking over his shoulder at us and noticing the two of us gape at him, Ezra whips around at inhuman speed so that he is now on all fours in front of us. He brings his face close and says seductively, "Should we pack up and leave?" Marshall clears his throat and removes his hand from my thigh.

"Nope," I simply state, swallowing hard.

"Alright," he says and goes back to rummaging as if nothing just happened. He finds what he is looking for and jumps to his feet, holding the bottle of sunscreen over his head like some dorky video game character, dropping his calculated sex-God persona for a moment. "Aha! I found it," he announces, his voice bright and theatrical.

He unscrews the cap and turns to Marshall. "Alright, bro, you're up first. Can't have you burning out there," he says while gesturing with his thumb for Marshall to stand. Marshall gives me a sidelong glance but doesn't protest. He flips his cap around while he stands, then shrugs out of his shirt with a quiet efficiency that sends my pulse skittering. How he took that shirt off with such effortless grace without catching the brim of his cap was so unfathomable; he could probably write another PhD dissertation on the math of it. His lean, defined muscles catch the sunlight, and I have to fight the urge to stare openly. He stands still as Ezra squirts a generous amount of sunscreen into his hands, the stark white lotion contrasting against his tanned skin. The sight of them—so effortlessly handsome in the sunlight—has my heart doing little flips.

Ezra's hands move confidently over Marshall's back, spreading the lotion with long, practiced strokes. Ezra says, his tone conversational, "Skin cancer is no joke." They both look at me, ensuring I am watching them, and I know immediately that this is all just some little show for me. These two are up to something. I imagine there is a notebook somewhere on Ezra's desk with the words "*Operation Seduce Adley and Get Her to Stop Being Upset with Ezra*" scrawled on it. If that's their game, I can play along. They can play the naughty boys trying to seduce me, and I'll play the still-angry girlfriend who is doing her damnedest to resist them.

"I understand," Marshall says, his tone steady yet tinged with amusement. He looks at me for a moment, and I immediately bury my face in my book, though it is clear I'm not fooling anyone. My cheeks burn despite the refreshing breeze, and I suspect maybe I am fooling myself that I can keep this up.

"Adley, are you watching this?" Ezra calls out, catching me off guard. My head snaps up, and he grins at me, wicked and knowing. "Are you enjoying the view?" *Yes. God, yes.* I'm not the only one. A small crowd has started to form around us.

"Yes, the ducks are super cute," I say, trying to sound nonchalant even as my face burns hotter. Ezra's laugh rings out, and he turns back to Marshall, adding a playful slap to his shoulder once he is done.

"Your turn," Marshall says, taking the bottle from Ezra. He is more methodical, his movements slower as he spreads the lotion over Ezra's shoulders and back. Ezra, in true Ezra fashion, strikes a dramatic pose, flexing his muscles as though he is modeling for a photoshoot. I hear audible gasps, and at first, I think it's me, but then I realize it's someone from the crowd.

"You could at least pretend to take this seriously," Marshall says, his tone dry but affectionate.

"Why?" Ezra replies, flashing a grin over his shoulder. "Adley's enjoying herself. Aren't you, Adley?" As Marshall rubs lotion on Ezra, his gentle strokes rock Ezra forward and backward, reminding me of all the naughty things I wish he was doing to me right now.

I pretend to be not entirely engrossed in their show and roll my eyes with exaggeration, then say with a laugh, "Yes, this book is quite enjoyable." I look back down at it, or at least I pretend to.

"Oh really, babe. What's it about?" Ezra asks me, knowing full well I have no fucking idea. The book could be upside down right now for all I know.

When they are finally done, Ezra tosses the sunscreen onto the blanket and turns to me with a mock-serious expression. "Now, Adley, have you applied your sunscreen? Or do we need to assist?"

"I'll manage, thanks," I say quickly, though the mental image is enough to make my heart race. Ezra smirks, clearly pleased with himself, while Marshall gives me a small, knowing smile.

"Alright then," Ezra says, clapping his hands together. "Stay tuned,

Adley. You're about to witness greatness." He bends down in front of me to grab the frisbee from the picnic basket. Giving me a mischievous wink.

"Let's give the crowd something to talk about, Marshall," he says, slapping Marshall's ass as they walk away. A passing jogger literally stops in his tracks at the sight.

Marshall sighs, "You're insufferable."

"But you love me anyway," Ezra replies, tossing the frisbee into the air and catching it with a dramatic spin. Marshall rolls his eyes but follows him toward the open grass.

EZRA

I feel Adley's eyes on me. I lean into Marshall's space and give a conspiratorial whisper, loud enough for him to hear through that ugly hat, "It looks like *Operation Honey Trap Adley* is working." I glance back at her. Her eyes are locked in on us, watching us walk away.

I shake my ass and tail at Adley with a wink. She blushes and looks back down at her book. I can tell by the way she's shifting that she's resisting the urge to plunge her fingers into her panties. The thought arouses me, but I gotta keep it together. I can't fuck her in front of this crowd of people who are now lustfully watching Marshall and me walk away—even though I doubt they would care. While our honey trap was explicitly for Adley, I relish the fact that we caught a few more flies. The more eyes I get on me today, the more desirable she'll find me, and the more desirable I'll find myself. Win-win.

Marshall gives me his usual side-eye but says nothing, which I take as a win. He's not as hard to read as he thinks; I know he is still annoyed about the fight. The thing I said about fucking him… that was a line I shouldn't have crossed—it came out of a deep part of my psyche that I didn't realize was even there.

I'll admit it: I've got a flamboyant theatricality. Today's plan has multiple parts. Part 1: Get Adley to relax and fully forgive me. Seduce her, then live happily ever after buried deep in her cunt. Part 2a: Let Marshall see the ducks and enjoy the sun. Part 2b (which Marshall has not been let in on): Get him to forgive me, too. Seduce him, as well. Part 3: Draw a crowd to build my confidence and ensure I can perform well for my mates tonight.

The plan is flawless and will obviously go off without a hitch. A picnic in the park, the sun shining just right, my hair catching the light like the sun was made with the explicit purpose of shining on it—perfect. I'd chosen this spot by the pond because it had the perfect balance of natural beauty and foot traffic—enough to be seen but not so crowded that we couldn't enjoy ourselves.

Marshall squints at the ducks like he is mentally organizing them into one of his beloved spreadsheets. It's why his art is fantastic but also why he needs me to push him out of his head now and then.

There is something in Adley's voice today that's making me hopeful. She is trying. After everything that went down a few nights ago, I wasn't sure if she'd want to spend the day with us. But here she is, sitting on the blanket with that little paperback she'd brought, looking… like she's DTF. *I wonder if she's reading smut.*

I spin the frisbee like I don't have a care in the world. But cares are all I've got right now. I need to perform a delicate dance of keeping my two emotional mates happy. While yes, I do have a goal of getting my dick wet, I care more about their happiness. The dick-wetting part is an added bonus.

If I'm honest with myself, I don't know that I have ever put a mate's happiness above my own. *Sarah was right to push me.* I shake my head, trying to remove the memories and not focus on that.

MARSHALL

There's something about parks—their calming rhythm—that I truly value, particularly lake parks. I suppose it's good I found myself in the land of ten thousand lakes. I could spend all day observing the wind creating ripples on the water while the ducks paddle leisurely across it.

It feels like the park's calm is a backdrop to something more fragile today. We are here to move past the argument simmering between the three of us over the last few days. It was emotional and scary. I thought Ezra was going to leave. I also thought Adley was going to slap him. However, they keep returning to it and cannot let it go entirely. We'll have a pleasant conversation about something mundane, and then one of them will bring up the fight. Ezra turns the arguments into a performance, deflecting the emotions away. Adley tries to dissect them logically. I… well, I try to stay out of it until I can't anymore.

As I follow Ezra to help him enact his grand *Operation Honey Trap Adley* plan, I wonder why I always just go along with whatever he wants. I'm not above wanting to sleep with her. But I also very much want us all to get along again. I look back at her. She has her laptop bag with her, which doesn't surprise me. When she's not in the throes of depression, she's always working, coding, and fixing things. Sometimes, it seems like she can fix anything—except us. She can't seem to fix us. Adley rarely lets herself relax, and after the tension of the past few days, I expect her to be guarded. But there she is, settling onto the blanket with a paperback in her hands. I feel a flicker of relief.

She looks at us, and her eyes glaze like they do when she wants to sleep with us. *Maybe this will work.*

"See?" Ezra's voice cuts through my thoughts, as it always does. I nod my head but don't bother responding. Ezra's dramatics are part of who he is, and I learned long ago trying to temper him is like trying to bottle a storm. Instead, I'll help enact this silly plan that somehow involves us playing frisbee and gathering a crowd.

I longingly look to the ducks because as much as I want to please my mates, I just want to sit on the water's edge and watch the babies float by. *They're so cute.* But I suppose I have to get used to what I want always being of lesser importance than what they want. This relationship has an unspoken hierarchy, and I've inexplicably found myself at the bottom.

37

EZRA

I jog ahead of Marshall, "Alright, bro, let's show them what we've got!"

Marshall rolls his eyes for the hundredth time today as he slowly follows behind me. He acts like he doesn't want to get involved in my schemes, but he always follows me into them anyway—he's a good sport like that. I know people are watching; I can feel their eyes just like I can feel Adley's. Who could blame them? But their eyes aren't the ones I'm most interested in right now. I need Adley to see us. I need to get her riled up into a lustful frenzy over how athletically superior her mates are.

After a sufficient amount of space is between Marshall and me, I spin around and hurl the frisbee at him—ensuring I get lots of lift on it. As it flies through the air, it occurs to me that my mates are the brainy, intellectual type—the type not known for their coordination and athleticism. Dorks, if you will.

My worries are almost instantly quelled when Marshall catches my throw with effortless precision. His movements are so smooth they almost look rehearsed. *He looks so cool.*

Of course, I can't let that nerd show me up when he lobs it back. The frisbee soars through the air, a perfect arc against the blue sky. I follow its trajectory, its weight familiar in my hands, even before I jump and twist mid-air to snag it. The sound of the wind rushing past my ears, the sun glinting off my expensive watch—everything feels just right. *This is my element.* The small crowd nearby claps, and I shoot them a wink. This is what I'm good at: taking something ordinary and making it extraordinary.

"Try to keep up, bro," I call, spinning the frisbee in my hands before sending it back to him with a dramatic flick of my wrist. It is a flawless throw, the kind of throw that makes anyone watching wonder if I do this professionally.

Marshall catches it without breaking a sweat. There is no flare, no showmanship, just efficient precision. I find his disregard for presentation annoying sometimes. It's this difference in our personalities that makes him feel simultaneously like a cockblock and a wingman. If he weren't my mate, I'd do everything in my power right now to reduce him to rubble, knock him lower so I look taller. But he is my mate. And I no longer hate that about him. I won't step on him—we'll lift each other. Not just to impress Adley but also for the crowd—not that he wants the crowd's attention. But I can use his presence to make the crowd adore us—well, specifically me.

And there is a crowd. There always is, even if they don't realize it at first. People pause mid-walk, their disgusting dogs tugging on leashes. I wish they'd move on. I don't have the same hangups as Marshall about dogs, but I still don't like them. A group of teens on bikes slows, their phones out, gasping, "It's Ezra!" A jogger stops completely, pretending to adjust her shoelaces but clearly watching me. I picked this spot for a reason. The park's open field is a stage, and I know how to work it.

This time, the frisbee returns to me with a little extra spin—Marshall's subtle way of keeping me on my toes. I leap into the air, twisting mid-jump to catch it behind my back. The crowd murmurs, a ripple of admiration that fuels me like nothing else.

I jog backward a few steps, turning to look at Adley. She sits on the blanket, her book open on her lap, but her eyes… are they on me? For a moment, I am sure they are. Her gaze lingers, and I feel that familiar warmth in my chest. Adley isn't like the others; her attention isn't easy to grab. When she looks at me, it isn't because I am performing. It is because she sees… me. Or at least, that's what I want to believe.

I smile and throw the frisbee again, with an exaggerated spin that makes it curve dramatically before settling into Marshall's hands. I turn back to Adley, hoping to catch her reaction, but she is already looking down at her book. The moment passes, and I feel a pang of frustration.

"You're going to throw your shoulder out with that spin," Marshall says as he walks toward me, his tone flat, but I can read the teasing in it.

"Don't worry about my shoulder," I reply, grinning. "Worry about keeping up, old man." He hates it when I refer to the fact that he's older than me despite being born seven years after me. *Oh, the joys of space and time travel.*

I throw the frisbee again, this time high and far, forcing Marshall to sprint for it. As he takes off, I turn back to the impromptu audience. The jogger is closer now, her hands on her hips as she catches her breath. "You're really good," she says, her voice carrying just enough to make sure I hear.

"Thanks," I reply, flashing her a quick smile. "Years of practice."

"You're Ezra From Another World, right?" she adds, stepping closer.

"Do you live near here?"

"Nah, doll, I'm from another world, remember?" I say, half-joking. She laughs, the kind of laugh people give when they're unsure if you're serious. She reaches for my arm, but I skillfully dodge her grasp by raising my hand to Marshall, indicating I want him to throw it back and pretending I didn't notice her reach. I hope he will throw it closer to Adley and away from this jogger so I can break from this conversation.

Undeterred, though slightly embarrassed, she lifts her chest and attempts to speak to me again. *I should get Adley an outfit like that.* Before she can say more, Marshall returns, frisbee in hand. *Bro, why didn't you just throw it?*

"Are we done?" he asks, his tone neutral but with an edge that only I would catch. He thinks I'm flirting. I look to Adley to see if she sees this woman talking to me, but she isn't currently watching. That's good. I don't want her to see me talking to this woman; I want her to see me being a frisbee-catching sex god.

"Just chatting," I say, brushing off the moment as I take the frisbee from him.

If Adley isn't watching, then I will make her notice me. "Ready for something big?" I ask Marshall, not waiting for his answer before launching the frisbee high toward Adley. I run after it, leaping just as it begins to descend. My fingers close around the edge, and I tuck into a roll, landing near Adley's blanket edge. I spring up, startling Adley—who is staring at me with that same look she gives me right before she takes my dick into her mouth.

The crowd claps, a few even cheer, and I shoot them a theatrical bow, but for once, I don't care. My audience doesn't matter. *Only Adley. Only Marshall.*

"Babe, I thought you wanted to read your book. If you keep staring at me like that, you'll lose your place," I waggle my eyebrows at her before running off toward the lake's edge, where Marshall lingers.

Marshall strolls toward me, shaking his head and smiling. "You're ridiculous," he says.

"But it's working," I reply, tossing the frisbee back to him.

ADLEY

Ezra is strutting around like he's god's gift to frisbee, and I can't help but laugh at him. I wish I could get a glimpse into that blowhard's head. Don't get me wrong, he looks great, but he's hamming it up so hard it's obvious he thinks this little show will solve all of our relationship problems. The funnier thing is that it's actually working, but not for the reasons he likely believes it is. It's working because it's adorable how the two of them are trying so hard to woo me right now. The look on his face when I saw him leap and tumble to catch that frisbee in the most extra way he possibly could was so adorably hopeful. This whole spectacle reminds me why I love them—both of them.

I cannot stop watching them, and I've made zero progress on this book I'm trying to read. In fact, I've made negative progress; I've had to go back a bunch of pages because their antics are so distracting that it's erasing my memories of anything other than them. The two of them move quickly, their throws sharp and catches effortless. Ezra's energy is magnetic, pulling in everyone within a hundred-foot radius. Marshall, quieter but no less graceful, has a way of commanding attention without trying. Together, they are impossible not to watch. And clearly, I am not the only one who thinks so. A small crowd gathers, murmurs of appreciation carrying across the field. I marvel that no one seems to care about Ezra's ears and tail. An impossibly beautiful jogger is chatting up Ezra, and I'm trying not to let my jealousy get the better of me.

I guess I'll just watch them. This book isn't happening. I close it and toss it to the side. I shift to the most comfortable position, ready to lean back and enjoy the warm sun, the soft blanket, and the show. They notice me discarding my book, and the looks on their faces make all the angst of the last few days fall away—Ezra's megawatt grin and Marshall's quiet, steady gaze.

"The view's nice, huh?" a voice says, breaking through my thoughts. I look up to see a woman standing nearby with an adorable corgi puppy. The dog sniffs at the edge of the blanket, its tail wagging furiously. The woman smiles, her face open and friendly. She looks about my age, with short, dark hair and a practical, no-nonsense air about her.

"Yeah, the lake is beautiful," I say.

"Girl, you and I both know I wasn't talking about the lake," she laughs. "Good choice," she says, pointing at the book I tossed aside. "That's one of my favorites."

"Really?" I ask, looking up surprised. "I haven't made much progress because…" I say, gesturing vaguely towards the guys, "but I've heard it's good."

"Hard to concentrate with all that going on," she says, nodding toward Ezra and Marshall. "They're… impressive, aren't they?"

I laugh softly, feeling a blush creep up my neck. "They're definitely something."

"I'm Tina," she says, extending a hand.

"Adley," I reply, shaking her hand.

"This is Ein." Ein, apparently deciding I am friend material, flops onto his back for a belly rub.

"Like *Cowboy Bebop*?" I ask, scratching his belly.

'Exactly like *Cowboy Bebop*!" she says. "I'm a data analyst, so of course I have to have a data dog," she says with a laugh, and I laugh with her.

"Do you mind if I sit and chat for a minute?"

"Oh, yeah, sure. That'd be great."

"Do you live around here?" she asks. "I don't think I've seen you before."

"Yeah, I live a few blocks from here," I say. "But I… don't really get out much."

"Ein and I love this park," Tina says. "Great spot for reading, obviously." She gestures to the book. "What kind of books are you into?"

"Oh, umm… cozy murder mysteries and… smut… as you already know," I laugh, referencing the fact that the book I tossed aside is notoriously smutty.

Tina's face lights up. "Ha, yeah. I saw you sitting here with that book, and I figured any woman willing to openly read that in public is the kind of woman I want to be friends with! Then I saw the Sailor Moon bag, and I just knew I had to talk to you. I got nervous when you said you hadn't made it far; I was scared you didn't know how smutty it was, and I showed my pervy hand too soon," she laughs.

"Oh, no, I know how smutty it is," I laugh, reassuring her.

"You should join my book club! We're just a bunch of smut nerds. It's a fun time. Gives us all a good excuse to get together, drink wine, and talk about…" she whispers conspiratorially, "dragon dick," then laughs maniacally.

"Really?!" I say, the idea sparking something warm and hopeful inside me. "That sounds amazing. I… I've been wanting to meet people, but it's hard to know where to start."

"Let me text you the details. We're meeting next Friday. If you can't make it, we should meet for brunch or something," she says, reaching for her phone.

"I'd love that," I say, unable to hide the excitement in my voice. While we exchange numbers, Ein rests his head on my knee.

"He likes you," Tina says, smiling.

"He's adorable," I say, scratching behind Ein's ears. My attention drifts back to Ezra and Marshall for a moment. Ezra executes another dramatic catch, and the crowd responds with scattered applause. I catch the way a woman near the edge of the field claps a little too enthusiastically, her eyes glued to him. My chest tightens again, but Ezra turns, his gaze finding mine. He looks horrified that I have a dog in my lap, but his face softens, and he grins at me with a wink.

"Is that one yours?" Tina asks, nodding toward Ezra.

"Both of them," I say before I can think better of it. Her eyebrows lift in surprise.

"Damn, girl, I knew I was going to like you. You've got excellent taste," she says, laughing.

I smile, feeling a rush of gratitude for her easy acceptance. "Thanks. They… mean a lot to me."

Tina stands and says, "Well, Ein and I have to get back to our walk. I'll text you about the book club. It was nice meeting you, Adley."

"You, too," I say, waving as she and Ein walk away.

Oh, my God! Did I just make a friend?

I pick up my book again, grinning, excited to meet whomever Tina calls her friends. I look at the guys, and the crowd has dispersed a bit. The guys look at me and seem relieved the dog is gone. I smile at them and am excited by how effortless my smile feels. At this moment, I am deliriously happy.

A woman with a stroller lingers near them, as she adjusts her bra and checks her reflection in a handheld mirror. My chest tightens, and a sour pang floods me. All the hope and excitement I was feeling drains from me. *Veronica.*

MARSHALL

"Don't hold back, bro!" Ezra calls, attempting to get me to do some exaggerated thing to make him look extra cool. He already looks pretty cool, though. Ezra's movements are graceful and poised, with an edge of danger.

He crouches slightly, waiting for my throw. It feels calculated, almost predatory. I, unlike him, have no idea how to make throwing a plastic disc look cool. I particularly don't know how to throw it so that he looks cool while catching it. He grins at me, a beacon of confidence and mischief.

He sways back and forth, muscles taut, body coiled like a spring ready to explode—waiting impatiently for me. I throw it far away from him to ensure he has as much space as he needs to do whatever little dance he chooses. Ezra moves as if everyone is watching him—because they usually are. Everything he does is an audition, performance, and this game of catch is no different. I always prefer precision to spectacle, and my throws reflect that. I know precisely where the frisbee lands each time, and Ezra's dramatic catches only make me roll my eyes. But when he pulls off a ridiculous mid-air twist, I can't help but watch in awe. He has a way of making the impossible look effortless.

I throw the frisbee, a sharp, precise arc I know he'll catch. Ezra doesn't just catch it; he leaps for it, twisting mid-air as though the laws of gravity are mere suggestions. The frisbee snaps into his hand with a satisfying thud, and he lands lightly, almost silently, on the balls of his feet. Applause ripples from a group of onlookers, and I sigh. There is always an audience. Something I am trying to get used to.

Every movement is done in a way that is practiced, planned, and perfectly executed to meet precisely what those watching want from him. Having known him for a while now and being the person he confides his plans to, I know it's not as effortless as he wants people to think—he's planned the whole thing. Ezra's antics aren't random; they are calculated. Part of me finds it exhausting. Another part… well, I can't deny he is captivating.

"Is that all you've got?" Ezra teases, spinning the frisbee on one finger before sending it back to me with a theatrical flick. The crowd murmurs again, drawn in by his energy. He basks in it, head tilting slightly, preening in the sunlight. His hair catches the light, golden and shimmering, and my heart skips at his attractiveness.

I catch the frisbee with a quick, efficient movement, keeping my focus on the task. But my eyes wander for a moment—not to the crowd, Ezra, or even Adley, but to the ducks gliding across the pond nearby. Their feathers shimmer in iridescent greens and browns, catching my eyes and calling forth something primal within me. I could watch them all day—their quiet presence starkly contrasts Ezra's vibrant performance. A duck dips its head beneath the water, emerging with a small splash, utterly unbothered by the racket he is stirring. *I want to join them.*

"Bro, come on," Ezra urges, breaking into my thoughts. He claps his hands dramatically. I throw the frisbee again, this time with more force. Ezra darts to meet it, moving with the kind of agility that isn't possible for Adley's species—he really should tone it down a bit. He leaps, arches, and twirls mid-air, the frisbee clutched triumphantly in one hand. The jogger chatting with him gasps audibly, and Ezra's grin widens. She stays nearby as he jogs back toward me, her gaze fixed on him. I hope that Adley doesn't get jealous. *I'm a little jealous.*

"You're incredible," she says, stepping closer. Her tone is light but pointed, and her interest is evident.

"Thanks," Ezra says, flashing her a dazzling smile. It is polite but detached; he is used to this kind of attention. He flicks the frisbee back to me without missing a beat, already preparing for his next move. The jogger lingers, hoping for more, but Ezra has already returned to the game.

I catch the frisbee and almost ram into a woman with a stroller. I spin and do a somersault onto the ground to stop plowing into her and her stroller. "Great catch," she says, her voice warm, her eyes scanning me with curiosity. I'm pretty proud of the move and wonder if I looked like a video game character dodging an attack.

"That's what I'm talking about, dude!" Ezra says. I blush, and I wonder if he notices. Of course, he does. Ezra notices everything, even when he pretends not to.

I stand, brushing myself off, and the woman comes closer, saying, "Hi, I'm Veronica." I nod, offering a small smile, but don't say anything. I just throw the frisbee to Ezra and back away from her.

"Have we met before?" she asks.

"No," I reply, trying to get away from her.

"Are you sure? You look so familiar," she says. Why is she bothering me? She's in the way.

"I can assure you, we do not know each other. Please go over there so I do not run into you," I say, pointing far away. *Is she hitting on me? Is this normal in this world? For women with babies to so aggressively hit on you?*

I don't like this woman talking to me. I don't like it when strangers who are not my mates speak to me. I look back at the ducks. I try to focus on their quiet movements. One duck flaps its wings, droplets scattering in the sunlight, and I feel a strange sense of calm watching them. *They're so cute.* I want to leap into the water and snatch one close to my chest. Hug it.

"Do you and your friend play here often? I'm here all the time. Maybe that's why you look so familiar," she says. *Please leave me alone.* I look toward Adley, and she has a stricken, horrified look. *Fuck. Is she jealous because of me now? No!*

I hold my hands up to her and say, moving further away, "He is not my friend; he's my—"

"Marshall," Ezra calls, snapping my attention to him. "Try this one!" He hurls the frisbee high and to my left, a trajectory indicating it will land far away from me. I sprint for it, catching it just before it hits the ground. My heart races, not from the exertion but from the pestering of that woman and that sinking look on Adley's face.

When I look up, I see Adley staring at me. Her book rests on her lap, forgotten. Our eyes meet, and I feel a flicker of connection—a quiet acknowledgment amid Ezra's spectacle. I realize he threw it exactly into her line of sight. This, like everything he does, was a planned, calculated move. But, instead of looking impressed, she is… crying?

"Nice save, bro," Ezra says, jogging over. He claps me on the back, his touch lingering a beat longer than necessary.

"Ez," I say to him, drawing his attention to Adley.

"Can y'all sit with me?" she asks, her voice cracking and tears rolling.

"What did that demon dog do to you?" Ezra asks, rushing to her side.

38

ADLEY

I didn't expect to see Veronica today—not here, not like this. Even before she removed her hat and glasses to flirt with Marshall, I knew it was her from her movements. Veronica and I used to be inseparable. We moved here together—big dreams to get away from our shitty little town. But that was before she decided to fuck my boyfriend. My chest is tight, and my mouth is dry. *The stroller. Oh, my God, the baby! I can't breathe.*

Ezra rushes around me, looking around my body for wounds. "What did the dog do? I was watching that little shit. I'm so sorry. I must have taken my eyes off him for a second. Oh, my God, I can smell him on you."

Veronica watched them come over here. She's standing there, staring at me, obviously recognizing me. A flash of decision enters her face, and she pushes the stroller toward me. *She's coming this way!*

Ezra flops onto the ground next to me and rubs his face against my leg, where the dog was. He grabs my hand and runs it through his hair. Then, he stands and kicks his feet on the blanket where the dog once was.

I stand. I want to turn around, run away, and pretend I haven't seen her. But I can't. I am rooted to the spot. My feet refuse to move as some invisible force holds me in place. She is fast approaching. Her gaze flicks nervously back and forth as her pace quickens.

"Ezra!" Marshall shouts—speaking to him in a tone he rarely uses with him anymore. Ezra immediately takes notice. "It wasn't the dog," he says, staring at Veronica. Ezra follows his gaze.

"Do you know her, babe?" Ezra asks.

"We have to go," I croak through tight breaths as she approaches.

Marshall understands what's going on well before Ezra. He pushes Ezra off the blanket and tries to bundle it up. "Bro, what the fuck," Ezra says.

"That's Veronica!" Marshall hisses to him.

"Oh, shit," Ezra says and hustles me off the blanket and behind the tree so Marshall can finish his work and I can hide. He gathers our stuff and grabs my hand ready to pull me away when a soft voice calls out from the other side of the tree, "Adley?" *Shit.*

I lean around and peer behind the tree. There she is, standing a few feet away from me. Veronica removes her sunglasses, and her wide blue eyes are fixed on me, a mixture of guilt and hesitation across her face. Her face is a little fuller. Her eyes are puffy, and she looks tired. I glance down at the sleeping baby in the stroller that Veronica grips in front of herself—likely the reason she looks tired. *Fuck.*

"Adley," she says softly, her voice stabs into me like a familiar knife.

I want to run, but curiosity and the lingering fragments of our friendship root me in place. "Veronica."

She shifts her weight, glancing down at her feet before meeting my gaze again. "Can we talk? Just for a minute?"

My heart hammers in my chest—a mixture of despair, resentment, and rage.

The guys stand frozen behind me, awaiting my signal. Their hurried movements now stopped as they crouched to clean up our stuff. I want to call her a cunt. I want to scream and rage at her. But something about the glint in her eye softens me to her. "Fine," I say, my tone cold.

The guys look at me expectantly. I tell them, "It's okay, I'll be just a minute. No need for us to leave." And give them a reassuring smile—even though I think I might be lying. They both nod and lay our stuff back out.

Veronica yammers at me, "I… I wasn't sure if I'd ever see you here. I didn't even know if you still lived around here. You never post on social media anymore and blocked me from everything…"

"What do you want, Veronica?" I ask curtly.

She takes a deep breath, her fingers fidgeting with the stroller's handle. "I wanted to apologize. For Bryce. For what I did to you."

Her words hang in the air, and my brain doesn't know what to do with them. I have imagined this moment a thousand times, but now that it is happening, I don't know how to feel. The anger that has burned so hot for so long is still there, but the raw vulnerability in her voice dulls it. I open and close my hands at my side, trying to release some of this awful feeling building in my chest through my fingers.

"I know I don't deserve your forgiveness," she continues, trembling. "I know you've painted me out to be some cold-hearted villain in your head. And there's some truth to it; believe me, I hate myself for what I did more than you probably could, but I was just as lonely as you were. I'm not trying to excuse my actions. But… but I'm sorry, Adley. I really am," she says. "I regret it every day. Deep down, I knew what I was doing would hurt you. I did, but… I tried to convince myself it wouldn't. I convinced myself I loved him more than you did… I don't know what I was thinking. But… hurting you wasn't why I did it."

I think back to the moment I saw them together—the look on her face. I've always thought she looked proud. But was pride really what she was feeling? Was it a shame? Was it fear? I saw them, and I went so white hot with rage I didn't even talk to her. Has my rage and my sadness clouded my memory? Am I the unreliable narrator of my past?

She hesitates, glancing down at her feet before meeting my eyes again. "And… I know. I know that the two of you hooked up after… after I… after he and I… after we got engaged." She swallows hard, her eyes glistening.

My stomach drops, and a rush of shame floods my cheeks. I open my mouth to protest, but the words catch in my throat. She isn't wrong. I did do that. Do I even have a right to be angry when I did the same thing?

"Listen, I get it. He was yours first, and I stole him. I hurt you first. I destroyed our friendship for him and didn't deserve your kindness after that. But… we were having a baby and going to get married…" They were going to get married? Does that mean they didn't?

I can't look at her anymore. Her eyes bore into me; all I see is my cruelty, arrogance, and hypocrisy. The pain and sadness that drove me to him—is she saying she made similar mistakes? My eyes fix on the sleeping baby. *Did I break up your family?*

"I'm sorry. I am… not proud of that. I wanted to hurt you. It was… cruel of me," I croak, finally admitting it to myself.

A sad smile quirks on her face, "Thank you. That means a lot, Adley."

The weight in my chest shifts. It's no longer a burning, seething rage. It's a whirlwind of guilt, sadness, and loss.

"And… I thought you would like to know," she sighs. "He left me. For someone else. So, I got what was coming to me." She lets out a self-deprecating laugh.

Another flood of emotion hits me like a bag of bricks. He left her? He destroyed me, he destroyed our friendship, and then he fucking left her with a baby?

"I guess I should have seen it coming," she continued, her voice thick with emotion. "He's an asshole. I can't believe how stupid I was. I was so lonely and so… he convinced… it doesn't matter," she says, shaking her head. She looks down at the stroller, and her expression softens, "But, I have Ellie, so I can't regret it too much… if that makes sense. She's the one good thing that came out of all this." *Is she the only good thing?*

I look down at the sleeping baby. Her nose squinches, and her tiny hands flex like mine when I'm nervous. And yeah, it does make sense.

"I don't expect you to forgive me," Veronica says. "I just needed you to know that I'm sorry. And I forgive you for sleeping with him. I wanted you to know that he and I are not together—but that's not your fault." She lets out a long sigh as if an enormous weight has been removed from her chest.

I look at her face—beautiful and haunted by guilt. And it seems real. I believe her. I don't know if I can hate her anymore. For the first time, I feel something other than anger toward her. I feel pity.

"I don't hate you," I say slowly, the words surprising even me. "But I… I don't forgive you…"

She nods, tears slipping down her cheeks. "I understand. Thank you for hearing me out."

She grabs the stroller tighter and twists the handles. "Okay, well, so long, Adley," she says as she turns, wiping her nose on her sleeve.

"Veronica, wait!" I stop her. "Mittens. Is… is she okay? What did he do with her?"

Her face lights up, "She's wonderful! I have her!" But her expression pains again when she says, "Oh, I… I suppose you want her back." The tears roll faster down her face now. *Yes, I do. I do want her back.* I miss her desperately, just like I miss Veronica. I miss them both with every fiber of my fucking being. But… I have Marshall and Ezra.

When I look at Marshall and Ezra, my heart feels less lonely. The floodgates of my tears break as I shake my head vigorously. I can't take Mittens from her. She needs Mittens more than I do.

"No… no. You… you take care of her," I bawl, not wanting to say it, but feeling like I should.

"Thank you… thank you, Adley," she says—her tears now containing a mixture of happiness.

Before she leaves, I ask, "But… maybe… maybe I can visit her sometime. Visit you sometime?"

"We'd like that," she says and turns to leave.

I turn to Marshall and Ezra, my heart cracking open into a million pieces. I sink into their shared embrace and bawl into their chests.

39

ADLEY

Like the tide retreating from the storm, the swell of emotions in me subsides, and I blink back my tears. I pull my face away from Marshall's chest. My eyes adjust to the bright afternoon sun, and I cringe at the wet splotch I left where my face was. However, Marshall hands me a napkin before I can say anything about it. I wipe my face and his shoulder.

People walk past, and I can feel their eyes on me—a blubbering idiot engulfed by two shirtless hotties. I pull away slightly, but neither of them releases their embrace on me, and I'm still held in a tangle of powerful arms. A soft purr emanates through their warm bodies and comforts me from all angles. Marshall's thumb presses small soothing circles into my back, and Ezra's face presses into my shoulder.

"You okay, babe?" Ezra asks, his expression a mix of concern and tentative relief. His golden hair catches the sunlight as his anxious movements scan my face for any lingering signs of distress.

"Yeah, I'm sorry, guys," I state, though my voice is hoarse from crying. I hide my face between them, trying to be seen by no one but them.

"Why are you sorry?" Marshall asks—solid, unmoving. His steady presence is in direct conflict with Ezra's fidgety one. *Marshall, my pragmatic rock.*

"Because I know y'all had some big elaborate plan to seduce me, and I once again ruined it," I say, as tears threaten to pour out again.

"I have no idea what you're talking about, babe," Ezra says, looking guilty.

"Really? So, what was with all the lotioning and showboating?"

"Have you met me? This is how I always act," Ezra says, still not wanting to let go of the ruse. I look to Marshall because I know he'll admit to it.

"It is true. He does always act like that," Marshall says.

"See!" Ezra shrugs, pointing at Marshall. "Babe, you already know I'm extra."

"Are you ready to go home now?" Marshall asks.

"Actually, no, I'd like to stay and eat the food we brought. I feel much better," I say with a smile.

"Are you sure? You're not doing a fake smile?" Marshall asks, studying my face.

"Yeah, I actually… I actually feel… fantastic. That was a very freeing conversation. I feel… hopeful. Grateful," I say.

"Yeah?" Ezra asks.

"Yeah. I realize that I'm so fucking grateful Bryce cheated on me. I mean, I wish it hadn't been with Veronica, but… when Veronica mentioned Ellie being the one good thing that came out of it… I realized I have two good things," I say, smiling at them. "I love you both so much."

"We love you, too," they both say in unison. One in an excited, eager way. The other in a steady, powerful way. They kiss me on my temples—multiple quick kisses on one side and one slow, firm one on the other.

I giggle because these two are so different. Interestingly, they are both perfect yet so different. I shift from their embrace so we can speak more freely.

"Thank you for being such great boyfriends and taking care of me," I say earnestly. I am so incredibly grateful at this moment, and all the tears are now gone.

"We're a team, babe. We all take care of each other," Ezra says.

I smile at the word 'team'. Because I think we actually are. I'm ready to move on and drop all of the things that have held me back from being fully in this with them.

"Anyway, I'm sorry I ruined the day," I sigh, picking at the blanket beneath me.

"Nonsense, nothing is ruined," Marshall says as if I'm being ridiculous.

"Exactly. And besides, if there were some grand Adley wooing plan, do you think a few tears could stop it? Nah, it would have contingency plans," Ezra says with a glint in his eyes.

"Oh, really? So, what would these hypothetical contingency plans be?" I ask with a laugh.

"Well, it would involve stuffing you with all your favorite foods while we douse you in compliments," Ezra says, leaning forward and pulling the picnic basket closer to us.

Ezra's face gets deathly serious for a moment. "Adley, Marshall, I'm really sorry about what I said… about the pact… about you putting out. That was… it's not how I feel about you two."

"I know," I say, and I do. Marshall nods.

"And I'm sorry, too, Ezra. I appreciate everything you do. I will stop waiting for you to leave. I will stop suspecting your help and love is conditional. I will… I will let you help me…"

"So does that mean the two of you are going to work on the game, for real?" Ezra asks.

"Yes, if you're okay with that," I say to Ezra. "And if you're okay with it," I say to Marshall.

Marshall nods, and Ezra says, "Of course, babe. I want the two of you to do this together."

"We do it together. All of us," I say, brushing Ezra's cheek.

"Sounds great, babe," he says, smirking at me.

EZRA

"Bro, I think you were right about my shoulder," I say, rolling my shoulder as we walk in the door.

"Well, you are 42," Marshall says with a smirk. "You can't run around like that anymore."

"What! Bro, no, I'm fucking not. I'm 32."

"To me, you're 42," he shrugs while putting the basket on the table. He's getting me back for that "old man" quip earlier.

"Whatever, dude, my youth literally transcends time and space," I laugh.

"Well, since Marshall technically came from five years in the future, here, you're 37, and Marshall's only 30," Adley smirks.

"Oh, yeah, that's true. If we consider our actual birth years and the current year of this universe," Marshall says.

"What?! That's not fair! Age is based on how long your body has existed! If we consider that, my body is the youngest one here," I say, hands on my hip, puffing out my chest. "Going five years into the future doesn't make me five years older." *Does it? This math is hurting my head.*

"You're only saying that because you're the oldest on either timeline," Adley giggles at me teasingly.

"It's not funny, babe!" I say as I grab her and pull her close, breathing in her neck the way I always do. A sharp twinge in my shoulder causes me to grimace. I rub my neck, trying to relieve the pain.

"Aww, Ez, you went too hard," she says, rubbing it for me and pulling her pelvis into me.

"I could never go too hard for you, babe," I say, my dick rising at the sight and smell of her. God, I need her.

"Let's go lie down and… rub that out," she says with that glint in her eyes.

My eyes meet with Marshall's as we silently acknowledge the success of *Operation Honey Trap Adley*.

I might as well ham this up. "Oww. It hurts so much, Adley," I say with a feigned whimper—even though it does actually hurt.

"Aww, you poor baby. We will take care of you. Right, Marshall?"

The only time he's good at this roleplaying stuff is after he's had some alcohol in him, so I'm surprised when he says, "Well, we both are doctors." It's lame, but he's trying. "Not that kind of doctor, though," he says, unable to stop himself.

I give him an exacerbated smirk and attempt to put things back on track. "Are the two of you going to let me just lie back while you do all the work of… massaging me?" I ask. Honestly, my shoulder hurts so much that I think I need it. *Fuck. I am getting old.*

Adley guides me into the bedroom, with Marshall trailing closely behind us. As we reach the bed, she sits me on its soft, inviting surface. My back twinges, and I stifle a wince. Her lips reach my neck, planting a tender kiss that sends my tail on end. Her kisses slowly travel up to my chin, leaving a path of warmth in their wake.

Marshall positions himself behind Adley, gripping her hips against him. I grab the lower part of Adley's back with a deep, insatiable hunger. I pull her close, wrapping myself around her and burying my face between her breasts. I relish their softness as I nuzzle in deeper. I take a deep breath, letting her scent fill my lungs—a deeply missed sensation. "Oh, babe, I missed you," I whisper, my voice muffled against her skin.

Her fingers comb through my hair as she arches her back in pleasure, leaning her head back against Marshall's chest. As she does so, she runs her fingers around the ridges of my ears, gently petting them between her fingers and tugging when she gets to the tip—an action she knows will elicit a response from me. A low moan escapes my lips as my dick begs to be inside her.

Meanwhile, Marshall's powerful hands find their way to the tense muscles of my neck and shoulders. He applies firm pressure with skilled precision, massaging at the knots forming. Each kneading stroke from his fingers melt away the stiffness accumulated over the day. Marshall and I purr, inciting a deep moan in Adley—she leans her head back and relishes in it.

Adley grabs my shirt, pulling it over my head and causing my shoulder to bark in pain. A moan of agony escapes me, and Marshall says, "I told you so."

"Small price to pay, bro," I say, ready to lose myself to the pleasure I suspect is about to be inflicted on me.

I try to stand, but they both push me down gently. "Lie on your stomach," she commands. I attempt a cool flip to my stomach, which is interrupted by the pain building in my back. *Jesus, this sucks.* "Relax, let us take care of you," Adley whispers.

The smell of my and Marshall's sweat combine, mixed with the heavy scent of our arousal. Marshall deftly lifts her shirt, revealing her full breasts nestled securely within an unassuming bra; I can't help but thrust my dick harder into the mattress beneath me. My hands grip the bedsheets, knuckles white from the intensity of my arousal. Their eyes lock with mine, and I can see the desire reflected in their depths.

"Take off her pants," I gasp, pressing my hand hard against my throbbing erection over my shorts. My desire is ravenous.

He gets to his knees in front of her, and with a deliberate slide of his hands, he slowly guides her pants down her thighs. Her breasts heave with gasping breaths as she reaches for his hair. I can't help but groan again, my cock aching to be buried inside her wet cunt.

"Turn her to me. Take off the rest," I say. He gets behind her and unhooks her bra, letting it fall to the floor. He lifts her breasts, cupping them in his hands and presenting them to me. He pinches her nipples until they harden between his fingers. She bites her lip and closes her eyes, her breathing becoming heavier as he caresses her breasts. Her hand instinctively reaches for her pussy, sliding her fingers inside herself as he continues to touch her.

With her free hand, she strokes my tail in long, fluid motions from root to tip, each stroke bringing more pleasure. I can sense her arousal growing with every passing moment as she rubs herself harder and faster. Her hips gyrate, moving in rhythm with her hand as Marshall continues to fondle and squeeze her breasts. He kisses her neck, and I want to taste her, too—to feel the warmth of her skin against my lips, the sweet scent of arousal that lingers in the air as she touches herself. I want to taste them both. The thought of running my lips over their naked bodies makes my heart pound faster in my chest.

"The panties. Now!" I say, unable to wait any longer to see that miraculous cunt.

Still kneeling, Marshall's fingers gently trace down her body, causing her to moan and writhe. With a deliberate slowness, his fingers hook into her panties and pull them down. I drink in every detail of her body, and Marshall gently spreads her lips for me to get a better look at her swollen pussy glistened with need.

"Fucking perfect," I breathe into the pillow, my grip tightening around my dick. It feels like I am about to explode with the pent-up desire building up for so long.

"Now, take his clothes off," I say, recognizing that, at this moment, I want to feel the press of both of their skin against mine. She turns to do so, giving me a view of that beautiful, tailless ass. She lifts his shirt over his head, revealing his muscular chest. Her lips part as she takes in the sight before her, and then she leans forward to place a gentle kiss on his taut pecs. He groans in pleasure, a testament to the intense sensation of her soft lips on his skin.

She pulls his shorts and underwear down in a single fluid motion, causing his dick to stand to attention as it pops out from behind the confines of his clothing. It twitches as she reaches out to touch it. She marvels at it for a moment before bending over, her ass now in my face, and places a soft kiss on the sensitive tip of his dick. He moans in delight, as it's been a long time since he has felt the tenderness of her kisses on his dick, too.

The moment she stands at full height, he grips her waist tightly and slams his body into her with passionate fervor. They kiss passionately, and she moans into his mouth as they grind into each other.

She breaks from his embrace, and they turn their attention back to me. She quickly slides my shorts and underwear down, adding them to their pile of discarded clothing. She crawls onto the bed, spreading her legs wide, straddling me, and positioning her entrance over my tail. She grinds her body against my back. Pressing her tits into my sore muscles and slicking my tail with her damp desire.

Our hearts pound in unison, but before my orgasm releases itself all over the bed, she rolls off me, moving to the side like a well-coordinated gymnast. Marshall kneels on the floor beside me, placing his strong hands firmly on my back. He applies intense pressure that borders on pain. Adley kneels beside me on the bed and applies softer pressure wherever his hands are not.

I hum in pleasure, savoring their touch as they manipulate my stiff muscles with precision. Are…they in sync? Is this how Adley feels when Marshall and I coordinate our movements to please her? This is awesome!

ADLEY

Ezra's body is taut with desire as he lies with his face down, moaning into the pillow. My fingers press into his flesh, kneading and caressing his muscles, tense with anticipation. Marshall's firm and confident touch mirrors mine as he massages Ezra's broad shoulders.

Ezra's body writhes beneath our hands, and I can tell he is torn between enjoying the massage and the desire to fuck. The room is thick with tension, filled with the sounds of our heavy breathing, their purrs, and Ezra's low moans as Marshall and I explore Ezra's body.

My hands drift lower, tracing a path down Ezra's spine and across his lower back, then gliding up his tail in a slow, fluid motion. As I do so, Marshall rubs his back. But once I reach the tip, Marshall's hand replaces mine, and he runs his hand down the length of Ezra's tail. Our movements, a synchronized choreography, wave across the entire length of his spine. This elicits a low growl deep within Ezra's chest as he arches into our touch.

"I can't take it anymore," Ezra gasps, his voice muffled by the pillow. He rolls onto his back, breaking away from our teasing touches. His cock stands tall and proud, throbbing with need, and he can't help but stroke it slowly.

Marshall, his gaze burning with heat, kneels at the edge of the bed. He watches us both intently, waiting for direction before acting, as he always does.

Their purrs increase in volume and frequency when Ezra says, "I need to taste you." Ezra reaches for my hips and tugs me toward his face. Marshall's eyes linger on Ezra's stiff cock, clearly longing to taste him as well, but he holds himself back, not daring to act without permission.

Silently, I urge Marshall to ask for what he wants by glancing between the two of them. But he won't. Our exchange doesn't go unnoticed by Ezra, who studies Marshall for a moment before meeting his gaze, nodding toward his erection, and saying, "Go ahead."

Marshall's eyes widen with excitement at realizing what Ezra is telling him he can do. Hesitantly at first, he reaches out with one hand to grasp the base of Ezra's cock while his other hand cups his balls gently. His lips meet the swollen head of Ezra's member in a delicate kiss before sinking further, taking more of him into his mouth.

Ezra's moan is unrestrained and filled with pleasure as Marshall works on him, swallowing him whole. "Adley," he groans impatiently, "get on my face." With an urgency fueled by lust and anticipation, he gropes my ass and pulls me towards him until I straddle his face. My thighs press against the sides of his head, and he digs his fingers into my ass, no longer concerned about aggravating his injured shoulder.

His skilled tongue whirls around my sensitive flesh, guided by the firm grip on my hips as he moves me in passionate circles. Each teasing lick and thrust sends waves of pleasure through my body, building and intensifying with every touch.

My breath becomes ragged as the pleasure builds within me. My muscles tense and pulse with anticipation as I grab the headboard and grind deeper into Ezra's face, my orgasm ready to release. His body jolts below me as he pumps into Marshall's face.

"Wait," Ezra gasps, coming up for air, his breath hitching in his throat. "Marshall, not without Marshall," he insists, making it clear that we can't come without him. He gently removes me from his face, and Marshall gazes up at me with eager eyes. I gracefully slide off the bed. I nudge Marshall to the side so that I can take his place around Ezra's cock.

Marshall stands behind me, unsure of what the plan is. I point my ass at him and exclaim, "Take me with everything you've got, Alpha Marshall!" Spreading my legs invitingly as I lower my head to take Ezra's swollen, throbbing member between my lips. Marshall doesn't hesitate for a second. He raises his hand to his mouth, coating his palm with saliva before delivering a sharp, sensual slap to my backside. His thick length plunges deep inside me, stretching and filling me in that familiar way I missed more than I realized. His slick hand finds its way to my sensitive clit, working it in aggressive circles as he drives himself relentlessly into me.

About to lose myself to the pleasure of Marshall's cock and eager to please both of them equally, I devote my attention to Ezra's erection, bobbing my head along its length and swirling my tongue around its pulsating tip. Beneath me, Ezra writhes and moans in pleasure, his fingers gripping the sheets tightly. Knowing precisely what will throw him over the edge, I carefully slip a finger inside his tight opening. "Holy shit!" he exclaims as a fresh wave of pleasure washes over him.

Just as I feel the first hot spurts of Ezra's release fill my mouth and coat my tongue, Marshall follows suit within me—a shuddering crescendo as our bodies convulse together in unison. I ride out the wave of euphoria as my orgasm releases itself, feeling every twitch from his throbbing cock buried deep within me.

We crumble onto the bed, locked in a tangled embrace. As our heartbeats gradually slow down and our breathing evens out, Ezra whispers into my neck, "I missed you two."

40

EZRA

The jazzy music is replaced by an ominous crashing sound when "Epilogue Cleared" appears on the screen. Marshall grips the controller, his eyes glazed as the screen illuminates his face. He looks the way I feel: dumbfounded.

"What was with the dog?" Marshall asks, still gripping the controller, unable to accept the game is over.

"I bet he was the real villain," I say, suspicious of it.

Adley laughs, "He helped you the whole game!"

I squint at her, wanting to argue but knowing I'd have no leg to stand on. "I just have a bad feeling about him," I say, without any evidence to support my claim.

"I agree with Ezra," Marshall says. "That dog was nefarious."

"You two just hate all dogs!" Adley says.

"That dog was evil. I think your… human-ness blinds you, and whatever it is about your species that draws you to dogs," I say.

"Whatever. You two are ridiculous," she laughs and returns to the code she was writing on her laptop.

Marshall and I look at each other with a shared resolve. This is one point on which we will always agree: the dog is always going to be the villain in any story.

I return my gaze to the screen. Marshall is still on the save prompt, not selecting anything—contemplating the fever dream of a game we just finished. It's the first game we've beaten together. It says, "Do you want to save? Yes/no."

I look at him. I really look at him.

"Hey, Marshall," I say as a feeling swells within me.

He looks at me with that stare that bores into me. It's strange, really, how things can change in a moment. How can one conversation, one look, shift everything you thought you knew about yourself?

"Yeah?" he asks, already knowing I've got something I want to say.

"You know, I was just thinking… York and Zach's relationship is a lot like ours."

A curious expression crosses his face. "How so?" he asks, but I think he already knows the answer. He is the smart one, after all—but he struggles with metaphor, so maybe he won't get it. I suppose, in this case, it is a simile.

"Like them, we're outsiders who take care of each other," I say. "And like them, we have this bond that… that those that don't understand would call magical, but those who do would just call science…"

Marshall blinks, turns to me, and puts the controller on the table. A quiet tension lingers in the air, which has been building for a while now.

"York and Zach need each other. They're always there for one another, even when they don't always understand each other. But they can't escape each other either. They're both fractured, and in a way, they help each other stay whole. And they're kind of like two pieces of a puzzle…" I say, trailing off.

Adley stops typing and looks at us expectantly over the rim of her laptop. She bites her lip, anticipating my next words.

It's weird. The truth can hit you when you least expect it. I thought… I thought I understood this relationship. I thought I knew where we all stood. I thought I knew how I felt about Marshall. But tonight, sitting on the couch with him and Adley, I feel like something shifted—something I can't ignore any longer. Something that's been there a long time, but I was too afraid to admit.

Adley closes the laptop and sets it aside to watch us.

Marshall shifts uncomfortably, unsure how to respond.

"What are you saying?" Marshall asks flatly, his expression unreadable. But I can read it. *I know him.*

"I think I'm saying…"

This is more than a friendship.

"I think I'm York, and you're Zach," I say barely above a whisper. *Just say it. You can do it, Ezra.*

I continue, "We're always there for each other. Even when things get weird… We love the same girl. We… we love…"

My chest tightens. Something I never thought I'd say outright…

My breath catches in my throat. My heart pounds. I look back at the screen. It still says, "Do you want to save? Yes/no." *Yes.*

"We love each other," I finally say. Then, after a long, dramatic pause, "I love you."

"Are you joking?" Marshall asks.

Adley squeals quietly, kicking her feet and hiding behind her hands.

I muster all the seriousness I can and answer, "No. I am not joking. I love you, bro… Marshall. I love you, Marshall."

"I love you, too, Ezra," he says in his flat voice, which conveys enough meaning to me because I can feel it.

I reach out, grabbing his leg. "I'm sorry it took me so long to say it. I know you've been waiting for me to say it," I murmur. "I was just… scared, I guess."

I take a deep breath, and Adley still holds hers, glancing back and forth between us, waiting for us to signal it's okay to talk.

I take a deep breath, "Adley, I love you, too. I love you both so fucking much," the words come more effortlessly now like a weight has been lifted off my chest.

Adley's eyes sparkle, and she squeals in excitement. "I love you, too," she says without hesitation, her voice full of affection. She leaps upon us. Pulling us into an embrace and showering us with kisses. "And I love you, Marshall. Both of you."

Marshall smiles, his eyes glistening, smiling in a carefree way that I've never seen. "I love you both, too. I always have. We're a team."

"Oh, my God, Ezra! I can't believe *Deadly Premonition* made you realize you love Marshall," Adley says through sobs.

=^..^= ♥ =^..^=

"Okay, what if Astrid has this ethereal aura that appears around her when she's using her powers?" Adley suggests, tapping at the drawing on the tablet in front of Marshall.

Marshall chews on the end of his stylus, considering the concept. "Yes, and it could change colors to reflect the unique abilities!" he adds, excitement in his voice that rarely presents itself.

I stretch languidly, awoken by the sounds of their excitable discussion. Their teamwork is quite remarkable. I enjoy curling up in my ailo form on the chair behind them and often fall asleep to the rhythmic tapping of Adley coding and scratching of Marshall's stylus. The past few weeks have felt almost magical; it seems we are finally in harmony and have resolved our previous issues. Our communication has greatly improved, and everything is going wonderfully.

Adley leans in closer, her gaze fixed on the evolving design. "And her armor—with her tits exposed like this, would that really be helpful?" she says, pointing at the open chest design.

"Um, well, it won't stop her from getting stabbed in the heart," Marshall says with a hint of doubt; I suspect he recognizes that his design is flawed.

"Then what's the point?" Adley asks.

"Her stomach is protected," he says flatly. *Bro, that will not win you this argument.*

"So, she can't be disemboweled?"

"Exactly. The bowels are very important to protect."

Adley sighs, "But so is the heart, Marshall."

"I already animated her in this outfit. If I change it, I would have to redo the animation."

"What, bro? Let me see!" I say, jumping onto the desk. He opens another program and hits play.

"Nice, bro!" I purr as I those perfect tits bounce on his screen.

"Marshall! You perv! Is this why you are fighting so hard to keep this outfit?" Adley shrieks, pointing at the character's bouncing tits.

"What?" he says, looking up at her blankly before returning to the animated loop.

"Why do her tits bounce so much?! That is unrealistic," she says incredulously.

"Yours bounce like that," he says flatly.

"They absolutely do not," she says, folding her arms in front of her chest. *You can hide them all you want, babe. We're both looking at them.*

"Why don't you jump and prove him wrong, babe," I say, knowing she can't understand me.

"I don't even want to know what he said. Y'all are both sex-craved pervs," she says, pretending like she doesn't love it.

I transform and grab her, whispering, "I said, 'Why don't you jump around and prove him wrong.'" I bend her over the table slightly, grabbing at her tits and kissing her neck. She swats me away with a giggle.

"Plus, if she's wearing armor, why would they bounce like that? Wouldn't this part hold them up? It's just not realistic," she says, ignoring my sexual advances, too concerned with winning the argument. For now, anyway.

"You know, I was thinking, the way you've described Astrid, I don't think she'd be wearing armor anyway," I say, leaning my arm on Marshall's chair, angling myself toward both of them. He breaks his gaze from his tablet to glance at my dick.

"What? What would she wear?" she asks.

"She's going to go fight this guy but wants to be stealthy, right? She doesn't want him to know she's going there to fight him. She wants him to think she's there to fuck, right?"

"Yeah," she says, furrowing her eyebrows at me.

"So, she wouldn't be wearing armor. I mean, if I saw this hottie come up to me in that armor, yeah, I'd want to fuck her. But that outfit definitely doesn't give me the vibe that she wants to fuck me, you know?" I say, shrugging.

Adley looks down at the animated, bouncing tits loop. "You're right, Ezra. I've been picturing her in armor, but it doesn't make much sense."

"So, there you have it, bro," I say to Marshall. "Astrid won't be wearing armor, so you can make her tits bounce as much as you want. Adley's armor-restricts-bounce argument is now moot." I shoot him some finger guns to really drive home the point.

He looks at me incredulously. He knows I will never win an argument with Adley this easily.

"No, he still needs to tone them down," she laughs.

"Bummer," Marshall says, looking like he might actually cry.

"Sorry, bro. She's wrong, but she's the boss. It is what it is," I say dejectedly, patting his shoulder.

"Y'all are not going to drop this, are you?"

"Babe, I'm telling you. I see those tits bounce every single day. And that is a perfect rendition. But… if you want to prove me wrong, by all means," I say, bowing.

As the mischief sparkles in her eyes, I can sense what's about to unfold. Gently nudging me back, she declares with determination, "Okay, I'll show you. I'm going to bounce on that cock, and you'll see. You'll see they don't bounce that much."

My low purr of arousal blends with the hum of the powerful PCs and is soon echoed by Marshall's. With staggering agility, he leaps to his feet behind her, deftly sliding his hands underneath her shirt to cup her breasts. "I need a demonstration as well," he murmurs, grazing her neck with his lips. "As the animator, I need reference."

Her playful voice challenges him. "Are you calling me reference art?"

My laughter echoes as I chime in, "Babe, you're the most exquisite masterpiece I've ever laid eyes on." Since she and Marshall have been earnestly working on the game, I have seen a side of Adley that brings me infinite joy. She's confident and seductive. And horny as hell.

Her commanding voice instructs us both. "Ezra, lie down on the floor. Marshall, sit at your desk and sketch this scene. Clearly, we can't rely on your memory alone."

Marshall nods and sits at his desk. He frees his erect cock with one hand and grips his stylus with the other, awaiting her orders.

"Okay, Marshall," she asserts firmly, "I'll be demonstrating from various angles. Make sure you observe intently." He simply nods in response, stroking himself deliberately.

As I lie on the floor, already completely nude from my recent transformation, my arousal stands prominently at attention. The summer heat has transformed what was once a frigid hellscape into an inferno of desire. Consequently, Adley often dons sundresses for relief from the sweltering atmosphere—and for easy access to indulge in our insatiable lust. *She's so efficient.*

Today happens to be one of those days.

"Now," she begins while adjusting her attire, "I'll first demonstrate with clothing supporting my breasts." She slowly lowers the neckline of her sundress, lifting her enticing breasts above the fabric, allowing them to rest on the garment's edge.

I giddily await her smooth cunt's lips around my cock.

ADLEY

As Marshall's eyes lock with mine, the intensity of his gaze drives me forward. He grips a stylus with one hand and slowly strokes his erect member with the other.

Ezra lies on the ground, grinning like a fool as I stand over him, lifting my dress to reveal my nakedness. "Oops, it seems I forgot to wear panties today," I tease, feigning surprise at my lack of underwear, even though they both knew I wasn't wearing any.

Ezra's hands tenderly caress my ankles while I position myself above him. Slowly descending, I let just the tip of Ezra's erection touch me, eliciting a whimper of anticipation from him as I tease his cock at my entrance. I pretend to ignore him. "Okay, Marshall, this will be the forward angle. Are you ready?" I ask.

Marshall nods, his thumb gently circling his head. He's probably picturing himself in Ezra's place. "Okay, first, walking speed," I announce as I gradually lower myself onto Ezra's girth. The sensation causes him to moan passionately while I feel the reverberations of his purr deep within my walls.

Maintaining a measured pace with subtle movements of my thighs, I ask Marshall, "Are you getting this, Marshall?" His affirmative response comes through gritted teeth as he continues pumping his hand in tune with my rhythm while fervently sketching me and Ezra.

Marshall draws quickly, at an otherworldly speed, and after only a short time, he is done drawing.

"Done," he says.

"Okay, now jogging speed," I say and move myself faster up and down Ezra's cock. Marshall's strokes increase in tempo as he quickly completes the following illustration.

"Done."

"Now for a full sprint," I say, bouncing even faster.

"Oh, fuck," Ezra says, gripping my hips, assisting me with the movement—unable to restrain himself any longer.

"Done," Marshall says after a long moment.

I lean down and kiss Ezra and grind hard on him, moving in deep, sweeping circles as I rub my clit against his pelvis. I'm enjoying myself so much, but I don't know how long I can keep up this scenario before Ezra or I come.

"Okay, now from the side. Ezra, sit on the chair," I command, and he obeys, sitting on his couch. "Ready, Marshall?"

"Yes," he responds.

"Walking speed," I say as I lower myself onto Ezra's shaft, facing away to present my side to Marshall. Our bodies connect with a gentle rhythm. Marshall's eyes lock on us. Ezra gropes everywhere but my breasts, instinctively knowing if he did, I would bat his hands away. Ezra's hands slide down my spine until they plant themselves firmly in the small of my back, providing me with the support I need to rock against him. I can feel every inch of his thickness filling me up as our pace remains steady and deliberate.

Ezra's other hand travels between us, expertly navigating where our two bodies connect. With masterful precision, he traces slow circles around my clit—each revolution sending waves of warm pleasure throughout my entire body.

Marshall's eyes remain locked on my breasts, not even breaking to look at the tablet he can draw on from muscle memory alone. He continues to stroke himself, and his face flushes as beads of sweat slowly form on his temple.

"Done," Marshall says.

"Jogging speed," as I increase my speed.

"Done."

"Running speed," I say and bounce on Ezra's cock as hard and as fast as I can. Building the pleasure within myself as he hits deep inside me. "You getting this, Marshall?" I ask as Marshall loses focus, captivated by the sight before him and lost to the pleasure of his own touch.

"Marshall?" I ask in a slightly chastising way.

"Sorry, Adley, but I am having trouble seeing. I need to get a closer look," he says with an uncharacteristically devious smirk.

"Fine," I say, feigning annoyance, rising from Ezra's lap and making my way to Marshall. Ezra grunts as his hand replaces me around his girth.

I turn Marshall's chair to face me and lean forward, licking away the precum built on the tip. Marshall, impatient from my teasing, grabs my hips and pulls me toward him, guiding me to sink slowly onto his dick. Marshall always revels in the sight of our bodies joining together. As I hover slightly above him, his hands grip my waist, guiding my movements, his eyes laser-focused on the moment when he enters me. He pumps my body up and down, unable to break his gaze from our bodies colliding.

I reprimand him gently, "Marshall, you're supposed to be referencing my tits, remember?" He quickly regains his composure and finishes the drawing.

"Done," he says when the drawing is complete. He lets out a relieved sigh as he grabs me and guides me up and down his length, now ready to lose himself to the pleasure.

Ezra retrieves a nearby bottle of lubricant and prepares himself, standing above me with anticipation in his eyes. With my permission, he positions himself behind me and gently enters me from behind. They move inside me; the pace increases rapidly as I let them take the lead. Time seems to slow down as we reach our climax together, shared ecstasy overwhelming us in perfect harmony. The room fills with our impassioned cries as we reach the edges of our pleasure.

"You're right, Adley. They do not bounce that much," Marshall says.

"See!" I say, excited to have been correct.

"They bounce much more," he says with a smirk while Ezra snickers into my shoulder.

41

EZRA

Tonight's the night—it's going to be epic. I've got the rings in my pocket. Everything about tonight is going to be perfect. *It has to be perfect.* They don't suspect anything. They think I'm just being the way I always am—extra. So that's good.

We've talked about what we'd do, how we'd combine the ceremonies of our cultures: a mate marking and a wedding. We've talked about kids—if they're possible. We've talked about everything. The only thing left is to just fucking do it. Adley's culture makes a whole spectacle of the asking. And since spectacle might as well be my middle name, I've taken it into my hands to be the one to do it.

I've been planning this for weeks. Every little detail, every moment leading up to this one, has been carefully thought out. The location, the clothes, the rings, the speech, the timing—*it all has to be perfect.*

I couldn't find the perfect restaurant, so I orchestrated one. I found one that was close enough. It has every possible meat choice, Adley's favorite vegetable (bleh), Adley's favorite wine, Marshall's favorite sake, a corner wrap-around booth perfect for three, and is expensive (that part is for me). When I came a few weeks ago to check the place out, it was too loud, too crowded, too bright; my easily overstimulated mates need things just right to feel comfortable. So, I booked out half the restaurant and paid extra to have the lights and music turned down. Romantic. Cozy. *Perfect.*

I lied and told them we were celebrating a recent contract. Marshall hasn't been helping as much with the contracts now that he and Adley are so focused on the game, so he didn't realize the contract we are supposedly celebrating isn't even all that great. Since they think we are celebrating the contract, ensuring we all looked fabulous isn't that weird. I just brushed it off as being extra, and they accepted that as an excuse.

I'm looking amazing—because I always do. But Adley and Marshall are glowing more than usual—courtesy of a spa day and designer clothes I picked out for them. *Perfect.*

And then there's the rings. Marshall's was easy—an unassuming tungsten black band. Adley's took some effort. I wanted to get her the biggest, flashiest thing I could find, but I quickly realized that would be a very, very bad idea—okay, maybe not quickly. I definitely almost bought it. But the clerk asked, "What does she like?" and I realized the ring should be something Adley likes, not something I like. So, I asked Adley's new friend Tina for help. Apparently, it's not that weird for women to get drunk at brunch and discuss such preferences. So, thanks to Tina's help, I got Adley a 3 karat rose gold pillow cut diamond. And then, of course, I got myself a ring because I can't be the only one walking around without a symbol that says "taken—soon to be super taken." *Perfect.*

And then there's the speech. That part will be easy. I've rehearsed it enough times to know it as well as I know the gentle curve of the small of Adley's back and the little scar that runs on the inside of Marshall's ear. *Perfect.*

The last thing is the timing. Which—so far, is not perfect and causing a cold sweat to mess up my perfect hair. *Where the fuck is the waiter?* I coordinated everything with the owner of the restaurant down to the timing of the food and drinks; everything needed to happen at just the right time. I glance at my Rolex. The waiter was supposed to be here fifteen minutes ago. *Fuck.* I'm planning to propose during dessert. I had the timing all planned out. I calculated the time to make and eat Marshall and Adley's usual orders. But now, since the waiter is late, I'm running the risk of my mates overindulging in alcohol and being a bit too inebriated by the time deserts roll around. *Fuck.* They'll know something is up if I try cutting them off.

I reach for my whiskey, and my hand trembles, causing the ice to clink gently. I look nervously around for the waiter.

"You okay, Ez?" Adley asks, fingering the edge of her wine glass languidly. *Fuck, she must sense my anxiety. Relax, Ezra. Cool as a cucumber.* Easier said than done. I've never been this nervous in my life. And, unfortunately, when I'm nervous about something, they're the ones that usually calm me down. I'm a fidgety guy, but I must appear extra jittery right now. *Make a joke.*

"Oh, yeah, I'm fine. You two are just so hot you're killing me," I announce with a grin, giving them both a once-over. I lean back and put my arms across the back of the booth. I attempt to cross my ankle over my knee, but my knee hits the table. *Ouch, fuck.*

Marshall does that absolutely-fucking-adorable thing he does, where his tail and ears shoot upright whenever you compliment him, his sake has not kicked in yet. But Adley? Her wine has, and she's loose and open to flirty banter. She giggles at me; I'm not sure if she's laughing at my comment or the fact that I just banged my knee on the table trying to look cool. It doesn't matter. I'm not embarrassed either way. I've never felt this comfortable with anyone. *I love her so much.*

"Oh, yeah, how exactly are we killing you, Ezra?" Adley asks, leaning toward me and placing her hand on my thigh. Her dress glitters and sparkles even in the dim light. Her shoulders are bare.

"Well, those tits are so stunning I feel like you knocked me out with that baseball bat of yours," I say, leaning forward and leering at her.

She lifts her tits so they rest on the table and leans forward, "These tits?"

"Careful, babe, you keep that up, and I won't be the only thing knocked out in this restaurant. Marshall and I will start purring, and we'll knock the whole fucking place out."

"Well, we can't have that, now, can we?" she says, leaning into me, her hand trailing up my leg.

"No, we can't," I say, seductively sipping my whiskey.

Marshall looks stiff and uncomfortable, smiling and pulling at the sleeves. The Rolex I gave him peeking out momentarily. But stiff and uncomfortable is kind of his whole thing. I'll check in on him anyway. He's probably just nervous to have his ears and tail out. We finally convinced him it was safe to do so. It's not uncommon now to see people wearing replicas of my ears and tail—and I get a 10% cut for every one sold—well, the officially licensed ones anyway. But since his ears and tail don't match mine, he's been reluctant.

"Marsh, how's the jacket? Not too itchy?"

"No, it feels good," he says, fidgeting a little but smiling at my concern.

"That's too bad," I say with a smirk.

"Huh?"

"He's going to say something about wanting you to take it off," Adley laughs.

"Hey! Babe! Don't go stealing my lines," I laugh.

"I'm sorry, Ez, but you're going to need to get some new ones. They're getting predictable," she teases.

"Wow, babe, you wound me," I say, feigning insult and sipping my whiskey again. "I can't help it that you're both so hot you've turned me into a broken record who can only think about ripping off your clothes and fucking you."

"You're incorrigible," Marshall says, shaking his head but clearly enjoying the attention.

I wave it off dramatically, making sure to keep the energy light and playful. "I'm just telling the truth. I hope the waiter gets here soon. If I don't get some meat in me soon…"

"Don't you dare say it," Adley says, rolling her eyes but still can't hide the little smile tugging at the corner of her mouth. *I love that smile.* She hasn't had quite enough wine to let me say lurid stuff in public without gentle chastising. Another two glasses and she'll be the one making meat stuffing jokes.

"Stop flattering us so much," she says, clearly not buying it but not complaining either.

"Flattering?" I laugh, shaking my head. "I'm just speaking facts, babe. You two are literal works of art, and I'm just lucky enough to be sitting here witnessing it."

Marshall smirks. "Okay, okay. You're laying it on thick tonight, huh?"

"Yeah, Ez, you're being extra, extra tonight," Adley says.

"Can you blame me?" I ask with a raised brow, leaning forward and fixing my gaze on them.

"Oh my god, Ezra," Adley says, rolling her eyes, but her lips are still curled into that adorable smile. "You're impossible."

"Impossible to resist," I shoot back with a wink.

But even with all the compliments, the flirty banter, the easy laughter—my heart is hammering in my chest. I need the perfect moment, and I can't risk messing this up. I need to ask them. They're the love of my life, both of them. Together, we've built something incredible, and this… this will be the next step.

Where the fuck is the waiter? I touch the box in my chest pocket that holds the rings—ensuring it's still there and careful they don't notice the nervous twitch.

Our server finally returns to the table. He stands poised, a professional smile plastered on his face. His hands are clasped firmly behind his back. He's one of the ones that likes to impress you with his amazing memory. His eyes flick to Adley's tits but linger on Marshall. *I get it, bro; they're hot.*

"Are you ready for me to take your order?" he asks.

I nod to Marshall and Adley, signaling they can go first. Marshall nervously flips through his menu, trying to muster up the courage to speak to a stranger. I should just order for him. He gets the same thing every time. Filet mignon. Rare. How many he orders depends on the following variables: their size, how hungry he is, and how nervous he is. But, given their size, how much we ate throughout the day, and all the preparations I took to make this comfortable, he'll order four.

"Oh, um, may I have...," he flicks through the menu, "the foie gras for a starter. And for my main, I'd like the wagyu ribeye, rare, with the roasted bone marrow on the side. Umm, I'd also like the rack of lamb rare," he flicks through the menu further, "and the bison tenderloin rare," he closes the menu looking particularly proud of himself. *WHAT?!*

The waiter looks at him agape, just as surprised as I am. *Did you get all of that, bro? I already forgot.* "And for the sides, sir," the waiter asks.

"No sides, just the meat," Marshall says flatly.

"Of course, sir," the waiter replies.

"Oh, do you have a dessert menu?" he asks.

"Actually, sir, we don't have a printed dessert menu. But we do have a dessert cart with a wonderful selection. I can bring that over when you are done with your meal for you to make a selection."

"Oh, that would be great!" Marshall beams. He's speaking to this man quite freely and comfortably. Fuck. I forgot the fourth variable: Alpha Marshall. Shit, he is drunker than I thought. I glance at my watch. Yeah, this is all going to go to shit.

"And may I have another of these?" Marshall asks, tapping at his glass. I groan and put my head in my hand. *This is all going to go to shit, isn't it?*

=^..^= ♥ =^..^=

We're finishing up the meal. And the time for my big speech is fast approaching. So far, nothing has gone as planned. Adley ordered her usual petite filet with that aptly named ass-paragus, but other than that, it's been curveball after curveball.

By the time the waiter asked what I wanted, I was so flustered I just responded, "What he's having." It sounded good, and honestly, it has been good. The food and the whiskey have left me feeling a bit less on edge. My nerves are soothed a bit.

It won't be perfect. But that's fine. It can be almost perfect. All that matters is I ask them. It's time to work up my nerves. But first, I have to get them to stop talking about the game and start talking about me.

They've been animatedly talking about the game since we got our starters, and now it's time to take back control of this conversation.

Time for *Operation Propose to My Mates, Live Happily Ever After.*

I lean toward them, propping my chin on my hand, and give them my most devilish grin. I focus my gaze and try to give off my most irresistible vibe. But they don't even look at me. *Sigh.*

"You know," I say, letting my voice drop to a low, suggestive tone, "if I had known dinner would involve so much talk about… sprites and tilemaps, I would have brought that laser pointer to distract you two."

Adley gives me a tipsy giggle and playfully rubs my leg, but I don't think she even fully heard me because her eyes are glued to the napkin Marshall is scribbling on. He looks to be sketching out character designs for the game. *Typical.*

I'm going to get their attention, one way or another, even if I gotta whip my dick out on this table—which, believe me, I am 100% not above. I stretch my arms across the back of the booth, flexing my muscles, presenting myself like the present I am. They don't look up. Marshall continues to sketch, and Adley points at the napkin, saying, "That should be a bit to the left." *Alright, time to get them focused on me.*

"So, I was actually thinking about the time with the laser pointer. That was fun, huh?" I say.

Adley's eyes flick to me, and she smiles only slightly. "Yeah," she lets out a soft, exhale, half-laugh, "It was fun, Ez; maybe we can do it again sometime." Then she looks back down at the fucking sketch.

I sip my whiskey—trying to let the warmth calm my nerves.

Okay, let's get them to talk dirty to me, "What should we do tonight? We could try that—"

"Marshall and I were going to tweak some of the walk cycles of the NPCs when we got home…" Adley says then looks at me, "Oh, did you have more planned that you wanted to do tonight?"

Seriously, they were going to keep working? Well, they don't know I'm planning to propose. They'd stop working to spend time with me and celebrate… right?

"Well, I was hoping we could take a shower together," I say.

"Really?" Adley asks, taken aback. "After being in the spa all day?" she laughs with a hiccup, returning her eyes back on the sketch. *Seriously?! Babe?!*

Can you not tell I'm trying to seduce you?

I let my shoulders drop, trying to mask the disappointment that's beginning to overwhelm me.

What the fuck is he sketching that's so interesting? It better be my cock. "Are you drawing that character that looks like me?" I ask, leaning forward to glance down.

"No, it's the one that looks like Marshall," Adley says.

I should just tell them what I want. No games. Just tell them I want them to focus on me. They'll get it.

"Could you maybe stop drawing on the napkin for a minute?" I ask.

"Oh, yeah, good point," Marshall murmurs.

He pulls out his phone and stylus. Are you fucking kidding me? I blink, holding back a bitter laugh. *Really?*

"*Helloooo,*" I say, waving a hand between them. "Anyone going to tell me I look good tonight, or should I just assume you're taking it for granted?"

Marshall smirks, finally glancing at me. "You always look good, Ezra. It's kind of your whole thing."

"Yeah, but tonight…" I say, trailing off.

Adley's voice opens in realization, "Oh, Ezra, I'm sorry. We're ignoring you. We're so close to being done and we forgot how focused we get."

"I was just hoping for tonight to be about us," I say.

"I'm sorry, Ezra," Marshall says. "I'll be present." He puts the phone back in his pocket.

Adley creeps her hand higher up my thigh and looks at me deviously, "I'm sorry, too, Ezra. Let's talk about you."

"My favorite subject," I say with a chuckle. *It's okay, Ezra. You got the topic on track. Sure, you had to practically beg them to notice you, but they still love you. Get them to lavish you with compliments, turn the conversation to our relationship, how you're actually the lucky one, then pop that fucking question.*

The waiter appears at the edge of our table, his movements smooth and practiced as he carries an elegant dessert tray laden with decadent treats. My heart, which has been thundering in my chest all night, skips a beat.

Fuck. I'm running out of time.

The waiter announces with a cheerful tone, completely unaware of the tension I am drowning in, "On the tray tonight, we have our gold-dusted chocolate truffles, handmade with flavors…"

My heart pounds in my chest.

"Next, here is our vanilla bean cheesecake, topped with…"
Where is it?
"Here's the seasonal fruit tart, featuring…"
It's not on the tray.
"This is our champagne sorbet, served in an elegant…"
The owner assured me they'd have vanilla ice cream.
"And finally, our gold flake crème brûlée, a silky custard…"
The world around me spins. Is literally nothing going to go right tonight?
"Do any of these catch your eye?" the waiter asks us expectantly.
"Oh, wow! I've never had a dessert covered in gold. Ezra, should I get the gold-dusted chocolate truffles?" Adley asks me.
"Definitely, babe!" I respond, knowing they only have this on the menu because I specifically requested it for her.
I lean into the waiter. "Umm, do you have a vanilla bean ice cream? I called ahead about it, and he said—"
The waiter's eyes light up in recognition. "Oh… sir. Someone wrote down vanilla bean cheesecake. I am so sorry."
"Oh, no, it's fine. It's okay. Thank you," I say. Thank God I didn't ask them to put the rings in the dessert. I had planned to but Tina talked me out of it.
Marshall looks at me, "Did you try to get me ice cream, Ez?"
"Yeah," I shrug, dejected.
Marshall looks at me with appreciation, then he says to the waiter, "I'll have the cheesecake, please."
"Crème brûlée, please," I say, fighting back the awful pain in my chest. Why is nothing going the way I wanted it to?
"Thanks," we all say as the waiter leaves.

My crème brûlée sits mostly untouched. Marshall seems to have liked his cheesecake and Adley is still nibbling at her dessert. *Fuck. It's fine. All that matters is that I ask them. They're not talking about their game. They seem to be enjoying the desert. I just gotta ask.*
This feels like as good a time as any. I should do it now.
"So," I say, trying to sound casual, though I'm pretty sure my voice comes out shaky despite my best efforts, "I've been thinking about something. You

two really are perfect, you know that?"

They both smile at me and let me continue.

I grin, but inside, my stomach does somersaults. "I'm so lucky to have not one but two perfect mates. I wanted to ask you something."

I clear my throat and steel myself.

They look at me expectantly. *Both so beautiful.* My eyes water with love.

I reach into my pocket and place my hand on the box. I have to pull it out at just the right moment. "Marshall, Adley, I—"

"Oh, my God! It's Ezra from another world!" a squeal interrupts, cutting through the air like a knife. I freeze mid-sentence, turning to see a woman standing at the edge of our table, her eyes wide and sparkling.

Fuck.

MARSHALL

Adley leans into me and whispers, "Marshall, is it just me, or has Ezra been acting squirrely all night."

"Squirrely?" I ask.

"Jumpy. On edge."

"Oh, like a squirrel," I state.

She doesn't make me feel dumb, she simply smiles at me, puts her hand on my knee, and leans her tits into my chest, to reassure me it's okay.

Ezra keeps glancing back at us while talking to the admirer. His face is not as animated as usual. He really does seem to be trying harder than usual to get rid of the fan.

I consider her question for a moment. He acted strangely when I ordered something other than my usual. He kept making comments to us all night about how we all should "not drink too much"—something he'd usually never say. I know he loves that new watch, but I don't think I've ever seen him actually use it to check the time before tonight. And then there was the ice cream thing. What was that about?

"Yes, he has been acting strangely," I say.

Her face is alight with excitement.

"What?" I ask.

She makes me lean down so I can put my ear closer to her face. Her breath in my ear causes my dick to stiffen.

"I think he's going to propose to us," she says with an excited giggle.

"What? Really?" I ask.

"Yeah, did you see how he was reaching for something in his pocket?"

"I did see that."

"I'm going to say 'yes.' What about you?"

"Of course," I whisper, pulling her into a hug.

This night is perfect.

EZRA

This night is a fucking disaster.

I have to get this fan out of here. This restaurant really let me down. They were supposed to keep this area clear for me and keep people away. I glance around, looking for someone to save me, but I guess I'm just going to have to keep talking to this woman.

I look back at my mates. Their desserts are mostly gone now. They're snuggling together, hugging, whispering. They've returned to their own conversation without me…

My stomach twists, but I maintain the forced smile I am giving to the fan chattering away at me. She's beaming, clutching her phone to her chest, secretly taking pictures of me. Why do they do that? Just take the picture. "…thought that was so awesome. I can't believe I'm meeting you! Could I get a quick picture?"

"Of course," I say. I glance at Marshall and Adley, but they'd already turned back to each other, no doubt their conversation about tilemaps and color palettes picking up without missing a beat.

I slide out the booth to stand with her for a picture and tower over her. She swoons, because they all do, then says, "Oh my God. You're even hotter in person," because they all say that, too.

From the corner of my eye, I watch Marshall and Adley. Their voices have dipped into a quiet, animated discussion—probably about their game—and I feel a sharp pang of frustration. Whatever they're talking about is making them happier than I have been making them.

"Thanks, doll," I say, trying to keep the encounter short and sweet. "I really appreciate it."

"Your tail looks so real. Can I touch it?"

"Oh, I'd rather—"

She grips it tightly, running her hand from base to tip. This happens occasionally, and normally, I'm prepared for it. I ensure that I have my body turned just right when I'm near the ones who seem grabby. But she surprises me. *What is with this chick? She just went for it. No flirting, nothing.* And I'm seriously off my game today. So, when she does this, my body lurches forward in her direction, shooting my dick straight up and pointing my face at her tits.

Fuck. I catch myself and pretend to have tripped. "Sorry about that. I really suck at keeping my balance today. You startled me," I say, grinning and rubbing the back of my neck.

My ruse is unsuccessful. She steps closer, brushing her hair behind her ear and leaning slightly toward me, her voice dropping into an unmistakably suggestive tone. "You know, I'm free right now if you'd like for me to um… suck, too."

My brain stalls for a moment. "Uh... that's really nice of you, but I'm here with my—"

"Oh, your friends?" she interrupts, glancing at Marshall and Adley. A sly smile tugs at her lips. "They make such a cute couple."

My stomach twists. "No, actually—" A cute couple?

She cuts me off again, her eyes raking over me. "You know, being the third wheel isn't half as fun as being the center of attention. I can make you feel so good." *Third wheel? Center of attention?*

I plaster on a smile that feels like it might crack under the strain. "That's flattering, but I'm good, thanks."

I look at Adley and Marshall. They haven't even noticed a woman is blatantly propositioning their boyfriend. I know I've told them in the past not to worry about these things, but a little jealousy on their face every once in a while would be nice… wouldn't it? Right now, I'd give anything for them to leap from the booth and defend my honor… compromised as that honor may be.

She hands me a pen and paper. Do people just walk around with this stuff on hand? "What's your name?" I ask, and before she gets any further ideas I indicate, "For the autograph?"

With a wink and stroke of my hand, I sign it before returning it to her. She finally leaves after receiving it. My jaw hurts from how tight I was gritting my teeth while in her presence.

I sink back into my seat, my head spinning.

Still snuggled together, they stop their conversation and turn their attention to me.

"Ezra," Adley asks. "What were you going to ask us?"

The fan's words planted a seed, now growing into sharp, cutting, self-doubt. I stare at them, my chest tightening.

They're a couple...

I'm a third wheel…

I'm not the center of attention…

I force a grin, my heart heavy as I brush a hand through my hair. "Oh, nothing. I don't even remember," I say, laughing while leaning back into the booth.

I think maybe I'm not the most important thing in their life anymore.

Marshall looks at me crossly. "You're acting weird tonight."

Adley squints at me like she's considering me. "Okay," she says, and her brows stitch.

Why do they seem upset with me? They're probably just annoyed that I'm interrupting their conversation.

As their voices fade into game talk once more, I slip my hand into my pocket, feeling the velvet box still there, unopened.

42

EZRA

I lean against the doorframe, trying to hide the desperation in my voice. "Hey, Marshall," I call, "Wanna' play *Deadly Premonition 2* with me?"

He doesn't answer. The rhythmic tapping of his keys and stylus fills the silence instead.

"Marshall," I repeat, walking over to his desk and leaning against the back of his chair.

Finally, he lifts his head just enough to acknowledge me. He's wearing those noise-canceling headphones I got him. They lie turned atop his head, like a crown across his brow. He lifts a cup, causing his ear to spring back into shape atop his head. His eyes are still fixed on the screen.

"What's up?" he asks, his voice muffled with concentration.

I want to be understanding. I want to comprehend why he is so lost in this project and why the game seems to be the only thing that matters to him these days. But that doesn't stop the sting in my chest, the feeling of being invisible while he works on something we all care about.

"Come hang out with me. Let's play *Deadly Premonition 2*," I try to make it sound casual, but the weight of my words hangs in the air.

He glances at me for a fraction of a second, then back at the screen. "Um, later, okay? I really want to finish this character."

"Okay. I have some contracts I need your help with. Could you look at them with me later? After my live stream?"

"Yeah," he says, and I don't even know if he heard me. He puts his headphones back over his ears.

I stand there for a moment, watching him work, a wave of helplessness washing over me. It isn't just the game. It isn't just him being lost in his work—it is the unspoken feeling that he isn't even aware of how much I am trying to connect. That I am slipping further and further away.

Fuck. I'll go see what Adley's up to. Where is she?

=^..^= ♥ =^..^=

Alright. Time to woo my woman. She's sitting on the couch in the living room—at her spot—laptop open, coding away.

"Hey, Adley! Can I hang with you?" She looks up, her tired eyes lighting up for a moment.

"Sure, Ez," she says, smiling.

"I was thinking of lighting a fire and reading. Is that cool with you?"

"A fire? Is it cold enough outside for one?" She looks at me, confused.

"It's for the aesthetic, babe," I say, realizing this is a stupid fucking plan.

She looks at the fireplace momentarily, and I think she may say no. But she returns her gaze to me and puts on that fake smile of hers. *Fuck.* "Sure, that sounds great!" *It most assuredly does not sound great, Adley. Why are you lying to me?*

"Don't worry, babe. I won't bother you," I say, faking my own smile.

She nods and returns to her code.

I'm not proud of how much I struggle getting this stupid fucking fire going. *Great idea, Ez. Show her how fucking pathetic you are, and she'll definitely want to spend time with you.*

I grab her book club book from the bedroom and sit beside her on the couch. I place my head on her shoulder and open the book.

"That's what you're reading, Ez?" she smirks, peeking at me from over the rim of her laptop.

"Yeah," I say with a smirk, "I was thinking maybe it was time I take a page out of Marshall's book and do some research. Figure out who Alpha Ezra is."

"Well, I think maybe you should try a different book, though," she laughs.

"What? It says Alpha right in the title."

"Yeah, but that one's about werewolves—" she says.

I throw it across the room. "Gross, Adley!"

She laughs at me. *I love the sound of that laugh—even when it's at my expense.* "Sorry, Ez, I didn't pick it," she says before her fingers return to their furious typing.

I put my head back on her shoulder, but she shrugs me off after only a moment. "Ez, I'm sorry, but you're kind of hurting my shoulder."

"Oh… um, okay."

She doesn't seem to hear the frustration in my voice as she buries herself back into her laptop, typing at that speed that seems unachievable. The soft light of the screen illuminates her face making her look like an angel. I want to kiss her, but she is fully focused on her work.

She always liked it when I sat with her in my ailo form. I transform, leaving my clothes on the floor, and jump beside her. I can't sit on her lap, but I can sit beside her. I lean against her leg, staring into the fire and watching the flames twist and turn.

Great job wooing your woman, Ez. You won't be fucking her like this.

I don't really know what I thought would happen. Would she see me reading and then want to blow me? I don't know. But it is clear the game is more important than me.

She strokes my back.

I look at her, hopeful. Is she going to hang out with me now?

"Oh, babe, I was about to give up," I say. "I'm so lonely right now."

"Ez, I'm sorry, but it's really hot in here with the fire, and I need to go use the computer in the office."

"Oh, yeah, you can't understand me like this…"

"Hey, I know you're feeling lonely. I promise we are so, so, so close to being done with the game." She rubs my ear between her fingers before packing up and leaving.

I sit here for a long time. Watching the fire burn out.

The ache in my chest swells as the fire's embers flicker out. Has their love for me flickered out? What happened? I was so happy just a few days ago.

=^..^= ♥ =^..^=

I've just finished recording a live video, where I boisterously chatted with fans. I log off with a wink and immediately slide from my seat to the floor—exhausted by the constant performance.

The work has gotten hard. Marshall hasn't had as much time to help me with the admin work related to my various videos and endorsements. I spend most of my time sorting through emails or interacting with fans on live, stuck in decision paralysis, unable to pick work to do without Marshall's guidance and stupid fucking color-coded spreadsheet. I miss it. I miss the look on his face when he showed it to me, telling me about the various leads he's hunted down for me.

This all feels so familiar: all alone, with no one but the fans on the other side of the screen. *I can't go down this path again.*

Upstairs is dead silent—as if I am home alone. My heart sinks as memories of my parents leaving me without even saying goodbye flood my mind. I'm comforted when I hear gentle tapping: Adley programming. I peek through their office door. Marshall's drawing of the three of us is pinned to the wall between them above their heads.

They both are so focused on their work that they don't notice me standing at the door behind them. Their posture is terrible—it just looks uncomfortable. They both have stuffed animals in their laps and wear noise-canceling headphones to drown out the world— drowning me out.

"Hey, guys. I'm done with my stream. Let's hang out." Neither look up.

They can't hear me.

"GUYS!" I stomp so the floor will vibrate under them.

They startle and look at me with that blank stare they give me when they've been hyper-focused, and I've interrupted. I give them both a moment for their brains to catch up to the fact that I've addressed them.

In sync, they remove their headphones and smile. They are so similar in many ways. It's adorable, but it's also lonely.

ADLEY

"Done with the game yet?" Ezra asks, bursting into the room, looking annoyed.

What's his problem? Is he mad I'm reading werewolf smut? I shift uncomfortably. His presence is heavy as he looms behind our chairs.

"Marshall, you said you'd help me with some contracts after my stream," Ezra's voice is tinged with impatience.

Marshall glances up, his brow creasing as he meets Ezra's glare. "Can it wait?"

"Wait?!" Ezra's voice raises to a tone I have not heard him use with Marshall in a long time. It's sharp with frustration. "It's not a hobby, Marshall. These contracts are our livelihood."

"Right, right," Marshall says, though his attention had already drifted back to the tablet, "Right after I finish this up…"

Ezra bristles, his hands clenching at his sides. His voice carries the weight of restrained irritation. "You always say that, but 'after' keeps getting pushed back. You're supposed to be my administrative assistant, bro."

A hollow ache spreads through my chest. He said "bro" with such disdain.

I chime in, "Marshall, it's getting late. Why don't we finish this up tomorrow? Ezra needs your help."

"Just a minute, I just need to..." Marshall says, fully turning to the tablet and trailing off.

Ezra huffs and walks out.

Fuck.

"Marshall, you... you can't do that to him. You know how he is," I say. Marshall looks up at me, realization crossing his face.

"Oh, he thinks I rejected him."

"Yeah," I say.

"When I finish this piece, the game is done."

I sigh and put my head on my desk, "I think this is about dinner the other night."

"He has been acting... weird since then," Marshall says, putting his stylus down.

"The more I think about it, the more I think we were right. He was going to propose."

Marshall looks perplexed, "But why didn't he?"

"I don't know. It was like he was waiting for the perfect moment... and then something happened."

Marshall asks, "Was it the ice cream?"

"I think that was part of it. He was on edge all night. I bet he had some grand plan that didn't pan out perfectly."

Marshall leans back, pushing his chair away from the desk, "Something scared him. Maybe he thought we would say no."

"Did we do something to make him think that?"

Marshall responds, "Did that fan say something to upset him?"

I sigh, "I don't know. Somehow, we rejected him... and," I add, unsure how to voice what has been on my mind for days, "ever since, he's been both needy and distant. It's like he's trying to get our attention, but when we give it to him, he just pulls away. I don't get it."

Marshall rubs his hand over his face in frustration. "We definitely fucked something up, but I have no idea what we did."

I reply, guilt twisting my stomach, "It's like he's got it in his head that we don't love him, and we only love the game or something."

A frown pulls at the corners of his lips. "He... does seem particularly upset if I bring up the game."

I stretch and walk over to the window, looking at the spot where I found

Ezra in the snow almost a year ago. *We were all doing so well. Weren't we?*

"Marshall, we've been so wrapped up in the game… we need to make time for him, too."

Marshall pushes himself away from his desk and walks over to me, his hand resting gently on my shoulder; he says, "I've got an idea."

EZRA

I enter the living room, unsure what to do. I really don't want to get back to work, but it's what I do when I am feeling lonely and anxious. I lie on the couch and pull out my phone. I turn to the side and bring my knees up to my chest—hugging them and peering at my phone over my knees.

I'm all alone.

No one wants me.

No one loves me.

The couch has practically swallowed me whole. The smoky smell from my feeble attempt at wooing Adley still lingers. The werewolf smut lies on the ground.

It didn't matter.

Nothing did.

I remind myself I wanted this. I wanted them to have purpose. I wanted them to feel like they too were doing something for the group. But instead, they found a way to exclude me from the thing that is most important to them. They found a way to make me not the most important thing. And that's probably the hardest part. The fact that I'm not the most important thing anymore. I want to be part of it. Be part of the collaboration. Part of the ideation.

I should just tell them how I feel. But I spend so much time and effort trying to anticipate their wants and needs, why can't they do that for me? I must not be as important to them as they are to me. And here we reach the crux of it.

Adley and Marshall—brilliant, unstoppable Adley and Marshall. They don't need me. They have each other, their incredible minds working in perfect sync.

I am just… here.

An accessory.

A distraction.

I put so much effort into my proposal plan—I wanted everything to be perfect for them. The fan from the restaurant's words still echo in my head: *They make such a cute couple.*

Friends.

The idea twists in my gut like a knife. What if that's all I really am to them? What if their confessions of love have been fleeting, some experiment they were already regretting?

Am I even their friend?

Giggles erupt from down the hall in Adley and Marshall's office.

They're having fun without me.

I open the camera and check my hair. My face is smushed against the couch and I look… hideous. I make a barfing face at myself and sit up, fixing my hair and rubbing my cheek to remove the indents starting to form from my face being against the couch.

I'll never be enough.

A red dot zooms across the floor. *What the fuck was that?!* I jump to my feet, driven by an instinct I can't quite control, launching myself toward it.

It skitters in front of my feet to the hallway in front of Adley and Marshall's office. The dot stops at the center of a heart-shaped pile made of small stuffed animals, cat toys, balls of paper, and Adley's action figures. At the center of the heart is a piece of paper with the following:

* *Operation Propose to Ezra* *
1. Find a laser pointer
2. Arrange tokens of leaving
3. Lure him to the hall
4. Propose
5. Live happily ever after

The red dot disappears, and I look up to see Adley and Marshall, each on one knee in front of me.

"Flawless plan," I say as a tear runs down my cheek.

ADLEY

I stand at the base of the stairs, looking in on Ezra's recording studio. "You ready, babe?" he asks me.

"Yep," I reply beaming at him.

He looks so cute with his gaming headphones on. His ears poke out, making it look like they're part of the headset. They aren't even plugged in—since he can't hear out the ears on the side of his head. He mostly wears them for aesthetic appeal. "Gotta look the part, babe," he's told me.

He clicks one of about a million buttons on a panel, and his face appears on the computer screen in front of him.

"Heeeeeellllloooo, everyone! I have an awesome announcement today. I've recently been brought on as the VP of Marketing for an awesome new video game that is coming out soon. It's up for preorder now."

VP of Marketing? I chuckle. Well, I guess he is.

"It's called Harem Hex Healer. Let me show you the character art!"

He clicks a button, and the character designed to look like Ezra appears on the screen. "Look at this guy. Look familiar? Haha, yeah! That's because he's based on me. The lead artist has no imagination. Ha! Just kidding, Marshall! He's giving me the stink eye right now.

"By the way, Marshall also made all of the Ezra emojis that my subscribers can use! The dude is obsessed with this beautiful mug. But can you blame him?" Ezra says, running his hand through his hair.

"Remember how I said he has no imagination? Check this guy out. That's the big bad. And guess who he looks like? You guessed it! Marshall!" he laughs hysterically while the character that looks like Marshall displays on the screen.

"He's a looker, huh? Not as cute as me, but real close, huh?" he says, cheesing and putting his thumb on his chin.

"How 'bout it, everyone. Wanna see the real thing? I know y'all do! I see you thirsty dolls in the chats, always sending me sweaty emojis. If we get enough preorders, maybe we'll give you yaoi lovin' gals some fan service. What do y'all say? How many fujoshi do I have in the crowd? Respond with the Ezra kissy face emoji if you're a fujoshi and want to see me and Marshall smooch!"

I'm watching his stream on mute so that I can see it from the perspective of the viewers, and he has thousands of women in the stream begging to see Marshall, begging to see the game, and begging to see his dick. *Ezra really needs a moderator.*

Ezra looks over his computer monitor, and Marshall is hiding in the corner, shaking his head.

"Aww, Mar-shoo is scawed!" he says, making the crying hand face.

"Dude, Adley and I told you we didn't want to be on camera," Marshall hisses.

"I know. I know. And I will respect Adley's wishes, but unfortunately for you, you're the exact kind of eye candy my target audience wants to see," Ezra says, finger-gunning toward Marshall.

"Come on, Ezra!" Marshall stomps, looking like a little kid.

"Ladies, I think maybe you're not making enough noise in the chat for him." He leans close like he's telling the chat a secret, "He's wearing grey sweatpants."

I watch the chat start blowing up with tons of emoticons and gifts being sent to Ezra.

Giggling, I wave at Marshall to go get on camera. He shakes his head and stands firmly in place.

"I'm going to let you in on a little secret, my little Ezronies. Marshall has forgotten one significant feature of my streaming setup. Which is really a shame because he's the one who put it together," he says, making an exaggerated shrug and pout.

Ezra clicks a button on the panel, and a light highlights Marshall. The screen changes to show Marshall standing, with a green screen behind him. The grey sweatpants are doing him all the favors. Ezra's face appears in a small rectangle on the bottom of the stream.

"Surprise!" Ezra says with a maniacal smile.

"That's right, ladies, that hottie is the lead artist on this project. Some of you have even asked me about him. He's always kind of lurking around me when I make appearances. Yeah, I know he's super hot, BrandyX32!"

Marshall stands there, frozen in absolute fear. His ears laid back on his head. He grabs his tail with both hands and holds it in front of his chest—like a little kid with a blanky and it is so fucking cute I almost cry.

"They want to know how tall you are, Marshall?" Ezra clicks another button, and the microphone above Marshall's head lights up. "The mic will pick you up. No problem now, Marshall. Tell them how tall you are."

Marshall does not budge. "He seems too scared to talk, everyone. I can tell you for a fact that he is a measly 6'1', a whole 2 inches shorter than me," Ezra says, making about two inches with his finger and thumb.

"That's not true! I'm 6'4", and you know it," Marshall snaps.

"Ha! I knew that would get you yapping," he says, pointing at him.

Marshall sighs deeply and looks incredibly defeated. "So, what? Am I supposed to dance or something?"

"No, no, no! Save that for your OnlyFans, Marshall. This isn't that kind of channel, despite what Katarina696969 may lead you to believe. Am I right, Katarina?!"

"I don't have an OnlyFans, Ezra!" Marshall barks.

"Which is something I still don't understand. Guys, I've been telling him for months to start one. But I digress. Tell them about the game, Marshall! I know you and Adley have a whole pitch, so pitch it! Tell us what the game is about?"

Ezra clicks a button, and the game's logo appears next to Marshall on the green screen.

He clicks another button, turning off his mic and camera. He then changes his tone to a reassuring one and addresses Marshall directly: "Hey, Marshall, just look at me. Talk to me, okay? Tell me about your game."

He clicks another button, and his face reappears on the screen. Marshall tells Ezra about the game, while Ezra nods and smiles at the camera.

"Oh, wow, that sounds super cool. And what platforms is it coming out on?" Ezra urges.

"Well, right now, just PC. But hopefully, if it does well, we'll release it on other platforms. We're a small two-person development team. My partner, Adley, is the programmer. It was her idea; I just made the characters," Marshall says.

"Just?! Come on, Marshall, that's not all you did! You designed this logo, right?" Ezra says.

"Oh, yeah, I did do that."

"And what about this scenery? Who made that?"

"I did…" Marshall says.

"Did you do all the art in the game?" Ezra asks.

"Almost all of it. Adley did some of the UI art," Marshall says, looking at me embarrassed.

"What about this? Did you draw this?" Ezra hits a button, and a shirtless picture of the character who looks like Ezra appears on the screen.

"Umm… yeah," Marshall says with a blush.

"What do you think, everyone? Do you think he's in love with me? Yeah, I love him, too," he says with a giggle. Marshall looks abashed. Ezra never reveals he's in a relationship with anyone. Ever.

"Oops, did I reveal a little secret about me? Well, the cat's out of the bag. No pun intended. I love Marshall! But that's not all. I also love drum roll, please, Adley… who shall remain off-screen because she requested it, and I respect her wishes—unlike Marshall's. Yeah, we have a power dynamic problem, but we're working on it. And guess what! We're getting married! No idea how all that's going to work out legally, but whatever," he shrugs. "Just like me to have a whole extra spouse, am I right?!" he says, emphasizing the word extra and turning to me with a wink.

"Hopefully, the fact that I'm doubly taken doesn't make me lose any fans out there," he says, pouting. "When I'm taken by a hottie like that, I'm sure y'all don't mind, though, right? How about it? Would y'all like to see us kiss?"

He looks at the screen, watching the alerts roll in, nodding and smiling as he reads the messages.

"Well, I did tell all you thirsty Ezronies that if we got enough pre-orders, I'd give you some yaoi fan service. Adley, what's the count?" he says, looking over his shoulder at me.

"Oh my God. We have over 20,000 preorders!" I reply.

"WOW. WOW, everyone! You really came through! I think that merits a little kiss; what do you think, Marshall?" Ezra asks.

Marshall stands frozen with a huge smile, speechlessly clutching his tail in shock.

Ezra gushes, "Look at that, everyone, my cute little tsundere boy is all mush inside. You melted his little heart." Ezra runs around the desk to stand next to Marshall. Ezra embraces Marshall and kisses him hard on the cheek.

Marshall turns to him and, with a calm determination, says, "I don't think that's exactly what the fans were asking for, Ezra."

Ezra makes the "oh" face, covering his mouth with his hand in feigned surprise. Marshall grabs him and kisses him forcefully, channeling Alpha Marshall for the occasion.

They stand, forehead to forehead, purring contently until they snap out of it.

"Well, that's it for now, everyone! I'll be back tomorrow and show you some gameplay footage! BYE!" Ezra says, tapping the button on the floor to his left. "Well, I think that went well," Ezra says calmly, no longer his exuberant showman self.

I run over to them and leap into their arms. "Oh my God, y'all!! That was amazing!"

Epilogue

ADLEY

I nervously fiddle with my veil as I look out to my backyard. Strings of fairy lights crisscross over the small gathering of friends and coworkers. Under an awning covered in delicate wildflowers, Ezra and Marshall stand waiting for me. It feels like a lifetime ago that I dug my way through the snow to find Ezra's lifeless ailo body in that exact spot.

We decided to combine the traditions of both our cultures and create our own flavor of "wedding" that combines a wedding and mate-marking ceremony. It's Valentine's Day—one of the few holidays shared by both cultures, albeit named Queen's Token Day to the Ailura. This day is right in the middle of their mating season, and many Ailura perform their mate-marking ceremonies on it. A wedding outside in Minnesota in February is maybe not the best idea, but the cold is like a fourth in our relationship.

Ezra and Marshall look so handsome, standing side by side, Marshall in pale yellow and Ezra in black. Marshall stands still, a statue, gripping his tail with both hands while Ezra leans on him, laughing, chatting with the intimate crowd. His animated movements and laughter are the only thing moving Marshall. I don't even know if he's blinking. Ezra picked out the tuxes because, of course, he did. I can still hear his boisterous laughter at Marshall's insistence that they switch. But Ezra assured him, it was for aesthetic balance. Ezra holds his phone above their heads and kisses Marshall on the cheek for a selfie. *Well, I guess I gotta save Marshall this time.*

An usher slides the glass door open for me. I take a deep breath, and with now-characteristic decisiveness, I step into the backyard to walk towards my mates. The same door I rushed through to save Ezra and Marshall threw himself at.

The music changes, and Ezra puts his phone in his pocket. Ezra's fidgeting ceases momentarily as he and Marshall lock hands and stand tall as two frozen statues.

Walking toward them, I momentarily look at the crowd and am grateful for my collected friends. Tina and the rest of the smutty book club members are all here on my side. Marshall and Ezra started a frisbee league after half the town started coming to watch them play every weekend. Ethan, the hot firefighter, joined and has become one of their best friends. Ethan and the rest of their team are smiling at me from the grooms' side. Veronica sits at the back of my side, quietly waving Ellie's little hand at me. Bryce isn't here—because fuck that dude.

And scattered throughout are people who work for the game studio we now all run together—including my ex-coworker Madelyn, whom I hired away from that shit show the moment we could afford employees. The game has done decidedly well. It was a little janky when we first released it—having been banged out (no pun intended) by two people in a short time. But it made enough money for us to hire people and make Whispering Whiskers a real company—just like I always dreamed. It did well in early access, and it's now officially released. We got offers from investors to sell the company, but we decided to keep it.

Everyone here knows about Ezra and Marshall's origins—which was surprisingly easy for people to accept. Ezra has this magnetism that makes people okay with whatever wackiness he tells them. So, when he explains that he's an interdimensional time traveler people tend to believe him. He always emphasizes that "time traveler" part and repeatedly explains he is actually 10 years younger than his birthday indicates. In the cases that people think he's just being extra full of shit, he pops into his ailo form and all doubts are instantly wiped.

But I don't look at the crowd long because they are not who I want to see. Ezra is no longer standing still, but is back to fidgeting, blubbering like a baby, and pulling a pocket square out to dab at his tears. Marshall wears his emotions in his ears and tail while standing as straight as he does. I laugh at how adorable my emotive men are.

When I reach them, they turn so we can all hold hands—forming a triangle. The officiate, not official because this isn't legal, says a few words, but honestly, I don't hear them. I'm too busy looking into their eyes. Marshall is now crying, and their tails wrap around my legs.

When the officiant says all he wants to say, a ring bearer approaches with three pillows—each with two rings on it. Mine with two men's wedding rings, both rose gold. Ezra's pillow has two rings, one for me and one for Marshall. They're both yellow gold with diamonds. Marshall's pillow has two rings: one for me and one for Ezra, both dark tungsten.

All crying now, we sloppily place the rings upon each other's fingers—we probably should have coordinated this better. But, after we are done fumbling, I have Ezra's ring on my left ring finger, and Marshall's on my right. Once the rings are in place, they bring my fingers to their mouths. They wrap their lips around the area between the first and second knuckles. "Okay," I whisper. They bite down simultaneously. It hurts, but not much, and the marks are small. They pull handkerchiefs from their pockets, and in perfect sync, they snap them open, wrapping them around my bleeding fingers.

We wait for the officiant to tell us to kiss, and when he does, we embrace and lock into a single kiss shared between us. They lift me between the two of them and hold me close. Their purrs vibrate through my whole body, and I am deliriously happy.

The officiant falls to the ground. And one by one, each of our guests slumps over in their chairs as their purr vibrates across the yard.

"Well, shit, I forgot about that," I say as I look around me at the guests slumped over.

=^..^= ♥ =^..^=

Want to accompany Adley, Ezra, and Marshall on their wedding night? Subscribe to my newsletter to receive the free novella Whispers, Whiskers, & Wedding Night (Cozy Clowder Chronicles Book 1.1).

https://www.imogenknowed.com/newsletter

A Note from the Author

Hello, readers! Thank you so much for taking the time to read Whispers, Whiskers, and Wine. I can't tell you how much it means to me that you made it all the way to the end!

This book took me longer to write than I expected—two years longer. It had at least five different versions—with completely different plots and structures. At first, Marshall was a cop who chased Ezra to Adley's world after Ezra accidentally murdered someone. I was not feeling it and sat on it for a long, long time.

Eventually, after going through my own series of emotional turmoil and self-discovery, I realized I wanted this book to be a slice-of-life between three fated mates. I wanted it to focus on the fact that they are all fated, doesn't mean they're instantly perfect for each other. I also love stories about visitors from other worlds experiencing ours. So, I wrote the book I needed—one that acknowledged we're all flawed but can still find meaningful love and still accomplish our goals—even if it takes us a little longer than we originally hoped. I deeply love these flawed characters, and in a sense, they saved me in the same way they saved each other.

I hope you enjoyed this book and loved the characters as much as I do. Please leave a review of Whispers, Whiskers, and Wine on Amazon and Goodreads.

Sign up for my newsletter at www.imogenknowed.com to learn about upcoming books in the Cozy Clowder Chronicles!

Special Thanks

I want to thank my husband for his unwavering support while I wrote this book. Without his support, I could not have hyper-focused on it, writing literally every moment of the day that I wasn't working or sleeping.

To my husband:

Thank you for enthusiastically discussing characters and plot with me. Thank you for being okay with the fact that my mind was lost to another world for a while. Thank you for always putting food in front of me when I get so lost in something I forget my own body has needs. Thank you for always being there to help me recover whenever my mind and body explode from the world being too loud, too distracting, and too scratchy. I love you.

About the Author

Imogen Knowed has suffered from insomnia since she was a little girl. So, she has a lot of free time on her hands—especially at night. She spends her days programming video games and her nights reading and writing smut. She particularly enjoys reading webtoons and is a dedicated follower of quite a few long-running series. When she's not writing smut or making video games, she's hanging out with her daughter, husband, dog, and/or three cats.

You can follow her on social media:
https://www.tiktok.com/@imogenknowed
https://www.instagram.com/imogenknowed/

www.ingramcontent.com/pod-product-compliance
Lightning Source LLC
LaVergne TN
LVHW010557100826
845148LV00014B/2747